Around the Way
Girls 10

Around the Way Girls 10

Ms. Michel Moore, Marlon P.S. White,
and Racquel Williams

www.urbanbooks.net

Urban Books, LLC
300 Farmingdale Road, NY-Route 109
Farmingdale, NY 11735

ISBN 13: 978-1-62286-771-4
ISBN 10: 1-62286-771-8

First Trade Paperback Printing January 2017
Printed in the United States of America

10 9 8 7 6 5 4 3 2 1

Distributed by Kensington Publishing Corp.
Submit Orders to:
Customer Service
400 Hahn Road
Westminster, MD 21157-4627
Phone: 1-800-733-3000
Fax: 1-800-659-2436

NOT WITH MY MAN

by

Ms. Michel Moore

CHAPTER ONE

"All right, y'all, strap up! Let's do this!" Holding a gun in one hand, he eagerly used the other to pull a mask down over his face so you could see nothing but his street-hardened pupils blinking every so often. "Remember, everybody, stay safe. And if you have to kill one if these sons of bitches inside to make sure you get back home to your family tonight then so be it. Shoot the shit outta a motherfucker! We'll deal with the fallout later."

"What in the hell." Sasha was startled. Her eyes widened. The thunderous sound she'd rapidly heard three times caused her to jump out of her skin. The loud commotion was followed up by multiple strange voices shouting. Instantly, her heart raced. Strangely her feet couldn't seem to move. She was frozen in fear of the unknown. Her home-cooked meal with special ingredients had been interrupted and she was helpless.

"Search warrant, Detroit Police Department. Let me see them damn hands. Search warrant. Hands in the air, now," the first officer entering the dwelling loudly demanded after his colleague rammed the front door. He was ready to kill if need be. If Sasha or anyone else who was behind the door they were taking put up any sort of opposition then so be it. The occupants' blood would be on his hands, blood he'd happily take full responsibility for if need be.

The rest of the brigade dressed in black stormed across the threshold, the door barely attached to one hinge. The last officer inside the otherwise quiet bungalow caused the solid oak door to break all the way from the frame. Just like that, it came crashing to the floor, causing another ear-splitting sound to bounce off the walls of the house.

"Oh, my God, what is this? What do you want? What did I do?" Sasha pleaded for answers. Dumbfounded in front of the stove preparing spaghetti, she prayed as the tears started to flow. Still holding the black handle of the skillet in hand, Sasha fought to make complete sentences. Shocked and confused, she was almost at a loss for words as the small army of tight-laced boots trampled throughout her entire house, guns drawn. Sasha wasn't expecting this unforeseen drama on her day off, or any other day for that matter. This occurrence, out of the blue, was nothing she was familiar with even though her husband was loyal to the street life.

"Get on the floor. Get down and get on the damn floor now. Right now," the cop shouted, pointing his department-issued revolver at her head. "Hurry up. Ain't nobody playing with you. Now move!" Seconds away from pulling the trigger he felt his own adrenalin pumping. It was go time and he was ready to put in work.

Rushing up to the thin-built female, he roughly grabbed her forearm. With one move, the trained officer of the law snatched Sasha away from the stove. Everything was moving so fast she couldn't catch up. She wanted to tell him they had the wrong house, but she couldn't. Before she could protest any further and even explain she was pregnant, he was slamming her face first onto the kitchen floor.

Seemingly on purpose, portions of the ground turkey she was browning on the stove tumbled down as well.

When some of the spicy seasoned meat landed dangerously close to Sasha's face, also getting entangled in her weave, no one said, "Excuse me." No one cared about the hot skillet that vindictively followed, melting a circular spot on the vinyl beige tile. If Sasha felt violated, disrespected, or slighted, so what? It was what it was to the Detroit Police Department Narcotics Taskforce. The comfort and security she was accustomed to having in her own home was of no concern to them. The joyful reality of just finding out she was almost two months along with child was not an issue to them at this point, even if they did know. Sasha Eubanks was merely one of two people residing at an address being raided. All that mattered to the taskforce was executing the search warrant and securing the premises.

Sasha's arms were swiftly pulled behind her back. She could feel her shoulder blades almost snap. The overzealous male cop then pressed his knee into her lower spine after holstering his weapon. The expectant mother screamed out in total agony as he applied more pressure. "Please! Please, stop! Stop! You're hurting me. My arms are hurting. Please, Officer, please stop!"

"Shut the hell up, lady, and do as you are told. Stop trying to resist and things will go a hellava lot easier for you."

Trying desperately to catch her breath, Sasha was glad she'd mopped earlier considering the side of her face was being smashed down and practically becoming part of the floor. Feeling the plastic ties being tightened around her tiny wrists was more than she could take. "Please, please, please," she managed to mutter in between the sobs. Tears poured out of each corner of her still wide eyes. Wanting to wipe her face, unfortunately the happy homemaker couldn't.

"Keep running that drug-dealing mouth of yours and you gonna get more than a knee in your back and being handcuffed." The cop made sure she saw he was not for showing any sympathy. "Now shut your damn mouth; that's my final damn warning!"

From floor level, Sasha helplessly watched her perfectly kept home being turned upside down. The loveseat and chair were flipped over and the rear material torn off both. The cushions on the couch were sliced open and a few antique vases smashed. Callously, the living room and dining area curtains were snatched down from the rods as if someone could actually be hiding behind the sheer panels, ready to pounce.

As her personal items were being trashed, Sasha remained silent. Normally feisty and outspoken, she had no choice. She had been warned multiple times to keep her mouth shut. If she didn't, she'd run the risk of being marched onto the front porch and stretched out on the grass until they'd finish sweeping the house. Not wanting to be paraded and put on display for her neighbors' ridicule, Sasha sucked it up. She asked the Almighty to give her strength while calling the over-the-top cops everything but the child of God in her head.

"Yeah, we got one good to go secured in the back," a voice proudly yelled out.

"We all clear in the basement."

"All clear on the upper level."

One by one, hearing taskforce members check in with each other, the cop towering over Sasha smirked. He was content. None of his team had been injured upon entry and there had been no gunplay, deadly or otherwise. Now that the entire house was deemed officer friendly it was time for phase two to be put in effect. Using one hand he grabbed Sasha's wrist, making the plastic ties tighter. Not caring about the excruciating pain the female claimed she was in, the cop jerked her upward until she was back to her feet.

"Please, Officer, please. My side is hurting." Her tears never once let up as she continued to beg for mercy.

"Didn't I tell you to shut your damn mouth?" Hell-bent on doing his job with as little emotion as possible, he stuck to proper protocol. Yanking her up from the floor, he roughly guided her into the living room. Sasha was instructed to take a seat on the couch that was missing all of its cushions. Taking longer to move than the officer wanted, Sasha was verbally assaulted, along with getting knocked in her shoulder. Once more, the terrified female was urged not to speak until spoken to.

Sitting on the far corner of the couch near the fireplace, Sasha heard her husband's voice getting louder. Focusing on the hallway, seconds later he appeared, being man-handled by two policemen. Not as accommodating to authority figures as his wife, Mario was going berserk. A two-time felon, with countless misdemeanors also under his belt, he'd been down this road before and he knew his rights.

"Sasha, don't say shit to these grimy, rotten mother-fuckers." He struggled to break free from the same type of plastic ties that held his wife. Seeing how the taskforce had destroyed his living room, Mario grew even more enraged. "These sons of bitches ain't got shit on me, bae; they ass just out here in these streets fucking with people like me and you in our house minding our own damn business. Old nothing-ass lames. That's why all the real ones be out here dumping on y'all coward asses, putting something hot in y'alls' heads."

"Yo, homeboy, didn't I tell your wannabe-tough ass to calm the fuck down in there talking that rah-rah bull-shit?" One of the cops shoved Mario in his back, causing him to stumble over the coffee table. When he fell to the floor, his jaw felt the brutal impact of another officer's fist sucker punch him. "Now slow your dumb ass down before you catch these hands from me; for real, too."

"Catch these hands? Who, me? Oh, so dig that, you wanna try to beat on a guy when they at a disadvantage all tied up, huh? You and me both know you only with that ho shit because I'm fucked up right about now." Mario's face started to immediately swell as he spoke. He frowned, trying to show his hands from the backside; but he couldn't. "If we was out on the block and I wasn't tied up it'd be on. I'd bust that ass for real, no questions asked, toe to toe. I ain't like Mike Brown. I don't just growl. I bite!"

As if on cue, all the cops within earshot laughed. Veterans and rookies alike had that same conversation almost word for word with every thug they were about to lock up. They'd heard that same line numerous times. Mario and the way he was stuntin' for their sake was amusing, if nothing more.

However, for Sasha, now slumped over on her side begging for God's mercy, wasn't shit funny. She was hysterical; her lower abdominal was aching and her fingertips were growing increasingly numb. She'd counted at least eleven strangers in her home, most covering their faces. None seemed to be listening to her constant pleas for help. When they finally got Mario to be quiet long enough, they had him sit on the couch next to Sasha.

"Why don't you sit your punk ass down next to your little crybaby girlfriend and relax? Let us do our damn job in peace."

"First of all, she's my wife, idiot, not my girlfriend," Mario angrily fired back, still ready to go a couple of rounds. "And, second of all, guess what? Fuck you and your damn job."

Once again the same renegade cop with a temper ran up from the rear of the couch. Slamming his closed fist into Mario's mouth, this time drawing blood, he smiled. The force of the blow caused the blood mixed with salvia to splatter on Sasha's face and shirt. Mario grimaced, still being a soldier, while Sasha cried.

Minutes later, two of the men searching the basement came upstairs. Acting as if they'd hit the four-digit dollar straight and dollar boxed, the mini-celebration started. Tossing a small, unzipped duffle bag on the coffee table, Mario looked dumbfounded as huge amounts of various pills came spilling out. He turned his face toward the wall, wishing that when he turned his head back the bag and all its illegal contents would have disappeared. Of course that didn't happen. Mario looked back to now see not only the bag and pills, but his rainy day stash shoebox.

"Damn, hell yeah. There's the freaking headshot right there," the lieutenant on duty announced, elated they hadn't been on a dummy mission and wouldn't be returning to the station empty-handed. "That along with the money that was located in the shoebox in the rear bedroom should be good enough to get your smart-talking ass locked back up. Then let's see who the tough guy is when you facing the judge."

Mario was forced to think quickly. The good day he'd had flicking a shitload of pills off had just gone all the way south. Caught red-handed, he had a serious screw face, much to their overall enjoyment. There was nothing that these police and several others would like to see more than him being returned to prison, caged up like an animal. Mario was not naïve to the system. The hardcore criminal knew the next time any judge laid eyes on him in their courtroom they were going to be banging him hard. "Man, fuck all that you talking about. Them pills ain't mine. Not them or that damn money. That shit ain't mine. Y'all faggots trying to set a young, innocent brother up."

"Oh, yeah, is that right?" the officer who'd body-slammed Sasha to the kitchen floor spoke out while grinning. "Then why don't you tell us all whose stuff this is? Solve the mystery for us all, please. We're waiting to be enlightened."

Mario was desperate. He didn't want to go back to prison, not today, tomorrow, or ever. Even though he could jail it if need be, eating cook-ups and walking the yard was not on his agenda. The hardened criminal was on the edge of being lost and buried in the system for years to come. He couldn't wrap his head around the thought.

Before Mario knew it, he'd blurted out the unforgivable: "You know what? Them is hers. Them her pills and the money. It must be, 'cause I ain't never seen the shit before in my life." Mario turned his body the best he could and looked over at his teary-eyed wife. The street thug showed no emotion. He was more than ready to throw Sasha under the bus if it meant he could walk away from this charge. "Damn, bae, where you get that type of money from? You been holding out on me or what?"

"Come on dude, is you really about to say fuck your girl like that? You's a real piece of work." All the other officers agreed, looking at Mario with contempt.

Sasha, of course, felt the same as the police: the very men who'd mistreated her and had just destroyed her home. Without a second thought, she gave her supposedly loyal, devoted husband the side-eye as well. *Oh, hell naw. Did he just say that? How could he? I've told him to get all these pills out of the house. He knows you never supposed to shit where you sleep at; hardheaded, lying-ass dummy got us both messed up. Now he's here trying to mess me over.* Still in pain, she lowered her head in disbelief. Mario had promised to love, honor, and cherish her the rest of their lives. Now here he sat, basically saying fuck her freedom and fuck her life. "Mario, really, how could you?" she sadly mumbled, turning her lowered head in disgust.

In the midst of all the unexpected turmoil that was taking place, Sasha closed her beet red eyes. In denial, she fought hard to tune out her terrible reality. Somehow, someway, she found a way to transport her mind back in time. Before the suspected female drug dealer knew it, she was reliving the day she met the now foul-intentioned Mario. Sasha and he were as different as night and day. Everyone, including them, always wondered what made them start dating, let alone decide to get married. The tighter she closed her eyes, the clearer those days became.

She and her best friend, Kat, were hanging out at the park after the Summer Jam concert. There was stop-and-go traffic around the strip. Every expensive car, rimmed, custom-painted truck, and wide-tire motorcycle you could imagine was in the constant parade around the bend. Sasha and her sidekick had been enjoying the late-evening goings-on and they were only minutes from getting in Kat's Ford Tempo with a huge dent on the driver's side door. It may have not been the best vehicle parked that night, but the two of them were content. It'd gotten them to the concert and to the park, and it was about to get them home. Dressed all in white, Sasha and Kat slowly strutted toward the car, hoping more than a few dudes wearing Nikes, wife beater tops, and sagging jeans would look their way.

Reaching the car, Kat removed her keys from her crossover bag. Seductively licking her lips at one of the guys riding by, she started smiling when he pulled over. Signaling her to come to the car, Kat pranced over as if she'd hit the lottery.

"What up, doe?"

"Hey."

"What's your name, girl?"

"Kat. What's yours?"

"They call me Dino."

"Oh, yeah? You east or west?" Kat asked, making sure to poke her ass out when leaning into the window.

"West like a motherfucker, NFL; we getting that money for sho," Dino proudly announced, elbowing his homeboy who was riding shotgun. "And, yo, who is your girl standing all off over there to the side with the big booty? Tell her to come this way. My peoples Mario wanna holler at her."

Sasha heard the obvious thug make reference to her, but she kept her distance. It was bad enough he'd gotten Kat at his car, and she ran the risk of getting snatched up, never to be heard from or seen again; but he had the raw nerve to make mention of her butt. Although she had been out all day at the concert and park behaving as if she were about that life, in all reality clearly she wasn't. Sasha was no more than a good girl, dedicated to school and her job. She was a virgin who didn't smoke or drink, and she hardly cursed, unless she was singing along with a rap song.

Mario had been laidback while Dino was talking. Taking full advantage of having the just-rolled blunt to himself, he finally leaned up after hearing his name referenced. Still bopping his head from side to side along with the music, Mario looked over Dino and past the female hanging all off into the window. Focusing his sights on Sasha, it took him all of three seconds to lean back into the passenger seat. It was apparent he was not interested, turning his head to the other side of the car. Just to make sure Dino didn't misunderstand his body language, Mario smirked, telling everyone interested or in earshot that he was good.

Even though Sasha wasn't stepping foot anywhere near the triple black Dodge Charger to have a face-to-face conversation with the bumpy-faced, blunt-smoking passenger, she was still a human with feelings. Instantly the good girl not willing to go bad got in her emotions about the way he'd publically snubbed her.

Only seconds from getting the courage to give him a piece of her mind, gunshots rang out, interrupting the night. Pandemonium ensued. Gaping holes were ripped through the doors of multiple vehicles. The loud sounds of bullets shattering windows and ear-piercing screams filled the air. Not knowing exactly where the source of the assault was coming from, people didn't know where to run or where to hide.

Hitting the ground like many others, Sasha covered her face and prayed. Her stomach pressed down onto the concrete, she peeked through her cupped hands and was stunned. She was speechless. Through all the feet she saw quickly scrambling around in search of safety, Sasha made out Kat. She was squatting down behind the door of the black Dodge Charger, which was now halfway open.

As Sasha quickly glanced to Kat's side, she saw the driver slumped over. Only held by the restraint of the seat belt, his upper body was dangling as the bullets continued to whiz by in every direction. Sasha wanted to scream out to Kat, yet she could not seem to get her mouth to form the words. Her throat had a huge lump in it and her mouth was dry. It was as if she and everyone trapped in the park were living in the middle of a bad horror movie.

Kat hopelessly stared back at Sasha like a deer trapped in headlights. She finally moved her lips, saying the words, "Help me." Kat wanted to just get up and dart over to her own vehicle where her best friend was, but she couldn't move.

With the barrage of gunfire seeming to get closer, Kat screamed out for help as Sasha sobbed, asking God for mercy. With her eyes temporarily closed in prayer, Sasha opened them to see Mario, the unruly passenger, swoop Kat off the ground. Practically dragging her with him, the two of them made it behind a bullet-riddled car two spaces away from where Sasha was taking refuge.

Mario yanked down a metal garbage can to further aid in shielding them from harm, apparently the same harm that had come to a motionless Dino. Like a small baby on hands and knees, Sasha swiftly crawled over to their makeshift bunker. It would be at least another three long, grueling, torturous minutes of uncertainty until silence after the gunshots once again filled the night air. That silence was then filled with the aftermath of tears, screams of the discovery of death, and sirens from police cars approaching.

Suffering from a few scrapes on her knees, thankfully Sasha was not injured. Kat, however, had been struck in the lower part of her leg; but strangely she didn't realize it until an overwhelming burning sensation started to occur. As she cried out in agonizing pain, Sasha cradled her head in her arms. Rocking back and forth, she repeated to Kat that it was going to be okay and help was on the way.

Mario had done his duty as a hood hero, getting the random female his boy was talking to out of the line of fire. Cautiously, he lifted his head to see if the coast was clear. Faced with the horrible sight of his comrade hanging out the door of the Charger, engine still running, sounds still blasting, Mario ran over to Dino's side. Reaching inside the car, he turned it off.

Struggling to unfasten his homeboy's seat belt, which was stretched to capacity, Mario was in tears. One minute they were just hanging out, talking shit, having *fun; and the next, this. Mario was distraught and confused as Dino's blood-soaked shirt was torn off him as paramedics attempted to save his life. Unfortunately, there was nothing they could do for the young man.*

Mario dropped his head and they covered the body with a sheet. Burying his face in his hands, Mario felt the awful moisture of Dino's blood slide down between his fingers. He was seconds away from having a total mental breakdown.

Sasha had made sure Kat was getting the medical attention she needed and she was now focused on Mario, who'd saved her best friend's life while putting his own in harm's way. Ironically, right before the gunfire erupted, Sasha wanted to spit on him after loudly cursing him out for being rude. Now the only thing the "good girl" wanted to do was go to "bad boy" Mario's side and reassure him that he was not alone. Without reservation, she did just that, consoling him.

In the days and weeks to follow, the unlikely duo had become inseparable. They had absolutely nothing in common other than the fact they'd survived an unthinkable, tragic attack. Holding on to the fact that deep down Sasha knew Mario could not possibly be as cold, callous, and ignorant as he often portrayed, especially reminiscing about the terror in the park, she found it in her heart to "work with him." Mario was a true womanizer, a chronic gambler, disrespectful to Sasha constantly on so many levels, and just an all-around coward who happened to display a bit of courage out of the blue that night. Yet, like most women who think they can change a man, Sasha was no exception to the rule. Before she knew what was happening, she'd asked Mario to get married and settle down.

Snapped back to the here and now that was taking place, Sasha continued to not understand how her husband could be such an asshole. Mario ignored his wife's obvious disapproval of what he'd claimed to be true. He stuck to his story about the cash and pills being hers. He repeated the inconceivable story the entire time the pair of them were being read their rights, arrested, and thrown in the back of two separate police cars.

Sasha was fighting what she knew was taking place. She kept reflecting on that night in the park and she prayed that side of Mario would emerge. Trying to be supportive, knowing that when it came down to it Mario would hopefully step up to the plate and do the right thing, Sasha never said a word in protest against her husband. Maybe it was because she was numb from what was happening, or in disbelief her man had basically made her out to be the fall guy. Whatever it was, the insurance claims broker, naïve to the streets, tried to gather herself together the best she could. Sasha knew now was not the time to fall completely apart. She just kept silent and waited for her court-appointed lawyer to be assigned to her case, just like the criminal television shows had taught her. If a fish doesn't want to get caught on the hook, all he has to do is keep his mouth shut; and that was what Sasha did.

CHAPTER TWO

"Okay, Mrs. Eubanks, do you understand fully what you're doing? What you're saying?" The lawyer shuffled through his paperwork, ensuring it was in order.

"Umm, yeah, I think so," she responded with butterflies in her stomach. She looked up at the clock over the door and thought she could hear each hand moving. It was as if her life were moving in slow motion as her attorney spoke.

Sasha had gone along with the story her husband gave to the cops who raided their home. She'd repeated it three times to the detectives working the case and once to Mario's parole officer. And now she was going to stand in front of a judge and swear it was the truth, the whole truth, and nothing but the truth. She would admit the pills and money seized belonged to her, not her spouse. Also any other drug paraphernalia that was discovered that day was solely hers. Sasha Eubanks would stand, left hand in the air, vowing Mario never knew she had any of those illegal items in their jointly owned home.

Since the day she'd been released on her own personal recognizance, Mario had been calling her constantly, singing in her ear, trying to get in her head. He reasoned with Sasha that if she went along with the game plan he was laying out, they'd both be good. He explained that by her never even having a traffic ticket, let alone any contact with the judicial system, she'd easily get a pass, a slap on the wrist. Not to mention the fact that she was pregnant would weigh heavy on any judge to show sympathy.

After forty-one hours of Mario sitting in the county jail on a parole violation, Sasha finally gave in. In true con-man style, he'd run every guilt trip on his wife he possibly could. Tugging at her heart strings, he even threw up the fact that she wouldn't want her child's father to have to see his firstborn from behind bars. Now here she was, minutes before going in front of the judge for sentencing on the crimes she really wasn't responsible for. However, just as Mario had said would happen, her lawyer set up a plea deal arrangement with the prosecuting attorney. In the deal, if Sasha would plead guilty, accepting all liability, she would get a six-month probation including some community service. No jail time would be served and her baby would be born at home as planned.

"You can't just think you are ready to go in there, Mrs. Eubanks. You have to be certain. The judge will be asking you a series of questions and you have to answer in accordance to what we have all agreed upon."

"I understand. I'm just nervous, I guess."

"Well, it's much too late to be nervous. The time for feeling that way was before you stepped up to the plate on these charges," the lawyer advised, standing up from behind the table in the private room they were in. "So get yourself together. They'll be calling our case next. I don't think we will have to wait too long. We should be in and out relatively fast."

Early along in her pregnancy, Sasha was not showing, but she kept rubbing her stomach just the same. She was a nervous wreck. Never being pregnant before, she prayed her rollercoaster emotions would not affect her baby. The time seemed to drag on, although it had only been minutes. Hearing her last name announced, the court bailiff signaled for Sasha and her attorney to enter the judge's domain. She took a deep breath, and then exhaled. Nauseated, she was ready to just get this entire thing over with and go home and get some rest.

Stepping inside the smaller-sized courtroom, she saw one of her three siblings, Regina, and Kat. They'd both begged her repeatedly not to take the fall for her pathetic troublemaking husband, but Mario had Sasha bamboozled. Kat tried to give him the benefit of the doubt considering what he'd done to help her, but she'd seen him firsthand do too many terrible things to her best friend. He swore he was done selling drugs, womanizing, and behaving as if his shit didn't stink. He promised he would be there for her and their unborn child, no more bullshit.

Yet, here it was. Less than ten hours after him making that claim, he was nowhere to be found. Sasha looked to the left and the right. A house didn't have to fall on her head. Not seeing Mario she'd realized she'd been played. Part of her wanted to change her mind and run out of the courtroom, yet she knew she'd gone too far in the process to back out. She'd just serve her expected probation and do her few community service hours like a champ. As for Mario, her supposed loving husband who'd left her out to dry, she'd deal with him later on, when she got home.

"The State of Michigan versus Sasha Lachelle Eubanks," the same bailiff who signaled them to enter the courtroom loudly spoke.

Terrified, Sasha stood. It felt like each of her steps was surrounded by quicksand. Following closely behind her lawyer, she took her place next to him at the podium. The prosecuting attorney who had just spoken to them both maybe an hour ago took his place as well. You could hear a pin drop as the judge read over a semi-huge stack of documents handed to him inside of a manila folder. Looking over his glasses a few times then shaking his head seemingly at Sasha, the judge kept them all standing at attention longer than usual. Finally he spoke.

"Yes, go ahead with your statements."

Each attorney took turns to introduce themselves for the court stenographer's records. After that the judge asked to once again briefly go over what was what and exactly what the two sides were proposing. Upon allowing them to finish, he removed his glasses.

"Okay, people. I do have the plea paperwork in front of me. And as far as I can tell both sides have chosen to enter into this agreement freely and willingly. Is that correct?"

"Yes, sir," the prosecutor agreed.

"Yes, it is, Judge," the defense attorney concurred.

"Well, before I render my decision on the acceptance of this plea, I'd like to hear from Ms. Eubanks." The judge glanced down at the stack of papers, quickly correcting himself: "Forgive me, the court definitely apologizes. That's Mrs. Eubanks. We wouldn't want to forget or be disrespectful to your union of marriage. Matter of fact, I'm just wondering, is Mr. Eubanks in the court with us this morning?"

Sasha felt her legs getting weak hearing the judge ask about Mario. The sharp pains she was having in her stomach all night started again. While part of her wished he were here by her side, helping her stand tall for the mess he'd gotten her into, the other side was elated he wasn't, having an awful feeling the judge was in a bad mood. "No, sorry, sir. He's not here this morning."

"Oh, I see. I guess he had other prior engagements more pressing than this proceeding. So be it. Let's move. Mrs. Eubanks, back to what exactly is your version of the events that took place that day once more?"

Sasha solemnly went on to repeat the same lie she'd been telling since Mario convinced her to take the rap. After she finished, the judge put his glasses back on. Wishing she could read his mind, Sasha waited for what was coming next. Feeling nauseated once more, she hoped he'd just hurry and tell her the number of community service days she was to serve, so she could go to the bathroom. Since finding out she was pregnant she was urinating and throwing up what seemed like every other hour.

"Okay, counselors. Although I appreciated the time that was spent to come up with this Fantasy Island plea deal, unfortunately I won't be accepting it at this time. It's not going to work for me."

Sasha was shocked, as were her sister and friend who were now sitting on the edges of their seats. Both lawyers had seen this type of thing occur time and time again and, as always, they rolled with the punches. The judge presiding over the case having another form of justice in mind, other than what the two sides had decided upon, was not unheard of.

"What's happening? I don't understand. What's going on?" Sasha confusedly rambled, blurting out question after question in the otherwise quiet courtroom.

"Excuse me, Mrs. Eubanks, but this isn't the proper time for you to be speaking. That ship has sailed. Maybe your attorney should advise you pertaining proper court protocol. I'm doing the talking now and you are doing listening. Is that understood?"

Sasha nodded that she did indeed understand.

"Forgive the interruption, Judge." The attorney fiddled with his ink pen, knowing that what was coming next was not going to go in his and his client's favor. "It's just my client has never been in trouble with the law before and has no knowledge of how the proper—"

"Please, sir. I have read all about your client's history prior to taking the bench. I certainly don't need a complete rundown of her personal history or lack of involvement with the law. I'm dealing with this case in front of me, nothing more and nothing less. Are we clear and done with all of the interruptions?"

"Yes, Your Honor." The lawyer nodded, dropping his head from being verbally admonished.

"Thank you. Now, as I was saying, this court finds that the defendant, Sasha Lachelle Eubanks, chose to plead guilty. I have a strong suspicion that's not the case and she is covering for someone else. But that was her choice. Now I have a choice to make as well. And the choice is Mrs. Eubanks will not be serving community service. She will not be placed on probation as her legal representation and our obviously very generous prosecutor's office overzealously agreed upon. I think the punishment must fit her crime, and fit the crime it will."

"What does he mean?" Sasha spoke out again before being swiftly hushed by her lawyer, allowing the judge to finish rendering his decision.

"Now the amount of pills that she was found to be guilty of having in her possession was clearly at felony levels. And although the defendant has no criminal record, the guidelines have several interpretations for sentencing at my discretion. And mine tells me at least twelve to eighteen months behind bars should be a good lesson. Mrs. Eubanks wants to be what the streets call a rider, or be into thug life, well, she should be right at home in a cell."

"Oh, no. Oh, my God," Sasha's sister cried out in disbelief, having to be comforted by Kat.

The judge looked over his glasses at the source of the outburst. Giving Regina and Kat a stern look before continuing, he motioned his head for the second bailiff standing in the rear to be on alert. "Now, as I was saying, the defendant is to be immediately taken into custody. She is to be held in the Wayne County Jail until such time as she is transferred to one of the women's prisons located here in Michigan to start serving her sentence. Bailiff." The judge signaled for him to escort Sasha out.

"I'm sorry. What did he say? What happened? I thought you said I was getting probation, that I would be home by lunch." She panicked, snatching her arm back from the bailiff's loose grip while still yelling at her lawyer. "Why did he say I was going to jail? Why did he say it? Please, Judge, listen, please. But I'm pregnant. I can't go to jail. I can't."

"Well, maybe that husband of yours, the infamous Mario Eubanks who seems to be too busy to grace us with his presence today, will find time to raise his child until you are free to assist."

"Please, Your Honor, please," Sasha screamed out as she could no longer hold the urine that trickled down her leg and into the side of her shoe.

"Good luck to you, Mrs. Eubanks. Court adjourned."

The judge was unmoved by Sasha's theatrics. He ignored the strong-smelling piss puddle that had formed on the courtroom floor. Over the years he'd seen plenty of defendants show out at sentencing and have to be restrained, so Mrs. Eubanks having a fit meant nothing. Many times the people who break the law so nonchalantly are the ones who scream injustice the loudest when punished.

CHAPTER THREE

From the very moment he'd heard the cops hit the front door and rush inside, Mario knew he was going to get knocked. His wife had told him repeatedly to clean house and not bring his work, a felony waiting to happen, home. But he didn't listen. Mario never did. He didn't trust anyone in the streets with his money or pills. Not in the mood to go back to jail, he grew more annoyed at his sometimes forgetful memory.

With small beads of perspiration in each crease of his forehead, he prayed he'd put the small duffle bag back in its hiding place, up in the far left corner ceiling tile, but he wasn't sure. His people had just called him, telling him they had a hookup he might want to check out. So he'd run upstairs and he was just about to get undressed and get in the shower when: boom.

Here the taskforce came, search warrant in hand. The first cop to enter his bedroom was met with a struggle. Mario wasn't going back to jail without a fight, so the officer pointing his gun at him mattered none. Mario went for it, knocking the pistol out of his hand. Before he could attempt to swing or try to go for the gun, a second officer entered the bedroom, tackling him off his feet. Brand new Jordans in the air, shirt torn, Mario took more than a few punches before giving up.

Marched into the living room, Mario was pissed seeing his girl in tears, knowing it was partially his fault.

Although he knew he wasn't the best man he could be to her, he still didn't like to see her hurt. It was like he was Dr. Jekyll and Mr. Hyde. One day he couldn't live without Sasha and he was thankful for all she did to hold him down each time he was locked up; the next day he was disgusted to even see her face, knowing all she was going to do was nag him half to death. Watching the officers berate her made him buck to get out of the plastic ties. He wanted nothing more than to protect her. Yet when his stash was discovered and the threat of doing hard time loomed over his head, Mario's beloved wife was first in line to be his Get Out of Jail Free card.

After both being arrested, Sasha had his back like he assumed she would no sooner than she touched back down. After a hot minute or two of Mario taking her on a guilt trip of what her future would be like without him in her or their baby's life, his pregnant wife folded. Mario had won another victory over her common sense. Sasha would stand tall and eat the charges just as he asked. Crazy in love, his good girl had done a lot of things since they'd been together to prove her devotion, much to the dislike of her family, especially her sister: cars in her name he'd crashed, credit cards he'd run up, random females texting his cell, and him slapping her around when he'd be drunk or high off the pills he was selling. Mario had no off button or filter to his behavior. As much as he tried to do right by Sasha, the streets and every-thing that came with running in them always seemed to be calling him. He couldn't seem to help himself.

Mario had been out of county lockup no more than twenty minutes when he had Sasha drop him off on the block. The more she protested, the more he tried to convince her he would only be a short time collecting what was due him. Mario claimed one of his boys had been working a bag for him and was ready to cash him out. Exhausted going word for word, she pulled the car over near the curb demanding he get out as soon as possible. With a one-track mind on getting money, Mario didn't let that brief threat of parole violation he'd just avoided thanks to his wife slow his hustle down. He was going to live life fast, reckless, and with no regard to the next man's problems, even Sasha's.

"Okay, six is the point." Mario snatched the dice up off the ground. After tossing a couple more twenties onto the pile of money, he grinned, shaking up the ivory-colored cubed pair. Skeeting a stream of spit through the side of his clenched teeth, he knew he was about to hit another lick. He'd been on the top for almost thirty minutes straight: a new hood record. Crapping out was not in his vocabulary or mindset.

After a few more shit-talking rolls, Mario and the guys who were riding with him celebrated. Counting his portion of the winnings, he was interrupted by his cell vibrating yet again. In between the back-to-back text messages he was receiving from Sasha, he was amazed her bugaboo ass hadn't broken his winning streak mojo. He knew what she wanted without even bothering to read another word or answer his line.

Caught up in the dice game, Mario would stay out all night if he was in his zone whether he was winning or losing. The more his cell jumped the angrier he got. He knew Sasha had court in a few hours. He knew it was his fault his pregnant wife was going to have a criminal record and probably would have to pick up trash on the side of the road as an added punishment. Mario tried to pretend he cared since that fateful afternoon the police violated their home but, in reality, he didn't. He had dodged the bullet, so to speak. And that was all that really mattered. So what if Sasha was embarrassed in front of her neighbors every time she stepped foot outside? Big deal if her parents, family, and friends warned her she'd be shunned if she kept standing by Mario. He was out for himself, and his wife would have to play her position with him or run the risk of having no position to play at all.

"Damn, girl, why in the fuck you keep getting at me like you crazy?"

"I'm sorry, excuse me." Sasha's tone was filled with arrogance and rightly so.

"Look, don't start with all that uppity tone and 'I'm sorry, excuse me' bullshit with me. I ain't in the zone for it. I'm out here trying to get this money and you all on a nigga's dick, ol' nagging ass."

"Mario, the dang sun is almost up. I've been calling and texting you all night. Do you know what today is?" Sasha sarcastically barked at her husband.

"Yeah, I know what today is. So? And? I mean, what you want me to do about it? The lawyer said the whole thang was gonna be one, two, three, and the shit will be over, in and out."

Second-guessing her decision of not just letting Mario go back to jail, Sasha took a deep breath before getting even more heated. "Okay, and so what if it is gonna be in and out? You don't think I want my husband to be by my side just for moral support if nothing else?"

"Man, that's what the lawyer is getting paid for: moral support," he announced, eager to get back in the game. "Besides, take one of your sisters or that nosey-ass best friend of yours who's always talking shit and trying to throw salt in a playa's game. I know they ain't doing shit but watching reruns of *Oprah,* taking notes on how to hate a man even more."

"Mario, please don't start with me about them; please, not now. I can't take all that on my plate, too. My head and stomach has been bothering me all night. I guess I'm nervous or scared or something. I don't know. But whatever, bae. So just tell me, are you coming home to get dressed and go with me to court or not?"

Mario's split personality was attempting to get out. He'd heard the sound of desperation and fear in Sasha's voice and he wanted to make everything all good like any normal husband would, especially considering the situation. With enough money won in his pocket to eat steak, lobster, and crab for a week straight, Mario could walk away and hold his head high with bragging rights until the next game. Wanting to do the right thing, he was seconds away from telling his loyal wife he was on the way home and she should lay his clothes out on the bed.

Sadly, just as he parted his lips to say those words he knew Sasha wanted to hear, a few of the fellas turned the corner, pulling up. Mario knew they had money and he couldn't resist the urge to try to break their pockets. "Umm, hey listen, just put my clothes on the bed. I might be running late, but court never starts on time."

"But, Mario," she whined, feeling another break in her already damaged heart.

"I gotcha, girl. We good. I'll be there."

It was nearing eleven when Mario's cell rang again. Naturally, he assumed it was Sasha having returned home from court, pissed. He knew he was going to be in the doghouse with his wife for what he'd done, or didn't do. The game had gotten so intense he couldn't break away from it no matter how much he wanted to. There was way too much money on the floor to bounce.

She'll be all right. I ain't even gonna trip. I'll make it up later. Mario planned to stop by the flea market and grab Sasha a couple of bootleg purses, and a Snickers and a red soda from the store. In past experiences with fucking over her emotions, Mario knew that she couldn't stay mad at him long. So he'd bless her with her favorites and wait it out. Not downplaying the disrespect and disregard he'd shown Sasha today by not showing up to be by her side in the shit storm he'd created, Mario knew this wait would be longer than the others. Unfortunately, he had no idea how long.

Not bothering to take his cell out his pocket, Mario made his moves and went home to take his verbal lumps from the wife. Bags in hand, he was relieved when he didn't see her car in the driveway. *Whew, okay, she ain't here waiting behind the door with a frying pan or a butcher knife.* With no shame for all the commotion he'd caused on the block since moving there, Mario arrogantly and dryly spoke to his elderly neighbors, daring them to act as if they couldn't speak back.

Inside the house, he placed the items on the dining room table so Sasha would see them when she first walked in. Wanting to just get it over with, he finally decided to return her calls. Falling back on the couch, Mario kicked his legs up, allowing his head to be cradled by the multicolored pillows. *What the fuck? All these calls is from Regina. What her wild ass wants?* Double tapping her name, Mario waited all of ten seconds before his sister-in-law answered. "Hey, girl, what up, doe? What it do?"

"What up, doe? Nigga, please," she barked like a drill sergeant trying to get his point across. "Don't 'what up, doe' me like it's all good. Where the hell your ass was at when my sister was getting locked up this damn morning? Why you wasn't there? Or better yet why you let her get fucked around from jump?"

Mario sat straight up. Maybe he wasn't hearing correctly. He couldn't be. He switched his cell to the other ear. To him it sounded like Regina's normally annoying voice said Sasha was locked up. But he knew that couldn't be the case. The lawyer had pretty much assured them that with her having no past contact with the law it was open and shut. "Whoa, whoa, hold up. Slow down, girl. What you say? Stop playing. Where the fuck is Sasha ass at?"

Regina, enraged, was in her feelings, as well she should have been. She not once let up on her justified rant. "You know where she is: locked the fuck up behind being so stupid. Her ass gotta do at least twelve to eighteen months for some shit you got her into." Her voice grew louder with each passing word she spoke about her little sister. "She's pregnant, you asshole. You know what that damn time fucking means? Do you? It means that baby gonna be born behind fucking bars, in damn jail. I swear to God you ain't about shit. Nigga, you all kinds of fucked up for this here bullshit!"

Now on his feet, Mario paced the floor, listening to Regina go off on him. Still in somewhat denial of what she said, he begged her to just slow down and calm down. He wanted her to tell him everything that happened at court with his wife. "Listen, Regina, just tell me what the hell popped off. The lawyer said they had the plea agreement all worked out."

"Well, if that was the damn case, somebody showl forgot to tell that judge that bullshit. 'Cause he banged my sister, hard." Still very much heated, she didn't know how she'd break the news to her elderly parents. Their last-born would be under the jurisdiction of the State of Michigan's prison system for some time to come. In the meantime, Regina explained to Mario word for word, blow by blow what happened at the court proceedings that he should have been the star of in the first place.

Ending the angrily charged conversation with his sister-in-law, Mario tried to contact the lawyer but was told he'd be out of the office for the rest of the day. Although Regina had just told him what happened to Sasha, he wanted to hear it from another reliable source. Maybe it wasn't two years; maybe she'd misunderstood and his wife would come bopping through the front door singing some damn Beyoncé or Mary J. song that she'd been blasting on the radio. Maybe she'd just gone shopping to get her mind off of all the bullshit he'd forced her to go through for the past month or so. Yeah, maybe that was it, he reasoned, dialing the courthouse for information.

"Yes, I need to know the status of Sasha Eubanks." Mario prayed this was no more than an awful joke his wife and her sister were playing on him to teach him a lesson for leaving Sasha hanging earlier. "Yes, E-u-b-a-n-k-s, Eubanks. She was supposed to be sentenced at nine this morning in Judge Raymond's courtroom. Was it rescheduled or something? This is her husband."

CHAPTER FOUR

It'd been a solid week since the judge had changed Sasha's life. The harsh reality that she was not coming home for an extended amount of time was starting to set in. Feeling like an animal trapped in a small box, she'd been forced to sleep on the floor on a pallet with one sheet and one blanket. The fact that she was with child meant nothing to them, just as it meant nothing to the judge. Her back aching or the need for extra food was just another thing on the long list of discomforts she'd dumbly chosen when "standing by her man." The overcrowding in the county jail was against regulations put in place by the federal government, but from the moment Sasha Eubanks was taken into custody all her civil rights flew out the window. She was just another prisoner waiting to get transferred to the penitentiary that would soon become her home for the next twelve months, at least.

"Hey, girl, what you in here for?" asked the overly thick female who slept in one of the few decent bunks.

"Who, me?" Sasha glanced up from the floor wishing she were back home in her pillow-top king-sized bed.

"Yeah, you, ladybug. Why you up in here? You look way too cute to be up here in the hot son of a bitch."

Sasha overlooked the fact that she was obviously being hit on. She had been basically ignored since getting brought up to the all-women inmate floor and she welcomed what she believed to be a friendly face. "They said I had some pills and some drug money, but they're wrong."

"They said," she sarcastically flipped out while sizing Sasha up. "Either you had some pills and that cash or you didn't. What the fuck? You bitches kill me coming all up in here and behind the wall acting like y'all innocent. Y'all be some fake wannabe pussies wanting to get fucked. So is that it, baby doll? You wanna get fucked?"

Sasha was speechless. She blankly stared at the girl, not knowing what to do or say next. A few of the other seasoned inmates couldn't hold their laughter. Many of them had watched the exact same thing pop off day after day in the overcrowded unit. They knew that the ballsy dyke was about to put her beast hand down on another newbie to the system. It wasn't their business to play bodyguard, so each turned a blind eye to what was sure to come next. Some were only there for a short time and they didn't need or want any additional trouble.

Shockingly, before Sasha knew what was happening next, the girl had stood up from her bunk. With ill intentions she towered over Sasha, tugging at her crotch area as if she had a dick. Much too light to fight and definitely too thin to win, Mario's wife looked to the other prisoners for assistance, but unfortunately she found none.

"Look, I don't know if you think I'm that way, but I'm not."

"Well, today your pretty ass is." Reaching down for Sasha's head, the determined dyke grinned knowing she was close to turning another straight female out.

Seconds away from being be sexually assaulted, one of the guards came to the cell gate, saving Sasha. "Hey, Eubanks, you have a visit. Your lawyer is here."

***

"The lawyer just left and things are all bad. I thought you said this wasn't gonna happen. You told me since I didn't have a record I wasn't gonna get in trouble. Why you lie to me like that? Huh? That's messed up, Mario, for real."

Aggravated, Sasha sobbed, pressing the receiver of the phone as close as she possibly could to her face. Rocking back and forth, her legs trembled. Her head had been throbbing nonstop since the judge had her taken away. Of course she was worried about her baby. She asked time and time again to see the nurse because she was suffering from stomach pains and a bad headache. But her request fell upon deaf ears. Told that things would be easier and her sentence would fly by when she was transferred from county jail, Sasha counted down the days until it was time for them to ride her out.

"I know I did, Sasha. I swear I ain't think shit was gonna pop off like it did. I'm just as fucked up behind this bullshit as you is."

"Yeah, okay, Mario, whatever." Her skepticism was evident as she ran her fingers through her nappy, untamed hair. "Just be honest and say you don't care about me or our baby."

"Naw, girl, for real, for real. I ain't bullshitting. Just calm down. Even the lawyer was fucked up in the head when the judge flipped the script like he did. He said him and ol' boy from the prosecutor's office had they deal all official and whatnot until the judge started acting a straight pussy on them and you."

Sasha's mind drifted back to that very moment in time when the judge delivered the verbal blow. "Yeah, he was being an asshole, that's for sure. But he kept asking where you were at. Like he knew we was lying or something. I mean, seriously, why was he doing all that?

Why? I don't understand. He was bugging like he was mad I was standing there instead of you. Why was that, Mario? Huh? Why?"

"Hold the fuck up. You acting like it's my damn fault ol' boy flipped the script on you, like I locked you up!"

"Are you serious, Mario? You did lock me up. It is your damn fault I'm here. That judge wanted to see you standing there, not me. I'm in this place paying the price for what you did."

"Damn, look, Sasha, I don't know why the judge ho ass was bugging. Maybe he caught his wife fucking the pizza delivery man the night before or somebody parked in his damn parking spot. How the fuck I know what was on that man's mind?" Mario immediately got on the defensive. His voice continued to rise as if he were the true victim and not his wife, whom he'd callously thrown under the bus.

"Yeah, you would say something like that, wouldn't you? That's all you think about is somebody cheating," she snapped, growing weary of his excuses and lies. For the next two years she would have to depend on him and her family to hold her down and she knew he wasn't up for the challenge. Sure, she'd proven her love for him when he was incarcerated, but Mario was cut from an entire different cloth. Disgusted, Sasha hung up in his ear, not caring that she still had a minute and fourteen seconds left on the facility-timed call.

Not being able to get her paperwork in order, the county jail officials could not verify that Sasha Eubanks could have any other visitors; that meant her husband—who, at this point, could drop dead—family, or friends. Besides her lawyer, who only had more bad news to deliver, she was isolated from her once almost perfect life.

Mario had been spending the first week of his wife's abrupt incarceration like some sort of a mini-vacation.

It was like Christmas, New Year's, and tax return time all rolled into one. Not bothering to come home for days on end, he was finally able to freely do everything and be everything his wife always accused him of. After having her foot on his neck for so long, Mario's true colors were showing bright and clear.

When it came down to it, deep inside, Mario loved Sasha; that much was true. He knew he'd gotten her locked up and she was now forced to be a soldier and tough it out, but he was out here in these streets free, and he had to live his life. So in spot-on dogmatic fashion the wannabe playa thug couldn't help but push up on every female who hopped, skipped, or jumped. He'd taken to hotels—five star ones at that—a few random strippers he'd met at the club. He caked with another couple of females at Red Lobster, and enticed another to suck his dick in the rear seat of Sasha's SUV, which was now his until further notice or until he missed a payment or two and the repo man came calling. Mario was living a bachelor's dream life, as if Sasha weren't suffering behind bars with his unborn baby growing in her stomach.

With his gambling problem now in full swing, Mario had also managed to start slowly draining Sasha's savings account. He didn't want to but he couldn't help himself. She had been stashing away a little here and a little there for the past few years and she was ready to splurge on her expected bundle of joy with or without Mario's help. Knowing what the bank statements showed, he knew he could hit a lick if he got what he needed.

Eagerly, the sinister-minded husband retrieved Sasha's personal property from the jail, including her purse. Asked by his wife to just put all her belongings up until she came home, Mario wasn't having it. That, of course, was not part of his game plan.

He searched like a trained detective through every item in her purse and wallet. Her credit cards were already maxed out thanks to Sasha's own hand, but the debit card was wide open for the taking. Having prior knowledge of her once cherished pin number, Mario was on. In his eyes, he'd hit the hood jackpot. Making numerous trips to the ATM had become a regular routine when he was falling short on bets or other needed items. Up until now Sasha had full control of her bank account, which would get a monthly deposit from a lawsuit settlement. Now that she was locked up, Mario was working under the low-key contingency that whatever was his wife's was his as well.

What the fuck? She just hung up on me and time wasn't even up. Damn, I know she pissed. And dang, for real for real, she should be. That girl ain't built for this type of bullshit, locked up like some animal. I was wrong as hell to even ask her to eat that charge, but hey. What's done is done. She locked up and I'm still out here and I gotta keep shit going, for her and me and my seed.

Mario's conscience was kicking into full overdrive as he paced the living room floor. In between all his hanging out with the fellas, cheating, and spending Sasha's cash, Mario made a promise to himself that no matter what dirt he would do over the next year, he would at least hold his wife down like she had done for him in the past. After all, she was going to be the mother of his child, the same woman who had stood up and taken the hard time that was rightfully his.

CHAPTER FIVE

Although it took a relatively short time for Sasha to be transferred to the women's prison from the county jail, it seemed like a lifetime. Cramped in the small Department of Corrections van, she felt every pothole on the packed highway of regular "free" people traveling here and there. As they drove by a Taco Bell, two McDonald's, and a Starbucks, it became painfully clear to Sasha that her once fairytale life was over, at least for twelve to eighteen months. Her baby would be born behind these walls and that was that. She would no longer be able to make her own decisions and come and go as she pleased. Thanks to her loving husband Mario, her life as well as the baby's were no longer theirs, but the Michigan Department of Corrections'.

Finally arriving at the front gates, the driver was met by a small group of guards. Realizing this was nothing like the movies, but real life, Sasha's soul ached to go home. Watching the guards exchange paperwork and give the thumbs-up as the huge metal mesh–fence monster was slid back so the van could gain entry, it got realer. Sasha gazed in the faces of the other three females who were on the ride in with her: one who started the journey off with her and the other two who were picked up from other jails. They collectively looked like four deer with their eyes caught in the headlights. It was apparently their first time doing real time in a prison as well. Sasha's stomach started dancing and her palms grew sweaty. This was about to be a nightmare come true.

"Okay, you inmates, off the van now," one guard ordered, swinging the side double doors open. "And hurry up. Let's get this thing done before count time. We need to be done and get you all processed before that."

One by one, they each stepped down onto the grounds and jurisdiction of the Huron Valley Women's Facility. Glancing back over her shoulder, Sasha looked at the fence and the huge stretch of green grass beyond it. Taking a deep breath, even the air felt different than when she was free.

Instructed to get in a line, single file, a pregnant Sasha was second to see the inside of the control center. Just as in the county jail she was processed and fingerprinted, and her picture was taken and she was strip-searched. Issued two state blue uniforms and an inmate number, Sasha Eubanks, now known as 998797, was marched to her cell.

The eyes of multitudes of other inmates were focused on her. Sasha tried to walk with her head held up high and showing no fear, but her lip quivered as she fought back the tears. Her worst nightmare had become a reality. The area she was in smelled like strong disinfectant and the lights were extremely bright. Sasha stood there, saying absolutely nothing, well after the gate had slammed shut. Slowly, she searched the cell for a friendly face like she had dumbly done back in the county jail, but she found none. Her emotions were scrambled. She hated Mario. How could she not? Sasha hated that she had gone against the advice of everyone who loved and cared about her. At this point she despised herself.

Clutching her extra uniform, bedding, and cosmetics bag, Sasha was in denial of what her world now consisted of. Five minutes after stepping foot inside the cubicle for eight women, Mario's pregnant wife screamed out. Her state-issued items fell to the floor. Sharp pains darted throughout her lower midsection. With both hands, the mother-to-be clutched her stomach, dropping to her knees. She was mentally drained and physically weak. The crotch area of her pants was starting to become drenched. Reaching one hand between her legs, Sasha felt extreme wetness. Bringing her hand up to her face, she saw it was covered in blood. She got dizzy. She was short of breath and couldn't speak. It was increasingly hard to breathe as the other inmates looked on. Then, suddenly, for Sasha everything went dark.

"Excuse me, nurse, but what time is it?"

"It's a little bit past four. Why you keep asking? Do you have somewhere to go? A hot date or something?" the nurse in the infirmary teased as if something were truly funny.

Sasha was still in excruciating pain. Both physically and mentally she was going through it. She'd regained consciousness the day before. Back to her wicked reality, she had discovered what had taken place. A pregnant woman's worst fear had occurred. Tragically, she'd lost her and Mario's baby. Not sure if it was stress, a physical defect with her body, or just God's way of telling her she wasn't ready to be a mother, Sasha mourned what could have been. Even though she was beyond pissed at Mario's terrible ass for placing her in this predicament, part of her still yearned to hear his voice. "Is there any way I can call my husband?"

"Call your husband?" The nurse paused from glancing down at Sasha's chart. "I'm sorry, dear, but we don't have phones in place just for inmates to use at their leisure. There's proper procedure and paperwork. Do you even have an approved calling list yet?"

"I understand that, miss, but this is an emergency."

"An emergency? How so? Your vitals are all good. You're stable, besides maybe a bit of discomfort to your abdomen. But that will definitely pass in a few days or so."

"Yes, but"—Sasha slightly turned her head to the side as if she was ashamed of what happened—"I just lost my baby; his baby. I need to tell him. He needs to know."

The nurse had seen this exact thing more times than she cared to recall. Prisoners would come to the infirmary and try to use their illnesses, no matter how minor or severe, to place a call home. Some, she felt, had valid reasons to want to hear a loved one's voice, while others were just on that bullshit. Either way it was against the facility rules and regulations to allow calls from that area. That's why she tried to make as many jokes as possible, to keep the women's spirits up. Although she went home to her husband and children every night, she could only imagine the torment any person felt not being able to do the same. "Look, dear. I'm sorry for your loss. I truly am. But unfortunately the officials here don't consider having a miscarriage an emergency. This is a women's prison so the warden and most of the staff have grown immune to much."

"Oh, my God. You people are heartless in here, like wild animals. I could never be so callous. I couldn't do your job or want your job even if it was the last thing on earth to do to make money. I couldn't live with myself being so mean to the next human."

Instantly the nurse was offended. She tried to be sympathetic to Sasha, but she'd crossed the line with the name-calling, indirect or otherwise. "Look, Eubanks, I'ma give you these two aspirins for pain; then you're on your own. By the time you get back to your cell, you should be able to use the inmate phones. Then I guess you can tell your husband about your bad luck."

"Wow, really? That's it?" Sasha quizzed with a growing attitude and a frown on her face.

"Okay, inmate. I'm warning you. Don't try to get out of order with me and catch a ticket in your first seventy-two hours. I was trying to be lenient just because, but you're no one special around here. Behind these walls you're just another female doing time, one who lost a baby. And, truth be told, if you cared so much about that child you wouldn't have broken the law and been in here in the first place. So suck it up, take these meds, and get yourself together to leave. I'm getting ready to finish up on your paperwork now."

Sasha practically snatched the extra-small paper container holding the aspirin out of the nurse's hand. Without bothering to drink any water, she threw the Styrofoam cup into the trash while chewing the yellow coated pills. With each slow movement of her jaw, Sasha mean mugged the nurse in deep thought. *I see how it is up in here. I lost my baby and no one cares. And if I tell Mario, he probably don't care either. It's just me against the world. If I want to make it through these next two years and get back to my normal life, I need to be anybody else but who I been. I can't keep being weak. That shit is a wrap.*

CHAPTER SIX

Regina had been going through a rough couple of weeks since Sasha's incarceration. She couldn't believe that she and her little sister could no longer go shopping. There would be no one to watch her small children. No one she could just pick up the phone to gossip with. That was a wrap. The only small glimmer of hope in this entire rotten situation was that she would be able to care for Sasha's baby when it was born. She knew Mario wasn't worth the skin God had blessed him with. The chances of him actually stepping up to the plate and doing the right thing were slim to none. Just as Mario turned his back on Sasha, Regina knew the dirty bastard would do the same to his child.

She and her little sister's best friend Kat had heard about Mario and his recent "financial windfall." The word was also out in the streets about all the different women he was running with. Mario was so reckless when it came to the jump-offs he was caking with that some had even posted pictures of him with them in hot tubs, at Cedar Point and, most disrespectfully chilling, at what seemed to be Sasha's living room.

Kat's uncle shot dice with Mario on the regular and kept her updated on the major hits in the pockets he'd suffer. Kat was surprised that Mario was even still alive let alone still gambling. Rumor had it he was still over $3,100 in the hole to Big Dae Dae. Everyone in the city knew Big Dae Dae didn't play when it came to his money and niggas had to come correct. And even though Mario had lost and paid the six feet five, 285-pound goon well over $9,000 in the past two weeks or so, he was still no exception to the rule. Mario had to leave him Sasha's SUV keys an entire seventy-two hours until he could get all the cash gathered he owed. He'd withdrawn all of the funds he could from the ATM daily and had even pawned his wife's wedding ring.

Kat was also told by her uncle that by the time Big Dae Dae returned Sasha's vehicle, it had been sideswiped on the passenger side door. The interior had a few huge blunt holes burned on the seats and it smelled like stale arm funk and Hennessy. Mario was no fool. He knew better than to bug out on Big Dae Dae about the returned condition. It wasn't worth the possible physical beat down let alone the possibility of being blackballed from all the high stakes traveling dice and card games that popped off throughout various locations in Detroit. Mario's gambling and bad luck was at fault, so he cowardly reasoned.

Without question or delay, Kat went straight to her best friend's sister with the 411. "My uncle said that ho-ass bitch-made nigga been over the way dogging Sasha's name. Dragging her through the mud saying that he got her trained better than any ho he ever fucked with. Saying she was on her hands and knees begging his ugly ass to do the time for him so he wouldn't go back."

"Are you fucking serious?" Regina reached for the television remote and pressed the mute button. After hushing her small children and sending them into the other room, she started going. "You mean to tell me this nickel-slick punk not only got my little sister sitting in jail for his dumb ass, he out here in the free world bragging about it? Where they do that bullshit at?"

"That's what I said," Kat agreed, equally heated.

"But that's all right though. It's all good, because when that visiting form bullshit go through, I'm gonna go see Sasha. I'ma be all on her head to divorce that lame. I told her not to marry his jailbird ass in the first place, but she wouldn't listen. Now she gonna bless that fool with a baby."

Kat interjected, "Please don't remind me about that situation before I throw up in my damn mouth. Every time I hear shit about what he out here doing with Sasha's money and with these hood rats I wanna just run up and sock him dead in the jaw myself. I know he looked out for me back in the day out at the park, but shit, that was then, this is now."

Regina couldn't wait until daybreak. No sooner than she dropped her kids off at daycare, she was on a mission. The angry sibling made it her business to go seek Mario out. After several drive-bys, the front blinds were finally open, indicating the late-night hood hustler was finally awake. Regina had caught him at the house, and now she wanted answers.

Irate, she questioned her brother-in-law about what she knew to be true. No doubt he lied and lied and lied. He claimed he'd been dropped off the night before and left Sasha's SUV parked at his boy's crib because he had been drinking and didn't want to drive. Regina knew her brother-in-law was full of it, but she had no concrete face-to-face facts to stand on, just Kat's secondhand info.

After warning Mario that she'd be checking in on her sister's house from time to time, she stormed onto the porch. Still exhausted from shooting dice until almost five in the morning, he shrugged his shoulders as Sasha's sister drove off.

Always in beast mode when it came to females only, Mario's first thought was to tell Regina, Kat, and whoever the fuck else to stay out of his damn business. He was grown and did whatever he wanted, whenever he wanted. However, he knew the nosey pair of women had the direct pipeline to his wife. If they were to go back running off at the mouth to Sasha, the inmate, already irritated with him, could easily arrange for her sister or aged parents to take over her business affairs. That would definitely include her bank savings accounts that received the monthly deposit from the lawsuit settlement. If Mario was to lose that, he'd not be able to maintain the bullshit lifestyle he'd grown accustomed to.

In the days to come, he managed to keep the SUV out of Regina's sight until the damage to the door was fixed and the vehicle was detailed. As for the holes, Sasha knew he smoked weed so he would say he'd done it by mistake if it was to ever come up. Nevertheless, Mario was chill knowing he had at least a year to cross that bridge before his loyal wife saw the SUV or freedom again.

"You have a call from Sasha, an inmate at the Michigan Department of Corrections. If you feel that this call is harassing in nature or unwanted, please press one. In order to accept calls from an inmate at the Michigan Department of Corrections, press two."

Mario was good and high off of half a blunt he'd smoked. A huge, goofy smile graced his face while he held the phone close to his ear. In spite of all of the reckless things he'd done since his wife had been locked up, he was still overjoyed to hear her voice. The last few times they'd spoken, Sasha was not giving him a break. Rightfully so, inmate 998797 made him feel guilty and like the piece of rotten shit human being he was for letting her take the fall. Quickly pressing the number two on his keypad, the pair was finally connected.

"Hello."

"Yeah, hello, Sasha? Is that you? What up, doe?"

"Yeah, it's me. What's going on?"

"Nothing much, girl. Just been lying back in the crib, that's all." Mario paused, trying to see if he could sense any strange vibe in her voice that indicated she knew he was lying. "I was just thinking about you and my seed. Are y'all okay up there? I called down to the county and they said you'd been transferred. How was the ride out? Are you still pissed with a nigga or what?"

"Naw, I'm not angry anymore. I made the decision to do what I did; so be it. But, umm, umm, well, I need to talk to you and I know I don't have long. The operator said fifteen minutes so I guess that's what it is."

Mario had been leaning back on the couch, but now he sat straight up. He had done enough time behind bars to know how fast those minutes would fly by. So he gave Sasha her time to get off her chest whatever it was she wanted before the call was terminated. "Go ahead, baby. Tell me what's going on. I'm listening."

Sasha was still weak. Her mindset felt out of sorts. The penitentiary aspirin she'd taken had zero affect on the pain and discomfort she was feeling. Wanting nothing more than to return to her cell and get some rest, Sasha, swiftly becoming depressed, fought back the tears. Having just decided that she had to develop a thicker skin to survive her two-year hiatus in hell, she heard Mario's voice and, just like that, her game plan was done. She began to fall completely apart. "Listen, Mario, I don't know what happened. Maybe I was stressed out. Maybe I was worried and didn't get enough rest. I don't know. The doctors said—"

"The doctors? What you mean doctors? What the fuck you talking about, Sasha?" Mario cut her off midsentence with a barrage of questions.

It didn't take Sasha long to break all the way down. "Mario"—her voice cracked as she spoke—"I lost the baby."

"Hold up. What you just say?" He stood, thinking he must have heard his wife wrong. Pacing back and forth from the living room to the dining room, the dining room to the kitchen, and the kitchen out onto the front porch, Mario grew agitated.

Sasha lowered her head. She prayed none of the other inmates would notice her dropping tears. It was bad enough she had passed out, but now she was determined to go hard. "I know you hurt, I guess. But God knows best. Maybe He didn't want my child being born behind bars like some caged animal. Maybe He felt like we wouldn't make good parents."

"Naw, bitch. Don't run that God bullshit on me. God ain't do that shit. Your janky ass probably did," Mario taunted, searching his pocket for a lighter. "The last time your dumb ass talked to me you was blowing that crazy shit out your dental, acting like I got you locked up."

"What?" Sasha paused, getting just as heated as her husband had become. "I know I didn't just tell you I lost our baby and you blaming me."

"And what? Who the fuck else I'm gonna blame?" Mario lit a Newport, taking a long pull. "You supposed to be the damn vessel for my seed and you done messed around and fucked that up. Thanks a lot, bitch."

At this point in the once private conversation, Sasha came totally out of her bag. Her voice grew louder with each passing word. The other inmates, as well as the guards, were now ear hustling whether they wanted to or not. The incarcerated, once pregnant female had lost the one thing that was giving her any small amount of hope the day before, and she definitely was not in the mood for Mario's judgments.

"Listen, you ho-ass piece of shit motherfucker. You got this game and me all the way twisted. I'm posted up in here doing this time because of your no-good black ass.

I stood up tall because you was too weak to be a man. If you would've had any type of balls it wouldn't be no way in hell you'd let your pregnant wife be up in this stanking place."

"Yo, Sasha, who in the fuck you talking to like that? You must have lost a lot of blood in your brain or something."

Sasha didn't care who was listening, looking, or concerned. She heard the "one minute left" warning speech on the phone and she went all the way in for the kill. "What you mean who the fuck I'm talking to like that? You, nigga, that's who. Remember you out there in them streets living because of me. Did you forget? That's my house, my SUV, my jewelry, and my money you spending. And you better put some money on my books before you be homeless and hungry. I pay them bills and put food in the house whether you nickel hustling or not. I swear on everything that . . . Hello? Hello? Hello?"

The inmates and the guards knew the new inmate had run out of time on her call, but they watched her still say hello several more times before she angrily slammed the receiver down.

"Hey, Eubanks, take it easy over there. That's prison property you trying to destroy." The second-shift guard would have written any other prisoners up, but he knew 998797 had just suffered a huge blow and was not thinking clearly. "Why don't you just go back to your bunk for a little while and get it together?"

Sasha gladly took his suggestion and did just that. Falling back onto the thin mattress, she locked her fingers behind her head. Staring up at the bright fluorescent lights, she closed her eyes, wishing she were anywhere but prison. In a matter of minutes, a few of the females who had been in the dayroom listening to her conversation interrupted, introducing themselves.

CHAPTER SEVEN

Angela Vega, known around the way as Angie V, was just getting to work. After spending practically all night in the emergency room with her small daughter, the youngest of three, she was exhausted. A single mother, she was forced to be the substitute father when all of her "baby daddies" chose to abandon her and their seeds. Pro-life in belief, she didn't believe in abortions. So if she was careless enough to get knocked up, she'd be woman enough to stand up, no matter what the circumstances were.

Sadly Angela Vega learned that harsh lesson and her right to life belief was tested early on. Once the academic head of her graduating class, Angie V didn't quite remember what exactly sidetracked her from her studies. One minute she was taking math and English tests and window-shopping for the perfect but affordable prom dress. Suddenly out of nowhere her young life was turned upside down.

Asked to help out on a special literacy project, the dedicated teen stayed after school on a few occasions later than the other participants. The next thing the virgin teacher's pet knew was that she was spread-eagled in the back of an empty classroom, both hands gripping the sides of a desk, with the principal's dick buried deep inside her womb from the rear. They both enjoyed the scandalous deed for weeks until they were discovered by the janitor. Having no morals, the janitor stood, broom in hand, bargaining that if sweet-faced Angela Vega didn't suck him off, he'd rat them out. Repulsed by the thought, she refused, even at the urging of the grimy-intentioned principal who didn't want to run the risk of losing his job, family, and possibly freedom.

Angie V knew she was dead wrong for banging a much older man, one married at that. However, no matter how book smart she may have been, her family's financial situation was shitty to say the least. Besides the mature sex he was blessing her with, gifts and money were major draws. For the first time since starting high school she was able to walk into a store and buy any dress or pair of sneakers she wanted.

She was caught all the way up, but it wasn't worth the fallout. Exposed to the vice principal, teachers on staff, students, and parents, Angela Vega was shunned and ridiculed, and her name was dragged through the mud. She was forced to leave school days after the local news caught wind of the story. Some said it was the educator's rightfully bitter wife, while some said it was a jealous student he was rumored to also be having relations with. Nevertheless, without enough credits to graduate, Angie was left with no school to attend in the district.

To make matters even worse, when the teen discovered she was knocked up by the married man, he opted to commit suicide, leaving her all alone to abort or have their illicit love child. The choice was hers. Angie V's oldest was born seven months later, prematurely.

Walmart's oversized parking lot was full when Angie V drove up in her late-model struggle buggy. That along with the fact that it was the third of the month was proof enough that this extra shift she was voluntarily working would be long. Like most single mothers she was barely making ends meet and did whatever, whenever, for the sake of her children.

Annoyed that her smock wasn't where she'd left it hanging the evening before, she finally located the blue and yellow vest. Slipping it on, she took a deep breath, then exhaled. Punching her employee code in the time clock, she was ready to start her shift. Dragging her weary body down the stairs, Angie V placed her cell on vibrate and tucked it deep down into her rear pocket. The managers frowned on employees using their phones during working hours, but Angie V had to ensure the young girl who babysat for her could get in touch if need be.

"Ms. Vega, you are on the self-service aisle today. I know you are used to ringing straight out on the register, but today is your lucky day. We need help down on this end."

Angela thanked the front end manager. She was tired from being at the hospital and up the night before with her sick child, and welcomed the slower-paced job detail. Time seemed to drag by, although in reality it had been three hours of the six-hour shift she'd volunteered for. Just as she reached in her back pocket to get out her cell on the sly, Angie V was met with an extremely confused customer. Approaching him, she immediately took notice he was holding an armful of items that could only feed a family of one. "Do you need some help?"

"Yeah, hell yeah." Mario had just about given up on purchasing the bottle of raspberry lemonade, bag of Doritos, cheese slices, jalapeño peppers, and can of stewed meat. "I keep trying to put this damn scan thing on the package across this thing and it seems like the bullshit ain't working for a fucking nigga like me. They make simple shit be more difficult than it need to be."

Angie V laughed to herself. It wasn't hard to recognize this guy was no more than an uneducated, uncouth street thug. The fact that he couldn't form a complete sentence without cursing was one of the dead giveaways. "Hold up a minute. Let me help you. Just put all your things down right here." She smiled, seeing he was now checking her out.

"Thanks, ma. I'm just a dude out here in this world trying to navigate through it. I need a good woman like you to help a brotha on this day-to-day bullshit. You see I already can't buy this food without your help. So what's up? You and me is made for each other."

"Oh, yeah, is that right?"

"Yeah, sweetie, it is." Mario schemed, wondering if he could maybe get some ass later.

"'Sweetie.'" Angie V turned up her nose, indicating she was offended as she started to scan his items.

"Damn, girl, you all acting uppity I see, working at Walmart and shit like you a lawyer or something. You need to get your ass off your shoulders and stop bugging out. You need a man like me to get you right."

"Look, sir, I'm finished with assisting you with your items. If there isn't anything else I can do for you . . ." Angie V started to walk off but was stopped by Mario's forearm blocking her path. "And please, sir, be so kind as to keep your body from touching mine and invading my personal space."

"Yo, shawty, slow your roll. Knock it off. A guy straight ain't mean shit by saying that." Mario was simple-minded. He knew all the right words to say to the common hood rat females he was used to kicking it with, but this girl was seemingly different, much different. The way she made sure to make keep eye contact with him when she spoke, and had no problem checking him, she reminded him of Sasha, his wife. The wife he was disrespecting by even trying to push up on the next female. The wife who was doing time behind bars that rightfully belonged to him.

But at this moment, like all the others that had passed since Sasha had been locked up, Mario didn't care. He was out for himself as always. He was on the hunt for some pussy from another random chick and he was gonna run game to get it, flat out. "Look, Miss Lady, I just wanna get to know you a little better. See what you and me can get popping. Let me at least take you out to dinner or something; maybe lunch." Mario reached into his pocket, pulling out what appeared to be a baby-sized knot. While attempting to stunt, he accidentally dropped his debit card, which of course had Sasha's name on it. Quickly, he swooped it up, hoping his soon-to-be conquest had not noticed.

Angie V was not a sack chaser by a long shot. After what had taken place between her and her oldest child's deceased father, she vowed never to be swayed by the glitter of gold again. However, just as time changes, so does one's circumstances. Her rent was past due and the lights were scheduled to be turned off in the next seven days. Even though she was getting a paycheck every two weeks and braiding hair when she could, Angie V and her three small children were still trapped in poverty. This guy was definitely not her type, but she wasn't looking for a man to settle down with and possibly become stepfather to her kids. Low on money for the bills, in a moment of weakness, she decided to take the easy way out.

Looking around as if the morality police were somewhere hiding ready to jump out and pounce, Angie V slowly lowered her guard. "Oh, yeah? You wanna take me out, huh?"

"Yeah, ma. Let me take you out tonight and grab something to eat."

"Then what?" She cut straight to the chase, not needing a meal but cold, hard cash for the rent and light bills.

Mario paused, licking his lips once more. She had been going hard since he stepped to her and now she was flipping the script like she was pushing up on him. He was no fool by a long shot and quickly figured out where this was going. Having nothing to lose, he went for it. "Then it can be whatever you want it to be. Shidddd, with me quiet as it's kept we ain't even gotta eat nothing. We can straight go somewhere and chill out; ya feel me?"

Angie V took out her cell and locked his number in. She hated herself and every second of what she was doing; but her kids having food in their stomachs and a roof over their heads was all that mattered. With shame in her tone, she gave into the devil's bait of temptation. It wasn't like she was a virgin, she reasoned, so one more dick she had to take for the team was what it would have to be. "Okay, so I get off at six-thirty this evening. You can meet me in the parking lot if you want. Is that good for you, Mr. Big Shit Talker?"

"Cool with me, baby doll, it ain't no thang."

She stared him directly in the eyes so there would be no misunderstanding about what was going to take place later. "All right, like I said, six-thirty, but I gotta go pick up my kids by no later than nine. And I wanna stop by and pay my DTE bill before that."

Mario grinned, knowing for sure he was gonna hit them guts later; at least, for a small fee. He'd be eating Angie's box instead of the jailhouse cook-up he had just purchased the items to make. "Your DTE bill, huh? How much is it?"

Angie V knew the overdue amount to avoid shutoff and the total bill owed. And since she was lowering herself to sell pussy she wasn't going to sell it that cheap. He had a knot, so paying whatever she said should not have been a problem. "It's $283 in total."

Mario wasn't accustomed to tricking off one third that amount on the rats from around the way he'd been running with as of late; but he could tell this female was like Sasha: different. "Okay, then, love, see you at six-thirty. I'll be on time and waiting."

As Mario left through the door, bag in hand, Angie V hated herself already but knew a real, true mother did what she had to do for the sake of her kids, right or wrong. She had no idea what she was getting herself into with dealing with him, but she knew she had no choice. It was fuck or starve. The decision was easy.

CHAPTER EIGHT

Regina traveled the same road her little sister had been on weeks earlier. She felt every pothole Sasha did and passed by every restaurant as well. The only difference was Regina was not in handcuffs and she was more than free to stop on that long, bumpy road when and if she pleased.

Finally arriving at the prison, Regina found a place to park. After emptying her pockets she got her driver's license out and stuffed it in her rear pocket. Leaving her purse stashed on the rear floor behind the passenger's seat, the older sibling was ready to make her first of what would be more visits to come. Going through the unsettling process, Regina was led to the visitor's room where Sasha was waiting, sitting off to the side.

"Oh, my God, Sasha. I'm so glad to see you. I miss you and so does Mom and Daddy."

"Me too. I miss you and them." Sasha was overcome by seeing a member of her family. She fought it, but she could no longer hold back the flow of waterworks. "I needed you so bad when I lost the baby. Regina, it was awful. This place is awful! I swear, you have no idea."

Regina dropped tears as well, seeing her sister go through it firsthand. "Sis, I can only imagine. I almost wanted to turn around and leave as soon as I saw that big-ass gate closing. But seeing my little sister is the only thing that matters to me. So I'm good."

The sisters hugged it out as other prisoners greeted their guests as well. No more than five minutes into the visit, Regina started spilling her guts. Not dry snitching on her brother-in-law, she came directly out, telling her little sister what Mario had been up to. Not one to mince words, Regina didn't leave out one single thing that she'd heard the womanizer had done over the past month or so. The multiple women he had been rumored to take to hotel rooms, the low-budget shopping sprees of sneakers and T-shirts, popping bottles at the club, taking strippers to his and Sasha's home, and his gambling losses. Regina gave her sibling an earful of Mario's indiscretions, leaving her almost in shock.

"Regina, are you freaking serious? Please tell me you lying. Please tell me this is a joke and you just pulling my leg."

"Naw, sis, I wish I were. But that nigga you married and all up in here doing time for is a no-good sack of shit! The whole city knows it but you. It ain't no big secret. He ain't even trying to hide his dirty-ass deeds."

Sasha was enraged but she knew she had to hold her composure. She couldn't run the risk of getting any tickets, which would add more time to her sentence. She'd already avoided two when she'd first arrived, thanks to the nurse and the guard letting her slide. However, she knew she had no more chances. Instead of screaming and yelling like she wanted to do, Sasha suffered in silence, knowing one day she'd get revenge on Mario for being the dog he was.

Trying their best to relax her mind, Sasha and Regina both enjoyed the rest of the visit, having come up with a plan to stop Mario from taking everything that Sasha had built and running it straight into the ground. When it was time for the visit to come to an end, Sasha sadly said her good-bye.

When Regina was let out of the secured visiting area, inmate Eubanks was led to the back then searched before returning to the common prisoner living area. Sasha rushed back to her unit with one thing and one thing only on her mind as she lay back on her bunk: plotting on Mario.

Minutes after the evening count time was completed, Sasha headed toward the phones. Punching in her pin code, she then dialed her supposedly loyal husband's number and waited for him to answer. *This motherfucker got me and the game twisted. If he think I'm just gonna sit back and let him play me, he dead wrong as two left feet.* Sasha's new beastlike attitude and disposition since arriving at prison was shining through and Mario was about to get a taste of it once more.

Regina rode back to the city, content that Mario would soon be relieved of all things he was in charge of that solely belonged to her little sister. At this point, it would be up to him whether he wanted to relinquish the power he felt he had the easy way or the hard way.

Regina was nothing like her sister. She was far from naïve and not ever in the mood for games of any sort. Although she had small children to tend to, she always found time to show up and show out at the Black Union Zodiacs, a motorcycle club she'd been a part of since being a teen. After trying for years to coax Sasha and Kat to join the club, known citywide, Regina finally stopped going every week after giving birth to her first child. But rest assured if she ever needed her brothers and sisters to come to her assistance they would have her back.

Snatching up her cell off the passenger seat, Regina placed a call to Kat, informing her how the visit went. Shortly after that, she was swinging by the babysitter's and then she was on her way home. *I can't wait for Sasha to call tonight and give me the word, 'cause when she do that's Mario's black ugly ass! He gonna feel me for fucking over my damn sister and running game.*

Kat was almost as ecstatic as Regina that Mario had been exposed. She wished she could have been there to see the expression on Sasha's face when she got the bad news and was forced to face the truth. It wasn't that she had any ill will toward her best friend; it was just that she had been telling Sasha for days, weeks, months, and even years that Mario was no good. That he was fucking her over and would never change. Time and time again, Kat had given Sasha ample opportunity to catch her beloved, cherished husband red-handed in some bullshit she had stumbled upon on the humble; but Sasha had declined, not wanting to face the obvious. At times Kat wondered if Sasha was just slow and dumb or just scared to face the truth. Whatever the case, Regina claimed she had finally broken down that naïve wall of denial that her little sister had when it came to Mario.

Rubbing the scar the bullet had left on her lower leg, Kat sucked her teeth and shook her head. She looked at the time on her cell phone, knowing that if all went as planned, Mario would be getting his eviction papers from her best friend's life once and for all. Like dominoes falling, Mario in turn would be going on what could probably be his last all-out, "balls to the wall" addicted gambling excursion with Sasha's finances later as well.

Calling her uncle, Kat gave Big Dae Dae a heads-up that Mario would be in the dice spot one final time, and to make sure he was there to break his pockets.

"Yeah, Unc, no doubt that slime ball nigga Mario probably gonna be betting big tonight. He about to get cut the fuck off so I know he gotsa go hard a few more times before my girl cuts the cord for good. Then you know when she cut him off, he done. So hit that fool in the head good!"

Big Dae Dae laughed at his niece. Over the years he'd seen both her and her mother hold a grudge over some of the simplest things a man could imagine. But Kat was going overboard with the hate and wanting revenge so he had to ask why. "Damn, Kat, I know the young'un a little clown with his shit, but you going extra on li'l homie who looked out for you back in the day. As far as I know he slanging them pills from time to time and a li'l bit of weed, but as far as his ass getting that bread from Sasha, that's between them two, Kat; don't you think?"

Kat shook her head as if he could see her through the phone. "Hell naw, it ain't between them when she too dumb to see the truth. What kinda friend would I be if I didn't put her up on his ho-ass shit?"

"If she was crazy enough to actually go to jail and do time for that lame, trust me, she already knows he ain't shit and she must like it. I'm telling you, Kat, you can't beat a couple no matter what kind of good intentions you may have."

"Fuck all that you talking about, Unc; and fuck Mario. Bust that nigga's ass later and share some of that cheese with your family!"

CHAPTER NINE

"You have a call from Sasha, an inmate at the Michigan Department of Corrections. If you feel that this call is harassing in nature or unwanted, please press one. In order to accept calls from an inmate at the Michigan Department of Corrections, press two."

Mario had just jumped out of the shower and he was drying off when his cell rang. Praying it was not a call from his mixed-breed soon-to-be jump-off cancelling their "paid date," he grabbed his phone. Recognizing the strange three-digit exchange flashing on the screen, he knew it was a call from prison.

Even though the last time he had spoken to his wife he'd gotten handed his ass on a silver platter, Mario still wanted to hear her voice. He assumed she received the JPay payment he'd put on her books earlier while at Walmart, and he hoped that she was pleased. Sure, he was going to bang another female's lights out shortly, but that didn't take anything away from her and them. He was still going to hold her down the best he could just like she'd done for him. Fuck what her sister and best friend thought; he would have his wife's back and make her believe she was the only one for him. Excited, he pressed two so they could be connected.

"Hello." Sasha's seething attitude could automatically be heard through her voice.

"Hey, baby doll. I was hoping you'd call a nigga."

"Oh, yeah, is that right? You was hoping I was calling you for what? To tell you where some more money is stashed at that you can lose to Kat's uncle? To tell you where I got another SUV at that you can tear up? Or to give you my blessings for fucking around with all them hoes I heard you been running with since I been gone?"

It was apparent that her best friend, or Regina, or someone else from the outside had made a visit, sent a letter, or something because the cat was out the bag, so to speak. Mario couldn't get a single word in. Sasha had been going off on him since the word hello and she had not let up. She was hell-bent on getting her money's worth for this fifteen minutes and Mario was not going to stop her, even though he tried.

"Bae, stop—"

"Don't 'bae' me. And don't tell me to stop. You fake as fuck," Sasha raged as her voice got louder and more determined with each passing word. "So since you out in the real world being so damn fake, I got a good-ass idea for your black ass. Why don't you do that shit on your own dime?"

"Say what?" Mario stopped drying off and sat down on the side of the bed.

"You heard me loud and clear, Mario. We done and so is you using my money."

Mario had to think quickly to hold on to what he had. He had grown accustomed to doing dirt and getting away with it, so for Sasha to check him, even from behind bars, he was shocked. The last few times they had spoken, his once tame-mouth wife had been coming out of her bag and acting a fool. He knew he had those verbal attacks and so much more coming for all the stunts he'd pulled over the years, but hearing her say she was done with him was still a blow to his ego. "Look, bae, I'm confused.

How am I supposed to be using your money? I've been doing exactly what we talked about when you was back in the county. I paid the light bill. I paid the water bill. I paid the summer taxes on the house and I paid the SUV note."

"Oh, yeah?" Sasha stopped yelling long enough to listen to Mario's claims of responsibility.

Mario knew his wife like the back of his hand. The con man husband knew that if Sasha closed her mouth long enough to hear what he was saying, he could run game like he always did. "Yes, bae. I've been out here doing everything I'm supposed to do. I love the shit out of you. The only thing I forgot was a few days I forgot to water your flowers and when they looked weepy and shit a nigga went to Home Depot to get some spray for them."

"You've been watering my flowers?" Sasha's rant slowed down and Mario took that same window of opportunity to get in where he fitted in.

"Of course I have, bae. I know how much those crazy growing plants mean to you. And I've been making sure to pay the lawn people to keep your parents' grass cut every week just like before. I'm doing everything right, Sasha, and you keep hollering at me and now accusing me of bullshit. I know I should've stood up, but I was fucked up in the head. I wasn't thinking clear. I'm sorry, Sasha. If I could take it all back, I would. I even asked the lawyer, but he said it was too late. You can ask him. He ain't gonna lie."

"Yeah, well, it's just that to my understanding you been out there shooting dice, getting drunk, and dealing with all sorts of females." Sasha's original tone had come down at least three or four octaves and her husband kept laying it on thick.

Mario grinned, knowing he was making headway. "Yeah, you mean like the old lady at Walmart who helped me send that money to you today? Is that the type of females you talking about?"

"Money? Walmart? What are you talking about now, Mario?"

Mario stood up from the bed and started to get dress in his new fit. He knew his wife was back on his line and she was ripe to hear, accept, and eat any bullshit he was serving. "You know, baby doll, the same way you used to put money on my books through JPay with your debit card? Well, they got the shit hooked up so a nigga can just slide through Walmart and hook they peoples up. That's what I did today, earlier."

"You did? On your own without me asking you to? I can't believe it."

"Yes, bae. And yeah, I ain't gonna lie. You know me. I have been shooting dice, but I been winning. I swear on everything I been knocking niggas in the head. The money I sent to you today was mine. I won that shit. So whichever one of them bitter-minded bitches who been filling your head with that garbage about me is just hating," Mario proclaimed, lacing up his new sneakers that had just been purchased by Sasha's settlement check from the first of the month.

"Well, I heard differently. I heard you lost big time and pawned my damn SUV to Kat's uncle and he had an accident," Sasha suspiciously quizzed, wondering why her sister or best friend would lie on her man.

"I did what? Girl, that's fucking lie! Your nosey-ass sister came over here early one morning talking that mess Kat had told her. And I bet she can't tell you she saw that SUV with one dent on it."

"Well, she didn't say she actually saw it firsthand, so—"

"So there the fuck you have it. More of Kat's famous fables and lies. Look, Sasha, I might not be the best hus-band in the world but I'm always gonna have your back from this point on. I know you love a nigga. I see you's a straight-up soldier." Still running game, he sprayed on some cologne. Ironically it was his wife's favorite scent on him. As Mario stood posted in the full-length mirror admiring himself, he was glad when the prerecorded voice timer cut in, alerting them there was only one minute remaining in the call. He was close to running late in meeting up with Angie V and he didn't want to run the risk of missing out on banging out her back.

"Well, it's almost count time, so when it's over I'm going to call you back so we can finish talking and I can figure out what I'm going—"

Seconds later Mario smiled as Sasha was cut off. *I swear that dumb bitch be getting on my last nerve. I'm trying to be cool, but she pressing me too much about what the next ho say. Her sister's and Kat's good grimy asses need to go get some dick and chill the fuck out.* Grabbing the SUV keys off the dining room table scattered with mail, Mario set the burglar alarm and darted off the front porch.

Mario pulled up in the parking lot. After driving around for five minutes, he finally found a space somewhat near the entrance. Checking his cell phone, the married cunt hound was glad Angie V had not hit him up to back out of their impending date. Taking a quick look down at the time then back at the door repeatedly, his manhood started to jump. Since Sasha was gone he'd gotten more than his fair share of pussy, but was truly anticipating this.

It was nearing six-thirty and Mario now had his eyes focused on the door. Hoping there was no rear employee door, he counted down the seconds turning into minutes.

Ten minutes went by and he was just about to give up hope when Angie V emerged from the double door exit. Holding a few bags in her hand, she headed to what Mario knew must've been her car. Amazed that the rust bucket she'd opened the door of even started, let alone was safe to drive on the street, he drove around, blocking her path. Blowing the horn twice, Mario signaled to her.

"Hey, Miss Lady. What's going on with you?"

"Oh, hey." Angie V acted as if she barely wanted to speak or even hold her head up to look Mario in his face.

"I know you ain't forget about me, have you? A dude like me been waiting all day. So what's the deal? We good or what?" Mario tapped the side of his hand on the steering wheel, watching every move Angie V made.

Wanting nothing more than to back out of the reckless impromptu arrangement she'd made, struggling single mother Angela Vega was seconds away from doing just that when her babysitter called. The girl was demanding to get paid this evening when the kids were picked up. Wanting to take the money owed to the babysitter and pay the overdue portion of the light bill, Angie V knew that was no longer an option. The girl had been more than patient. She'd been waiting for weeks, allowing Angela to get caught up on some other bills she claimed she had to pay. But enough was enough. The babysitter knew if she didn't put her foot down she'd never see a dime, because it was clear the mother of three would never be debt free. So having run out of ideas of how to keep her little family out of the dark, Angie swallowed her pride. Her pussy now officially had a price tag on it.

"Yeah, we good." She tried to smile at Mario but her jaws hurt to do so.

"Okay, cool. That's what's up. So you gonna ride with me or what?" Mario clasped his hands together and started rubbing them as if he was scheming on a come up.

"Naw, I'm gonna follow you. Just lead the way," she announced, tossing the bags she was carrying in the rear seat of her car.

"You sure?" Mario asked, wondering if her vehicle could keep up with him. And of course as bad as he was yearning for laying Angie V down on a bed, he didn't want to run the risk of her backing out and changing her mind while she was trailing him to the room. If she was sitting right next to him, even if she was feeling apprehensive and having second thoughts, he'd be there to coax her back on the right track of happily giving up the ass.

Moments later they were en route to the hotel. Mario felt it was best not to go too far out of the way to get a room so she would feel comfortable. He wanted to ask her if she wanted something to eat or drink, but by the way she was acting before they pulled off, he left well enough alone. Besides, fuck spending more cash than needed for her benefit. Mario would keep it strictly business with her, just the way she appeared to want it: cash and carry. She was a freak and would be treated as such.

Only minutes away from his destination, Mario looked in his rearview mirror. She was at least five or six cars behind. He knew Angie V was having a hard time keeping up with him through traffic. Slowing down, he waited for her to catch up; then he drove a few more miles before turning into the parking lot of a Red Roof Inn. He hoped she wasn't one of them wannabe uppity females who acted as if they needed to fuck in a five-star room but lived in a no-star dump. Yet, considering Angie V was slinging pussy to him, a stranger, and God knows who else to pay bills, he figured she was far from picky.

Mario pulled over to the side of the building and parked. Grabbing his wallet out of the console of Sasha's SUV, he jumped out. Trying to have as much swag as possible, he walked over to Angie V's car, which smelled as if it was overheating. Mario ignored the small amount of steam that spilled out of the side of the hood. Her car problems were just that: her problems. He'd signed on to buy some ass to help her pay her light bill, nothing more and nothing less. Mario's mindset was that he could give three shits if that motherfucker blew the hell up with her and her kids in it after he done getting the pussy. With his wife locked up for at least the next year, he had no real strings or attachments out in the world. He lived his life in an out-for-self manner, and that's how it was going to stay.

"Yo, I'm about to go in here and pay for this room and get the key. We still good, right?" Mario double-checked, not wanting to waste money he could easily use on a dice game later that night. He was already parting with two and some change on some pussy that might not be all of that so anything else was out of the question.

Just hanging up from talking to the babysitter, assuring her she'd be paid tonight, Angie V was content. She had made peace with what she was about to do. In a short amount of time she would have the money for not one but two bills she owed. Although this was not what she wanted to do, it was what she had to do to make ends meet. So for that reason she would put on a brave face, swallow her pride, among other things, and handle her grown woman business. "Yeah, I already told you we're good. Why would I follow you here if I wasn't good?" she smartly replied, trying to get her mind right.

Smiling, Mario came out of the registration office with the small envelope containing the plastic key. Informing his female companion to follow him around to room 217, she complied. Parking side by side in the empty parking lot, Angie V got out of her vehicle first.

Damn, ol' girl ready like a motherfucker. I see she ain't trying to hold a nigga up. "What up, doe baby doll, you ready to chill or what?" Mario grinned, opened his car door, and placed one foot down on the pavement.

"Yeah, but gimme a few minutes to get cleaned up." Angie V held the bags she'd thrown in the back seat.

"Cleaned up?"

"Yeah. I just got off work, remember? I need to at least wash my face and hands and whatever else. Is that cool with you or what?" Waiting for him to have the nerve to protest, she planted one hand firmly on her hip shifting all her weight to one side.

Before Mario could respond, his cell started to ring. Out of the side of his eye he saw it was one of the numbers his wife would call from. *Damn this worrisome bitch again. Shit, let me spin her real quick.* Without further hesitation he hurried, handing Angie V the key. "Yeah, love, go ahead and do you. I gotta take this call. It's some business I got popping off. Then we gonna go hard." Before any other words could be exchanged Mario put his foot and leg back in the SUV and rolled the window up. Listening to the prerecorded voice prompt do its thing, the sworn master manipulator made sure the radio was down and the air conditioning was on low.

"Hello."

"Hey, bae. I was waiting for you to call back. You was cut off before you could finish what you was saying," he lied, reclining his seat, wishing he had a blunt to blow before he got with Angie V.

"Yeah, I know and I damn straight wasn't done getting off into your lying ass." Sasha was back on the same tip from earlier. Having had time to think about what Regina had told her and the act that she knew her husband was putting on, she was heated. All the work he'd put in trying to song and dance her about him doing this or that, including watering her houseplants that were more than likely dead, was out the window.

Mario was getting fed up with Sasha going in on him each and every time they spoke. Sure, he loved all the benefits that came with being married to his wife. She was smart and had her shit all the way together. And, no matter what, she was loyal. If Mario never believed how loyal Sasha was before, her present living conditions and current mailing address sealed that deal. He wanted to go easy on her, but she was making it hard for him to hold back.

Knowing he had some hot, strange pussy only a few yards away good to go, Mario decided to be real brief with his meal-ticket spouse. "Okay, look, I done had enough of you talking to me like your ass crazy and I ain't about shit. Now I done told you earlier ain't nobody out here in these streets fucking you over. I'm out here doing what the fuck I can to make you happy and make shit right from behind that coward stunt I pulled to get you locked up in the first place. So for real for real, you ain't got too many more times to get loud and talk to me like I'm your kid. I'm messed up in the head enough about you losing my son and you keep wasting money running off at the mouth about what your sister and that tramp Kat said. Now if you want me to get the fuck on out your life and let you be, just say that shit and get it over with. 'Cause, truth be told, a nigga like me sick and tired of feeling like a failure. I let my wife down and I gotta live with that the rest of my life it we together or not."

Sasha was dumbfounded. She didn't know what to say or what to think. Mario had flipped the script on her yet again. With all intentions of telling him to leave her house, only taking his clothes, park the SUV in her parents' driveway with the key underneath the mat, and turn over her ATM card to Regina, Sasha was left holding the receiver in the middle of the prepaid call, trying to come to terms with what was just said.

Mario was right. She had been treating him like pure filth when the truth of the matter was she had free will to stand up and say the money and pills were not hers but his; however, she chose not to do so. So what if he was the driving force in coaxing her to give up her freedom in exchange for his. No one had a gun to her head. Sasha was just dumb and in love and that was her fault, not his.

"Okay, Mario, listen. I don't know how you want or even expect for me to carry this bullshit. I'm nothing like you. You're used to being caged up like some wild animal; I'm not. Especially for something I didn't do. So yeah, I'm pissed. Yeah, I'm listening to what people have to say about what you out there doing. And if memory serves me correct, you had no problem acting the same way when you was locked up."

Mario looked at the clock on the dashboard. He knew that between him and Sasha talking shit to one another they had eaten up at least half of the time on the call. Now if he could only get through the next seven or so minutes in peace with his agitated wife, he could go into room 217, fuck the dog shit out of Angie V, and get his money's worth. He had let Sasha have her say knowing full well his wife was weak minded as hell and would never truly want him to leave her side, in jail or not.

"Bae, do you love me or not? Do you wanna still be my wife or what? 'Cause if the answer is no, I can get the same lawyer who's on your case to file divorce papers and have you served in there. Now is that what it's gonna be? I hope not, because a nigga really love you and wanna do the right thing by you, if you just give me a chance." Mario poured it on thick, knowing full well that even if Sasha did say it was over and she wanted a divorce, he would empty her bank accounts and sell all the contents of the home they shared before she even could think about freedom.

"You know I love you," Sasha replied almost in tears as she gripped up on the receiver.

"Well, then stop tripping, my baby, and hold tight. My parole officer said since I'm so close to getting off I can reach out to the warden and sign special paperwork to allow me to come visit your pretty self sooner than you think. You just need to write him as well. A nigga love you, Sasha, with all my heart; and I'm always gonna make sure you good, you feel me?"

"Mario," Sasha whined.

"Naw, Sasha, cut all the extra bullshit out. I ain't trying to hear it. Now call me daddy and tell me you understand how much I love you." Mario looked up and saw Angie V crack the room door. She was waving for him to come inside, obviously done with what she had to do. Using his free hand, the compulsive liar tugged down on his growing manhood in anticipation of what was soon to come from his new curvaceous friend, when he ended the emotionally charged conversation with his incarcerated wife.

"Yes, daddy, I understand." Sasha gave in, knowing no matter what she'd heard or would hear was happening in the streets in the near future, nine out of ten times she'd stay Mrs. Mario Eubanks.

"Are you sure?" he asked again, turning the SUV off.

"Yes, daddy, I'm sure," she dumbly replied, once more feeling as if she was wanted.

Seconds later time was almost up; one minute was left. While Sasha was sad wanting to call back for the third time that day just to hear his voice, Mario urged her to go lie down and relax her mind; and he was going to do the same. When the line finally went dead, Mario practically jumped out of the SUV.

Adjusting his already rock-hard dick, he bolted up the stairs and into the hotel room. Stepping foot inside, he saw Angie V standing on the far side of the room fully clothed. Immediately his dick started to soften. He was confused. "Hey now, what's wrong? Why you standing over there with your damn clothes on?"

Angie V had downed three long gulps of wine she had gotten from her job. She'd needed a minute or two to get her head right, and she had. While Mario was out in the SUV talking to whomever, she was standing in the mirror talking herself into having sex with a stranger and praying it didn't drag her back into the destructive black hole behavior that had her single and struggling now with three kids and no man in her life to help toe the line. "I'm saying you getting all loud and whatnot, but haven't you forgotten about something?"

Seeing her standing there with her hand out, it hit Mario what she was talking about. Caught up in dealing with his wife and her issues, he'd not paid Angie V the fee they'd agreed upon. Back in the hood he was a beast with the hoes. He would throw them a li'l something something when he got finished getting down, getting his dick wet. And not an amount they wanted, but what he decided the pussy or head was worth. "What's good, baby doll, you don't trust me? You think I ain't got you?"

"Excuse me, Mario, but on the real, I don't even know you. I really don't know how you do what you do when you do it. All I know is I'ma need my money up front before we go any further." Angie V was feeling the wine flow through her veins and she was not up for any games. She was on a tight schedule and had to pick up her kids from the babysitter and pay DTE before nine.

Mario smiled as if he were the first pick on draft day. He then tossed his keys onto the nightstand. Stuffing his hand deep into his blue jeans pocket, he pulled out that same small knot of cash he had earlier, minus the amount he'd spent on getting the room. "I told you back at your job, money ain't no thang with me. You hang with me, you always gonna be good. I'm always gonna look out."

Peeling off the price promised, he placed the currency on the dresser. Walking back to the other side of the room, he turned the deadbolt on the door for extra security. It was now show time. He'd been anticipating this very moment. Mario then took off his shirt, revealing a red ink tattoo across the right side of his chest reading SASHA. Angie V didn't bother to ask who exactly Sasha was and Mario didn't feel the need to volunteer. All he knew was he was about to get busy with the smart-mouth cashier from Walmart who swore her shit didn't stink.

Unzipping his pants, Mario allowed them to drop to his ankles. With his sneakers still on, he turned his baseball cap to the rear. With his eyes glued on Angie V, he was back hard in no time flat. His heart raced as he slowly stroked the shaft of his curved cock. "Okay, my baby, get naked and come crawl over here and suck daddy's big black dick. You on my clock and payroll now! I want some of that good head I know you working with. Bitches like you who talk all that shit always have the best head, and pussy, too."

CHAPTER TEN

Sasha's mind was racing a mile a minute. Mario had managed to do what he was so good at doing for so long where she was concerned: running game. He had her not only majorly confused, but sucker stroking as well. This had been her life with him from day one. Part of her was deeply in love with Mario and always would be, while the other part knew her man was up to no good. She knew her sister and best friend would not be just making up things her husband was accused of doing. What would either of them have to gain? She knew they only had her best interests at heart.

But now she was going to feel like she let both of them down, because she hadn't stuck to the game plan she and Regina had come up with and agreed upon. Mario had mind fucked her as always. She didn't understand why she was so weak when it came to him, but she was. Sasha could be standing in the room with her husband while he was butt banging the next three females and he could convince her she had not seen what she thought she had seen. He always had that power over her and she hated it. She was locked behind bars while he ran free because of his strange mental hold over her.

"Hey, young'un, how was your phone call? You over there looking like somebody ran over your dog."

"I'm good, Trina. It's just that my husband is always trying to double-talk me to death. I mean I know he's lying, but what can I do? I'm locked up and he's not."

Trina was an OG at the prison. She had been in and out of the system for years. Sadly, this time around, Trina was doing a thirty-year flat bid and would probably never live to see the outside again. She had caught her man messing around with her young niece and killed them both in a fit of rage. Charged with only two counts of manslaughter, the prosecutor took into consideration the unprecedented circumstances that caused the already unstable ex-felon to snap. Nevertheless, Trina had to be severely punished. "Girl, now you know better than to get me to talking about lying husbands. That bullshit right there is my specialty. Now you know I gotta get me something to snack on for this conversation right here."

Sasha had momentarily forgotten who she was talking to. Although she had only been there in that unit for what some would consider a short amount of time, Trina had talked her to death about every single case she'd caught and every single one she hadn't. At first it was something to do to pass the time. Then it became annoying. Feeling sorry that Trina's family had left her for dead, when Sasha tried to close her eyes and get her mind right, as Mario had suggested, she knew why Trina would never shut the fuck up. Sasha put her headphones on and tuned out not only her OG bunkie, who got an attitude, but everyone else as well. She had to think, not only about what Mario had said, but what Regina would say when they spoke again.

Angie V wanted nothing more than to be offended at the way Mario was talking to her. In any other circumstance, he'd get the business for being so rude and obnoxious. Yet since she had lowered herself and her standards to accept money for her body and sexual favors, she'd opened up the doors for the unacceptable to become acceptable. Normally no man could fix his mouth to even tell her to crawl; her three baby daddies were no exception. That was the most disrespectful thing a person could or would ask the next person to do, besides getting spit on or kicked up the ass. Now here Mario stood, pants down to his ankles, dick at full attention, demanding the $283 he had placed over on the dresser entitled him to more than just pussy and head, but Angie V's pride and dignity as well.

Rightfully deciding not to do as asked, Angie V walked over to Mario instead of crawling. Fighting back the tears, she was glad she'd gulped down the wine to take the edge off. Blacking out, she dropped to her knees. The carpet felt like small bristles and his private area had a strong scent of cologne as if he'd paid special attention to that area anticipating a female would be lurking down in that general direction. Taking Mario's stiff dick in her hand, she licked on the tip then the head. Closing her eyes she then started to suck and jerk at his piece, hoping he would bust a nut and not want to have sex. Unfortunately for Angie V, all the deep throat sucking and fast hand jerking she was doing only made Mario more eager to bend her over on the edge of the bed and put in work; and, for his $283, he slipped a condom on and did just that.

The more she seemed to resist and keep her pussy tight, the more enjoyment he got. Ramming his paid companion as if there were no tomorrow in sight, Mario finally screamed out in pleasure. Feeling his dick go limp inside of her and the condom loosen up from around his shaft, Angie V was relived it was over, or so she thought.

Mario was not done, as he pulled off the rubber loaded with thick cum. He tossed it on the floor, allowing the sticky substance to leak out on the carpet. Yanking her body all the way onto the bed, Mario spread her legs.

He'd imagined what she tasted like since first laying eyes on her. Angie V was soon squirming, caught up in how good Mario's tongue game truly was; but she was still off in her emotions. As he reached his hands up to cup each of her breasts while eating her out, he took a small break to look at her face.

"What's wrong, ma? You ain't feeling this shit?"

Angie V didn't mutter a word as tears fell from both eyes, trickling down her cheeks. Right then and there something strange came over Mario. He stopped devouring the cat, and stood. Staring down at the completely nude female, he knew that she was different from anyone else he'd tricked with. While some bitches fucked because they had white livers for sex, and others did it just for sport, Angie V was dead serious when she said she had to pay bills and needed the money bad. There was no new pair of sneakers being released, or a new iPhone that just came out she wanted to stunt with. Angela Vega had a much different agenda. She was selling ass to survive.

That truth became painfully clear to Mario as he had a brief flashback to the life his now deceased mother used to be forced to live. When alive, she had been much like Angie V in the way that she would do and say just about anything to make sure her kids had what they needed. Tragically, one night when walking home from her third job cleaning office buildings, she was gang raped and killed by a group of intoxicated factory workers who had just finished their shift and were out celebrating one of them taking the company-offered buyout. Never having dealt with the pain of losing his mother, or his older sister to a drug overdose, or his best friend in the world, Dino, Mario gave himself strong doses of hood therapy by smoking as much weed as he could and fucking around with as many females as possible, not caring that he was even married to Sasha.

Not bothering to ask her what was wrong, Mario got up. His demeanor was solemn as he headed toward the bathroom. Instead of taking a long, hot shower in the room he'd paid for, he wet a washcloth. With the quickness, he cleaned his private area after washing his face. No more words were exchanged between the two as Mario got dressed and left through the door.

In shame, Angie V got up and gathered her clothes, which Mario had tossed here and there in his rush to get what he paid for. Hearing what she believed to be his SUV's door shut, the engine start, and Mario pull off, she cried even harder at what she had done and who she felt she had become again: a common slut just like in high school. When she finally got herself together to leave she reached for the money that was on the dresser. There was no longer $283 dollars there, but $500.

CHAPTER ELEVEN

Nightfall came and Kat was sitting on the edge of the couch waiting for her uncle to check in with her with the good news. Ever since Regina had called telling her the plan that Sasha and she had come up with to get rid of Mario once and for all, she was happy. He would finally get what was coming to him, which was nothing.

As she fumbled with the remote, as well as her cell, Kat knew when her uncle's customized ringtone went off she'd be elated. Not only because Mario's no-good, slick, wannabe ass had just had his pockets run once again by Big Dae Dae, but also because she was going to get a cut of the winnings. She knew it was kind of foul to be benefiting from his loss, taking into full consideration that it was Sasha's money he was gambling with; but in Kat's distorted way of thinking someone was going to get that cheese, so why not her?

It was getting later and later and still there was no call. Kat had watched two and a half On Demand episodes of *Power* and there'd been no word from her family. She wanted to text him and ask what was really good, but she knew better. He had warned her plenty of times before not to disturb him during a game. If there was money on the floor, him answering might jinx his luck.

Going into the kitchen to get a late night bowl of cereal, Kat fumed as she puzzled about what was going on at the dice game that had her uncle so tied up he couldn't give her an update. She figured he could bust Mario down

easily. The entire squad who shot with him would joke
about his constant bad luck but his wild-minded eager-
ness to keep at it until the gamble gods finally would
bless him with a win or two. Emptying the last bit of the
cereal from the box and into a bowl, Kat prayed tonight
wasn't Mario's time in line to receive such a blessing. She
knew he definitely didn't deserve it, not after how he had
played her best friend.

Pouring the milk almost to the edge of the bowl, Kat
smiled seeing the cereal was completely submerged, just
as she liked it. Using both hands to carry it, she slowly
walked back into the living room trying not to spill a drop.
Only yards away from the coffee table, that dream was
short-lived. Startled by the sound of her cell flashing and
ringing, she stumbled, shifting half of the contents out of
the bowl and spilling them onto the floor. *Fuck! Son of
a bitch!* Kat was pissed. Carefully placing down the now
half-empty bowl, she snatched her cell up off the couch.
Finally this nigga calling! "Hey, Unc, what's the good
word? We all the way up or what?"

With the noise of fellas still very much off into the
game, Big Dae Dae stepped away from the commotion.
Standing on the front porch of the spot, he gave his
sister's child the bad news he knew she didn't want to
hear. "Yo, your peoples ain't show up tonight."

"What the fuck you mean he ain't show up?" Kat quizzed
as if she didn't believe him.

"Hey now, Katherine." He deliberately called her by her
government name to let his much younger niece know he
was serious. "Watch your damn mouth and remember
who the hell you talking to. I'm not one of your friends
you run with."

"Sorry, my bad," Kat apologized, not because she was
sorry but because she wanted to know what went on at
the dice game tonight.

"It ain't no thang. We good. Now just what I said, I been here since seven getting shit all the way in and that little nigga ain't darkened the doorstep to shoot, fade, or just stand around being a spectator. So apparently your little Inch High, Private Eye ESP information is off. And I know he ain't at no other real game, because this the only one jumping off tonight."

Kat didn't laugh as her uncle joked and teased. She didn't find shit funny, not tonight and not ever where Sasha's husband was concerned. First, because she wanted Mario to get what she felt he had coming. And, secondly, she needed her share of that come up money to pay her cell phone bill. Sure, she had plenty of free phones with government-issued minutes, but this time she was really going to try to keep up payments on this prepaid Android. "Well, how long you gonna be there? Maybe his dumb ass somewhere tricking with some hood rat and gonna fall through later. I know he gonna be betting big. I know he is. Sasha done handed that nigga his walking papers and I know he gonna clown with her money."

"Well, if he do come by here, my black ass won't be here to see it. I done crapped out way too many times for the night. Your favorite uncle about to call it. It's a wrap for me and all that revenge shit your delusional ass on. I done told you that you can't beat a couple. They be having crazy bonds and ties we can't even fathom."

Kat wanted to beg him to stay, but she didn't. She knew when her uncle said he was done he meant just that. So she reasoned with herself that tomorrow would be another day and Mario's dice-addicted ass would show up sooner rather than later, ready to give away more of Sasha's hard-earned money.

Ending the conversation with Big Dae Dae, she stuck her spoon into the bowl of cereal, or what remained of it. Seconds after putting the crunchy treat in her mouth, Kat spit it out, realizing it was soggy. She couldn't win for losing tonight. Her entire attitude was fucked and, in her mind, it was all Mario's fault.

CHAPTER TWELVE

Several days and nights had passed and still there was no sign of Mario. Big Dae Dae had done what he and the rest of the hardcore gamblers had done over the past week or so. They had made their rounds hitting up the various high-stakes games scattered throughout the city, especially on the east side of Detroit. But, as he reported by to Kat almost daily, Mario had been AWOL. Kat didn't understand. She was confused. That was nothing like Mario. From what she knew about him from not only her uncle but Sasha as well, Mario could not stay away from his addiction to the taste of taking chances. To her understanding, that was how he ended up in jail so much: taking dumb notions and risks that were uncalled for when there was no need.

Wishing she could talk to Sasha and see exactly where her head was at in this whole sordid situation, unfortunately she couldn't. When she didn't get her cut from her uncle the other night, she had no funds to pay her cell bill and her phone was turned off. Sasha had written to her and informed Kat that she could have only so many numbers on her approved call list. She didn't want to waste a slot on one of Kat's many numbers that would change or run out of minutes in a few days.

Confused, Kat decided to finally call Regina and see if she had seen or heard anything from not only Sasha, but Mario as well. Dialing Regina's number, before being connected, Kat was informed she only had six minutes remaining on the 250 free minutes flip phone. So that of course meant she had to talk quick.

"Hey, Kat. I was just thinking about calling you."

"Oh, yeah, okay then. That's what's up." Kat was glad Regina and she were on the same page.

"Have you heard or seen our little punk-ass boy lately?"

"Naw, not me or my uncle. He said it's like Mario done went underground and stopped coming around for some reason. What about you? Have you seen him?"

Regina hushed one of her crying kids in the background so that she could hear better. "Naw. I was gonna drive by the house later on. That's why I'm glad you called when you did so I could check in. You know your ass be having so many damn numbers a bitch never know how to get up with you."

"You right and I swear I'm gonna get my shit together because I need to be able to holler at Sasha. Have you talked to her any more or gone to see her again?"

"Naw, Kat. She ain't called me back like she was supposed to and I'm getting worried. I know she got money on her books, 'cause I put that shit on it my damn self," Regina announced, now pacing the floor as she spoke, getting more worried by the moment. "I hope when I left she ain't nut the fuck up about what I told her. I mean, she was acting like she had it all together and whatnot, but you know Sasha. She's a ticking time bomb underneath all that nicey-nice exterior. She's liable to have fought a bitch in there or run off at the mouth to a guard and gotten thrown in the hole. With her, ain't no telling. All I know is she should have called by now and told me what was good when she got at Mario's slime ball ass."

Kat agreed with her best friend's sister. "Yeah, when she gets mad, it ain't no stopping her, that's for sure."

"Well, after I get dressed and get the kids together, I'ma do a drive-by over to the house and see if I see Mario's punk ass posted up."

Before Kat could reply, the line went dead. Her six minutes had expired. Tossing that cell in a drawer, she searched through several others to see if they had any minutes left so she could call Regina back.

Things had been hectic for Mario. Strangely, since his sexual encounter with Angie V, he was starting to see things in another light. He had not been out late at night in days and had not even thought twice about picking up a pair of dice. Everything that he claimed he did when he spoke to Sasha he was busting his ass trying to accomplish. He had cleaned the entire house, including the bathroom, which had become beyond filthy. He tried his hardest to bring her plants back to life, even though he knew it was a losing battle. The grass that was overgrown in the rear of the house and the weeds that had taken over the driveway were now gone. Mario had gone to Home Depot and purchased a lawn mower himself, instead of paying the next man to do what he should have been doing as a man all along.

Nightly, instead of running the streets, he would talk to his wife twice, maybe three times, begging her to call back if time ran out. Mario was content for the first time in his always wild life and he didn't know why. Sure, he was still using Sasha's money; but now it was for something positive to help them both. The only thing he could attribute the abrupt change to was the sight of Angie V's tears. She looked just like his mother sobbing late at night, wondering how she was going to make ends meet, while she thought he and his now deceased older sister were asleep; and it haunted him. Whatever the reason was for the change, Sasha was living the best she could in the celebration, never having seen this side of him even in the beginning of their relationship.

Backing out of the driveway, Mario threw up his hand and spoke to the neighbors as if he had not been a disrespectful menace to all of them since he and his wife first moved on the block. Not knowing what to make of his actions, they just waved back, praying this behavior would continue. Mario drove a few miles through traffic, not once having the usual road rage he'd incur.

Pulling up in the parking lot of Walmart, he found a place to park in the always crowded lot; and he not once complained. Going inside, he headed to the rear of the store, grabbing a bottle of orange juice and a package of lunch meat. After scanning the two items through the self-checkout and paying, the sworn womanizer never once wondered where Angie V might have been. As he headed up to the customer service counter, however, she spotted him.

Her heart raced, knowing he would probably come over to her and try to buy some more pussy. Or he would say that the extra cash he'd left on the dresser that evening was a down payment on some more head. But that didn't happen. He didn't look in her direction, not once. He handled his business and left straight out of the store. Angie V was relieved she didn't have to have that scene with him, but still she was confused as to why he hadn't even bothered to look her way.

"I just sent you some more money to put on the phone and I wrote you a damn dumb-ass note online. So check it out when you can," Mario told Sasha, who had called on his drive to pick up his carry-out from the restaurant.

"I love you, Mario." She smiled from ear to ear, finally knowing that although her husband had let her down, he was trying his best to make amends. She had no worries in life, except for of course breaking the news to her older sister that she and Mario were going to try to work things out despite what she was told he had been up to since her incarceration. Sasha had not called her for days on end, and she dreaded reading the letter from Regina that had arrived in mail call earlier.

Having gotten her children ready for the day, Regina strapped them in their car seats. Ready to make the ride across town, she decided to ride in silence apart from the chatter of her babies. She was not in the mood to hear the radio blasting rap song lyrics about this or that. Regina knew that at a drop of a dime she could be incited. She didn't want to take a chance on a song coming on that instantly put her in clown mode. At this point she was just doing a drive-by to check on her sister's house and make sure it was still standing and that Mario had not illegally sold it to the highest bidder.

Only one block away from the house, a strange number flashed across her cell phone screen. Not hiding from anyone, including the bill collectors, Regina answered. It was Kat calling back from yet another random number.

"Hey, sorry about that earlier. My joint ran out of minutes. You know how it is."

"Naw, honey, you got me twisted. I don't know how it is." Regina could only shake her head in denial. "I swear, you young girls kill me. Between you and my sister I don't know who is the craziest. She in jail for some fool who don't give a fuck about her and you can't keep a phone on to save your life."

Kat laughed. "Fuck all that. I ain't going to jail for nobody, not even Jesus."

"I heard that." Regina laughed back. "Well, me and the kids is right down the street from Sasha's so I'm about to check it out and see what's good. Holler back at me later. That is, if you can come up on any more minutes," Regina taunted before hanging up.

Pulling up in front of the house, she was shocked. Regina couldn't believe what her eyes were seeing. The front grass was cut and the weeds were out of the drive-way. The water sprinkler was going back and forth full blast as if white people lived there and didn't care how high the bill would be. If she didn't know any better, she would have thought Sasha was back at home making sure her surroundings were on point.

Regina got out of her vehicle, leaving her now asleep children inside still strapped in their car seats. She made her way around to the rear of the house and was amazed even more. The back grass was cut as well. Propped up against the black plastic garbage can was an empty box that a lawn mower had come in. *What in the entire hell?*

Regina walked back down the driveway and saw one of her sister's neighbors watching her every move. She spoke to him and soon found out that Mario had been the one to cut the yard and was taking out the garbage to the curb on time. Regina couldn't believe her wayward brother-in-law's actions. From the moment her sister had introduced him, Regina, like their parents, knew Mario was no more than a lowlife opportunistic high school dropout looking for a come up. *That nigga is bugging. He must be up to some real shit this time.*

Stepping foot on the porch, she saw that all the sales papers, which were piled up in the corner that last time she was there chin checking Mario, were gone. Peeping in the window, the house appeared to be clean. The strong smell of Pine-Sol filled the area. *His lazy, no-good ass cleaning and shit. Oh hell naw! I need to talk to my damn sister. I hope she get that letter and call a bitch back, 'cause this shit ain't right.*

CHAPTER THIRTEEN

A solid month had flown by since Sasha had received the letter her sister mailed. She had read it repeatedly and was at a loss for words. The four-page letter detailed each and every thing that Regina had known Mario to be involved in. While some of his wrongdoings were beyond contempt, others were not as severe.

Sasha was depressed for days and wanted nothing more than to kill herself. But thanks to Trina and a few more inmates convincing her to stay with Mario, at least until she got out and could do things for herself, Sasha kept it together. Countless times she wanted to write her sister back or at least call and explain her actions, but she knew Regina. She knew how hard she was when it came to forgiveness and how stupid she thought she had been for taking the time for Mario in the first place. In light of all the things that had been revealed, how could she say that she and her husband just wanted to be left alone until further notice? Sasha couldn't bring herself to make that call or write that letter. Instead she said nothing and did nothing. She acted as if Regina, along with her elderly parents, didn't exist. She reasoned that when she got out of jail she'd make things right with them all.

"You have a call from Sasha, an inmate at the Michigan Department of Corrections. If you feel that this call is harassing in nature or unwanted, please press one. In order to accept calls from an inmate at the Michigan Department of Corrections, press two."

Listening to that recording and pressing the number two had become a regular thing in Mario's life. Trying his hardest to do the right thing by his wife, he smiled when hearing her voice. "Hey, baby, what's going on?"

"Nothing much, boo-boo. Just this damn Trina keeps hitting me up for noodles and candy bars every other day. I mean, it's not like I can't let her hold some until she get her money, so she claim, it's just that I know she running game. She ain't got no peoples or no money coming."

"Yeah, well, do what you can. But don't be letting motherfuckers in there think you soft and they can run over you."

"Me, soft? Naw, fuck all that. Never again. Ain't no bitch on this earth taking shit that belong to me, not even my freedom."

Mario noticed with each day that passed that his once shy, quiet wife had turned into a boisterous beast. He knew with the way Sasha spoke and behaved now, he would most definitely have hell on his hands if he even attempted to try to persuade her to take any more time for him. What once would have been easy for him to lie and get away with had become a no-go. She was on him heavy about everything. If she said she was going to call at 1:00 p.m. right after count and he didn't answer on the first ring, she went ham. When Mario said he was writing her a letter, she had better get it in mail call in the next few days. Sasha was on his head; and the strange part about it was Mario seemed not to mind one bit. He had to finally respect her for standing up to his bad boy ways and outlandish antics. He needed structure in his life and she was giving him that, even if it was long distance from a jail cell.

"Come on now, calm down, baby doll. You getting all worked up and aggressive for nothing. But on another note, I saw your sister earlier today."

"What? Regina? When? What did she say? Did she ask about me?" Sasha fired off question after question waiting anxiously for a reply.

Mario had mixed feelings about telling his wife about the unplanned encounter because he knew she was caught up in the middle. And it was all because of him. "You know normally the guy who cuts your parents' grass stops by here and picks up the money, but this morning he said his truck was acting funny and he didn't think he could make it way across town to our house."

"And?"

"And so I drove over there to give him his bread. No sooner than I pulled up in front of your parents' house, Regina had pulled up too."

"Okay, Mario, and? What happened then? What she say? What you say?"

"I ain't say nothing and neither did she. I just stuck my hand out the window and gave ol' boy his cash. She just mean mugged the fuck outta me until I pulled off. I swear to God she was still setting me on fire with her eyes when I turned the damn corner. When I say your sister hates the shit outta my fucking ass, that's for real!"

Sasha was sad. She felt some sort of way. How could she not? Although she knew her and Regina's relationship would probably never be the same since she had not gotten back to her, Sasha still felt there was chance. Wherever there was love there was still hope. She thought that her older sibling would still put all bullshit aside to ask if she was at least okay and maintaining behind bars, if nothing else. But inmate number 998797 apparently was dead wrong in her thinking. Blood wasn't thicker than water. Blood was just what it was: blood. Nothing more and nothing less.

***

Mario was exhausted. Not only had he done a lot of work in and around the house, he had been having phone sex with his wife the better half of the day. Just because he didn't actually have her there in person to touch, hold, and bang didn't mean he wasn't just as tired beating his meat until it exploded.

Needing to make a trip to Walmart, he felt as if the SUV had a mind of its own and was steering itself. With one task at hand, Mario slowly strolled up to the customer service counter. Just like all the multiple times prior, he added funds to Sasha's JPay account. All the calls she was making were adding up. Mario knew for a fact he'd put more than $400 on her books in the last three weeks. With his receipt in hand, he turned to leave and was suddenly face to face with none other than Angie V. Even though he knew she worked there, he was still shocked to see her. Mario, however, didn't say a word. He just stood there. After a few brief moments of silence, she was the one who finally broke the ice.

"Oh, hey, Mario."

"Hey, girl, what's good with you?"

Having seen him come and go, Angie V had been ashamed for weeks to run into Mario. After what had taken place between the two, she felt he would look at her as if she was no more than a piece of trash. "I'm okay, I guess. I've been wanting to call you to say thank for what you did for me that day; but I didn't know if it was all right to call."

Feeling guilty for the first time in history for fucking behind his wife's back, Mario stuffed the JPay receipt in his pocket as if Sasha could magically hear what was being said through the paper. "Naw, it's all good. It wasn't no thang. I was glad to be able to help. Everybody needs somebody sometime or another, even if it's just to talk." He couldn't help but have a flashback to his mother, whom he'd been thinking a lot about since he and Angie V hooked up.

Angie V was relieved Mario didn't judge her or the freaky circumstances that originally brought them together. Through standing there talking, she also noticed something different from before about Mario's demeanor. He seemed much more settled and more laidback. His bad boy swag status was now more that of a grown-ass man. "Thanks for being so cool about it. You think I could give you my number and maybe we could talk sometime?"

Mario didn't refuse. Immediately, he pulled his cell out his back pocket. As she called out her number, he punched in the digits and locked it in. Exchanging a few more words, Mario knew he had to get back to the SUV and head home because Sasha was going to be calling him after the last count for the night was over. When he left through the door, Mario had no idea whatsoever that he had been spotted the very moment he walked through the front door of the store and watched like a hawk until the time he'd left.

"Look at this sneaky-ass bum, all up in Walmart trying to mack bitches." Kat was furious as she hissed under her breath so no one else could hear. "And check out this mixed-breed thirsty tramp all on his trail like he ain't married to my best friend. I should just run up and sock the ho dead in the jaw." Like Regina, she had had no contact with Sasha either, but that was still her road dawg and best friend.

This was the first time in weeks anyone had seen Mario out and about. Although he was not officially hiding, he was trying his hardest to make shit right with his wife. He knew the streets were a major distraction and so were females, especially Angie V. Yet he took her number just the same.

Kat couldn't wait to tell Regina who she'd just seen and what he had done. But just her luck, the free minutes on the last cell she had that had not expired didn't flip over until midnight. So snitching on Sasha's husband would have to temporarily wait. In the meantime, though, Kat pretended like she needed assistance finding an item so Angie V could help her. Striking up general conversation, Kat looked at her name tag: ANGELA. She also discovered the whore had three kids and no man at home. *If this thing thinks she gonna get my girl's husband to be her kids' new daddy, she straight up fried in the brain.*

CHAPTER FOURTEEN

"'Mr. Mario Eubanks, after careful consideration of your application dated July 12, 2016, to visit Sasha Lachelle Eubanks, inmate number 998797, unfortunately at this time we cannot grant your request. As you are currently a felon registered to be on parole and under the jurisdiction of the State of Michigan Department of Corrections until September 15, 2016, we find it to be against our general code of conduct. After the terms of your parole are completed and all monies due to the State of Michigan are satisfied, we will accept and review any new applications to visit Sasha Lachelle Eubanks, inmate 998797.'"

"That's some bullshit! I hate these sons of bitches!" Sasha was livid after listening to Mario read the denied request for him to come and see her. It was hard enough being away from family and friends, but now the warden had shot down any chance she had of seeing her husband. They had both written letters as Mario's parole officer had instructed them to do. Yet, as luck would have it, they crapped out. The only thing they could do was, as the letter stated, try again in a few months when he got off paper. There was no guarantee that application would be approved, but it was the only hope they had of a face-to-face reunion before Sasha was released.

"Just stay calm. They love to push a nigga's buttons up in there so they can write your ass a ticket and hold your black ass longer."

"Look, Mario, for real I'm not going to let this get me down, I swear I'm not. I'm about to get off this phone with you, go in the dayroom, and play checkers. I'm good."

Mario had wanted to see Sasha just as bad as she wanted to see him, but he was used to being in jail and isolated from people. She was a rookie to the act of jailing it. Now that Sasha had decided to give him a break, he welcomed a calm peace of mind. Dealing with her on a daily basis was starting to take a toll on him mentally.

Having not been out to the cemetery in years, Mario had the strong urge to visit his mother's gravesite. After taking a quick shower, he got dressed. Making sure he brought the garbage can back from the curb, he jumped in the SUV and sped off. After making one stop at the florist, Mario was finally on his way to make the cross-town, somber drive to what people in the city of Detroit called the welfare cemetery.

Driving through the entrance, Mario automatically busted out crying. It was if he couldn't control the tears. Overcome with emotion, twenty minutes or so later he got himself all the way back right. Getting out of the SUV, the warmness of the late evening sun hit his face as he walked to the cemetery office. It had been a long time since he'd been out here and he needed to know the ID marker number to locate his mother's grave. Unlike most cemeteries that had tombstones, fancy headstones, and marble benches, the welfare facility for the most part had small ground-mounted oval shapes of thick tin that had numbers embedded in them. If a person buried there was blessed enough to have anything other than that, it was because some agency, church, or group had taken up a collection way after the burial.

Told his mother's ID number was B-107, Mario was then pointed toward that secluded area and informed to start looking to the right of the huge oak tree.

"And by the way, son," the caretaker warned as Mario left through the door, "I just want to let you know it's been some time since I've been able to get around that way and take care of the grass and whatnot. So you may see more than a few weeds over in section B, but don't worry. I'll take care of it before long. We're just shorthanded."

Mario left his SUV where it was. Although there seemed to be a small road that could take him to the far other side of the place where his mother was, it seemed too narrow for the SUV to get through. Cutting through what was once an already makeshift trail, he labored across the tall grass growing wild. Once near the tree that was mentioned as a landmark point, Mario started looking down but, as he was warned, the weeds covered the majority of the graves and their allotted numbers. There was no choice if he wanted to find 107; he would have to practically get on his knees and pull the weeds. Without hesitation, Mario did just that.

"102, 103, 106, 107," he counted out loud until seeing the number he was searching for. "Mama, I miss you so much." The distraught son started crying once more while cleaning the marker all the way off.

As he sat there in meditation, Mario was interrupted by the sound of someone else trampling across the grass. When he looked up, he couldn't believe his eyes. "Bitch, what in the fuck is your ass doing here?"

"It's a free country, boy. I can come and go as I please, not like Sasha's dumb ass that's on lockdown thanks to you."

"Are you following me or something? Why is you even here? Damn!"

"Like I said, it's a free country. And if you don't like me being here seeing what your sneaky ass is up to then make me leave. Matter of fact, why don't you go and get that bitch Angela with three kids who work at Walmart to help you make me leave? How about that bullshit? Do that, playboy!"

Mario was heated. He couldn't believe the out-cold over-the-top nerve of this female. Not only had she apparently been stalking him to some degree to know anything about Angie V, here he was posted at his mother's gravesite and this lunatic good-hating-ass ho popped up out of nowhere.

Infuriated, Mario stood. Leaning over, he knocked a bit of dirt off his knee area. He attempted to get it together, but he could not. The left side of his head near his temple was pounding. The veins in his forehead could surely be seen. It was beginning to feel as if a set of hands from were reaching up out of a grave and strangling him. Mario was beside himself. No matter how much he tried to fight it, he felt an overwhelming urge to punch this tramp in the throat.

Focusing in on Kat's smug expression, he felt a rage come over him. He'd only felt this feeling once before in his entire life. It was the same anger, resentment, and desire to do great bodily harm to someone he'd experienced when finding out his mother had been murdered. Now, ironically standing near his mother's grave, he wanted to give Kat the same fate she had succumbed to: death.

Taking a few steps toward his wife's best friend, Mario had blood in his eyes. "I swear to God I'm tired of you always being all up in my business, in Sasha business, and everything else. Now why is you following me?"

"Boy, I wasn't following your stupid ass. My peoples live right across the street from this raggedy-ass son of a bitch and I saw my best friend SUV drive in. So, yeah, I'm gonna see where my best friend SUV was going." Kat was no fool, taking two steps back for her own safety as she talked cash hot fire shit. Right away, she sensed and visually saw that Mario was minutes, probably seconds, away from snapping. It was written all over his face. However, when it came down to it she didn't care. She had wanted to do battle with him for years. The fact that he looked out for her back at the park that day meant absolutely nothing to Kat. She, just like Mario, had her own self-destructive, paranoid demons lurking that made her behave the way she did.

Mario was emotionally drained. He was fed up. He was finished with listening to Kat always having something to say about her best friend. Now it was going to be his time to talk and Sasha's best friend was going to hear him loud and clear. "Okay, bitch, you wanna just keep coming at me over and over again like I'm some sort of lame!"

"You is a lame, with your punk ass," she continued to taunt him, not believing that fat meat was greasy.

Mario lunged at Kat, yanking her by her shirt. She struggled and squirmed trying to get away from his strong grip, but couldn't. Mario didn't say a word. He didn't have to. Balling up his fist, he then brought his arm back and smiled. Before Kat knew what was happening next, his fist had made direct contact with her jaw. She was rattled for sure, but still up on her feet thanks to him holding her shirt. Now using his open hand, Mario slapped her around a few good times before letting her go. Kat was semi-delirious, but she was a trooper at best. The side of her face was swelling and had turned a dark shade of red, showing through her dark, rich chocolate skin.

"Why in the hell is you always on a nigga worried about what I'm doing and what the fuck me and my wife doing? Why, bitch? What's your damn problem?" Mario ran back up on her ready to fight even more. Kat tried her best to stand tall, but she was starting to be weak. The blows Mario had put on her were crucial. He yanked Kat up toward him and their bodies were now pressed against each other's. "Why won't you stop? What's your damn problem with me?"

Mario and Kat both stopped. There was a strange vibe between them, one that neither one of them could or wanted to explain. Next thing, the two sworn enemies were embraced in a deep, passionate kiss. That kiss led to them groping and their hands searching each other's private parts. Mario wanted to stop, but couldn't. Kat tried to pull away but the throbbing in between her legs wouldn't allow it to happen. The unlikely pair was stuck doing what they both knew was wrong and would hurt Sasha if she ever found out.

As they fell to the ground, Kat landed on top of Mario. She could feel the hard, strong print of his manhood fighting to get out of his blue jeans. It all made sense to her. Kat now knew why Sasha and the rest of the females he was messing around with were so in love with him. Mario had been blessed with a big dick. Wanting to see what it felt like, Kat helped him unzip his pants and reveal his big-headed gift from God. As she started sucking and licking the pole, Mario's hand found its way down her shorts, fingers moving her panties to the side and exploring her cat. The raw freak feelings were quickly escalating to be too much to hold back.

Seconds later, Sasha's husband and best friend were disrespectfully having sex on top of Mario's mother's grave. Grunting and groping, the two went at it as if they were teenagers sneaking to get it in before one of their parents came home from work and caught them in the act. In one final thrust, Mario found himself ready to bust. Tossing a bruised-face Kat off his dick and onto the grave next to his mother's, he held his dick, allowing the hot stream of cum to shoot out on the thick, tall grass that surrounded them.

Mario lay back, trying to catch his breath. He was ashamed of what he had just done. Not only had he fucked his wife's grimy, snake-ass best friend, but on his mother's final resting place no less. He had done a lot of distasteful things in his lifetime, but this was by far the worst. Closing his eyes, Mario begged God and his mother to forgive him as he listened to Kat throwing up on the grave next to him. When she was done, she never spoke another word. She just got up, straightened up her clothes, and walked off.

CHAPTER FIFTEEN

Mario sat on the front porch of the house he and his wife shared. With his head lowered, he couldn't believe what he'd done hours earlier with Kat. He hated himself. He was trying so hard to turn over a new leaf and it was as if the devil himself took on the form of that slut to tempt him to do wrong. Now he was posted, sitting here messed up in the head that he had failed the test. There was no question Mario knew the first chance Kat got she would rat him out about what they'd done, even if it meant cutting her own head off. Kat lived her life every day for drama-filled bullshit like this. He knew the bigmouthed bitch would also tell Sasha what she somehow knew about Angie V. Mario was fucked in the game and knew it.

Depressed about what to do next or say when Sasha called him, Mario removed his cell from his pocket. He needed someone to talk to, someone who would not judge his self-destructive actions. Scrolling down the numbers in his contacts list, he came to the Ws. Smart enough not to put her actual name with her number, Mario pushed the contact, labeled Walmart, dialing Angie V's cell.

After it rang three or four times, his call went to voicemail. Not willing to give up his pursuit of talking to her, Mario dialed her number once more. This time it went straight to voicemail. Before he could try a third time, he received a notification ring that indicated he had a text message. Tapping the small envelope icon on the screen, Mario saw it was from Angie V saying that she was at work and couldn't talk at the time.

Knowing he had no business whatsoever wanting to confide in the next female he had fucked behind his wife's back about another female he'd also banged behind Sasha's back, Mario took this as a sign. He needed to just go in the house, take a shower, and get his mind together. There was no way he could talk to Sasha tonight; his conscience wouldn't let him. Mario didn't want to go back to his old ways of living and thinking, but it seemed as if that reckless lifestyle was calling him.

It had been a long few days for Sasha. First she received the awful, heartbreaking news that the warden had shot down any chances of her and Mario seeing one another. Then, after returning from the dayroom, she discovered one of the other inmates had broken into her foot locker. Missing was most of her food, cosmetics, a few wash-cloths, and all of her unused legal pads. Of course no one claimed to have seen anything, especially Trina's always nosey ass.

Sasha was boisterous, letting the entire unit know that whoever the desperate thief was who stole her belongings didn't do shit in the way of stopping her shine. She let them know that she could and would replace it all just as soon as she was able to order from the store. "I ain't like you needy-ass bitches who beg, borrow, and steal the next person's shit, or sit around waiting on a secure pack. I'm good and gonna stay good!"

Sasha was on a full-blown rant and rightly so. However, she was going to catch a few tickets and end up in the hole or on restrictions if she didn't settle down, as the guard on duty demanded. Attempting to calm her nerves, she just wanted to speak to Mario. She knew just hearing his voice would make things better.

Five minutes after the final count for the day was complete and the shift changed, Sasha headed to the phone area. By it being the first of the month, more inmates than usual had money on their books thanks to their people on the outside. Impatiently she waited her turn. She was ready to explode. If she didn't speak to her husband soon and tell him what these lowlife bitches had done to her, she was going to kill someone for sure.

As of late, Mario was the only one who could get her to see things in a different light. He was her strength as well as her lifeline to the outside. Since Sasha basically severed ties with Kat, Regina, and her parents, Mario was her world.

Punching in her secure pin number as she'd done so many times prior, she dialed her husband's number; but she received no answer. Not once. Not twice, but three, then four times. Having no choice but to let the next inmates waiting to place their calls go, Sasha got back in line over and over again until the phones were turned off and it was lights out.

Lying in her bunk, in the dark, eyes wide open, Sasha prayed nothing was wrong and nothing bad had happened to her king.

Sasha woke up with Mario on her mind. Without bothering to take a shower or eat breakfast, she went straight to the phones. The early-morning shift guards had still not turned them back on from the night before so she had to wait. Sasha had been locked up long enough to know there was no way to rush or strong-arm a guard to do anything they didn't want to do when they didn't want to do it. With arms folded, she leaned against the wall, waiting.

The moment she saw the switch go on, she wasted no time. She tried to call Mario. It went straight to voicemail this time, not even ringing. Slowly her heart was starting to break into tiny pieces.

Throughout the day, she didn't eat, didn't talk to anyone, and didn't go outside on the yard. Sasha didn't care about the dayroom, watching television, or showering. Her main focus was constantly running back and forth to the phones in between count times to try to call Mario. Each and every time that she would place the call, the outcome was the same. The guards and the inmates both found it amusing to see the high and mighty Sasha Eubanks, inmate 998797, be brought down a few notches and go through it.

Nearing the end of the day, Sasha could no longer take it. Her head was pounding and her heart was aching. She couldn't suffer going through another sleepless night wondering and worrying if her husband was dead or alive. It was too much for her to take and she knew it. They had been talking on the phone daily for months, and now bam, nothing, flat line. Beyond desperate to know what was going on in the outside world with Mario, Sasha had no choice and no other options. She decided to call her sister and see what she may have known or heard.

After a few rings Regina answered. Sasha kept her fingers crossed. She prayed her older sibling would be elated to hear from her and would not hold a grudge and accept the call. Thank God Regina did.

"What is it, Sasha?" she asked right off the bat without even bothering to say hello.

"Dang, sis, can't I just call you to see how you and the kids are? And how are Mom and Dad? It's been awhile."

"Check on us? Come on now, Sasha, with all that game you trying to run. Let's keep it real. If you really cared about your family you would've called or written." Regina went all the way in not holding her little sister up one bit.

"So like I said, what the hell you want, Sasha? This call ain't about family."

There was no sense beating around the bush. Regina could see clearly through her motive for the out-of-the-blue call. With that in mind, Sasha cut to the chase. "Well, it's just that I have been trying to call Mario and I keep getting his voicemail. I was wondering—"

"Oh, yeah, wondering what?" Regina fired back, shaking her head at the nerve of some people.

Sasha took a deep breath before asking, "I was wondering if you could go ride by my house and check on him and make sure he's okay."

"Are you fucking serious, Sasha? You ain't dealt with me or Mom or Dad in months. No calls, cards, or letters, but now your dumb, stupid ass calling asking me to go check on that pussy-hound punk who got you locked up in the first place. Girl, bye. You better get your life." Regina mocked her sister being so thirsty and desperate for a man cut like Mario was. "He probably somewhere laid up with that black Spanish chick he banging who work at Walmart!"

"Huh? What Spanish chick? What are you talking about?" Sasha had tears starting to fill her eyes. "Please, Regina, tell me what you're talking about."

"Come on now, little sister, you mean your so, so special husband you so worried about and up in there doing time for ain't tell you his new ho got that good hair and her three kids? I thought you knew that! If your best friend Kat knows, trust me, the entire city knows too. Wow, they say the wife is always the last to know, so I guess it's true. So, umm, back to your original question. Hell naw, bitch, I ain't going to check on no grown-ass man. Silly, you on your own with that mess. Now good-the-fuck-bye and enjoy the rest of your day! Oh, and by the way, Mom has cancer!"

Cancer! I know she just lying to hurt me even more. I'm not even gonna feed off into that. Sasha was left standing mute, holding the receiver in her hand. It was as if her legs couldn't move. She wanted to believe Regina was lying about the Spanish chick as well, but despite Mario's recent actions she knew who he really was: a dog.

Hysterical, she tried to call him once more in hopes of him denying what she had just heard, but again she was met with his voicemail. *I swear to God I'm gonna kill this nigga when I get out!* Furious, she slammed the phone down, almost knocking it off the wall. The guard on duty had just about enough of Sasha always prancing around the facility as if her shit didn't stink. With malice he wrote her three tickets, one that placed her on immediate LOP, which stood for "loss of privileges." Ordered to stay on her bunk, she was prohibited from going to the dayroom, going out on the yard and, most severely, using the phones for seven days. Sasha was sick with it as she curled up in a ball and cried and cried and cried.

CHAPTER SIXTEEN

It had been days and Mario strangely had not heard from his wife. After her calling the few times and him pushing ignore, he could only assume Kat had gotten in touch with her exposing the dirty deed they had done at the cemetery. For the first time in years, Mario had not stepped foot out of the house. He slept most of the day, having dreams about his mother. His appetite had increased and his depression had caused him to eat damn near everything that was in the refrigerator and freezer. Mario didn't know if he was coming or going. Several of his people had hit him up, texting the addresses to a few high-stakes dice games, but he wasn't in the mood to gamble. He felt like he'd lost his edge and urge for that some months back. He'd tried calling Angie V just to talk, but he could never seem to get in touch with her either.

Feeling like shit, as well as looking the part, Mario dragged himself off the couch. Jumping in the SUV, he noticed the tank was almost on empty and he still didn't want to stop to get gas. Turning into the Walmart parking lot, Mario had no reservations about pulling into a hand-icap space and daring any person young, old, male, or female to challenge him. As he sat there, he tried calling Angie V once more. He got the voicemail. He then texted and still got no response.

Going inside Walmart, Mario did his usual: he went straight to JPay to put some money on Sasha's books.

Even though she hadn't spoken to him for whatever reason, she was still his wife and he still owed it to her to make sure she was good while doing time. As he stood at the counter, he searched the checkout lines and all the cashiers to see if he saw Angie V. Finally he asked the older woman who always helped him at the JPay register if the Spanish chick Angie was working today. Without hesitation, she informed Mario that Angela Vega had taken ill a few days back and was off the schedule until further notice.

Holding his receipt in hand, he headed back out to the SUV. Before starting the engine, Mario texted Angie V once more, asking if everything was okay because he had heard she was ill, and what could he do to help. Tossing his cell onto the passenger seat, Mario hoped his friend replied as he drove to the gas station.

Kat was beside herself. Trapped in the house with her pride, she'd nursed her bruised face for days. Each and every time she stood in the mirror, she relived what she and Mario had done at the graveyard. While part of her still wanted to throw up in her mouth for the ultimate betrayal of her lifelong best friend, the other part could not help but fantasize about how good the sex was.

Naked in the shower, Kat let the hot water run down on top of her head and she got chill bumps as it trickled down the crack of her ass. It had been a long time since she'd had any real dick up inside of her and she hoped she wasn't sprung. It was one thing to have fucked the enemy, but to lust after him was another.

Reaching her hand out beyond the curtain, Kat grabbed her bullet-shaped companion and went to work. In and out, out and in, all she could think about was Mario. Kat knew it was wrong. She still hated his guts for the way he had always treated her best friend; and she even hated him for having sex with her as well even though they were equally at fault. As she was close to climax with her best friend's husband in mind, she swore to herself that the first opportunity she got to fuck over Mario and his smug world, she would. Knowing that his no-good, slick ass was trying to get with ol' girl at Walmart, Kat knew to start there. The only main thing that she wanted to preserve in the meantime was her relationship with Sasha, which she cherished almost more than life itself.

Mario left the gas station and headed back toward the house. After swinging by McDonald's he pulled in the driveway. As he sat there he wondered what Sasha was doing at that moment and if she would ever be able to forgive him for what he'd done as far as Kat was concerned. He had no way of knowing that his wife was on LOP and couldn't call, let alone that she knew absolutely nothing about Kat. He could only assume when Kat callously threw herself and him under the bus, he dragged Angie V along with them for the ride. Why wouldn't Kat be so vindictive to do so? That's who she was and who she always was since the moment she'd first stepped to the car out at the park trying to push up on his boy Dino and him. The fact that she was low-key whispering for both of them to have a threesome with her and forget about her ugly, boring-ass friend standing back over to the side was never brought up again, especially after all the gunfire and death that erupted seconds after she mentioned it. However, Mario never forgot what a snake Kat truly was and just how fake her loyalty was to Sasha; and the fact that he just fucked her proved he was right all along.

Mario finished off his fries before getting out of the SUV with his burger still in the bag. Walking up on the porch he paused as his cell phone went off. Looking down at the screen he saw, thank God, it was Angie V returning his text. She said that she had been extremely busy, and asked if he could call her after seven. Mario instantly replied yes with a smile on his face.

CHAPTER SEVENTEEN

Walking down the last few days of her prison-enforced restrictions, Sasha was trying hard to get over the hurt and pain caused by Mario not taking her calls. She also had come to terms with Regina turning her back on her, although technically she'd done it first. She was all cried out and had made up in her mind that she was not going to keep calling Mario. There was no need to keep making a fool out of herself. If he didn't want to be bothered with her after all she'd done to help him, then so be it. Sasha was not going to fret. She could have called the lawyer to get the paperwork together to have Mario removed from her house and his name taken off of other documents, but she didn't.

However, Sasha was extremely close to one of her friends who worked at the bank. Writing her a letter, she asked her if she could do her a huge favor. Knowing the type of person Sasha truly was outside of dealing with Mario and going to jail for him, the girl obliged. Putting a hold on Sasha's checking and savings accounts until she came into the bank and spoke personally with a customer service rep, all activity was suspended. That sudden suspension included the ATM card that Mario had been frequently using as if it were his hard-earned money accumulating, not his wife's.

That was the first thing Sasha did in the line of many to regain her dignity, self-respect, and pride. She knew that she had an out date. And one that was not too far away. That was the good thing. Sasha knew if she just let the outside world go on while she lived her life within the walls of the prison, she could stay focused and make early parole. With her being a first-time offender and trying to stay ticket free from this point on, she'd be back home in no time, especially with the overcrowding and budget cuts the corrections department was suffering from. Trina's good-begging ass had taught her one thing since being incarcerated and that was you can't control what you can't control.

It was nearing seven and Sasha sat back on her bunk and imagined how life would be when she went home. Mario would pay for leaving her for dead. It would only be a matter of time.

Mario stepped out of the shower feeling totally refreshed. He had used the trimmers to shave and he looked to be a new man in the mirror. With a towel wrapped around his midsection he put on deodorant, sprayed on some cologne, and fell back on the bed. He knew deep down inside he loved Sasha, but something in him would never allow him to fully commit. He had someone else on his radar and the thought of her consumed his mind.

Counting down the time until Angie V asked him to call, Mario checked his Instagram page, which he was hardly on. Created solely to look at thirst traps who posted pictures of their asses shaking and titties bopping, Mario grew bored with the social media pussy he could never touch.

Checking the time once more, it was exactly 7:00 p.m. Not trying to be or seem desperate, Mario waited ten more minutes before calling Angie V's number. Unlike the other recent times, she answered on the second ring.

"Hey, Mario. How are you?"

"I'm good now. Where you been hiding at? A guy been trying to get at you for a gang of days."

"I've been around. I just had some things I had to work out."

Mario was happy to hear her voice as if they had some bond between them other than an evening of paid fucking at the Red Roof Inn. "Well, I'm glad you decided to get back. I been thinking about you a lot over the past month or so. You got a brother kinda feeling you. So when I heard you was sick I was like whoa."

"Oh, yeah, well, please don't worry about me. I'm good." Angie V couldn't front. Considering her situation, she was feeling some sort of way about him as well.

Mario cut straight to the chase before she tried to end their conversation he had waited so long to have. "Okay, Angie, a nigga wanna lay eyes on you. So is that cool or what?"

Angie V wanted to say no, but she didn't. "Yeah, it's cool. It's just I don't have a babysitter."

"And?"

"And I don't let just anybody know where me and my kids lay our heads at."

"So I'm just anybody?"

"Ummmm, basically yeah, you are." She laughed.

"Damn, girl, okay then. How we gonna play it? 'Cause I wanna holler at you for real for real."

After a few minutes of them going back and forth, she gave in, giving Mario her address. Within the hour he was knocking at her front door with a pizza and hot wings in hand. After he met the kids and they ate, Angie V finally put them to bed. She was ecstatic that Mario and them got along so well. Trying to be a good mother, she hardly introduced them to men she had dated unless she felt they were about to be serious. Mario was the exception to the rule; well, kinda sorta.

With the kids tucked away for the night the two of them had a chance to talk. Before Mario knew what he was saying he'd told her all about his mother getting killed and him going to visit her grave for the first time in years. It goes without saying he left out the part about him having sex with Kat, his wife's best friend. Mario also lied to Angie V, saying that the tattoo across his heart saying SASHA was for his deceased mother, not his wife, very much alive in prison. The one thing he couldn't figure out and didn't want to ask was how Kat and she were even connected. Mario didn't want to ask and stir the pot of bullshit, so for the time being he just let it be.

Getting to know each other more and more, Mario could picture himself being with Angie V on a permanent basis. It was weird to him that because he saw her crying that day and it reminded him of his mother, he was willing to throw away everything that Sasha had built for them. He couldn't wrap his head around it. Mario had stopped shooting dice, drinking, and acting a fool. He fought hard to be the man his wife always wanted him to be; but in truth all along the dramatic change was for Angie V.

After hours of him being there, Mario had to use the bathroom. When he came out he took it upon himself to grab another soda out of the refrigerator so that Angie V would not have to get up. As he put his hand around the handle he was stopped by what was on the door. A decorative magnet held up a small black-and-white ultrasound. Mario couldn't understand why Angie V would have this hanging on the refrigerator door of all places; and exactly who did it belong to? With the thin, glossy photo in hand, he returned to the living room. Going over to the couch where she was sitting and messing with the television remote, Mario plopped down.

"Yo, Angie, who this right here belong to?"

Angela Vega, mother of three, looked dumbfounded. It had slipped her mind that the first indicator ultrasound was even up there. The only people who knew she was pregnant were her doctor and her three small kids. She had not even revealed that information to the baby's father, until now. "It's mine. It belongs to me."

Mario was confused. None of this made sense. She was knocked up by some nigga and she still had to sell him the pussy. His pipedream of maybe being with her had flown right out the window. "So, I mean, if you having a baby and whatnot, why you let me come over and chill with you? Ain't your baby daddy gonna be bugging out? I mean, I would if my girl did some ol' crazy disrespectful bullshit like that. And, damn, why you ain't have that lame help you out on them bills? What kinda dudes you be rocking out with?"

Angie V allowed Mario to go on and on until he shut up. Making sure he was done, she finally responded. "First of all, I didn't tell the father because I didn't think he would care. Secondly, I know at the end of the day I'm the one responsible for my baby, not him. So if he even asked me to get rid of it and have an abortion I would tell him to just beat it because me and my kids will be just fine."

"Don't you think he should know just the same?"

"Yeah, I do." She sat straight up, looking him in the eyes while taking the ultrasound out of his hands. "So okay, Mario, you're going to be a father."

It was dead silent in the room. Angie V waited for his response, but there was none. Mario just continued to sit there, jaw dropped open wide. He'd had different females back in the day try to put babies off on him, so he wasn't quick to say anything. As his mind went back to the time they had sex, he distinctly remembered using a condom. He easily recalled tossing it down on the side of the bed.

Taking all that in consideration, he finally spoke. "Look now, I like you and all. And I wouldn't mind kicking it with you despite you got them three kids back there." Mario pointed to the rear room where they were sleeping.

Offended by how he was speaking about her seeds, as if they were mere objects that lessened her value as a potential good woman or spouse, she went off. "See, that's why I didn't want to tell you in the first damn place. I know the circumstances of us getting together was really messed up right off rip. I realize that much. And the crazy fact that I got pregnant behind it made me salty at first too, because I definitely don't need another mouth to feed; but the bottom line is I'm going to have this baby." She placed her hand on her stomach, glancing down then back up at Mario. "And if you choose to be a part of your son's or daughter's life, then so be it. But if not, trust, I'll make a way."

"How you gonna make a way? Selling the next nigga pussy so they can be busting nuts all in my baby's face?" Mario was now on his feet, caught up in his manhood and emotions. He didn't know for sure if Angie V was running game, but he knew time would tell.

"Get the fuck out my house. I told you me and mines gonna be good, so go." Her arm was fully extended with her finger pointed at the door.

Mario swiftly obliged and he left to get in his SUV. Before starting the engine, he sat there in somewhat of a daze. Where half of his mind said the bitch was lying and just running game, the other half was kinda happy knowing he was going to have a chance to be a father again. Going back and forth with himself, Mario seem to forget one important factor to the sordid equation between him and Angie V: Sasha, who had just lost their child.

After sitting in the vehicle a good hour or so, thinking, Mario made up his mind. Seconds later he was pounding on Angie V's door. It took awhile, but when she did open the door dressed in nothing but her robe, Mario dropped to his knees, pressing his face and head on her stomach. "I'm gonna be here for you and my baby no matter what. That's my word."

CHAPTER EIGHTEEN

Months Later

Time seemed to fly by once Sasha had gotten her mind right and settled into her life at prison. She had made the best of it because she had no other options. Several times she pushed in her secured phone pin number and was going to try to call her husband, but she changed her mind. She had come to the conclusion, months back when Mario had cut her off, that he truly meant her no good. The conclusion was easy. He had set her up to take the fall so he could be free and live his life. Dumbly she fell for it because of the power of love.

Fighting with those demons was hard sometimes, but nothing like what she had to experience behind the walls of the prison that she had called home over the past year. Having no visits since Regina had come early on in her short bid, Sasha came to grips that she was out in the world by herself. The couple of letters she'd written to her elderly parents went unanswered, but she attributed that to her older sibling being vindictive since she basically took care of all their wants and needs and personal affairs.

As Sasha waited to speak to the case manager, she felt a strong sense of relief; the day she'd been waiting for since receiving her Under the Door parole decision paperwork in mail call. The favorable decision rendered made her realize once again that God was good and the devil couldn't hold her down any longer. She'd completed all the required classes she needed to take and now the only thing left to do was sign a few documents, making sure to cross the T's and dot the I's at that facility.

With the ride-out van filled with the other six inmates who were also going home that day, they were all transferred to the central release center to be processed out of the system and given instructions. After that was done, Sasha was given a debit card with the remainder of her account balance on it, fifteen dollars in cash, and a Greyhound bus ticket back to Detroit. She happily boarded the bus. No one knew she was coming home early, not her parents and Regina, not her best friend Kat, and definitely not her husband Mario, who'd left her for dead. Soon, they would all be surprised.

Mario had been living somewhat of a double life. Embracing the fact that Angie V was indeed carrying his seed, he did everything possible to make her sure her and her three children's lives were great. Even though Sasha had somehow found a way from behind the wall to cut him off from her purse strings, he still was a hustler and he went back to selling pills. This time, however, he didn't jack off his earnings on shooting dice and smoking weed; this go-around he helped pay bills, and he kept a smile on Angie V's face by always coming home and doing right by her. It was getting late into her pregnancy and she could no longer work, which was fine by Mario. He loved that for once in his life he was the true breadwinner and not his woman. He appreciated all that Sasha had eagerly done to make his lifestyle gravy, but it crippled him as a man.

Angie V still had no idea whatsoever that Mario, her man and soon-to-be baby daddy, was married. Mario was always with her and the kids, spending most if not all of his nights over at her house. She had not one clue.

Whenever he did say he was going home to check on his house, Mario had led her to believe he meant a small one-bedroom apartment he and his roommate shared, taking turns sleeping on the couch. Urging him to just give up that place and move in with her and the kids all the way, Mario reasoned with her that he would do just that as soon as the baby was born. In reality, he knew the clock was ticking and in six more months at least, Sasha would be on her way home and would force him out of the house they shared but she owned. Until then, he would play the game until it played itself out.

"Baby, I got a few moves I need to make; then I'll be back." Mario kissed her on the lips and then headed toward the door as Angie V sat on the couch with a big belly and a huge grin.

"Okay, Mario, but don't forget I have a doctor's appointment at two forty-five today and we have tickets to take the kids to the circus."

"Damn, is that today?"

"Yeah, crazy, it is and the kids been looking forward to it all week so don't be late. We can all go to the appointment together then go straight to the circus."

"Okay, baby, don't worry. I won't be late."

Sasha arrived at the bus station with no one to greet her. There was no welcome home or "Damn, I missed you." Just as it was while she was locked up, she was on her own. Using her state-issued debit card in the ATM, she griped at the overpriced service fee before withdrawing sixty dollars. Still dressed in the beige prison gear she was released in, she held a medium-sized bag containing the clothes she wore when she was taken into custody, which were now much too small, and some legal papers, along with a few other personal items. The rest of her belongings she left to Trina.

Hailing a cab, she gave the driver her address after being asked to put a deposit up front. She knew it was the way she was dressed that made him leery, but so be it. She had seventy-five dollars on her person, so she was good.

Arriving home, Sasha was relieved that at least the home she'd work so hard to purchase was still standing. The grass was cut and all in all it seemed to be well maintained. Walking up on the front porch, she took the mail out of the box, which had seemed to pile up. Her SUV was not in the driveway, so she could only assume her no-good husband was out running the streets like he always did.

Going around to the rear of the house, she reached up over the frame of the back door, retrieving the spare key she kept there if she ever got locked out. Once inside, Sasha smiled. She had made it back home and through the storm. Gathering all the mail off the table, she took it along with the mail she'd gotten out of the box and started to go through it while running some hot bathwater. Bill by bill, bank statement by bank statement, Sasha grew infuriated. She could hardly believe how much of her money her supposedly loyal husband had jacked off before she put a hold on her accounts. When the water was finally ready, Sasha stripped, tossing her clothes in the corner. She slid down in the marble tub and exhaled. She would deal with Mario whenever he showed up.

CHAPTER NINETEEN

Mario was trying to stay focused. Having made all his runs, he was tired but still had to keep it moving. Checking the time, he was running late to pick up Angie V and the kids, but he wanted to swing by the house and check on it. He hadn't done so in four days straight since cutting the grass.

When he pulled up in the driveway, a strange feeling came over him, but he didn't think anything of it as he stuck his key in the lock. Stepping inside, a familiar aroma circulated through the air filling his nostrils. *Naw, hell naw, couldn't be. I must be bugging!* A few steps later Mario was standing in the middle of the living room face to face with Sasha.

"Well, hello, Mario. How you been?" she asked with a smirk on her face. A few pounds heavier than when she went in, Sasha looked him square in the eyes, letting him know she was not in the mood for any games.

"Sasha." He could hardly get her name out as he was shocked and dumbfounded.

"What, Mario, no 'Hey, wife, welcome home'? No 'Thanks for going to jail for me while I run around and fuck other females who work at Walmart'? No 'Good looking out for letting me run through a gang of your money for months on end'? Come on, baby, at least act like you happy to see a bitch!"

Mario still hadn't moved from the spot on which he stood. He wasn't expecting to see Sasha standing in front of going ham, at least not for some months to come. Yet here she was. "Damn, girl. When you get out and why you ain't let anybody know you was coming home?"

"Anybody who? Not your sorry ass."

"Damn, Sasha, why you going so hard on a nigga?" Mario barked back, trying to defend the verbal attack he was under, but just happy she hadn't said anything about Kat as well. "You just getting home and already got me all fucked up!"

It was just like old times in their household. Mario would do or say things that were out of order and Sasha would have to cut off into his ass. Toxic as ever, the arguing went on nonstop for at least thirty minutes while Angie V blew up Mario's cell. Well off into a hour of who did what and to whom, the arguing turned into a physical altercation. Seven punches, three slaps, an attempted kick to the groin, and Mario getting a huge glob of spit in his face, the husband and wife were soon embraced on the kitchen floor fucking like wild animals in heat. When both had exhaustingly climaxed, Sasha lay there, mad at herself for giving in to her overwhelming need for dick, while Mario plotted how to get out of the house and back to Angie V, who had called and texted countless times.

It was daybreak and Sasha had not let Mario out of her sight. As much as she had planned to be done with him when she came home, it was like he was her addiction. She had fallen back in love with her husband just like that and she was willing to fight any bitch who even thought of coming between them. That included the mystery Spanish tramp she grilled Mario about, who he of course denied.

No doubt, there was no way in hell fire Mario could break the news to her about his "new woman." Or the hurtful reality that they had a child on the way, especially since Sasha was so gung ho about making another baby all the time they were having sex throughout the night. Mario was torn. And at this point he had to get to Angie V and give her some sort of explanation for his twenty-four-hour absence and make things right in that household. "Hey, bae, I need to go take care of a few things real quick. I'll be back soon."

Sasha got up from the bed, wrapping the sheet around her naked body. Walking over to look out the bedroom window, she looked outside, overjoyed to be home. "Welp, that's good and all, Mario, but you gonna have to find another way to do whatever it is that you do. I need to do some running of my own. So, bottom line, I'ma need you to run me my SUV keys, homeboy. Oh, and by the way the dick was good and I needed it for sure. But we ain't done talking about how you played me when I was gone. Round two later when we both get back home, so get ready!"

Mario was angry he would no longer have a vehicle to drive, but what could he say? After all, the SUV was Sasha's. He was just glad that while his wife was taking another bath he was able to sneak out the door and toss Angie V's daughter's car seat in the trash can next door before it was seen. It was not hard to notice that Sasha was not the same mild-mannered woman she had been before spending time in jail. Something told Mario to tread lightly. His wife was tired of his lies and manipulations.

CHAPTER TWENTY

Sasha had to get used to driving all over again. Her SUV's interior had definitely seen better days when she got inside and checked it out, but she overlooked it since she was on a mission. Although she wanted to see her parents, and even Regina's evil ass, she had to touch base with Kat. If anyone could put her up on game and give her the true, raw 411 on what Mario had really been up to, it would be her best friend. Kat knew just about everybody and everything that went on in the city.

Since Kat was bad with money and paying bills, Sasha had given up on contacting her at one of the multiple cell phone numbers she had for her. Instead, Sasha decided, just as she done to Mario, she'd pop up on her BFF. Minutes later she was turning into the apartment complex Kat lived in with her stepmother since childhood. After blowing the horn twice with no one coming to the window, Sasha got out and knocked on the door. Seconds later Kat flung the door open and had the biggest smile known to man plastered across her face.

"Awww snap, you home! My girl is home like a motherfucker! Damn, sis, hug a bitch! Damn, I'm geeked as hell."

Sasha was happy at least one person was glad to see she'd made it home through the dark storm. Going inside the apartment, she shared with Kat a few things that had jumped off while she was locked up, but more importantly she told her she had come to get some much needed intel. "So dig this. I talked to Regina a few months back and she told me Mario was supposed to be messing around with some low-budget bitch who work at Walmart. Is that bullshit true? Tell me what you heard."

Relieved that her best friend didn't know what took place between her and Mario, Kat had no problem ratting him out about Angela, where she stayed, and the fact that she found out the chick was supposed to be knocked up with Mario's baby. Kat could easily tell that Sasha, with her new beastlike attitude, was pissed.

"Where the fuck that bitch at? Ain't no ho having a baby by my husband." Sasha had brought all the courage and newfound prison mentality home with her and she was ready to do battle with anyone at anytime. "A baby. A fucking baby! Hell naw, not with my man!" Just like their old teenager days, Sasha and Kat jumped in the ride, ready to clown and tear some shit up.

"I'm telling you I was locked up all night. They took my phone, my money, everything. They even towed the damn SUV. That's why I had to catch a cab."

Throughout all the time Mario was explaining, Angie V knew he was lying. First of all, he had on different clothes than when he left. Secondly, he had shaved. And, lastly, he smelled like fresh soap. She knew Mario thought he was slick sometimes in the things he'd say and do over the past few months since they had been dealing with one another exclusively, but this time took the cake. There was no way in hell she believed he was locked up, but where he'd left the SUV was a mystery in itself.

As she let him go on and on making the lie more elaborate, there was a knock at the door. "We'll finish this later." She held her bulging stomach as she waddled toward the door. "That must be the maintenance man about the leak in the sink you keep saying you can fix."

Mario took that welcomed interruption as a way to go in the bedroom and gather his thoughts. Just as Angie V had been blowing up his cell when he was with Sasha the night before, now his wife was doing the same thing.

CHAPTER TWENTY-ONE

Standing shoulder to shoulder, Sasha and Kat both braced themselves, not readily knowing what or who they'd find behind the door. Being close to two degrees away from a hood detective, Kat had found out where Angie V laid her head at some time back after she and Mario had sex at the graveyard. She needed an insurance policy to get his ass stomped out just in case he snitched on them to her best friend. Thankfully he hadn't. As they stood silently there, waiting, each could hear voices arguing in the house, then footsteps getting closer. When the door finally swung open, Kat smiled while Sasha was ready to kill seeing Angie V's stomach.

"Hey, what are you doing here?" Angie V asked, vaguely remembering Kat from back at the store.

"We're here for the baby shower," Sasha snidely answered before Kat got a chance to reply.

"Baby shower, huh? I'm confused. What are you talking about? Matter of fact, who are you?"

Kat gladly intervened, responding to the million dollar question. "Oh, sorry, my bad for being so damn rude. This here is my best friend, Sasha."

"Sasha?" The pregnant mother of three paused when hearing that name.

"Yeah, Sasha. Mario's wife!"

Just as Kat finished making the impromptu introductions, the man of the hour emerged from the bedroom. "Oh, hell naw. What in the fuck is y'all doing here?"

"Pump your brakes, nigga. I was about to ask you the same damn thing," Sasha blurted out, revealing she had a pistol in her purse. As she backed Angie V and Mario all the way over to the couch, Kat followed her friend's lead, standing guard at the front door.

"Okay, Sasha, so you got a fucking gun, waving it around like you crazy or some shit. Now what?"

"Mario, who are these people?" Angie V pleaded, terrified for not only herself but her three innocent children who were in their bedroom watching cartoons.

"Yeah, Mario, boo-boo, tell your little pregnant jump-off who we are, especially me."

Mario turned up his lip as all three of the women stared at him, waiting for him to speak.

"What's wrong, you big liar? I know you ain't forgot who I am. I mean, damn, baby, we only been married three years and together five."

Angie V couldn't believe her ears. After all this time of her and Mario being together she had been sleeping with a complete stranger. Here she was thinking they had a chance at a real life as one and, in reality, she was pregnant by a married man. "I asked you who Sasha was and you said your mother!"

"His mother?" Sasha giggled, shaking her head. "Nigga, you going straight to hell for lying on the dead. And, bitch, what makes you think you can have a baby by another woman's husband and think it's all good? It's rules to this shit, sweetie!"

"Yeah, but I didn't know anything about you or that he was married until just now." Angie kept nervously rubbing her stomach.

Sasha laughed once more, gripping the handle of the pistol. "Well, just like his dead mama, you should've done your homework on me and him. So that's on you!"

Kat wanted to laugh too, yet the sheer mention of Mario's deceased mother made her feel uneasy about their secret encounter on top of the woman's grave. Instead she turned her head, just glad that Mario was finally getting his just due.

Angie V rubbed her stomach as if she was comforting her unborn child for having such a shit bag for a daddy. Sasha, however, was growing madder by the moment seeing her husband and his pregnant ho sit next to each other as if they were a couple and she was the outsider. Mario noticed the look in her eye and tried to bring a peaceful resolution to this before someone got hurt.

"Look, Angie, I didn't really lie to you; you never asked. Plus, she was in jail all this time."

"Are you serious? You mean because I never thought to ask a man who sleeps in my bed each and every night, pays all of my bills, and takes care of my kids as if they're his own is married, I'm wrong? A man who cries almost every day saying how happy he is I'm carrying his seed, I should ask is he married?"

A loud sound suddenly rocked the inside of the living room and the entire house. It was quickly followed by two more. Kat jumped back and Mario defensively held his hands and arms up. With malice in her heart, Sasha grinned as Angie V slumped over on the couch holding her stomach, which now had a huge, gaping hole in it. Finding some weird sense of revenge upon the next female who thought it was okay to have a baby by her husband, she then aimed the gun at Mario, who was now begging for his life and asking Kat to get her girl.

"So you two lovebirds just gonna argue in front of me like I'm not standing here with a gun, huh? Come on now, Mario, you must think I'm the same dumb-ass bitch who went to jail for you! The same bitch who was pregnant with your baby and who you left for dead while you over here playing house, downgrading with this hood trash! Well, guess what, I'm not her anymore. Things change and so do people! So you can beg all you want to live while her and y'all precious baby bleed out! Then you can see how it feels to slowly suffer when someone you love leaves your black ass all alone."

Mario had tears streaming down his face. He wanted to jump up and try to bum-rush Sasha, but he didn't want to take his hand off of the gunshot wound in Angie V's stomach, which he was now holding in hopes of stopping the heavy flow of blood. When Sasha watched her husband's pregnant jump-off take her last breath, she fired another round off into Mario's skull. She had no remorse. Jail had made her cold to the world.

Turning around, she saw one of Angie V's three children standing in the hallway crying. "Get your little bastard ass back in that bedroom before you be next!" Hearing sirens in the distance, Sasha then turned to Kat, asking her what she wanted to do.

Kat hadn't signed on to be an accessory to two murders, but since she was desperately in love with her best friend and had been since childhood, she'd ride with Sasha all the way to hell if need be. Mario was gone and out of the picture for good. So, in her eyes, even though Sasha was not gay, there was no one standing in their way to be a couple.

As they rushed out the front door and to the SUV, a police car spotted them both. Kat unfortunately fell on the curb and twisted her ankle trying to run, ending her *Thelma & Louise* fantasy. Sasha, however, kept it moving. Throwing the SUV in drive, she recklessly sped off with the cop trailing close behind.

Getting up to speeds of more than a hundred miles an hour through residential streets, Mario's wife wiped the tears from her eyes, thinking of what her once perfect, calm life had become. Sasha Eubanks, inmate 998797, had been home, released no more than forty-eight hours on parole before killing two people; and she was now going to be apprehended and returned to prison, sadly never seeing her elderly parents or sister while free, all because of a no-good man!

THE END

THE ULTIMATE REVENGE

by

Marlon P.S. White

CHAPTER ONE

"Oh, hell naw, you little ungrateful bitch. You got a lot of damn nerve after I took you in off the streets. Now guess what? Get all that shit you came here with together now. You and that garbage bag full of raggedy clothes that barely cover your ass need to get the fuck out my house. And hurry up before I really get mad. I swear to God, you just like your good-for-nothing, dead-ass mama." Rissa's aunt stood in her personal space, nose to nose, yelling. "She wasn't about nothing, and neither is you!"

Rissa felt like she was having an awful nightmare and couldn't wake up. She was depressed how her life was going. At the same time, she was hurt that her own flesh and blood wouldn't believe her. For the last three weeks Rissa was being stalked inside of the house and she'd had enough of the awful situation. That's when all hell broke loose. Rissa told her aunt that Mackey, her husband who always behaved weird, was forcing himself on her every morning after her aunt went to work. Knowing it was wrong, she thought she was doing the right thing by snitching. Instead, here she stood with her aunt throwing her out and hawking in her face.

Rissa turned her head away from her aunt and wiped the spit off with the palm of her hand. "Auntie, why you doing this to me? He's the one who's sick and messed up in the mind. I didn't do nothing."

"You young, hot-in-the-pants whores are all the same. See a good, married man and wanna try to steal him for yourself."

"Are you serious right now? Please, Auntie, you can't be. What you doing and saying is so wrong." Sick to her inner core, Rissa had flashbacks of Mackey forcing himself inside of her as she tried relentlessly to no avail to fight him off. Only 125 pounds fully clothed up against a grown man weighing in at an easy 245 pounds, if not more, it was easy to guess who would come out on top of the battle. Rissa had no chance whatsoever and no easy win in sight. She was no match for Mackey to defend herself against him, and the sad part about it was he knew it.

Sinisterly, he would roughly smash his hand over her mouth, warning her that if she dared told her aunt, she wouldn't believe her and what was taking place right now would happen. She would be kicked out with no place to go because no one else wanted to be bothered with her or cared about her.

"Yeah, Rissa, as long as you give me this sweet, tight little pussy you will always have a place to stay. You'll have food to eat and a roof over your head. See, your aunt loves me. She believes I can do no wrong. Whatever I tell her to do, you see it. You're not blind. She obeys me. Truth be told, she the best bitch I ever had in my life." He constantly taunted his niece by marriage until she could take no more.

That's when Rissa gathered enough courage to prove him wrong about what he was saying about her mother's sister. Rissa was dumbfounded and confused at her aunt's reaction to this unthinkable situation. The naïve niece just knew her aunt would have her back and she would either kill Mackey with her bare hands or at least call the police immediately to protect her from him.

But the wife, in denial, hadn't done anything like that. In fact, she'd done the complete opposite. Rissa was almost hysterical, pleading with her kin to believe what she'd exposed about Mackey. The more Rissa revealed details to prove she was telling the truth, the more her claims of sexual abuse fell upon deaf ears. "Auntie, I'm not lying. I swear to God I'm not. He told me if I said anything you wouldn't believe me, but I told him you would. I told him you would believe me because I was telling the truth. Why would I make something like this up, Auntie? Why?" Rissa sobbed with a face full of tears streaming down her cheeks.

Mackey was cold as ice. Arms folded, he stood behind his wife, smirking at his young victim who was going through it. Picking at his dirty fingernails, he was confident things would go just as he said if Rissa exposed him for the pedophile monster he truly was. The more Rissa spewed out what they both knew to be the truth, the more his wife defended him, just as he predicted. "Come on now, baby. That little nappy-headed bitch lying. What the hell I look like dealing with her when I got you here with me?" Mackey grinned, grabbing his dick, licking his lips at Rissa.

Tears flowed even harder down Rissa's otherwise innocent face as she watched Mackey over her aunt's shoulder antagonizing her as if the entire thing was a joke. Fed up, she couldn't take it anymore. She put her hands over her mouth to muffle the scream she could no longer hold in. Turning away, she ran to the bathroom. Of course her auntie was dead on her heels. Rissa quickly slammed the door in her face, feeling as if she wanted to throw up her breakfast, lunch, and dinner. Not knowing what she was going to do next, Rissa panicked, walking around in circles as her aunt's balled-up fist could be heard pounding on the bathroom door.

"You gotta go, you fast-ass little ho. You're not gonna fuck my happy home up. That's what's wrong with y'all young bitches nowadays. Always in a grown man's face thinking they want that fresh perch smelly cat between y'all legs. You gonna learn today. You been acting twice your age smelling your own pussy since you turned a damn teenager." Auntie was livid and meant every word she was saying as Mackey backed her up rant. "So guess what, wannabe grown ass. You got ten minutes to be the fuck out of my house. You hear me, bitch? Ten minutes!"

Rissa slowed down her pacing. With her head hurting, she took several deep breaths trying to regain her composure. With both palms covering her ears she sat on the side of the bathtub. As she rocked back and forth her mind was racing trying to figure out her next move.

She knew staying under her aunt's roof with that monster Mackey was totally out of the question. One, because her aunt was throwing her out; and, two, Rissa knew it was no longer safe. *Where will I go? Who can I call? Should I go to the police and turn him in? Will I end up in a foster home, lost in the system 'til my eighteenth birthday?* As the questions shot through her brain like skyrockets, she had no other choice but to boss up as her aunt was now back banging on the locked door.

Knowing good and well becoming a part of the system was not in her future, Rissa decided to take her chances on the streets of Detroit rather than be a ward of the state. Having felt alone in the world since her mother died, she stood. Going over to the mirror, the anguished teen placed her hands on each side of the bathroom sink, taking a good look at herself. Reaching for her washrag, she wiped the tears off her face, knowing she was done crying over bullshit she couldn't change. Rissa took a long, deep breath. Eyes bloodshot, she calmly looked around the bathroom until she found her hairbrush. Blocking out the awful world behind the door, she slowly brushed her long black hair to the back as she always wore it. Rissa kept staring at herself in the mirror, remembering being posted at her mother's hospital bedside the day before she died of kidney failure.

"Baby, I'm not afraid of dying. My God has sent for me and I know I won't suffer anymore. I just pray and ask Him to look after my only child. Lord knows there's a lot of wolves in this world masking themselves in sheep's clothing."

La Rissa Ford didn't understand what her mother's words meant in that dire moment in time. But today she fully understood what her mama meant. Mackey was that big, bad wolf in sheep's clothing. Rissa started to hate her aunt, and Mackey most of all, because the two of them stood at her dying mother's bedside and promised to take care of her. Now Rissa realized why Mackey was so gung ho with taking her into his household. His shady motives were now all too clear. He had been plotting on taking advantage of her from jump.

"No dude gonna ever touch me or do what the fuck he wanna do with me ever again unless I let him. I'll die first. I swear on my dead mama's cremated ashes," Rissa angrily vowed as she unlocked the bathroom door ready to face whatever. Mad at the world and anyone against her well-being, Rissa swung the door open with so much force that the knob hit the wall, causing plaster to fall from the ceiling.

"Bitch, don't slam my doors. You ain't paying no bills around here," Mackey shouted from the living room couch where he spent most his time watching television while his wife worked.

"Welp, neither do you, nigga!" Rissa was heated. She marched out of the bathroom and went into the spare bedroom where she slept. Franticly, she gathered her belongings. In the heat of the moment, she began to cry again, mumbling hateful things toward her aunt and Mackey. "Both of you gonna pay for fucking me over. I know my mama turning over in her grave." Rissa closed her eyes and spoke out loud to her mother as if she could hear her. "I know you didn't know, Mama. I don't blame you."

Rissa knew her mother would have never allowed her to stay with her aunt if she knew what an awful monster her sister's husband was. The truth was her mother always got uneasy vibes about Mackey whenever he came around. Yet she couldn't quite figure out what it was about him that made her feel that way.

Linda Ford really had no other family to speak of. It was only her and her sister. Their parents had passed away years ago. Rissa never met her grandparents on her mother's side, only hearing stories from back in the day. As for her own father and his people, Rissa's mother told her that her dad was killed when she was barely three months old. Her father's side of the family had a knockdown drag-out dispute with Linda over the illegitimate bastard.

In denial of Rissa being their grandchild, her grandma let it be known plain and clear that her son had no children he knew of. She was a mean, hateful woman who could not be moved. Linda did everything she could to convince her that Rissa was their blood, even offering to get a DNA test and pay for it. With a cold heart, she wasn't trying to hear none of what Linda was claiming to be true.

When Rissa got older, around fourteen years old, she sought out her father's wicked-mouthed mother on her own. Sneaking through some of her mother's personal papers, she found the address. Gathering her courage, she went to find her truth and knocked on the woman's door. Anxiously, she waited for an answer. Overjoyed to finally come face to face with someone who looked kinda like she did, Rissa smiled. She then introduced herself, explaining to the woman her deceased son was her father.

Her grandmother went in on her hard, crushing all hope of Rissa ever knowing any of her daddy's side of the family. The bitter woman confusingly refused to accept the fact that her son had or could have a child to carry on his name. Rissa remembered the incident as if it had just happened.

"I'm gonna tell you this one time and one time only. Don't bring your little bum bitch ass back to my house no damn more with all this high drama shit. Your mama sent you barking up the wrong tree." The woman stopped ranting long enough to squint and lean forward. "Hell, you don't look nothing like my son, me, or nobody else in my gene pool, as a matter of fact. So fuck you and your conniving mama," the bitter old bitch barked at poor, broken-hearted Rissa.

That had done it for Rissa. She wanted no part of that woman from that point on. Ironically, she would find out later on down the line that she had a lot of her grandmother's evil streak in her when it came down to it.

Rissa glanced around the bedroom looking for anything of personal value she cared about taking with her. Seeing nothing, she picked up the lightweight trash bag off the floor and slung it over her shoulder. Having no choice, she was ready to head out of her aunt's house for good.

Before the pitiful teen got to the front door she had to walk by Mackey and her aunt. The two of them sat on the living room sofa, cuddled up, passing a Newport back and forth as if nothing major had been said. Side-eyeing Rissa, her aunt smirked, feeling as if she had accomplished something by turning her back on her deceased sister's only child. "Lock my door on your way out, lying-ass, loose bitch."

Rissa stayed focused. She looked straight ahead, trying her damn best not to say a word to either of them. However, when she reached the front door, Rissa stopped, turning around to give them a final piece of her mind. "Fuck both of y'all wack asses. You deserve each other, two fake niggas who ain't about shit. And, Auntie, you know my mama would beat your ass for letting him get away with doing me like he did, your own blood. But that's cool, though. I swear, I'ma be good. But y'all gonna fall; watch! Motherfuckers can't do people like y'all doing me. And when I get wherever I'm going, I'm calling the police on your nasty ass, believe that!"

Rissa's words were delivered with sheer ice. Superstitious, Mackey and her aunt both felt fearful that Rissa had just cursed them, but they tried to laugh it off as she walked out the door for good. Mackey also hoped she would not actually call the cops and turn him in.

CHAPTER TWO

"Dang, I guess I'm on my own, Mama," Rissa said, looking up at the evening sky as she walked up the block with tears still in her eyes. Having no idea what her next move was, Rissa got several blocks away from the house. Having to stop to catch her breath because she was walking so fast, her mind was going a hundred miles an hour in all directions. She got sick to her stomach. Her entire world was turned upside down. She had no plan and no real money to speak of. Distraught, she doubled over, throwing up on the sidewalk and part of the curb. Rissa wiped the vomit away with the back of her thin North Face jacket sleeve. The cool April air was comforting to her, at least, as she sweated. Getting back on her square, she steadied herself and looked around to see where she was. The street signs read Gratiot and Gunston; she'd walked all the way from Eight Mile Road and hadn't realized it.

Searching for a safe place to rest her burning legs, Rissa also needed some water to rinse her mouth out. Her first mindset was to drink out of someone's water hose, but actually finding a person in the hood with a hose let alone a faucet tap that worked was impossible. Bag back over her shoulder, she went into the gas station on a nearby corner to buy a bottle of water. Crazy as it may seem, it was jumping and it was located right across the street from the police department's ninth precinct.

This area was known in Detroit as the Red Zone, where anything was subject to pop off. There were always drug deals being made, panhandlers posting up and begging for a dime, a quarter, a cigarette, or something. Before you could get out of the car good and walk inside the station you were attacked.

Rissa went to the cooler and got a dollar water. Then she headed back to the front to cash out. On her way in she'd noticed the two Arabs working behind the counter eyeing her trash bag over her shoulder extremely hard while they tended to customers. When it was her turn to pay for what she was buying she pulled out a dollar that was tucked in her rear pocket and eyeballed them back. "What the fuck you keep looking at my bag for?"

"Why you so rude, sweetie? I do something to you? I say nothing wrong to you," the Arab at the first register spoke in broken English with lust in his eyes.

Rissa couldn't stand them because they were always disrespectful to black women with all that sweetie, honey, baby bullshit. But as soon as a nigga knocked one of their bitches off, it was a problem. Rissa sucked her teeth and rolled her eyes at the dude. She then paid for the water and turned to walk out but was stopped at the entrance.

"Girl, what up? What you doing at the trap station?" Wanda cried out in joy to see her road dog.

Rissa perked up quick when she saw Wanda. "I was about to ask your ass the same thang." Rissa smiled as they hugged each other. Wanda and Rissa had met in ninth grade and had been jam tight ever since. At one point when you would see one you would see the other.

"What are you about to do, go to your auntie crib?" Wanda asked, assuming that had to be her homegirl's move.

Rissa dropped her head an inch and shook it side to side. "No. I bounced from that bitch house. Her and my slime ball uncle be on that bullshit, especially him," Rissa announced sadly as she got a huge lump in her throat.

An off-brand nigga came through the door high as fuck. He walked between them like they were invisible. As he bumped Rissa's shoulder her garbage bag full of all she now owned in the world fell to the ground. Wanda and Rissa went ham on him. There was no way in hell anyone in the hood would allow the next person to be so rude and not go off, damn the consequences.

"Hey, nigga, damn. Have you lost your fucking mind or what? Where the fuck they do that bullshit at?" Wanda was pissed, immediately bending down to help her friend pick up her bag.

Rissa looked up, giving him a death stare. "Yeah, that was messed up. You gotta be high off something strong as hell, shit."

"Damn, my bad, ladies. A brother a little wasted tonight," he apologized with smug grin plastered across his clean-shaven face. Then he yelled out to the cashier to give him a fresh back wood blunt. After he got it he hurried back out the door ready for the rest of his night.

"Okay, sis, now back to what we was talking about before that fool came in. So when did you move out?" Wanda quizzed with surprise.

"I guess about an hour ago," Rissa replied, knowing her life would never be the same. She hated Mackey for what he had been doing to her and she hated her aunt, her own flesh and blood even, doubly for not believing her. Yet and still, Rissa still couldn't help but feel a bit of sadness not knowing what her future would hold.

"Damn, girl, that's all the way fucked up." Wanda hugged Rissa tightly in an attempt to comfort her. Out of curiosity, she asked her childhood friend what happened and why she wasn't going to be living with her aunt anymore. Rissa was already beyond upset. She had been through enough emotional turmoil for the night and didn't want any more tears. She knew good and well her eyes were already redder than fire. Throwing her bag back over her shoulder, Rissa told Wanda she'd tell her later, which was all she had to say. They had been running together long enough throughout the years to know that was code for "Bitch, hold tight. I'll tell you when I get high."

"Okay, damn all the sad shit; so what is you about to do? I need to turn up and get my mind right, girl," Rissa gleefully said, trying to take her thoughts off of the earlier events.

Wanda looked at her watch and smiled. "Girl, go to my house. My mama and brother left driving to Florida this morning. Her cousin died."

"Oh, wow. That's messed up. Sorry to hear that and for your loss." Rissa gave her a sad look as they walked out the door of the gas station together.

"Fall back, bitch, don't be sorry. I didn't like his old, crusty, good-black-face-hating ass anyways," Wanda shrieked, waving her hand from side to side.

As the friends laughed, both the girls' attention was drawn to their left. Off to the side of the wall, they noticed the same rude nigga who cut between them inside then took a cop. He was cursing into his cell phone while he held it like a microphone trying to be more than extra.

"Fuck that, homeboy, if you ain't high you didn't buy it from me. It's whatever, my dude. I'm out here in these streets like a real G every day and night, you can believe that!" He was obviously agitated the louder he got.

Rissa and her girl side-eyed him for trying to front for a few young, giggling females who had no business even being out this time of night and posted at the hot box gas station at that. Ready to get in their own zone, they kept it moving.

Bending the corner, Rissa saw Wanda's boyfriend Chad parked off to the side of the lot. He was gangster leaned back in his old-school Cutlass that sat up high on rims. The two friends were horse playing, talking shit about this and that. Rissa was glad to have someone to talk to who wasn't as fake as she'd just found out her aunt was. Almost a few yards away from the car, Chad began franticly motioning for his girl and Rissa to hurry up and get inside.

"I told her ass I didn't like this gas station shit always popping off up here," Chad said out loud to himself as he leaned over from the driver's side, pushing the passenger door open.

Obviously the girls weren't paying attention to their surroundings. But thankfully Chad was. Knowing the reputation of where they were, Chad was focused on the black Hell Cat as soon as it turned off of Gunston into the gas station lot. Watching the play about to go down, he saw the vehicle whip right up on the dude who was just on his cell phone a second ago truly going ham on someone or perpetrating it. Just the same, something wasn't right. Chad had a bad feeling come over him as soon as the Hell Cat's tires came to a screeching halt.

"Hey, y'all, hurry the fuck up! Now," he demanded, putting bass in his voice.

"Look at this nigga, girl, trying to be all bossy. Boy, don't be rushing us. We coming," Wanda yelled at Chad, who was giving them a crazed look.

"You must have told that nigga he getting some wet-wet tonight the way he rushing a bitch," Rissa teased, switching the bag to her other shoulder.

Both the girls were smiling, oblivious to the scene playing out behind them. The rude, bigmouthed cash-talking guy at the gas station was frozen in fear. With his hands up, grimacing, warm piss started to run down his pant leg. He was caught with his dick out, exposed. The front passenger in the Hell Cat had a .40-cal. with an extended clip aimed at his head. He appeared to be short on patience and long on determination, demanding his twenty-five dollars back he gave him for the nothing-ass weed he had copped not even ten minutes earlier.

"Damn, dawg, it ain't that serious for all that. You ain't gotta be pointing that thang at a nigga face and whatnot."

"It wasn't that serious until you was screaming at me that you was about that life and my little twenty-five dollars wasn't about shit. It was serious then so let's keep that convo on tap," the passenger yelled back at his soon-to-be victim.

"Man, quit playing. Bust that bitch-ass nigga, man. He was talking that tough-tone shit on the phone a minute ago. Now look at him, all pissy and shit," the driver mocked, begging his boy to just go ahead and put in that work so they could peel out.

As the soon-to-be high-profile but common crime was taking place, Chad got more animated, pointing at the situation popping off behind the girls. Finally when bullets were seconds away from flying, the mouthy duo caught on to Chad and what he was trying to say. Looking back, they saw the real murderous drama unfolding.

Rissa and Wanda jointly let out high-pitched screams and ran full speed to Chad's car. Practically diving inside, their hearts raced. Chad called them both all kinds of dumb hoes for not paying attention to what was going on around them at all times in Detroit. Rissa ducked down in the back seat, peeking out the window. Chad hit the gas, making the Cutlass leave a trail of burned rubber tracks off of the side of the gas station onto Gratiot.

Rissa witnessed the rude guy attempt to reach toward his waist as if he had his own peacemaker. However, it was much too late to call himself taking a stand. The man who he had sold the garbage weed to didn't double back to be friends but enemies of the boy's family and friends. Countless numbers of flashes lit the night air followed by the ear-splitting eruption of loud gunshots coming from the Hell Cat the guy stood just feet away from. It was like looking at an oncoming train wreck. Part of Rissa wanted to just turn her head in the other direction and thank God it wasn't her getting cruelly put to sleep, while the other part had to watch the inevitability. All three of them knew the bigmouthed dude was dead before he hit the ground.

Oh well, add another one to the homicide statistics of Detroit, Rissa thought. She had zoned out. She forgot she was in the car with Wanda and Chad. Her heart raced and her adrenalin was on a hundred. Finally she was snapped back to reality by Chad's continued ranting. "Chad, you my nigga and all but shut the fuck up, bro; we get it. Pay attention to our surroundings," Rissa repeated with sarcasm.

Chad was always overprotective of females, especially the ones closest to him. "Okay, y'all think it's all fun and games, until ya ass end up in some random clown's trunk buck-ass-naked and literally fucked up."

Wanda sucked her teeth and rolled her eyes at her man. He took his eyes off the road long enough to side-eye her. Rissa then yelled from the back seat, "Where's the weed at? Roll up! Put some smoke in the air. A bitch need to get her mind right."

Wanda reached over and snatched the quarter sack of bud off of Chad's lap. Then she prepped the back wood to be filled with weed. Finally rolled and lit, she hit it hard then passed it over her shoulder to Rissa. Rissa took it and looked at it good before she went any further. Then she cussed Wanda out for doing a fucked-up job rolling up as always. Rissa hit the weed hard causing her chest to fill up with the meds she craved. Rissa held the smoke in as long as she could. When she was no longer able to hold it in, she exhaled, blowing weed smoke out. The car filled up quickly with smoke.

Chad, the last to hit, could barely contain his excitement. "Damn, that shit smells funky; pass that shit!"

Way before the blunt was equally passed among the three, they were high as fuck and in a Snoop Dogg tranquil state of mind ready for whatever the rest of the evening had in store for them.

The trio finally made it to Wanda's mother's house. They exited the old school car and went inside. Once inside Chad went to the icebox to grab a drink to quench the case of cotton mouth he was experiencing. He found just what he needed: a pitcher of cherry Kool-Aid. In the hood it's everybody's favorite thirst quencher. Chad gulped down the ice cold Kool-Aid, giving life back to his mouth and pleasure to his taste buds.

Wanda and Rissa sat in the living room discussing Bobby, who was Rissa's special boo thang. As they did, it was time to put something else in the air again. The pair moved like a well-oiled machine. Rissa cleaned the tobacco out of the blunt while Wanda broke down the kush. It was rolled and blazed up in no time at all. Chad then joined them in the living room and pretended not to be listening to their conversation as he gladly took his turn when the blunt came around to him.

"So what you gonna do, girl, fuck with him or not?" Wanda quizzed Rissa.

"I don't know what to do, but I got a lot of issues going on in my life right now." She looked over at the plastic garbage bag sitting over in the corner of the room containing her stuff. "Plus, he cool and all but his baby mama drama ain't for me because I'll drag that bitch from east to west if she don't stay in the baby mama section where she belongs. You feel me, bitch?" Rissa said, looking Wanda dead in her eyes, signaling she meant business about the entire situation.

"I heard that, girl. 'Cause if I were to ever be in them shoes, I'm not going to hold a ho up," Wanda said as she glared at Chad. He didn't say a word in regard to her remarks. He was still acting as if he wasn't paying them any mind.

CHAPTER THREE

Chad was relieved to hear a knock at his girlfriend's mother's front door. He got up to see who it was. The girls ceased their conversation and focused on the door waiting to see who it was. Chad unlocked the screen and stepped to the side. Bobby came through the door with a brown paper bag clutched under his arm and a fat blunt dangling between his lips. He said, "What up, bro," to Chad as he grabbed hold of his hand shaking it firmly.

"What up, big head one and big head two?" Bobby referred to Rissa and Wanda. They sounded like a couple of schoolgirls as they said hey to Bobby simultaneously. Then the girls gave each other a sour look.

The blunt in his mouth bounced up and down as he walked a few feet to the coffee table and put the brown paper bag on it. "Y'all dead up in here. Turn up in this bitch." Bobby tried to emulate Future, halfway singing a bar of one of his songs. "'We got that good kush and alcohol.'"

"Boy, please stop messing that man's song up and pour me a drink. God knows I need one after that failed attempt you just made to carry a note."

The four of them burst out laughing together and so the night began to be filled with enjoyment among the four friends. For Rissa it was a temporary distraction from the real-world issues she held deep within: molestation, family betrayal, and being homeless. The music was loud, drinks were flowing, and kush stayed in the air.

The later it got, the higher they all got. At around a quarter of 2:00 a.m. Wanda and Chad announced it was a wrap for the two of them and that they were going to bed. Wanda gave Bobby the "go ahead" look to crash at her crib. She was secretly rooting for him to finally give Rissa some dick. She thought the two of them would be great for one another. He and she already had a bond that couldn't be broken. Time had proven that Bobby was always there for Rissa in her most difficult times. Basically he had been her young knight in shining armor.

Chad and Wanda stumbled to her bedroom not to be seen until the next morning. Rissa and Bobby were straightening up the living room as best they could due to the blitzed condition they were in. Out of nowhere Rissa was ready to confess what had become an unspeakable subject. Yet it was tearing her up inside. She had to tell someone and next to Wanda he'd always been her confidant.

"Bobby, I wanna tell you something but I don't know how you'll look at me afterward." Rissa sat on the sofa and put her head down.

Bobby sat next to her and held her hand telling her to look at him. "What's the matter? What going on?" He could see the hurt in Rissa despite all the weed and alcohol she had put in the air and taken to the head. Bobby put his hand under her chin, lifted her head back up, and turned it toward him. Tears slowly steamed down her flawless brown skin. Seeing her crying made him grow even more concerned. "Shorty, what's the deal with you? Talk to me. You know you always can talk to me," he pleaded.

She wiped her face with the back of her hand and stared at Bobby for a long time before she spoke. "I don't got nowhere to live. Wanda said I can chill here with her 'til her mom get back from outta town, but after that I don't know what I'm gonna do."

Bobby was perplexed. "What? I don't understand. I thought it was all good at your aunt's crib. You're not living there anymore? What happened?"

Rissa shook her head from side to side and covered her face with her hands. She was ashamed to tell him for fear he wouldn't want her anymore or he would think she brought the situation with Mackey on herself. "Promise me you won't look at me any different if I tell you. Swear to God, Bobby."

Bobby's heart raced. His thoughts were all over the place fearing the worst. The first thing that came to mind was Rissa was going to tell him she was knocked up by some bum-ass nigga. He had already come to the conclusion that if she was pregnant he still wanted her and he'd step up and help her with the baby.

"Promise me, Bobby. Promise me," Rissa repeatedly begged him.

"Just fucking tell me, girl. I promise I won't look at you some type of way. If you don't know by now, I'm not your average dude you used to talking with or dealing with. We're better than that dumb shit," Bobby scolded her for not trusting in him and their longtime bond.

Rissa dropped her head once more and the tears flowed even harder down her cheeks. She shook her head back and forth, closed her eyes, and pictured Mackey doing the unthinkable things to her he'd done. "He raped me," she blurted out, sobbing so hard Bobby was in denial of what he had just heard.

"What?" Bobby jumped to his feet. He paused briefly before speaking again. He couldn't believe the words that just came out of her mouth. "Who did it?" he demanded to know as he grew angrier. Rissa wouldn't say who raped her. She had wrapped her arms around herself and rocked back and forth. She was ashamed to tell him who had violated her as he kept at her for an answer. "Who in the fuck did it, Rissa? Who?"

Bobby grabbed her firmly and stopped her from rocking. He wanted her to see his eyes and know he was not in the mood for stalling. "Look at me, Rissa, look at me!" he shouted, enraged. Reluctantly, Rissa looked up at Bobby. "Who hurt you, baby girl? You can tell me." He then changed his facial expression and spoke in a caring, soothing tone as tears of anger began to form in his eyes.

"Mackey," Rissa said through clenched teeth as she pulled away from Bobby. She began to tell him everything that had happened, from beginning to end. Bobby wanted to collapse out of anger and disbelief. He sat next to Rissa, hunched over with his elbows resting on his knees like a prize fighter waiting for the bell to ring. By the time Rissa was finished confessing to Bobby the terrible truths that had happened, the hurt tears in his eyes had turned to blood.

The alcohol and fury inside of Bobby mixed a dangerous cocktail. "Did you go to or call the police?" he questioned Rissa as if he were the police himself.

Rissa explained that no, she didn't go to the police because she was afraid of being taken by the state and bounced around group homes until she turned eighteen. Bobby shook his head that he agreed with her reasoning. He assured her everything would be okay and no matter what, as always, he had her back. At the same time he was formulating a plan of revenge. Mackey and her aunt had to pay dearly, and soon.

Rissa and Bobby both were emotionally drained. Blazing up, they decided to blow another blunt and try to get some rest. Rissa had drifted off to sleep in Bobby's arms on the sofa fairly quickly once they had gotten comfortable. Bobby, on the other hand, was restless and still seething. All he could think about was how he could kill Mackey and not catch a case.

Bobby wasn't a stranger to doing dirt. He had his fair share of run-ins with the law, because he had to fend for himself most of his young life. He would shake a bag to eat if need be. He'd even hit licks here and there when the block was slow or hot. Having been through so much he knew how to be grimy and tonight was one of those nights.

Bobby tried not to think about all the garbage Rissa told him Mackey did to her. But every time he closed his eyes, images of her being raped tormented him. Bobby recalled what Rissa told him what Mackey had said to her, that nobody would believe her, not even her aunt if she told her. Bobby thought, *I believe her, you sick motherfucker,* as he eased off the sofa carefully so he wouldn't wake Rissa.

Knowing she would stop him from acting on the evil intentions racing in his head if she woke up, he grabbed a blunt that was already rolled and the almost empty bottle of liquor off the coffee table. Ready to go on a mission, he crept out of the house. Once outside he got in his car and fumbled around in his pocket until he had found his keys. He started the car, put his foot on the brake, then put it in drive.

He shook his head from side to side trying to correct his blurry vision before he pulled away from the curb. Halfway up the block Bobby swerved from right to left. He straightened the car out and then guzzled down the rest of the liquid courage. Not giving a fuck, he tossed the empty bottle on the passenger side floorboard. When he reached the main street he didn't give a damn about traffic lights or stop signs. Intoxicated and determined to act a fool, he only stopped when he had reached his destination. Bobby sat two doors down from Rissa's aunt's house, watching it like he was expecting Mackey to walk out at any time, even though it was 3:21 a.m.

***

Dawn had just broken when Rissa began to stir. Her head was pounding, her mouth was dry, and she reeked of weed and alcohol. She rubbed her eyes with the tips of her fingers to clear the sleep out of them both. Her hair was a mess all over her head. She sat up on the edge of the sofa keeping her back to Bobby who was asleep behind her. She tried to remember what all happened the night before. Rissa knew one thing for sure: they all got shit-face wasted. Then she recalled telling Bobby everything about Mackey and her aunt. Her heart thumped in her chest hard. *Oh, my God, he's still here. Does he still want me? Does he think I'm ruined?* She panicked, never looking back at Bobby.

Suddenly Rissa realized the back of her blouse was sticky and moist. *Damn, I'm sweaty as fuck,* she thought as she reached her hand back to feel herself. When she drew her hand back in front of her all she saw was red. Rissa stared at the colored, sticky substance, puzzled. Turning slightly and looking behind her, she saw Bobby covered in the red as well. Suddenly it hit Rissa hard like a ton of bricks falling from the sky. There was blood on her back and blood all over him too.

Stunned, she fell to the floor and tried to call his name but the words were stuck in her throat. Rissa was having a panic attack. Her eyes were bucked wide open. She couldn't breathe. She looked like she was going to go straight into full cardiac arrest. *Is he dead? Is he shot? What in the entire hell happened to Bobby?* were her thoughts but her mouth couldn't formulate the words.

After a few tense minutes, she gathered herself. Now able to breathe she eased over to Bobby lying on the sofa. As Rissa got closer she could see he wasn't dead because his chest moved up and down. A sense of relief came over her. "Bobby," she yelled in his face as she shook him again and again until he responded.

"What? Huh? What's the matter? Why are you yelling in my face?" Bobby fired back with agitation growing in his tone.

"Boy, what's wrong with you? Is your ass hurt or what? What happened to you?" Rissa bombarded him with question after question, not waiting for an answer to the first one.

"Slow down, ma. What are you saying?" Bobby replied groggily, having no clue what she was talking about. Yawning, he sat up slowly as if he had gone ten rounds with Mike Tyson. He wiped his face with both his hands, trying to make sense of what was going on with Rissa and why was she so frantic.

"Look at your hands, Bobby." Rissa spoke in a whisper with a shocked facial expression.

Bobby looked at his hands and then his bloody clothing. "What the fuck?" he questioned himself out loud not knowing what to think or say. Then, suddenly, flashes of the night before came to him in bits and pieces like a bad movie with poor reception. *Oh, shit!* Then he remembered everything: where the blood came from and whose it was. "Damn, I fucked up, Rissa. I fucked all the way up. But I did it for you. I swear on everything I love, I did the bullshit for you," Bobby declared, still bewildered, holding his face downward.

"What do you mean you did it for me?" Rissa demanded to know what he was talking about while deep down inside she really was afraid to know the truth.

Bobby sat on the sofa with both of his hands on his head trying to remember everything that took place step by step. Once he put it all together he began to tell Rissa how he got the blood on himself and who the blood belonged to. "He needed to be dealt with. He can't keep walking God's green earth. If he'll do it to you he'll do it to somebody else. Ain't no telling how many others he done victimized throughout the years." Bobby tried justifying his actions.

Surprised and shocked, Rissa gasped for air with her mouth wide open. "No, you didn't, Bobby. Tell me you lying." Secretly Rissa was more than pleased to know Mackey got what he had coming. But she acted like she was upset. "You just hurt him real bad; that's why you got blood all on you, right?" Little by little she was trying to draw details out of Bobby.

"He might be just hurt. I really don't know; well, not for sure," Bobby stated, rubbing both hands over his face.

"Well, damn, tell me from the beginning. Start from when you got there." Rissa wanted to hear the story blow by blow.

"Okay, Rissa, I remember sitting in my car smoking a blunt; then it was like something came over me. I was so damned pissed off when you told me what you told me. I was just gonna go and bang on your aunt's front door and when he came to answer it I was gonna snatch his bitch ass out the door and beat his nasty ass. But the next thing I remember is being up in the house."

"Bobby, how did you get in?" Rissa confusedly asked.

"I think I went in through the bathroom window. Yeah, yeah, I did," Bobby stated, remembering much more clearly. "I crept to their bedroom, your aunt and Mackey ho ass, and I saw them both 'sleep."

Rissa swallowed the lump in her throat. "Oh, my God, Bobby, no, you didn't!"

Bobby started to regain all his memory of the fatal night before the more he exposed. "Yeah, girl, I remember noticing how huge his ass was compared to you. I thought of you not being able to fight him off and how you must have felt. A nigga got straight beyond irate. I was creeping around looking for something heavy to bust him upside his head with but I ain't see nothing. It was darker than a motherfucker in that son of a bitch. But anyway, I went in the kitchen and I think grabbed a butcher knife out the dish rack. Then I tiptoed back in the room and that shit was crazy as hell. Neither one of them woke up."

Rissa was almost speechless. She couldn't believe her ears. "Bobby, no, you didn't. Please tell me you lying to me."

"Nope. That shit was wild now I think about it. I stood over Mackey then I gripped the knife tight with both hands and held it up high over my head. I swear it was like my heart was beating so hard and loud in chest, I thought they heard it and was gonna wake up. I kept expecting your aunt to wake up and scream or some cornball horror movie shit like that."

Rissa was captivated by Bobby's step-by-step account of what happened. She stared at him not blinking an eye. In her mind she could see everything clearly just like she was in the bedroom with the knife in her own hand.

"Just before I plunged the knife down I thought should I put it in his chest or his neck. My mind was racing. I knew if I hit him in the chest he might eat it. You know he might take the blow and fight hard if I miss his heart. And in the middle of the night in the next man's crib, ain't nobody got time to be fucking tussling." Bobby's face was contorted as he talked, clenching his teeth together. "Rissa, I promise. Before I knew it, with everything I had in me I gave it to his chomo ass right in his throat. I got him good while he was lying on his back all open to the elements. Shiddd, I felt the knife hit a bone or something. I couldn't see all that good 'cause, like I said, it was dark in the room. But I know for sure for sure, he grabbed his throat and made gurgling sounds. At that point, I just kept stabbing him over and over again until I was tired. The blood on the blade was seriously flying back on me."

Rissa took her hand away from covering her dropped jaw. "Tell me this shit ain't real, Bobby. Tell me you just making this up to make me feel better."

"Naw, this shit was real as hell. Blood squirted out his neck. He was trying to get away from me; that's when she woke up and started screaming."

Rissa made a gasping sound out of surprise. She was wondering what her aunt was doing while Bobby butchered Mackey. Now she was about to find out. Bobby went on in detail. "Your aunt was yelling, 'Get out of my house,' 'Oh, my God,' and all that holier-than-thou shit. I told that bitch as I leaped across the bed on her, 'God can't save your ass 'cause it belongs to me.' She screamed my name out loud, Rissa. She knew who I was. By that time Mackey was done. He was hanging halfway off the bed, face down. So I grabbed your aunt by her hair when she tried to get away. We both ended up on the bedroom floor. I was all on top of her. Yeah, for real she fought me but I knew and she knew it was a done deal for her ass. I stabbed her I don't know how many times, but it was a lot. She kept screaming, 'Why, Lord? Why?' I said, 'Because you're a sorry, lowdown piece of shit harboring this fuckin' rapist.' I asked her how many people she let him rape, before I slit her throat to the bone. Then I just watched her bleed out."

Bobby turned to face Rissa and looked her in her eye letting her know how deep his devotion was to her. "Look, I did it for you. I'd do anything for you. I hope you know that."

Rissa was astounded. She didn't know what to say as she just stood there, blank-faced.

"Well, okay, Rissa, say something. I mean, what do I do now?"

Rissa finally snapped out of her trance and she knew she had to think fast. "Okay, first we gotta get you cleaned up." Rissa went and looked in the room where

Wanda and Chad slept. Seeing the pair were both still asleep she went back to the living room and got Bobby. Hand in hand they went into the bathroom.

"Okay, take off all your clothes; hurry up." She turned on the shower, making sure the water was on hot. It was the first time she had seen Bobby completely naked and she wasn't mad at him about it. He had a well-built, athletic body and his oversized dick was the icing on the cake. "Get in the shower and wash up good as you can. I mean, underneath your fingernails, behind your ears, and even in between your toes. The whole nine; scrub."

When Bobby stepped into the now steaming-hot shower, Rissa took everything except his shoes and put it into a trash bag. She then went into Wanda's brother's bedroom and rifled through his closet and grabbed whatever shirt and pants she thought would fit Bobby. She went back into the bathroom and set the jeans and T-shirt on the toilet top. "Okay, here's something for you to put on real quick," Rissa announced to Bobby, who was still in the shower.

Just then, she recalled she had blood on herself as well. Without hesitation she stripped her top and jeans off and got in the shower with Bobby. It was the first time Bobby had seen what was underneath Rissa's hoodie and pants as well. He tried to control his manhood as best he could. There was an awkward silence between to two as they bathed. Neither knew how to act or what to say or do.

Rissa was wondering if the entire scenario was real or if she was still asleep. Did Bobby really kill Mackey and her aunt like he said? Bobby's words repeatedly echoed in her mind. *"I did it for you, Rissa."* If this wasn't a dream, the young girl justified the unthinkable by telling herself the monsters who had pretended to love and care about her deserved to die, both of them. *I hope they suffered and felt every cut, slash, and stab! Fuck them!*

Then her mind went back to Bobby, who was standing directly in front of her naked and wet. *Damn, I wanna fuck him. But do I give the nigga some pussy now or what?* Rissa dropped the washrag and practically threw herself on Bobby, kissing him like she never did before. He returned the favor, gripping her well-shaped ass. "Okay, Bobby, I'm ready for you now."

As he spun her around, bending her over and smiling, he slid his dick inside of her still tight cat. Bobby had already killed for her and hadn't even gotten the pussy. Rissa could only imagine what he would be willing to do now.

When they finished banging for the first time, the two got dressed, Bobby in his borrowed clothes and Rissa in something she'd grabbed out of her garbage bag suitcase. After cleaning up the little blood that was still on the sofa, they stood back together seeing if it passed their eagle-eye inspection. "Okay now, Bobby. None of this ever happened except for that good dick you gave me in the shower. Do you understand?"

Bobby shook his head up and down in agreement with Rissa, wishing he could hit it once more.

CHAPTER FOUR

"So at approximately six forty-five this morning a call came in from a neighbor who said she believed someone had broken into the house next door to her because the bathroom window was wide open. She said she wasn't a hundred percent sure but she thinks blood is on the window frame." Homicide Detective Goodhouse gave his partner of eight years, Sims, the rundown of the initial 911 call. He had just arrived at the scene and needed to get caught up to speed.

"What do we got inside?" Sims motioned toward the house taped off in yellow.

"Two DOA victims. A man and a female. It's very gruesome. Maybe a crime of passion. From first investigation, looks like the perp came in through the window," Goodhouse speculated, showing Sims the point of entry. "Looks like the perp came in this way and left the same. Back and front doors are locked with deadbolts. They haven't appeared to be tampered with at all. Now come on inside and take a look at this." The detective, who'd been first on the scene, led as his longtime partner trailed.

"Holy shit," Sims remarked as he pulled a handkerchief out of his sport coat's inside pocket and covered his nose and mouth. There was an odor of death in the air mixed with the everyday filth of the hood dwelling. Other crime scene officers milled about. One was taking photos of Mackey and Rissa's aunt while another was dusting for fingerprints.

Goodhouse leaned down to get a closer look at the stab wounds when he recognized Mackey. "Who the fuck did you two piss off to fuck y'all over like this?"

Sims asked Goodhouse if he knew the victims. He lied, saying no, but in fact he did know the male. Then he went and inspected the female's body. He was in disbelief at how whoever had murdered her cut her throat down to the bone, almost severing her head. Goodhouse shook his head from side to side and rubbed his chin. *This is really messed up.* He started to ponder how he would break the news to his woman, and that all hell would pop off when she heard about Mackey.

A crime lab technician walked up to him, interrupting his thoughts. "We're ready to wrap this up here. The meat wagon's en route to pick them up and put 'em on ice. It looks to me like both vics sustained over a hundred stab wounds each. Maybe more, but there's so much blood at this point we can't really tell until the coroner cleans them up and performs an autopsy," the man nonchalantly explained, having grown used to gory scenes such as this.

"Okay, great. Wrap it up," Goodhouse agreed to the head crime scene technician. Being the thorough detective he was, he decided to backtrack over the crime scene once more, starting with the perp's entry. As he carefully canvassed the patch of overgrown yard under the window, the detective noticed a piece of plastic in the scrubs of grass. When he picked it up he realized it was a photo ID. While he was examining it, his partner came from behind.

"What do you got? You find something?" Sims wondered, hoping he'd discovered a clue to help solve the double homicide case.

"No, it's nothing. We all good here," Goodhouse claimed, slipping the ID into his sport coat pocket.

"Well, I got a phone number from the neighbor for the next of kin for the dead woman, a La Rissa Ford. The neighbor said the girl babysat for her sometimes and she lives with the aunt."

"Okay, Sims. I'll do the honor notifying her of her aunt's untimely demise while you get a line on the next of kin for the dead man," the dirty homicide detective told his sidekick as if he were giving him the easier task of the two. Sims tore Rissa's phone number out of his notepad and gave it to Goodhouse.

Later that day around five in the evening Rissa's cell phone rang. She looked at the incoming call on her screen. It was a number that she didn't know. Reluctantly, she answered it. "Hello."

"Yes, good evening. Is this La Rissa Ford?"

"Yes, this is she; and who are you?" she casually replied.

"Yes, my name is Detective Rob Goodhouse. I'm with the Detroit Police Department. It's very important I speak with you as soon as possible. Can you come down to DPD headquarters as soon as you can?" he spoke sternly, maintaining his tone.

Rissa's heart hammered in her chest. She knew the call was coming sooner or later. She had to get herself together. This was it. She cleared her throat and took a deep breath. "I'm sorry, Detective whoever you said you was, but what do you need to talk to me about, sir? I'm confused. And as a matter of fact, who gave you my number? Is this a damn joke or some shit?"

"Look, Miss Ford. I can assure you this is no joke. And as far as what I need to speak to you about, I'd rather explain it to you in person. And if you don't have transportation to get here I'll arrange for a car to pick you up. How does that sound?"

"Well, I can get down there by myself. I don't need no ride or nothing," Rissa rudely exclaimed. "But, once again, what is this about? Tell me something."

"Miss Ford, when you get here, just ask for Detective Goodhouse and someone will help you immediately," the homicide cop explained, not revealing any details including the fact that he was a homicide detective.

Rissa gave in, telling him she would be there shortly and she hung up the phone before the man could say anything else. She was a little uneasy from the phone call she knew would come. She got herself together then called Bobby and told him what was up. She was going to have Wanda drive her downtown to see what the detective had to say. Without question, Bobby was shaken, but Rissa reassured him everything would be okay. He had her back and she was definitely going to have his. What happened to Mackey and her aunt had to happen. Rissa just hoped that Bobby had left no indication of who he was.

Wanda watched Rissa's facial expression change from "Who is this calling me?" to "What do you need to talk to me for?" to "I don't know what's going on and I'll tell you later," after she talked to the detective and then Bobby. When she hung up the phone with Bobby, Wanda had a million and one questions for her best friend.

"Bitch, what the fuck is going on? What the hell the police want you to talk to you for? Ho, you got some warrants I don't know about?"

"Girl, I don't know what's going on," Rissa lied to Wanda, not knowing how she would deal with knowing Bobby butchered Mackey and her aunt. So of course she kept it from Wanda until she knew she could handle that type of information. Not everyone was built the same.

Wanda grabbed her car keys off the table and headed to the door. Rissa was on her heels. They jumped in Wanda's late-model Sunbird and were on their way. Ten minutes later they were in downtown Detroit pulling up at police headquarters. Rissa went to the front desk and asked the officer in uniform for Detective Goodhouse while Wanda fell slightly behind.

The uniformed officer asked Rissa her full name and she gave it to him freely. "Okay, so you're here to see Detective Goodhouse with homicide?"

Rissa and Wanda said, "Homicide?" out loud at the same time and looked at each other, wide-eyed. "Yeah, that's what he told me his name was, but he didn't say shit about no homicide. This dude got me all the way fucked up."

Wanda eased next to Rissa and whispered, "Bitch, who you killed?" while the officer made a phone call.

Rissa sucked her teeth at her friend even playing like that in front of the damn police. "Umm, let me think. Nobody, bitch."

Wanda laughed it off and gave her the side-eye as she walked to the chairs in the waiting area and sat down with her lips twisted up. She was still mean mugging Rissa as she stood at the officer's desk. When the cop hung up the phone and then told Rissa to have a seat, she came and sat next to Wanda.

Wanda was still on Rissa's head for information. "Okay, when they put you in that little-ass room don't say shit! Don't be like them dummies on *The First 48* and get to telling on yourself and confessing to shit. If it were me I'll make them do their job. I'm lawyering up soon as the first syllable of a question roll off his tongue. Yup, I'ma be like, 'Lawyer! Don't talk to me.' Sure would." Wanda rattled on talking and talking as if Rissa weren't under enough stress.

Rissa snapped her head back, twisting her neck. "Shut the fuck up, chatty patty, with your irritating ass. I can't even think straight with you all in my ear and shit. That's why I wanted your nosey ass to stay in the damn car."

Wanda was about to start up talking again when they both noticed a slim brown-skinned man with a tan sport coat, slacks, and tie approaching the officer sitting at the front desk. The cop behind the desk pointed in their direction. Then Detective Goodhouse walked briskly toward the now nervous pair. Before he got up to them he said with authority, "Yes, which one of you is La Rissa Ford?"

Rissa stood up and copped an attitude before he could say anything else. "Yeah, what's this about? You didn't say anything on the phone about no homicide."

"Well, young lady, I feel when there is a death in the family, loved ones should be notified in person."

Rissa already knew what time it was but she played her position, acting dumb. "Notify? Dead? What is you talking about, sir?" Rissa said, acting like she was in denial. "Who you talking about dead? I don't get it."

"Ma'am, I'm sorry to tell you your aunt Sara Ford was murdered sometime this morning along with her live-in boyfriend," Goodhouse said solemnly, having delivered this sort of news time and time again.

Rissa went in playing her part. She broke down crying, falling out on the floor. Wanda tried to pick her up and couldn't, finally ending up on the floor with her friend. People in the lobby passing by them were staring and whispering. One lady with a little boy remarked that their behavior make no sense at all acting a fool in public, that they were them millennium kids they'd been talking about on the news, with no home training. As she shook her head and ushered her little boy away quickly, a female officer saw the commotion and came over to the scene to help Goodhouse get the situation under control.

After Rissa was consoled she was escorted to an interview room in the back of the building, where the tragic news should have been delivered from jump. She was then grilled, and asked a thousand questions about her whereabouts at the time of the murders. Rissa cooperated, freely answering each one with either "I don't know," or "Sorry, I can't help you." The interview lasted almost two grueling hours.

"Okay, so can I go now? I've told y'all everything I think y'all want to know. I'm tired, my head hurting, and I'm hungry. I know my rights. If I'm not under arrest for something, y'all can't hold me," Rissa spat at the two detectives with an attitude. "I watch *Law & Order* and seen every episode of *The Wire*."

"Just give us a second; we'll be right back." Goodhouse and a rookie detective stepped out of the interview room, leaving Rissa to stew.

"This is some bullshit," Rissa hissed, huffing and puffing with her arms folded across her chest.

The two detectives stood in a cubicle watching Rissa on a video monitor. "What do you think?" the rookie asked Goodhouse for his opinion.

"Naw, she didn't do it. She doesn't fit the bill. No way there's' blood on her hands. Cut her loose and let her know we'll be in touch if we have any more questions."

When the rookie walked away to go cut Rissa loose, the dirty cop took the ID out of his pocket and looked at it carefully. He didn't tell him he had a good idea who had committed the murders. That information, along with who he knew would pay good money for having it, was his little secret. Goodhouse couldn't care less about clearing the bodies off the books.

***

Wanda sped her struggle buggy as fast as it would go up the 94 expressway. Rissa sat in the passenger seat bitching and moaning about how the police had treated her like a suspect instead of just informing her of her aunt's untimely departure from the living. Wanda couldn't be in the interview room so she had been waiting patiently in the lobby for the whole two hours so she could be the first to get the tea before Rissa told anyone else. "Okay, now, what did they say, girl? Do they think you killed them or something? Did they do you like they do dudes on television and try beating the truth out that ass?" she teased, trying to break the tension up.

Rissa forced a smile, coming to the realization her aunt was truly gone. "Man, they did that good cop bad cop act. They just wasting they time knowing damn well I ain't killed no two people. Police kept asking me the same fucking question over and over but in different ways trying to trip me up like I'm gonna change my story. They had me so mad I wanted to snatch out his hand the ink pen he was writing with and stab his ass in the neck. Real talk, doe, fuck my aunt and that scum bag nigga Mackey. They got just what God intended for them to have: a blade served cold." Rissa smirked with her eyes narrowed and anger dripping from her lip. "I hope both their rotten, stankin' souls go straight to hell with a pretty pink bow tied tight."

A chill crept up Wanda's back. She had never heard Rissa be so cold before in all the years they had been friends. "Bitch, you need a hug? That was your aunt, your family," she reminded Rissa. Wanda eased her car off the freeway and came to a stop at the red light. When it turned green she made a quick left. "Damn, sis, what the hell went on over there to make you so cold, Rissa? You going in extra hard on they deceased asses, like you don't even care."

Rissa fell silent for two blocks. When she finally spoke again, she had tears in her eyes, tears she never shed for her aunt let alone Mackey. "Okay, Wanda, I never got a chance to tell you why I really got the fuck away from that house. Mackey raped me more than once and my aunt chose to believe him over me. So that's why I'm glad they're both dead. Those tears weren't real tears of pain or hurt back at the police station; they was tears of joy they was gone off this earth!" Rissa knew in that instant, riding with Wanda in the car, she would be forever changed mentally the way she viewed the world and the people in it.

"Oh, my God, Rissa, you could have told me. I can only imagine how you feel going through that type of bullshit. Girl, I'm here for you," Wanda said sincerely. They got out of the car and gave one another a hug. Rissa had to call Bobby, so Wanda told her it was okay, and she went inside the house, giving her some much needed privacy.

Rissa pulled out her cell phone and went to the call log. Finding Bobby's number she pressed down on his name. The phone rang twice before he picked up.

"What up, doe?" Bobby said, greeting Rissa.

"Hey, I just came from DPD headquarters talking to a homicide detective, Good something the fuck or other. I can't remember the last name right. Anyway, he wanted to notify me of my aunt's and that piece of shit's deaths. The police brought your name up," Rissa announced to his dismay.

"What? Why? What did he say? Is they looking for me or what?" Bobby was rattled as he sat on the front porch of his mama's house, nervously smoking a blunt.

"Just keep calm, okay? I don't think they know you did it or they would have gone hard on me; but, it wasn't like that." Rissa tried to convince Bobby he was good and in the clear.

"Rissa, I'm tripping over here. I'm paranoid thinking the SWAT team gonna hit the block at any minute on my damn head." Bobby looked around and up and down the street, taking a strong pull on the weed, filling his lungs with high-grade THC. "I feel like everybody watching me and shit."

"Boy, lay off that weed. Stop bugging out. Remember, act normal. Do everything you used to doing; don't change nothing. Okay? They don't suspect you. If it comes down to it I'm your alibi. You were with me all night, simple as that. I'll stand up for you like you do and did for me, Bobby. I got you," Rissa vowed as she walked back and forth on the sidewalk in front of Wanda's house as she scanned the block feeling a little uneasy herself.

After talking to Rissa, Bobby loosened up and began to feel a little bit relaxed. He had smoked a whole blunt by the time they got off the phone. All he wanted to do now was lie back and munch on some junk food. And that's just what he did as if he hadn't committed a double homicide less than forty-eight hours ago.

CHAPTER FIVE

Two weeks had gone by since the investigation into the double homicide of Sara Ford and Mackey started. Detective Goodhouse, the lead on the case, was a veteran of the DPD and slated to retire in less than two years with full benefits and a pension. But for old Goodhouse that would not be enough to live off of. In his eyes it never was and never could be. For him, it was like for all the blood, sweat, and brain power he had put in all these years closing cases on some of Detroit's most abhorrent murders, he deserved much more and he was going to get his fair share of money out of the mud, so to speak, by hook or by crook.

Detective Goodhouse casually drove the speed limit on Jefferson Avenue when he reached Van Dyke. He made a left then drove through the run-down section of the hood that, it seemed, the City of Detroit had forgotten long ago. Then the detective made a quick right; then, suddenly, the scenery went from run-down and ghetto to upscale in a blink of an eye. *Yeah, I should be living like this.* He marveled at the well-kept lawns and mansion-like homes that were located inside the area of town known as Indian Village.

Finally at his destination, he pulled into a driveway with an eight-foot-tall wrought-iron gate surrounding the house. The home was historic in appearance as if time had stood still. A camera sat atop a portion of the brick pillar connected to the gate. Goodhouse looked up at it, showing his face; and, just like magic, the gate slowly opened.

When there was room enough for the detective's department-issued police car to pass through, he pressed the gas pedal gently and drove up the circular driveway to the front door and parked his car. *She better have my cash on deck or she ain't getting zilch. I'll pass this on to the next suit and tie who's thirsty for a case in homicide.*

When he got to the door he didn't have to knock. A middle-aged woman appeared, simply telling him, "Come right this way. The lady of the house has been waiting for you." Goodhouse had seen the woman many times but still couldn't get past the fact that she was creepy as fuck.

She showed him to the same office space she always did when he came to see none other than Detroit's most notorious madam, Valerie Whiteside. Goodhouse was told to make himself comfortable, also as he always was told each time. A good ten minutes passed like always then Madam Valerie appeared as if she were some superstar.

"Hello, Valerie," the detective greeted her, waiting for a response.

There was no return in pleasantries. She sat down behind her huge office desk and just looked at him with a blank face. "Look, I don't want to hear no small talk or anything else. Now who killed my damn brother Mackey?"

The detective exhaled hard, dreading this meeting. "Well, I've done my homework. He's a young nut, obviously, to commit a double murder on people sleeping in bed in the wee hours of the morning."

"Look, Goodhouse, stop fucking around with me and give me what you told me you had for me," Valerie shouted as she opened the top desk drawer. Reaching in, she took out a thick white envelope and tossed it to him. He caught it then opened the envelope, thumbing through the multiple twenty dollar bills.

"Okay, Valerie, how much is it?" the detective asked, not looking up at her and still focused on the currency.

"It's five thousand dollars. Now, run what I've got coming, Detective. Playtime's over," Valerie said harshly. She meant nothing but business.

Sliding his hand into his pocket, the detective pulled out what he found at the crime scene—Bobby's identification card—and looked at it one last time before handing it over.

"Are you sure you don't just want to let DPD catch up with the piece of shit and lock him up for good?" the detective questioned her. "I mean, I've seen Mackey's jacket. He wasn't no angel by far either." Goodhouse went on to name the crimes Mackey had done time for: sentenced four to ten years for first-degree criminal sexual conduct when he was younger than thirteen years old; sentenced five to fifteen years for armed robbery. Goodhouse was about to name another case he did time for when Madam Valerie snapped.

Standing up in a rage, she swiped everything off the desk to the floor. "I don't give a goddamn if he murdered Jesus Himself and took a shit on the cross he carried. He's still my fucking brother, you son of a bitch. I want his murderer dead, do you hear me? Do you want the job or not? It pays twenty-five thousand dollars. Half of it now, and the other half when he's zipped up in a body bag," Madam Valerie shouted in a murderous tone.

"I would, but it's not conducive to my pension plan. So I'm good and will pass," Goodhouse said, cowering in front of the madam.

"You're useless. Get the fuck out before I really lose my temper with your pussy ass," Valerie snarled, meaning every word she spat.

Throwing his hands up in defeat, he quickly backed out of her office, not wanting a problem. Keeping each step quiet, he ran to his vehicle. As soon as Detective Goodhouse slid in, he got tough again and sounded off to himself. "Fuck that cunt! I would put a case on her conniving ass if she didn't have dirt on half of the top city officials."

His hands were tied because she had his number as well. Goodhouse thought back to how he became Madam Valerie's flunky in the first place. Drunk at a hole in the wall one night, he struck gold with a young woman and got off into some young pussy. Taking her to a short-stay she'd already rented, shorty was all about business from the first step through the door. She hit her knees, sucked him off 'til he quivered, and then fucked him 'til he busted back-to-back nuts.

Goodhouse's dick got hard at the thought of ol' girl, though it shouldn't have. Her suburban sex game was the reason he and his wife of ten years divorced. After fucking li'l ma that night, Goodhouse didn't go home to his wife. And, making matters worse, he found out the whole thing was a setup from the jump.

Shortly after the incident, a package with no return address arrived to him with pictures inside of it of him fucking the underage girl. He damn near pissed his pants. Having sex with a minor carried a heavy sentence and bad reputation that Goodhouse didn't want to carry or own up to. Wrapped around the pictures was a note instructing him of when and where to meet the sender. Madam Valerie told him face to face that she'd expose his dirty secret if he refused to play by her rules.

Pounding his fist on the side of his head, disgusted and pissed, he headed toward the DPD headquarters trying to get a game face on. Madam Valerie had just pulled Detective Goodhouse's ho card. She was straight. She had what she needed in her hand: the address of the man who had murdered her brother.

Staring at Bobby's picture on the ID, she made a vow to herself and him to deal with the killer swiftly. Opening the top desk drawer, she removed a cell phone. Wanting to avoid ever getting caught up, she only used it when she needed to have some dirt done. And today was a good day to have some dirt done. Dialing the digits from memory, she hit call and tapped Bobby's ID on the desk, waiting for the person's voice she so desperately wanted to hear.

Hearing a few knocks on the door, Valerie looked up with agitation in her eyes at Kimmy barging into the room without being welcomed or okayed. As she kneeled down to pick up the small stack of papers and the few other things that were scattered on the floor from Valerie's earlier tantrum, Valerie snapped on Kimmy as well.

"Leave all of that and go. I don't care to be bothered at the moment so come back later. Please," Valerie ordered Kimmy, uncaring of how her attitude had come across.

"Yes, Madam, I'm sorry. Can I get anything for you?" Kimmy apologized and questioned sincerely.

"No, Kimmy. I'm fine. Now, please go," Madam said, looking away with watery eyes.

Only coming into the room in the first place because she'd heard Madam and the detective having a disagreement, Kimmy had wanted to be nosey. She hadn't been able to make out the argument word for word, but she knew something was going on that was serious. However, seeing that Valerie was highly agitated and emotional, Kimmy didn't want to push the limit. Leaving the room without another word, she closed the door behind herself, then made sure the coast was clear for her to glue her ear up to the door.

Kimmy was Valerie's number one girl. Not only did she bring in major money, but Kimmy was down for setting up dudes whenever asked to, no questions asked.

The two of them met when Kimmy was seventeen and out turning tricks on the dangerous strip of Woodward Avenue. Madam Valerie showed Kimmy a safer way to get money, and put her up for sale to a better clientele. That was years ago. Kimmy was twenty-five now.

Kimmy had the looks and the body thirsty men paid top dollar to get a taste of. She was just the type Madam Valerie sponsored: the perfect prototype of a bad bitch willing to get down and dirty. She had grown fond of Kimmy because she could deal with any type of client, in any arena. Whether it was an athlete, a Wall Street worker, or a big business mogul, just to name a few, Kimmy could work their dick and the money from their wallets with ease. Madam Valerie had schooled all of her girls to be pros, but Kimmy had surpassed all of her expectations.

What the madam didn't know, however, was that she had trained Kimmy all too well. When the moneymaker with no morals wasn't busting it wide open for whatever bidder she was called to trick for, Kimmy kept her lips sealed and paid close attention to everything about the business that went on around her. While Madam Valerie thought she was manipulating Kimmy and getting rich off of her, Kimmy had figured out how to become more powerful than her teacher.

Rolling Earl was laid back in his pickup truck at Lakewood Park getting his dick voraciously sucked when his phone began to ring. The no-gag-reflex head he was getting from Lady Lips was so good that he chose to ignore the sound of his ringing phone. All he could focus on was Ms. LL's lips sliding up and down his shaft.

Calling back to back, the more Rolling Earl's phone continued to ring without an answer, the more infuriated

Madame Valerie got. She hated not getting instant reactions from people. Tapping Bobby's identification card harder and faster on her desktop, she mumbled obscene words underneath her breath, reaching a point of infuriation.

Praising and degrading LL at the same time, Rolling Earl gripped the top of her head to the point of his fingertips hurting. "Bless this slab of meat like it's ordained by Jesus Himself. Only blessings can come to you from all walks of life with head this fucking good. You hear me, bitch?"

Rolling Earl was on the brink of one hell of a nut when his phone started sounding off again. Holding LL's head still with one hand, he swooped his phone up and answered it, yelling at the caller not knowing who it was. His mind was too wrapped up in his dick sliding down shorty's throat. "Whoever this is, don't call my phone back for at least ten mo' minutes. I'm trying to get this nut off." He hung up and tossed the phone onto the dashboard.

Hearing Rolling Earl hang up on her, Madam Valerie held the phone in her hand in pure disbelief. Almost surprised, she had to remind herself of what type of thug she was dealing with, who was a lowlife who was out for himself with no home training, and disrespectful. He was a backstabbing snake who would dead his own mother for the right price. Yet and still, knowing where the bodies he'd killed were buried around Detroit, Madam Valerie had him under her thumb and she knew it.

Rolling Earl's cell phone started dancing across the dashboard. Instead of LL being distracted, she started sucking to the tune, putting on a super head show. Rolling Earl was mesmerized. With his eyes rolling to the back of his head and his body shaking, LL hummed on his hardness and made him lose his cool. Her skills

were so off the chart that Rolling Earl couldn't hold
back a second longer, and he finally busted the nut he so
desperately needed and wanted. It wasn't until LL licked
and swallowed every drop of his thick white cream did he
put his dick back in his drawers, pull up his pants, and
tend to his hotbox phone.

"Yeah, damn. Obviously you've got a problem with following fuckin' directions, but fuck it. How can I fucking
help you?" He spoke recklessly into the phone, again not
caring who was on the receiving end.

"That's why you stay broke. You can't keep yo' dick
in your fucking pants, you two-bit, wannabe-ass pimp."
She laughed sarcastically. "Money calling you, but you'd
rather get a blow job by a ho who couldn't pay your cell
phone bill if she strolled the strip day and night. I guess
you don't need this work," Madam Valerie fussed and
grunted.

Rolling Earl recognized Valerie's voice as soon as the
first syllable escaped her mouth. He knew how she got
down and he knew a big payday was in his reach if she
was calling on him to put in work. He got right to the
point. "How much does it pay?"

"Twenty-five grand. Half now, and the other half
when the job is done. How do you want your money? In
small bills or all hundreds?" She spoke with confidence,
knowing he wouldn't turn the offer down.

"You already know how I like mines. In small bills and
in a brown paper bag." He agreed to the deal, already
making plans for the cash. Rolling Earl had it bad for
clothes, hoes, and powder cocaine for his nose.

Covering the mouthpiece of the phone, he dismissed
LL from his car, whispering he'd hit her up later. Rolling
Earl might have been reckless, but he wasn't about to talk
money in front of a trick. As soon as she was out of his
ride, he tuned back into the conversation with Madam
Valerie.

"Tomorrow, be at my house at noon," she told Rolling Earl with ice in her voice.

"I'll be there. Be sure to have my money on deck," Rolling Earl snapped into the phone.

Madam Valerie hung up the phone disrespectfully before he could get another word in.

Rolling Earl laughed when he heard the phone line go dead, knowing he'd hit a nerve when he demanded that she have his money ready. Valerie wasn't the type of woman who liked to be nor took kindly to being bossed around.

Noon the next day, he sat across from Valerie in her home office, listening to her run down the job she needed him to carry out. On the other side of her home office door was Kimmy, ear hustling once again.

"Who's the mark?" Rolling Earl asked, ready to make the luck of whoever it was go bad real fast.

Handing him an envelope containing half of $25,000, she then stared hard into his eyes without blinking and responded, "I'll tell you like I always do. Don't fuck me over. Don't play with my money, Earl."

Rolling Earl stared right back into her eyes, not feeling the least bit intimidated. In fact, he felt the urge to pull his trusty 9 mm out of his waistband and plaster her brains all over the wall. The idea lingered on his mind for a few seconds when he thought about how much money he'd probably find stashed. No high-class ho of his knowledge regularly made bank deposits. "Save all that tough-titty bullshit for the next nigga, lady. You're paying me for a job to be done. The job gon' be done," he said, looking at Bobby's ID card. Without another word, he abruptly ended the meeting and went to exit the room.

Madam Valerie burned a hole in the back of his head as he walked away toward the door. As soon as he hit the door and turned right, he ran right into Kimmy, almost knocking her down to the floor. She'd been slipping on her pimping and moving too slow.

"Watch where the fuck you're going," Rolling Earl barked, glaring down at the five foot tall and visibly shaken Kimmy. As he kept walking, he looked back at her with disdain.

Kimmy apologized repeatedly as her heart raced uncontrollably. She knew he wasn't up for no games. It wasn't the first time she'd seen him at the house. Whenever he came up, whoever Madam Valerie had problems with came up dead or missing. So she didn't want no part of Rolling Earl.

CHAPTER SIX

Three weeks had passed and Rolling Earl had finally caught up with Bobby in the wrong place at the right time. Bobby had been going about his life like he was a normal young nigga about to go off to Job Corps. He and Rissa had become inseparable. She had even moved in with him and his mother. It was agreed that she would help Bobby's mom out with bills and the house until he was done learning a trade in welding at Job Corps. They were beyond happy and vowed to get married as soon as they could. But today, their whole lives changed unexpectedly.

After watching Bobby for weeks off and on, Rolling Earl was finally confident enough to make his move. And, besides all that, it was time for him to kill and collect his cash. Having already spent a few thousand of the initial half, he was itching to dead Bobby to collect the rest of his payout. Once, he had followed Bobby from a pickup basketball game at the YMCA to the gas station. He was even brazen enough to ask Bobby for a light for his blunt. At one point, Rolling Earl was seconds from taking him out of the game, but a carful of Bobby's boys pulled up on him with that young nigga rah-rah shit, drawing attention. The assassin was forced to pull back that day; but the perfect time had finally presented itself.

Today, Bobby was going off to Job Corps. He and Rissa were ecstatic for the change and the opportunity. Even Bobby's mother was overjoyed. Cooking him a feast featuring all of his favorite dishes, Bobby was able to invite all of his friends and family over for one big shindig. Everyone showed up and out, including Wanda and Chad. They ate like kings, celebrated Bobby's new journey, and wished him well every second until they all parted ways.

Though the night seemed to be a perfect start to the new life Bobby planned on making for himself with the help of the Job Corps program, Rissa couldn't ignore or find a reason for the gut-wrenching feeling she couldn't shake. She kept the unjustifiable feeling to herself, however, not wanting to ruin Bobby's sendoff night.

The very minute after the party was over, Rissa helped Bobby carry his luggage to his trunk. As they headed to the car, laughing about the night they'd just had, a car swerved up on the two of them out of nowhere. Rissa couldn't blink and Bobby couldn't suck in another breath of Detroit's polluted air before seeing a hollow barrel staring at them. As soon as Bobby lifted one of the bags into the air in an effort to block the attack, it was riddled with bullets. The shooter was sending a fireworks display of bullets into him without an ounce of remorse. Bobby was hit multiple times in the face, head, and chest; while Rissa only took one bullet to the shoulder and one to the leg. The two were left bleeding on the pavement in a cloud of engine smoke. But only one person rose after the shooter fled from the scene of the crime. Bobby died damn near instantly.

Bobby's mother was about to take a cosmetics bag out to him that he'd forgotten when she heard the barrage of gunfire sounding off. Falling to the floor, she covered her head until the shooting stopped, then rose and ran as fast as she could out the door and off the porch. Though she was hoping the gunshots came from a block over, perhaps, which was normal to hear around the clock in the hood, it was her worst fear that something tragic had occurred to either Bobby or Rissa. Each step she took toward the car, the louder her prayers to God got. All she wanted was for her son to be okay.

"No, God. No," she screamed in a panic, running full speed to the car where Bobby and Rissa lay in the street behind. Her heart fell from out her chest, her lungs collapsed, and her mind went blank for almost five seconds straight. She was in a shock of utter disbelief. Sliding like a pro baseball player in a World Series championship game, she slipped through the growing pool of blood that was spewing from her son's body, and she grabbed his dead corpse. It was still warm. Burying her head into Bobby's chest, she cried out in agonizing pain, the type of indescribable pain only a mother who buried a child could relate to.

Picking Bobby's body up off the pavement, she cradled his lifeless body and begged for what she knew really wasn't believable. She didn't even recognize her son. "Come on, baby, breath for Mama." Her voice was soft and soothing, as it was to him when he was a newborn baby fresh from her womb. Rocking Bobby's limp body back and forth like her movement would stimulate his heart to beat again, Bobby's mother was in shock. She refused to let him go.

Rissa lay right beside them with her head propped up on the curb. Though she was going in and out of consciousness, she still heard Bobby's mother pleading desperately to God not to take her son, and for someone to call 911 for help. And though she wished upon a star her friend could rise, she knew that would never be the case.

Moaning from the excruciating pain she was feeling from the gunshot wounds, tears streamed down her cheeks. Life for her kept going from bad to worse. She thought the open, gaping wounds were on fire and that she was being burned alive. She tried to scream out loud, but it wouldn't come out. She tried to move, but she couldn't. Rissa felt paralyzed. She even tried to pray that the sirens she heard getting louder and louder were coming her way; but she wasn't strong enough to look up. Rissa felt completely out of fight. Her eyes started drooping and she got weaker and weaker each second that passed by; and then she finally blacked out.

CHAPTER SEVEN

Slowly but steadily, Rissa was regaining consciousness. She fought to open her eyes when she heard voices and felt the presence of people around her. Finally opening one eye at a time, she saw blurry figures of people she assumed were doctors because of the white coats they wore and the clipboards they were writing on. Once they realized Rissa was stirring, one quickly moved to check her vitals while the other asked her questions she struggled to answer.

Hooked up to several different machines, the constant beeping of the heart monitor was driving Rissa crazy. "Please stop that damn thing from fucking beeping. It's too much," she complained with a raspy voice, shaking her head slowly from side to side as if she were being tormented. Rissa's mouth was dry and her throat hurt like hell. She wished for a nice cold glass of cherry Kool-Aid and a fat blunt to go with it, but she knew those hopes were temporarily out of her reach.

"Young lady, you are lucky to be alive. You lost a lot of blood and you have been in and out of consciousness for the last three days. In order to save you, we gave you four blood transfusions. And in order to keep you alive, that heart monitor has been working overtime. If the EMs hadn't gotten you here when they did, we wouldn't be looking at one another right now. You are in good care here at Henry Ford Hospital. We have the best doctors in the city and you'll be out of here in no time," the Chinese doctor spoke arrogantly.

Rissa heard him but was preoccupied with thoughts of Bobby shortly after the doctors cleared out of her hospital room.

Wanda and Chad made their way in to visit with her. Rissa was her day one and she broke down crying. Wanda had come to the hospital every day to be by her girl's side. When Rissa saw Chad, she cried even harder knowing she would never be able to be with Bobby again. Having a flashback to the first time all four of them met, she wished she could go back to the good ol' days when all they did was hang tough and blow weed. Rissa wished they could enjoy life again but, sadly, she knew life for at least her would never be the same.

Wanda hurried over to her bedside and leaned down, giving her girl a comforting hug; then she stood back up melting down all over again. She couldn't help it. Wanda felt bad for her girl. Not only for what she'd been through, but for the death of Bobby, too. Chad came up behind Wanda and put his arm around her. He was trying his best to soothe her. Rissa had an IV in both her arms and tubes were inserted in both her gunshot wounds to keep the fluid from building up in her body. Only when she'd come out of the coma did they remove the feeding tube. Two bullets were surgically removed, but Rissa would recover. For that, Wanda thanked God.

"Yo, sis, who did y'all like this? My dog is dead and you got shot and damn near died. Do you know the dude? Ray who lives up the block said he saw the whole clip pop off like a movie. He said there was only one cat in the car. I ain't no killa, but tell me you know who did my mans dirty, and I'll go see dude right fucking now. That's my word, sis." Chad wanted to get revenge on whoever was responsible for his friend's death.

Squeezing her eyes shut, Rissa shook her head back and forth. "I saw the guy. Ray was right; there was only one nigga. I looked him dead in his face a split second before he started letting off. Chad, I never saw the guy before; but if I ever see him again, I'll know it's him." Rissa started crying.

Unbeknownst to all three of them, Detective Goodhouse was standing right outside the doorway hanging on to every word they spoke about a murder he'd put into motion. In a few seconds, he was about to reveal himself as the detective assigned to working Bobby's homicide. He was the worst type of weapon: a double-edged sword.

After listening for a few seconds longer, he walked into the hospital room and was greeted with nothing but attitude. Twice looking over her shoulder, Wanda spun all the way around and mean mugged the detective with suspicion in her eyes. Looking him up and down, she wanted to know why he was there. Surprise was an understatement for how she felt. Reading Wanda's body language, Chad stood up on the defensive. Folding his arms across his chest and mean mugging the newcomer to the room, he knew something was on the floor but didn't know what.

Rissa looked past her homegirl and rolled her already dry eyes. "What are you doing here? I hope to tell me you caught the people who killed my family," she said, voice weak and strained. She might've been in a foggy state of mind from all the strong pain medication, but she wasn't so far gone not to know how to play her role.

"We meet again, Ms. Ford, much to my regret that it's under unfortunate circumstances," Goodhouse responded with a smug grin on his face. "I'm the lead investigator on the homicide of Bobby Martin. It's my understanding that you were his girlfriend." Careful with his choice of words, he'd chosen the word "were" to make a play on the past tense of their relationship. When he saw the weakness in Rissa's eyes build up even more, he moved to get her alone. "Can I have a moment alone with Ms. Ford? This will only take a minute," he demanded more than asked of Wanda and Chad.

"We ain't ate all day so we'll go to the hospital cafeteria and grab something to eat. By the time we get back, he should done and gone," Wanda responded with attitude, directing her statement toward the detective while talking to Chad. "Girl, we'll be back in a little while. I'll ask the nurses if you can have real food. If they say you can, I'll bring you something with a li'l flavor to try eating."

Rissa nodded up and down in agreement with her bestie. No sooner than Wanda and Chad left the room, Goodhouse flipped the script. The professional cop disappeared and the crooked snake with a badge showed his true colors.

He and Rissa were all alone. Pushing the room door closed, along with the blinds, he wanted the two of them to have absolute privacy. Then he walked back over to her bedside. "Let's cut to the chase. I found Bobby's ID outside of the window he climbed through. He either dropped it on the way in or on the way out. Either way, those are his bodies and his murder rap. I just put the warrant out for his arrest before I got called to roll out on his murder," Goodhouse lied, trying to manipulate Rissa. "I also think you helped kill them."

Rissa's heart monitor beeped loud and fast. She was scared as hell and mad at the same time. She couldn't believe the detective was coming for her. Rissa mustered up enough courage and strength to give Goodhouse a piece of her mind. "Look, mister, Bobby or me ain't have shit to do with my aunt's and her husband's murders. Do I look like I go around killing people? Let alone my own family? Get the fuck out of here with your Cracker Jack–ass detective bullshit and go find who really killed my family and my dude."

Rissa had had enough of the police for one day. She slowly reached for the nurse call button with her good arm. No longer did she feel safe alone with the detective. Goodhouse saw the call button in Rissa's hand, then grabbed her wrist and squeezed it hard so she wouldn't press the button. "You little bitch, watch your mouth. Maybe I already know who killed yo' li'l boyfriend and maybe I don't give a damn. Maybe I'll let him get away with murder. How about you come up dead and I'll be heading the investigation and know your killer personally but just don't give a fuck too?"

First looking into his eyes trying to read them, Rissa then tried pulling her wrist from his grip but he was too strong. Her heart pounded and sweat formed on her brows. She thought, *is this muthafucka for real? Is he that fucking crazy? Is he bluffing and just trying to scare me into giving Bobby up so he can close his case or what?*

Standing her ground, Rissa demanded that he let her go or she would scream. Goodhouse, though, only had the idea of being more aggressive. Suddenly, the room door opened and in walked one of her several nurses assigned to her critical case. First consumed with the information on the computer monitor, she asked to verify Rissa's name and date of birth so she could administer meds, but then she looked up to Rissa snatching her arm away from the cop to the point of her body jerking. Without a doubt or question, she knew something wasn't right. "What's going on in here?" Her voice was loaded with disapproval of what she'd witnessed.

Goodhouse was caught off guard. With his narrowed eyes locked in on Rissa, he backed away from her bedside. "Nothing; just helping my niece out is all. She was just about to call for a nurse because she's in a lot of pain. You must've sensed it," he spoke slyly, wearing an under-handed, sly smile.

The nurse side-eyed Goodhouse as she walked past him toward Rissa lying in bed. Goodhouse stepped out of her way and gave her a plastic look as if she were nobody. When she began taking Rissa's vital signs, she noticed the anxiety and look of concern on the young woman's face, and she began worrying herself.

"Get him out of here, please." Rissa moved her lips, mouthing the words.

The nurse wrinkled her face up and slightly nodded; then she frowned her face up into an "I ain't here for the bullshit" expression and cut into the detective. "Look, I don't know what's going on here, but I'm not buying she's your niece. If you don't leave now, I'm calling hospital security." She thought her threat would carry weight.

"Lady, I am security." Goodhouse pulled his credentials out and stuck them in her face.

She slapped the badge out of his hand and it hit the wall then fell to the floor. "That shit don't hold no weight with me."

Goodhouse was shocked. He picked his shield up off the floor and put it away back in his blazer pocket. "I should arrest your shit-wiping ass for interfering with an ongoing investigation," he said, trying to save face.

"Go on, do it. Your ass will be answering why I walked in on you sexually assaulting a heavily sedated unconscious woman." She refused to back down, concocting a wild story Goodhouse couldn't dare take lightly.

"That's a lie," Goodhouse barked.

"What you think? I don't know it? I'm the one who's gon' tell it. And, by then, it's gonna be even more believable. So how do you want to do this, pig?"

"You ain't shit but a crazy little bitch!" Goodhouse couldn't believe she had the audacity to threaten him.

"I've been called worse by better people. Anything else you'd like to call me other than a child of God? Go ahead.

I'm free and listening. I'll just add it to all the other statements I'm prepared to write on your crooked ass," the sassy nurse sassed, unbothered.

The cop's pride was bruised and he was hotter than Iraq. He couldn't do shit with the nurse. He knew it was in his best interest to get the fuck out of the room before the situation got any further out of hand.

Before the ol' dog tucked his tail and ran, though, he had a few parting words for Rissa. "I'll see you on the flipside. And, when I do, I'll have some shiny bracelets that'll look good on you." Mocking Rissa even more, he patted his police-issued handcuffs and stared at her with his cold and emotionless eyes before leaving the room. All Rissa and the nurse heard was his devilish laugh echoing from out in the hallway.

"What was that all about, Rissa? That is how you pronounce your name, right?" the nurse asked, reading through Rissa's medical chart.

"Yeah, that's how it's said. So what's your deal? Why you go so hard for me? I just asked you to get him out of here. You ain't have to go in like that for me."

"Girl, please. I didn't. I've been on my feet for eight hours with four more to go. These fucking patients and coworkers done worked my last damn nerve. He just happened to be in the right place at the wrong time. Plus, I just was playing NWA's song 'Fuck the Police' on my iPod." She smiled, pulling the small earphone out of her ear.

"Thanks anyway. He's an asshole as you can tell." Rissa told her something she already knew while returning the smile.

She revealed the real reason she spoke up. "Seriously, I have a daughter close to your age who you reminded me of at first glance."

Injecting some morphine into Rissa's IV, the potent medication took effect on her immediately. Eventually, Rissa drifted off into a euphoric bliss. The sleep and relief was much needed. The good nurse pulled the covers over Rissa properly, then cleaned up behind herself before leaving the room to finish her shift.

Shortly after, Wanda and Chad returned from getting food and found Rissa fast asleep. After placing her friend's food from the cafeteria on the nightstand beside her bed, Wanda ran her fingers through Rissa's long, black silky hair. "Get some rest, friend. I'll be here to see you early tomorrow, okay?" Then Wanda and Chad left the hospital for Rissa to rest and heal.

CHAPTER EIGHT

It was seven forty-five that evening when Rissa came out of a deep drug-induced sleep. When she finally got enough strength to open her eyes all the way, she saw Bobby's mother sitting in a chair close to her hospital bed. Nessa was dabbing a Kleenex at her crying eyes. Expectedly, she was taking the loss of her Bobby bad. Her heart was broken. He was her only child and the only one she could count on through the good and bad times. In her mind, there would never ever be good times again in her lifetime. With the police unable to tell her who killed her only son, she turned hurt into anger, and no one was exempt from feeling her wrath.

"Hello, Rissa," Nessa spoke all dry, glaring at Rissa intensely. That fatal day played again and again in her head as she looked at Rissa lying in the bed with tubes coming out of her hooked up to monitors. She wished Rissa was on that cold metal slab in the morgue instead of her baby boy. She loathed the day that Bobby brought her into her home. Rissa had no idea Nessa felt the way she did. But she was about to find out.

"Hello, Nessa," Rissa managed to say, rubbing her eyes with the one good hand she could move freely. She was about to ask Nessa how she was holding up when she was abruptly cut off in mid-thought.

Nessa broke down crying and yelling at her that she was the reason Bobby was dead, and that after she left the hospital today she never wanted to see Rissa again.

His mama caused so much drama that she had to be escorted out of the room and shown the hospital exit.

Rissa was blindsided. Never not once did she expect Nessa to react or snap on her like she had. Nessa had reached a level Rissa wasn't familiar with.

Rissa's mind was all over the map. She wondered where she could go when she got discharged, how she'd eat, how she'd get money for clothes, and, most trivial, how she'd get her hair done. Feeling overwhelmed by the continued and constant drama, Rissa cried uncontrollably. She was drained, starting to drown in self-pity.

Reaching for and pushing the call button for the nurse, she begged for more pain medication for her wounds when the dosage was really to help her drift away. She figured if she was asleep she wouldn't have to cope. Once the male nurse administered her a Valium, she swallowed it then rested her head back comfortably on the pillow. Rissa knew she was about to return to la-la land, where life didn't matter, in a few short minutes.

Dressed and waiting in the hallway for an attendant to wheel her downstairs to the waiting room of the hospital, six long days passed and the time had finally come for Rissa to be discharged. When she first woke up in the hospital after the incident, she'd wanted nothing more to go home. But after getting the visit from Nessa, she dreaded leaving the around-the-clock care facility. Rissa was homeless. She racked her brain, went through several panic attacks, but still didn't come up with an address she could go to and call home. She wished more than ever that Bobby was alive.

"Are you ready, ma'am?" the attendant questioned, ready to wheel her from where she wished she could crash for at least a few more nights.

"I guess so," Rissa muttered, hanging her head low. Regardless of what was ahead of her, she had to face it. Rissa was tired of that being the story of her life.

The two of them rode the elevator down together in complete silence, but the family on the elevator with them chattered about how happy they were for their loved one to be coming home. Rissa couldn't catch a break. Their happiness made her sadder. Sniffing a few times, even wiping the one tear that broke free from her eye, Rissa held it together but asked the attendant to push her faster and by the window in a corner so she could get away. She wanted to be by herself but she didn't. She wanted Bobby. She wanted her friends. For a moment, the young girl contemplated falling out and causing a scene so maybe, just maybe, they'd readmit her. Rissa was grasping at straws when, finally, a little luck came her way.

Wanda was waiting for her at the hospital exit. "Rissa, hey, guess who convinced their mother to let you stay with them until you're strong enough to take care of yourself? Yup, me. That's who," Wanda bragged, making Rissa's whole day.

Rissa was more than grateful. Had she been strong enough, she would've leaped from the wheelchair and tightly hugged her road dog for life. Wanda had just saved her life.

The road to recovery for Rissa was long and hard. She was forced to learn and accept a lot about herself. In addition to Rissa nursing her wounds, she had to recover from a bruised ego and a broken heart at the hands of Bobby's mother as well. Rissa wasn't permitted to attend Bobby's homegoing all because of her. It hurt her beyond belief she wasn't able to say good-bye. It confused as well as tore her up that Nessa could act out so viciously.

Wanda and Chad were able to attend, sent with a few words from Rissa to whisper into his ear, only to find out their friend had been cremated. The last visual those in attendance had of Bobby was a blown-up picture that was front and center in the room.

With the only person in the world who cared about her dead and gone, Rissa felt alone. She didn't have a choice but to grow up and accept her fate for what it was. She wasn't a girl any longer. For the way she was about to be out for herself and acting out in her world, only God would understand.

CHAPTER NINE

Almost a year had passed since all the tragedy had taken place to and around Rissa. Not only had she gone through hell recovering, but she also had tried working a few jobs to make a few dollars to survive. But, unfortunately, none of the jobs worked out for longer than a month or so at a time, if that. Developing an "I don't give a fuck" attitude, Rissa didn't care about holding them down or being responsible.

Rissa was at her second job waiting tables at Bucharest Grill when she met a beautiful young woman named Kimmy. Kimmy was with a well-groomed businessman suited up in a tailored suit with expensive-looking shoes. Rissa thought he was attractive and, of course, made of money, but she tried keeping her eyes in her head. It was hard, though. The mystery man was fawning all over her. Though he was there with Kimmy, seeming to be on a date, he couldn't stop watching Rissa. Seeing everything unfolding before her, Kimmy couldn't care less. Her only concern was money.

Rissa stood inside the kitchen door in a daze, looking out into the dining room at the beautiful young Kimmy entertaining the older man. She wore a nice white blouse, blue jeans, and red bottom high heels. As her coworkers buzzed around the kitchen, in and out of the door, Rissa stood gazing into space with a million thoughts on her mind. *He got to be paying her. She's too fine for him not to be. He doesn't look like any nigga she would fuck with on the daily if he weren't cashing her out. I'll bet a bitch's last dollar on that.* Curiosity had consumed Rissa with trying to figure out why a pretty girl like Kimmy was with the dude.

So caught up in her thoughts, Rissa hadn't realized Kimmy had risen from the table and was headed toward the bathroom. A little voice in Rissa's head told her to follow Kimmy. Pushing the kitchen door open with no regard, it swung into another coworker. "My bad," she said, keeping it moving nonetheless.

"Whatever, newbie. You almost knocked my whole tray of food over. I suggest you watch where you're going," the coworker shouted to Rissa's back.

Too focused on getting a private second with Kimmy, Rissa didn't respond or even acknowledge her coworker's advice.

"What am I thinking?" she muttered to herself, pushing the bathroom door open and entering.

Kimmy was in a stall on the phone with someone, talking about the date she was on. Rissa stood at the sink with her head cocked toward the conversation but pretending to wash her hands.

"Yeah, I got the money up front like always. He can't keep his hands to himself. Yeah, I know it's part of the service. He even offered to give me an extra thousand if I go back to his suite with him. I told him I'd have to clear it with you. I'm good with it if you are. That's settled then. When I get to his room, I'll call and give you the room number just in case something goes wrong." Kimmy ended the call from rambling, wiped herself, then flushed the toilet and came out of the stall. It's when she was in the mirror fixing her makeup that she noticed Rissa standing there and how pretty she was.

Looking Rissa over, she thought about how much of a finder's fee she would get for introducing her to Madam Valerie.

Standing beside Kimmy, not knowing how to spark up the conversation without seeming like a pussy eater, she blurted out the first thing she thought of. "Hey, girl. I like your shoes," she said coyly with a smile.

"Thank you. They might look good on a bitch foot, but my toes are damn near numb." Kimmy returned the smile with a laugh.

Feeling a good vibe between them, Rissa couldn't help herself from pushing forward with her real intentions. "Hey, can I ask you a question?" Hoping she wouldn't be left hanging by the beautiful girl, she was relieved when Kimmy stopped and turned around to face her.

"Sure you can, sweetheart," she answered, thinking she would be getting some extra cash to blow if Rissa asked for a taste of the good life. Being that Kimmy had been in the trickin' business for a while, she could spot thirst more than a mile away. Not to jump the gun, Kimmy waited to hear the question.

Rissa, not being the shy type, got to the point without coming across as disrespectful. "I saw the guy you came with and he don't seem like the typical type of nigga young girls our age deal with, unless there are benefits, if you know what I mean." Throwing the question out there, she tilted her head to the side and waited for an answer.

Kimmy just looked Rissa up and down slowly thinking she could make a lot of money for herself if she played her hand right. "If you're asking me whether he's a sugar daddy, he's not. He's a client." Kimmy wanted her to ask more questions so she baited her with short answers.

"What kind of client? What are you? I mean, what kind of job do you have where somebody your age has clients?" Rissa asked.

"The type where I want for nothing. I eat, dress, and live a charmed life every day. And your name is?" Kimmy was sure and confident of herself.

"I'm Rissa. What's your name?"

"You can call me Kimmy."

"I heard you on the phone in there." Rissa pointed to the toilet.

"So you were game tapping, huh?" Now Kimmy had her hand on her hip, teasing her hair with her free hand and smirking at Rissa.

"Well, you weren't exactly whispering. And I wouldn't say game tapping either. I'd say I was taking notes is all."

Both girls laughed. Kimmy told Rissa she liked her and they would hook up and talk more if she really wanted to get up on the game. They exchanged phone numbers and Kimmy told Rissa to be looking for a phone call sometime the next day. With that, Kimmy went back out to her date and prepared her mind for whatever he was planning on doing to her in his suite.

Rissa went back to waiting tables while daydreaming about living a life where she didn't have to struggle to survive. She was tired of walking on eggshells every-where, scared she'd be asked to leave Wanda's mother's home for wearing out her welcome. "Shit, I can fuck with men. Especially if all I have to do is kick it with them. I need a come up like right now. I need my own crib, car, and some better gear." Looking over at Kimmy's table, she saw Kimmy and the dude getting ready to leave. They made eye contact and Kimmy's lips moved. Rissa wasn't sure what she said, but she guessed she was saying again that she'd call her. In response, she smiled while nodding and waved good-bye.

When Rissa got back to Wanda's after her shift at work she told her all the gossip that went on among her coworkers, and they laughed and smoked weed for the longest. Then Rissa told Wanda about meeting Kimmy and what they had talked about. She even told her she would get the easy money if things turned out being on the up and up. Wanda told her that she was crazy and she asked Rissa what her mother would think if she were alive and knew what she was planning to do. Rissa got upset and told Wanda that she wasn't and she had to do what she had to do. Wanda tried to talk her out of dealing with Kimmy, but in reality Rissa's mind was already made up. Rissa knew her time had come and no one would talk her out of it.

The next afternoon around one, Rissa was still in bed with the covers over her head when Kimmy called her phone. She and Wanda had been up all night binge smoking weed and talking about the good and the bad things that could come from dealing with Kimmy. Wanda reminded her that there were crazy bastard killers with money, too, some who got off on taking pussy, beating on the girls, and some cases even ending up killing the girl. With all that being said, it didn't change Rissa mind. She wasn't scared at all. Since her mother died and she had been raped by her aunt's husband, and then she saw Bobby murdered in front of her, all sense of fear was lost forever.

Rissa took the cover from over her head, grabbing her phone off the nightstand, and she looked at the incoming call. She didn't recognize the number so she hesitated to answer it. Four rings in, she swiped the screen answering the call. "Hello," she said tiredly, still feeling the effects of last night's smoke fest.

"Girl, is you still in the bed? It's almost one o'clock in the afternoon. I've been up and out in the streets, sold some conversation, and made a grand already."

Rissa sat up, holding the phone to one ear while rubbing her eyes with the free hand. Her heart was beating fast and she was shocked that Kimmy had taken her seriously and was really hitting her up. "Kimmy? Is this Kimmy?"

"It's the one and only. Who else got game to give a bitch? Girl, you not gonna get shit given to you but dick lying up in bed all day. So do you want dick or dough?"

"No, I'm up. I was on my way to get in the shower when the phone rang," Rissa lied as she jumped out of bed half asleep, gathering things so she could get in the shower for real.

"Good. Now, meet at the Motor City Casino in forty-five minutes, unless you got to punch the clock," Kimmy said with a chuckle, taking a jab at Rissa's nine-to-five occupation.

"No, I'm off. I'll be there in thirty minutes. See you when I get there," Rissa replied as her heart raced. She was excited and anxious at the same time. Grabbing a rolled blunt from the night before Rissa headed to the bathroom to blaze up, shower, and hurry to get dressed.

CHAPTER TEN

Rissa got to the casino and purchased two meal tickets, then was seated, waiting for her newfound friend. She had a million and one questions that were running through her head. She wanted know just what type of johns or clients she might be dealing with, and how much she'd make off each guy she kept company with.

Rissa looked at the time on her phone, then texted Kimmy, telling her where to find her sitting. Kimmy texted back that she'd be there in two minutes. When Kimmy arrived at the table she and Rissa greeted each other with a hug. The two women then got down to business.

Kimmy asked Rissa what made her think she had what it took for this line of work. Rissa told her about her mother's death and about Bobby being killed in front of her. She also told her about her aunt and her aunt's husband being murdered before Bobby got killed. Rissa explained that she had no family and that she was staying with a girlfriend, and the friend's brother and mother stayed there too.

Kimmy was moved by Rissa's horrible story, which made her want to bring her into the fold even more. It was agreed that they would get started right away. Kimmy told her that she was about to change her world completely. Because she understood what she going through and she was a good people reader, the two of them clicked well together and seemed to really like each other. By the time they had finished eating and talking, Rissa had more than won Kimmy over. Kimmy asked Rissa if she had driven there. The answer was no; she had yet to be able to afford a car of her own.

Kimmy smiled. "Well, we're about to go and get all your shit from over there and you're moving in with me ASAP. I don't got no nigga or nobody living with me and I got plenty of room. So you good."

Rissa couldn't believe it. Things were moving way too fast and sounding too good to be true.

Rissa was riding in the passenger seat of Kimmy's BMW 745 on the way to Wanda's house to get her belongings. She was in awe of the vehicle. She dreamed of owning her own one day. Kimmy smiled as she drove, looking over at Rissa from time to time while she talked to her. She told Rissa she could have her own BMW, or Benz as a matter of fact, if she played the game right and didn't let the game play her. She assured her she would put her up on the do's and don'ts that came with this line of work.

"Rule number one," she told Rissa, "is don't ever deal in feelings. Rule number two: this is a job. We sell fantasy. Rule number three is that for your body, and clearly your pussy if you choose to sell it, you get top dollar. If you choose not to you'll make money, but not quick enough to stack up a nice chunk, and you won't attract the real check writers."

Rissa hung on every word Kimmy said. She soaked up as much as her brain could hold at the moment. She kept telling herself, *I can do this,* as they rode in the car.

When they reached Wanda's house Rissa rushed inside while Kimmy waited in the car. Kimmy called Madam Valerie and told her the girl she had spoken to her about was in and that she would be staying with her so she could be broken in before she was introduced to her. Kimmy ended the call when Rissa and a female came out on the front porch arguing.

Wanda was pleading with her best friend not to go with Kimmy because she had a really bad feeling. Rissa told her she would be okay and not to worry; she could take care of herself. Kimmy popped the trunk when she saw Rissa walking to the rear of the BMW. Rissa put two garbage bags inside then waved good-bye to her homegirl. Wanda watched them drive off with that same bad feeling in her gut she had when Rissa first told her what she was thinking of doing.

Kimmy pulled into the parking garage on Woodward where she owned a two-bedroom loft just minutes away from the new, up and coming part of Detroit. Kimmy drove into her own reserved parking spot then she and Rissa got out and went to the trunk and got her bags. They made small talk while Kimmy led the way to the elevator. When they got inside she pushed the button marked for the fifth floor.

Rissa and Kimmy rode the elevator in silence with wide grins on both their faces. When the elevator stopped, the bell chimed and the door opened. They walked a short distance to loft 501. Kimmy opened the door and they went inside and set the bags by the door.

Kimmy kicked off her heels and began to show Rissa around the loft. They stepped into the big, open living area with plush carpet, a huge wraparound sofa, and nice paintings hanging from the walls. Rissa looked to her right and saw the kitchen with marble countertops and state-of-the-art appliances. She ran her hand over the smooth surfaces, telling Kimmy that her place was gorgeous.

Kimmy took her in the room where she would be sleeping. Rissa was impressed even more. Kimmy told Rissa
she could have anything she wanted in life; all she had to
do was use the gift God had blessed her with to get it.

As the days passed, Kimmy and Rissa spent a lot of
time together and got to know each other well. Kimmy
treated Rissa like the little sister she always wanted. She
even broke down explaining how she came to have all
that she did. She told her how Madam Valerie took her
in and gave her the true pussy game. She expressed that
one day she would take the throne and be the new queen
of Detroit because Madam Valerie was getting weak and
old. Rissa asked Kimmy how was she able to do what she
did so well.

"She blackmails them with mostly pictures of them
with young girls or them in sex acts, even recorded calls.
But, trust and believe, when the old bitch falls, I'll be
there to be next in line. And you gonna be sitting at my
right hand making money too!"

CHAPTER ELEVEN

Three months had passed and Rissa was making more money than she had ever seen in her entire young life. She could have been bringing in much more money, but she wasn't comfortable enough yet to sleep with strange men. Kimmy had been urging her to step her game up and use her full potential. Besides, since she brought Rissa into the life, when her protégé made real money she would get a greater percentage on top of the finder's fee she had already gotten.

Madam Valerie was already pressing the issue. She had clients who had seen Rissa's portfolio among dozens of other girls', and they all requested to pay for her time and pleasure. Kimmy and Madam Valerie had made the decision that it was time for Rissa to meet the queen of Detroit personally. In other words, it was time for Rissa to shit or get off the pot. If Madam Valerie had her way, like most of the time, she was going to shit, wipe her ass, and move on to the next swinging dick with cash, check, or credit card.

Kimmy sat in Madam Valerie's comfortable home office inside of the Indian Village estate, waiting for Rissa to arrive. A half hour ago she had texted the address to her telling her to meet her there. Kimmy was on the phone taking a call from a client when Rissa was shown in by the housekeeper. Kimmy motioned with her hand for Rissa to sit in the chair next to her, which was positioned in front of Madam Valerie's huge, intimidating desk.

Kimmy put up her index finger, gesturing she would be a minute. Rissa took a seat, looking around, amazed at how well decorated the office was. She was wondering whose home this was when an old woman walked in, taking a seat behind the desk. Rissa greeted the woman with a hello, but she just looked through her as if she said nothing at all. That made Rissa uncomfortable as well as nervous. She tried her best not to stare at the woman but couldn't help it. She had a graceful beauty about her and she looked very intelligent, appearing to be about all business.

Kimmy finally ended her phone call and spoke to the older woman with all due respect. "Madam Valerie, this is Rissa, the girl I've been telling you so much about."

"I assumed that much. Now let's get down to the matter at hand. I am a very busy woman and I don't have all day to play childish games." Madam Valerie looked directly at Rissa while she sternly spoke. "Are you not being well paid for your time when you are entertaining clients of ours?"

Rissa had a lump in her throat when she tried to speak. She put her hand over her breast and cleared her throat and humbly replied, "Yes, ma'am, I am." Rissa was wondering what she was going to say next. But she didn't have to wonder long. Kimmy sat silently like a mother in a parent-teacher conference when the teacher is speaking to the student. Rissa looked to Kimmy and she gave her the "I told you so" face.

"Do you understand what type of business you're in or do you not? If you don't, let me clarify it with you in plain English. Ain't no business like ho business," Madam Valerie said all hood despite the fact that she was just speaking like an uppity white woman. "See, I'm an old ho and you remind me of myself when I first came into this life. I thought I could just be arm candy and get paid. Sure, I got money; then I stopped getting clients and it seemed overnight because my value had become worthless. Now once I got hip and realized I was sitting on a goldmine my whole world changed. And that's what you need to do, realize your worth before you become worthless and your services become no longer needed. Like I told Kimmy about you earlier today, you are going to either shit or get your pretty little ass off the pot and make room for the next best thing. The choice is yours." Madam Valerie took her attention off of Rissa and started going through papers on her desk ending the ho pep talk.

Rissa was at a total loss for words and was slightly offended that this old bitch was telling her she had to sell her pussy. Rissa thought it wasn't her fault that the old lady's pussy wasn't popping no more.

She and Kimmy stood up to leave when the housekeeper stuck her head in the room and announced that there was a Mr. Rolling Earl here to see Madam Valerie. The queen of Detroit told her to see him in, and that she'd been expecting him. Rissa and Kimmy faced each other and then walked up the hall as they headed to the front door. Kimmy put her arm around Rissa's shoulder in a comforting way.

"Bitch, you could have warned me when you texted me to come here," Rissa whispered, agitated.

"Let's get out of here first and we'll talk about it later," Kimmy stated, still playing the big sister role as her eyes appeared to be looking for something or someone.

Rissa shrugged her shoulder, causing Kimmy's arm to fall away from her. Rissa wasn't feeling Kimmy at the moment. And she felt she was acting funny ever since the housekeeper told Madam Valerie that Rolling Earl was there to see her. She had never seen Kimmy unnerved before so she cut into Kimmy.

"What's up with you? Why you acting shook? Do you know something I don't know?" Rissa wanted answers, not wanting to be in the dark.

"Yeah, I guess you can say that. Let's just hurry up and get out of here, okay?" Kimmy pleaded with Rissa as they moved faster toward the front door. Kimmy didn't want to spook Rissa by telling her who and what Rolling Earl was. She hoped to avoid seeing him on the way out.

But hope went out the window when she heard voices of a man and woman coming in their general direction. When the conversation got louder, Kimmy easily recognized the man's voice as Rolling Earl and her heart raced. The housekeeper and Rolling Earl were turning down the same hallway, coming from the opposite way. Kimmy knew they would cross paths in a matter of seconds and she dreaded being in his presence. He always looked at her foul with unwanted sexual intentions. Not to mention she knew he was a cold-blooded killer for hire.

"Well, well, well. Who do we have here?" Rolling Earl said, licking his dry lips while he stood in front of Rissa and Kimmy, blocking their path to the door out of the house. The housekeeper walked by the three of them and waited for him up the hall a ways. "Kimmy, baby, what's up? I want to make you an offer you can't refuse." He hissed like a treacherous snake when he talked.

"Look, guy, I'm not interested in nothing you have to say or offer," Kimmy fumed flatly with anger.

Rolling Earl then set his sights on Rissa, who was standing behind Kimmy with her head down slightly, trembling all over. "Damn, well, look at this one here. You must be new. I'd love to get a taste of you, sweet thang." He mocked Rissa, blowing a kiss at her through his dry, cracked lips.

Kimmy grabbed Rissa's hand and pushed passed Rolling Earl. For a moment, Rissa's legs were as heavy as sandbags and wouldn't move. Kimmy pulled harder on Rissa's hand and her legs suddenly came back to life. Rissa had just looked in the face of the man who killed Bobby and shot her in the leg and shoulder. She was mad and terrified, and she wanted revenge, but she held her composure.

Once they were outside Rissa snatched her hand free of Kimmy. She ran to her car parked in the driveway and didn't look back at her friend, who was calling out to her. She started the car and slapped it into drive, stomped on the gas, and headed toward the gate, almost sideswiping Kimmy's BMW. She jammed on the brakes, coming to a stop in front of the huge iron gate, which was slowly opening. When it had opened wide enough for her car to go through, Rissa mashed the gas and sped away.

When she got to Jefferson Avenue, her phone rang and rang. With tears of anger in her eyes she looked at her cell phone. Kimmy was calling her but she didn't answer. Rissa knew she had to think so she drove to Lakewood Park. She got out and walked at the water's edge. She had to figure out what the hell was going on. Why was the man who killed Bobby and shot her there? What business did he have with Madam Valerie? She had to get the answers and she knew who could give them to her. After gathering her thoughts Rissa got back in her car and headed toward the loft.

Kimmy was at home waiting for Rissa to come so they could talk about everything that had happened back at Madam Valerie's. Having to meet a client in a few hours she decided to take a shower and get her mind right; plus, she was confused about why Rissa had taken off like she did in the first place. Kimmy wasn't sure if it was because Madam Valerie had cut into her about stepping up and selling ass. Or was it Rolling Earl's creepy self who set her off? Either way, she was going to ask Rissa what it was just as soon as she got back to the loft.

Rissa had finally arrived back at the loft to find Kimmy fresh out of the shower and walking around the loft naked, getting ready to meet a client. Kimmy was laying the outfit she was going to wear out on the sofa. "Bitch, why you just break out on me like that earlier? I was trying to talk to you before you left." Kimmy was still irritated and confused.

"Sit down, girl. I need to talk to you about that," Rissa said with an emotionless, straight face. "Since day one I've been real with you. Can I trust you with some real shit or what?"

Kimmy sat down on the arm of the sofa and gave Rissa all her attention. "Sure, you can. If you didn't trust me and I didn't trust you, we wouldn't be living together and getting money together. Now dish. What's on your mind, sis?" Kimmy asked sincerely.

"What do y'all call him, that dude who was sweating us in the hallway at Madam Valerie's?"

Kimmy had guessed it by now. It was Rolling Earl who had Rissa off her square. "Why, have you seen him somewhere before or something?"

"Yeah, he's the guy who killed my boyfriend Bobby and shot me in the shoulder and leg." Rissa walked over to Kimmy and pulled the collar of her blouse to the side over her shoulder, exposing the bullet wound. Then she showed her the entrance and exit wounds in her leg. "I damn near bled out that day!"

Kimmy's eyes doubled in size and her jaw dropped. Her hand involuntary covered her mouth. "Oh, my God, Rissa, why would he kill your dude and shoot your ass, too? He acted like he ain't know who you was."

"So you telling me you don't know shit about Rolling Earl killing Bobby and shooting me?" Rissa asked, side-eyeing Kimmy.

"Look, Rissa, I don't fuck with that man. He ain't no good. He's Madam Valerie's flunky. If she's got problems with anybody she'll call him. But, seriously, what I don't understand is what issue would she have with you and your nigga that would make her put Rolling Earl in play in the first place?" Kimmy gave Rissa the look that meant she needed answers. "I mean, if you don't be honest, I can't help you the best I can. So you need to tell me everything about everything or you on your own," Kimmy urged, then hurried up to her bedroom to find her robe and put it on; and she shot back downstairs.

When she came back downstairs Rissa was sitting on the sofa with her head down. Kimmy sat next to her and then it began. Rissa told her everything about the incident when she woke up to blood everywhere on her and Bobby. Rissa was detailed, even describing the way Bobby killed her aunt and Mackey in their sleep. Kimmy was soon also told how the police contacted her and she went to speak to a detective named Goodhouse. Rissa held nothing back.

She told her that same detective, who was investigating her aunt's and Mackey's murders, was the same one on Bobby's homicide case. "That ho-ass nigga came to the hospital fucking with me. Telling me he knows me and Bobby killed my aunt and her common-law husband. And he was saying crazy shit like maybe he knows who killed my boyfriend but he won't do his job and he gonna let the killer walk." Rissa left nothing out, to say the least.

"Yeah, I know Goodhouse. I played him some years ago for Madam Valerie. He's one of her flunkies too. What the fuck have you gotten your ass into?" Kimmy puzzled, wondering what the big connection to Madam Valerie was.

Rissa's head began to hurt she was thinking so hard. She couldn't believe the police, Rolling Earl, and Madam

Valerie were all in on Bobby's murder. She was hot that these no-good bastards would have a hand in taking her Bobby away from her. "Kimmy, you gotta help me find out how this old bitch linked to killing my dude," Rissa pleaded, almost in tears.

Kimmy wanted to help Rissa find out the correlation to Madam Valerie's entailment, plus she wanted to know for her own satisfaction. She would be in deep shit if she slipped and got caught, yet she decided to help Rissa because she had grown to see her as a little sister she never had. And if she were in Rissa's shoes she would want someone to assist her to find out what the fuck was going on.

Kimmy didn't have any issue about Bobby killing Rissa's disloyal aunt and her foul-ass nigga. She hoped if something like that had happened to her she would have a stand-up man in her corner as well. "Okay, I'll see what I can find out. Just know I'm putting everything on the line fucking doing this for you. You do realize that, don't you?" Kimmy said seriously to Rissa, who had a faint smile on her face.

Rissa felt some type of relief. "Thank you, sis; you got my back and I got yours. Now how are we going to find out what the fuck is going on?" Rissa asked Kimmy, wondering what their next move would be.

"Well, for one, she keeps all her business and dirt in her office desk at the house. If I can get in her desk, I might find out what we want know and more. I just can't get caught, 'cause if I do I'm good as dead." Kimmy had a worried look like she might be having second thoughts.

"Yeah, but won't you need a key to get in the desk? If she got her life in there, won't it be locked?" Rissa whined, hoping Kimmy could pull off the secret, squirrelly stunt.

"Let me worry about that. There's definitely more than one way to skin a cat. Locks are made for law-abiding citizens and, baby girl, I ain't none of that." Kimmy winked at Rissa before telling her she had to call her client and push their date back a few hours because something had come up.

CHAPTER TWELVE

Kimmy pulled up into the horseshoe driveway of Madam Valerie's house, killed the engine, closed her eyes, and said a prayer. She knew Madam Valerie had prior engagements and wouldn't be home. Her being there wouldn't draw unwanted or unneeded attention because Kimmy was always there anyway as if it were her second home. All the help knew she came and went when she wanted to. Kimmy took a deep breath and got out of her car, and she went inside, straight to the home office.

The door was never locked so she was able to turn the knob and go right in, shutting the door behind her. Kimmy's heart was racing. For a few seconds, she stood with her back against the door, looking around the room. Valerie didn't have any photos of family on the desk or hanging from the walls. She claimed she didn't have any family to speak of so Kimmy never asked twice.

Kimmy went over to the desk and quickly looked at what papers and notes were on the desktop and she found nothing of great importance. She momentarily paused, paranoid that someone was coming. Realizing she was tripping, she then started checking the drawers to see if they were unlocked. None of them were.

Kimmy stood perfectly still, scanning the room. She saw what looked to be a manila envelope that was in between two books on the bookshelf. On a mission, she went over and pulled the envelope out. Luckily, it had already been opened. She took a folded paper out of the envelope and started reading it. The heading read DEATH CERTIFICATE FOR MACKEY WHITESIDE.

Kimmy couldn't believe her eyes. "This old casket-face-ready, lying bitch." Taking out her phone she quickly snapped pictures of the certificate. When she was putting it back exactly the way she found it, a housekeeper knocked on the door, startling her.

"Come back later! I'm on the phone!"

Kimmy heard footsteps walk away from the door. Making sure she had left thing as they were when she came in, Kimmy left with what she needed.

Without stopping anywhere else, she raced back to the loft. She couldn't wait to show Rissa what she'd found. For years Madam Valerie had been keeping the fact that she had a brother a big secret. *He must have been a real fuck up or she knew he was a rapist and didn't deal with him the long way. Wow.*

Rissa was pacing back and forth through the loft when Kimmy came home. She bum-rushed her before she got through the door. "What happened? Did you find anything? Was they on to you?" Rissa quizzed franticly.

"Bitch, calm down and have a seat. Fall back some," Kimmy ordered Rissa.

"I don't need to sit down. Just please tell me something I can live with," Rissa cried.

Kimmy shook her head from side to side and gave Rissa her iPhone. Kimmy watched Rissa's mouth drop wide open while she read the snapshot of the death certificate. It all made sense to Rissa now. Bobby killed her aunt and Madam Valerie's brother. She never knew any of Mackey's people or where he came from to even know he had a sister, let alone one who sold pussy for a living.

All she knew was he was a piece of shit, sick in the head, who liked taking pussy. Rissa was glad he was dead so he couldn't ruin nobody else's life. She had no remorse, only hatred and vengeance for those who had a hand in killing the love of her life.

"This old ho had Rolling Earl kill my Bobby, but she couldn't have known on her own that he did it." Rissa closed her eyes and thought back to Goodhouse first interviewing her at police headquarters. "He asked me if I knew Bobby. I told him yeah, and he left it alone. Aw, fuck, Kimmy, that's how the cop got on to Bobby."

"How?" Kimmy was still trying to connect the dots.

"The day after the murders happened, Bobby and me was looking for his ID but we couldn't find it. He was drunk as hell that night and lost it. We was hoping he didn't lose it at the murder scene. But I guess he did."

"And I'll put my bank account on it that Goodhouse found it and sold the information to Madam Valerie ass. From what you told me, around the time him and her got killed I walked in on Madam Valerie offering Goodhouse a fat envelope full of money."

Rissa was livid. "That scumbag-ass pig. If it weren't for him Bobby would still be alive. I realize it now what he was hinting at when he came to the hospital, rubbing it in my face that he was in charge of Bobby's murder investigation. He was telling me in so many words that he was the cause of Bobby getting killed and he knew the killer all along."

Rissa started bawling tears of anger. Kimmy hugged Rissa, comforting her. When Rissa got her mind right she stood straight up, drying her eyes. Then she looked Kimmy dead in her face and said, "Bitch, you ready to be the queen? That washed-up, decrepit ho gotsta to fall, and them two lowlife, shit-eating snakes gonna follow." Rissa vowed scorn and determination.

Kimmy put both hands over her face, contemplating. Rissa backed away from her and crossed her arms over her chest. "So, what's it gon' be? You said one day you gon' to sit on the throne. Your time is now, Kimmy. Or you gonna wait around until she cross you, use you up, and throw you away?" Rissa was trying to convince Kimmy to ride with her because she knew she couldn't bring them down without her.

Kimmy moved her hands from her face, looked at Rissa, and tilted her head to the side. "Bitch, let's get it did. I'm tired of being run. It's time I run some shit. Push comes to shove and it don't go over clean, I got enough money put up to dip out and start over. A bitch can slang pussy anywhere. Ol' girl done had me do some grimy shit to people I didn't care to do, and them things always on my conscience. I think I'll feel good and sleep better at night if I help knock the ol' ho off her pedestal and wear her crown. You got a plan or naw?" Kimmy said with a smirk.

"Yup. I damn sure do," Rissa announced, pacing the floor again. "Check this out: if we get her client list and the dirt she blackmailing people with, she powerless, right?"

"Yeah," Kimmy agreed. "So that's how we gonna do it; take all that shit. I can get it, too, right from under her nose. She trust me way more than she should, of course. That skank won't know what hit her." The scheming pair laughed out loud, sure of themselves.

"First we got to deal with the help: Goodhouse and Rolling Earl slimy ass. Without them, she weak. I'll handle Rolling Earl personally." Rissa wanted revenge. "Can you get to Goodhouse? He'll see me coming a mile away."

"Yup, sure can. I got to him once and fucked up his marriage. I'm sure he ain't forgot what Kimmy cakes can do in such a way. If I call he'll come running." She giggled with a devilish smile. "We got to move on them both at the same time starting tomorrow. Then we'll deal with Madam Valerie succubus ass in a major way she can't come back from."

CHAPTER THIRTEEN

The next day Rissa and Kimmy made their move on Rolling Earl and Detective Goodhouse. They'd stayed up all night plotting how shit was going to go down.

Kimmy had gotten in touch with Detective Goodhouse. She pretended she had gotten pulled over by the Detroit police and they found a small amount of cocaine. She didn't want Madam Valerie to know about it because she had been warned not to mess with drugs. She propositioned him with sex in exchange for him talking to his friends in the narcotics department to make the case go away. At first Goodhouse told Kimmy he couldn't do shit about her problem, until she reminded him how good the pussy was. Instantly, he gave in and agreed to help. Kimmy told him she would come to his place around six. He anxiously gave her his address and apartment number then hung up the phone.

Kimmy and Rissa celebrated after she hung up the phone. "Girl, I told you, didn't I? Any nigga who done tasted this bit of honey gonna always want to put his finger back in the jar," Kimmy said, proud of herself. She was really feeling herself knowing Goodhouse would still fuck with her knowing she was the true reason he was under Madam Valerie's thumb. She'd put Kimmy on him years ago when she was underage and he was still paying the piper. Both Kimmy and Rissa laughed and agreed that if they were dudes, they wouldn't get played and then turn around in no time, later trusting a bitch.

***

Rissa had gotten Rolling Earl's cell number from Kimmy. She could get anybody's as long as Madam Valerie trusted her. But the storm was brewing. Rissa took a page out of her new best friend's book. When she got Rolling Earl on the phone and heard his voice, her stomach turned. Flashes of him gunning Bobby down and shooting her were overwhelming, but she fought through it. She dug deep and shook the all-too-real images out of her mind, reminding herself that she was on a mission to avenge Bobby's death and her near-death experience.

"Yes, is this Rolling Earl?" Rissa asked in the sweetest girly voice she could muster up.

"Yeah. Who the fuck is this and how did you get my digits?" he snarled.

"Um, this is Rissa. We meet at Madam Valerie's house. I was with Kimmy. Do you remember me? Short with long hair, brown skin? That's how I got your number."

"Oh, yeah, the new booty. How could I forget such a tasty-looking thang like you? Now what the fuck can I do for you other than beat that pussy up?" he fired back disrespectfully.

Rissa cringed at the thought of him touching her. She turned to Kimmy sitting next to her and covered the phone. "I can't do this."

Kimmy encouraged her to keep talking.

"Well, ya see, I got a serious situation that, if I don't get rid of, might cost me my good health, if you know that I mean." She talked in code. "I was told you can help me for a fee, let's say twenty grand. I don't know who else could help me. I really need your help," Rissa whined, playing the "ho in distress" role to perfection.

Kimmy punched the air and jumped up and down, holding praise back for Rissa. She had Rolling Earl on the hook now. All she had to do was pull him in. The mention of twenty Gs was the type of language he could comprehend.

"Well, I might be willing to help you with that issue. But we need to talk face to face so we can get a clear understanding. You feel me, Tissa?" He called her the wrong name thinking he was talking slick.

"That's cool with me. Do you smoke? We can blow a few back woods and talk about the arrangements if you do. I'm free around six this evening. Is that good for you?" Rissa purred.

"Shit, I had some other shit on the floor 'round then, but business comes first. Meet me at Burns Park off Jefferson no later than six-fifteen. If your ass late, don't call my number no more. Got it?" Rolling Earl killed the line and rubbed his hands together, thinking of what all he was gonna cop with his come up if shit went his way.

Rissa carelessly tossed her cell phone on the sofa and flopped backward, relieved she'd pulled it off. "That was the easy part. The real test gonna come when I'm by myself with him." Rissa sounded worried.

Kimmy stroked Rissa's ego. "Bitch, you got this. You got that stuff you got from Chad still, right?"

Rissa pulled out a tiny clear Baggie with off-white powder in it, showing it to Kimmy.

CHAPTER FOURTEEN

It was five fifty-nine and Kimmy was standing in the hallway outside of Goodhouse's apartment door, reminding herself of the plan to find anything incriminating that could be used to get his ass locked up for a long time, or forever and a day. She had nothing particular in mind, which she thought was risky, to say the least. Nonetheless, she was game.

She took a deep breath and knocked on the door. Two seconds later Goodhouse opened the door half drunk with a drink in his hand. With a towel around his neck, dressed in a black jogging suit and gym shoes like his old ass had been working out, Kimmy laughed to herself how fake he was.

"Come in," he said, looking Kimmy up and down lustfully. When she walked by him and went inside, he suspiciously stuck his head out the door then looked up down the hallway. Seeing no one, he closed the door and dead bolted it with a single key.

Kimmy watched him put the key in his pocket. A bad feeling came over her instantly. She refused to let him know, though. Goodhouse set his drink down and walked up behind Kimmy and grabbed her by the arm. She told him not to be so rough. He ignored her, pushing her face first against the wall. Her heart raced. She asked him what he was doing and he said that he was covering his ass. He kicked her legs apart and ordered her to put her hands up on the wall.

"Whoa, what did I do?" Kimmy said, holding her hands up.

"Shut the fuck up. I didn't tell you to say shit," Goodhouse hissed as he ran his hand between her legs. She didn't have any panties on so he jammed his fingers in her pussy hard. She begged him to stop but he wouldn't. He pressed his mouth against her ear and bit down. Kimmy struggled to break free from his grip, but it was useless. He was too strong. She attempted to scream; however, he put his hand over her mouth, muffling all sounds.

Oh, my God, he's gonna kill me, flashed over and over in her head. She had to think fast. She then started to act like she was turned on. He asked her if she wanted more of the same and unhanded her. She was breathing hard and sweating. Goodhouse ordered her to get naked.

"Why you doing me like this? I thought we gon' turn up." She stripped, keeping focused on his every move.

"Oh, yeah, we is," Goodhouse replied with one side of mouth curled up and a crazed look in his eyes. "Kimmy, you must have forgotten how you fucked me over, costing me my marriage and dignity. Now that bitch got a foot on my neck for life. I've been waiting to get you in the right position at the right time."

"Come on, don't do this. I'm sorry she made me do it." Kimmy's tears streamed down her face, ruining her once beat makeup. Ashamed, she covered her titties and crossed her legs; however, in that very moment she decided she didn't want to die. She looked around for a weapon. Goodhouse peeped her intentions and smacked her across the living room. Titties and ass was everywhere. She was on the floor bleeding from her head and forearm from smashing through a glass end table. Goodhouse then ran across the room and stood over her.

"Get up, bitch," he demanded, reaching down to grab Kimmy by her weave. Unfortunately, he'd failed to see that she'd grabbed a piece of glass the size of a butcher knife. As he was reaching downward, she was swinging a deliberate death blow.

Kimmy lunged with the makeshift weapon at the monster. Making contact, she stabbed him deep into the side of the head with the sharp glass. She yanked down with all her might, causing a deep, gaping wound. Blood sprayed all on her naked body. The once highly decorated police detective fell to his knees, holding his head. He was in shock, his eyes the size of half dollars. Goodhouse looked at his hand and the huge amount of blood that covered it. The devil finally called his disciple home as Goodhouse fell over dead.

Kimmy was hysterical. She couldn't believe she'd just killed Goodhouse, a member of the Detroit Police Department. Kimmy remembered the key to get out of the apartment. Reaching under his motionless body, she went in the deceased officer's pocket, retrieving it. She scrambled to her feet and ran to the bathroom, leaving a trail of bloody footprints. Kimmy quickly showered, got dressed, and locked the door behind herself when she left. *I hope he rots away in that bitch before somebody find his snake ass.*

Rissa pulled into Burns Park where she saw Rolling Earl's truck parked close to the walkway. She pulled up beside him and killed the engine. Getting out of her car, she went to the front passenger side of his truck. He had been watching her from the very moment she pulled in. Rolling Earl was grinning like a cat from ear to ear when Rissa walked up. He hit the unlock button and she got in. The equally conniving pair got straight to business.

"Okay, so who's the mark?" Rolling Earl growled, ready to put in even more work.

"My ex-boyfriend," Rissa lied, wanting nothing more than to spit in his face. With no warning whatsoever, Rolling Earl reached over, pressing and rubbing his hand roughly up and down her shirt. "What the fuck you doing, nigga? Damn, feeling a bitch up? This pussy cost and we ain't here for that shit." Rissa pushed his hand away. She was disgusted by him even touching her. She wanted nothing more than to hurry up and carry out the plan, and then her life would be complete.

Rolling Earl dog checked Rissa and told her, "This ain't no game. I'm only making sure you ain't got a wire on in an attempt to set me up."

Rissa told him she wasn't no rat bitch out here in these streets. She let him know that she was not going to fuck her name up or put her life on the line being a snitch. Rolling Earl liked that she stood up and didn't back down. He relaxed and told her that they could do business with each other. He told Rissa he needed a photo of the dude she wanted killed, and he needed the cash. The murder-for-hire thug informed Rissa there would be absolutely no refunds if she changed her mind. Once the money exchanged hands, it was his to keep no matter what. Rissa quickly agreed to his terms, then asked him if he minded if she smoked a blunt. With a smile on his face, he told Rissa to blaze up because he needed to smoke as well. What Rolling Earl didn't know was this just might be the last time he blew in his life.

Rissa lit the blunt and pulled the smoke deep into her lungs. They casually talked shit, taking turns hitting the chronic. Rissa watched the blunt closely. When she reached a certain mark she knew to stop getting high. She'd laced the pre-rolled blunt with PCP, the off-white powder in the tiny Baggie she and Kimmy had been giggling about at the loft. Chad said anyone who smoked it would go nuts. Rissa was praying he was right.

When Rissa was only seconds away from making up some wild lie to get away from the man who had killed Bobby, Kimmy called, frantic. Telling Rolling Earl she had to take the call, Rissa excused herself. Kimmy was talking fast and Rissa couldn't understand half of what she was saying; but she heard the words "dead" and "Goodhouse."

Playing it off as if she were talking to her grandmother, Rissa announced to Earl that she had to go because it was an emergency. Rolling Earl shook his head up and down as he hit the blunt hard once more, then tried to pass it to Rissa. He was told that she was good and he could kill the rest of the blunt, and she would be in touch with both the picture and the cash.

Rissa stood at her car door and took one last look at the man who killed the love of her life. Rolling Earl paid her no mind as he started examining the blunt, smacking his lips like he tasted something funny. Rissa smirked at him, got in her car, and drove off. Now she just had to go see what happened with Kimmy and why she was taking so crazy. Rissa headed toward the loft, which was less than twelve minutes away.

Rissa got to the loft and busted through the door, calling out for Kimmy. Suddenly she emerged from the bathroom, nursing the cuts on her head and forearm. Rissa rushed to her side, inspecting the wounds she hadn't had when she left. Then, of course, she blitzed her with a million questions. Kimmy held nothing back, telling Rissa everything that happened to her in Goodhouse's apartment. She was terrified the police would be looking for her and she would spend the rest of her life locked up behind bars. Although messed up in the head, Kimmy reassured Rissa that she would still help her get the client and blackmail list from Madam Valerie; then she was leaving Detroit and never coming back.

They wanted to get the lists from Madam Valerie's office as soon as possible. The two were ready to go right then and there, but Kimmy didn't want her asking questions about the extremely visible cuts and whatnot. Thinking of a plan on top of their plan, she called Madam Valerie's phone, fishing for information about her whereabouts for the rest of the evening. Kimmy was informed she would be away for most of the night on important business. Madam Valerie was clueless to the plot that was going on behind her back to dethrone her; and it was much too soon for her to know anything about her crony Goodhouse being dead. His blood was probably still warm. In the meantime, they were ready to put in work. Rissa agreed to be the lookout while Kimmy got the lists and anything else that would cripple the old whore's operation for good.

CHAPTER FIFTEEN

It was two hours later. Rissa and Kimmy had gotten to Madam Valerie's house and they had no problem gaining access to the office. The housekeeper and anyone else who maintained the house didn't pay any attention to Kimmy's bandages. They did just as they'd planned. Rissa served as lookout. She closed the door and put her ear against it to hear anyone coming, especially Madam Valerie. Every now and then she would open the door and peek up and down the hallway.

Kimmy looked for a hidden spare key, or any way to get in the desk drawers without busting the locks. She tried using a letter opener and even a bobby pin to pick the lock. Kimmy tried everything; however, nothing worked. She was, without a doubt, frustrated. Rissa was also fed up. She ordered Kimmy to watch the door so she could take a shot at getting the locks open. Rissa dug deep in her blue jeans pocket, pulling out a pocketknife, and she flicked the blade out. When she got to the desk she attacked the locks with the knife. One by one the drawers popped open. Rissa grinned, knowing she had hit pay dirt.

Kimmy abandoned the door and rushed to Rissa's side. "Bitch, is you crazy? She gonna know somebody was in her shit," Kimmy whined.

"Duh, she gonna know when she sit her dried-up ass down behind this desk anyway. Now, grab all this shit and let's go," Rissa explained in a disgruntled whisper, handing Kimmy the Gucci backpack they'd brought with them. Franticly they pillaged the drawers, stuffing the backpack with folders labeled with the names of judges, police officers, city officials, and a host of major businessmen.

Once they had relieved Madam Valerie of her gold-mine, they were ready to make their exit from the office. Just a few feet from the door, with both their hearts pounding and expecting to be caught up in some type of fight for their lives, Kimmy reached for the doorknob. Before she could turn it, the housekeeper came from out of thin air, frightening both girls. Kimmy screamed and pissed herself. Rissa blacked out, stabbing at the creepy housekeeper. In reality, she meant them no harm. She had no idea what they had done as she fell to the floor.

"What is the meaning of this?" she asked, out of breath, holding her hand up defensively.

Rissa was standing over the housekeeper when it dawned on her that she had indeed mistakenly stabbed the old lady. Still filled with adrenalin, Rissa went in. "You old creeping bitch, you'll know next time to make some noise floating up on people like you crazy."

Rissa looked up and around for her girl. She didn't see her. The front door was wide open. Kimmy had got the fuck on when Rissa attacked the housekeeper. She wanted no part of that unwarranted act. She had had enough violence for one day. Rissa ran outside as well and jumped in the car with Kimmy. The person manning the iron gate opened it, oblivious to the thievery and attempted murder on the housekeeper that had just jumped off.

The duo didn't believe it would be safe to go back to the loft, so they drove out to Southfield and checked into the Residence Inn. They kicked back with the television on, and lay across the king-sized bed, going through piles of client and blackmail lists. It was unbelievable for Rissa to fathom who Madam Valerie had her hooks in on the con game tip. But not for Kimmy; she'd originally helped set some of them up for failure. As they dug deeper into the folders Rissa came upon to some documents with BANK OF AMERICA on them. "Look at these. Is these what I think they is?" Rissa said, excited.

"Let me see that shit," Kimmy said, unenthused until she read the bank documents along with account numbers, routing information, and PINs to all of Madam Valerie's money. "Bitch, we rich! We about to drain this ho for every dime she got." Immediately Kimmy got on the phone with the bank and locked the woman she'd whored for out of all her accounts, and changed everything so she controlled them.

Kimmy and Rissa were celebrating their come up when channel four's live breaking news interrupted the normal broadcast. The reporter was hyped up, telling the story about a man who was high on PCP walking in the middle of downtown Detroit's Hart Plaza. He waved an automatic firearm at people, ranting and raving about how many people he'd killed. Luckily, officers were on duty and shot the suspect several times, killing him at the scene.

Rissa and Kimmy jumped off the bed screaming, whooping, and doing the Running Man. "Got 'im!" Rissa said, high-fiving Kimmy.

When they had calmed down, Kimmy had an idea to call a client of hers, who happened to be Paul Curt, a federal judge and on the blackmail list. Rissa gasped. "No, come on, Kimmy. Everybody knows him. He ain't out there like that."

"No way, he's not on the hound train for pussy. Madam Valerie got him taking bribe money from some downtown development company that's buying up everything.

So I thought he might like to give the old shoe Madam Valerie a kick around or two." Kimmy grabbed her cell phone. "Watch this shit here. He calls me his pretty kitty." She dialed his number, and when he picked up she went into action. "Hello, Judge Sexy, how are you? Me, I'm just fine now that I hear your voice." She spoke softly and seductively. "I got something in my hands right now I believe you'd like to take a peek at."

"Is that so, pretty kitty?" the judge sang into the phone.

The next day Kimmy met with the judge for lunch and gave him his own file of blackmail information and all the other city officials' files that the notorious Madam Valerie had in her possession. Two weeks later Madam Valerie was standing in front of a federal judge, being arraigned under the RICO Act, facing several of the same charges famed mobster and crime boss John Gotti had gotten got life for, including human trafficking and a host of other charges. If she was found guilty she'd never see the light of day again.

Rissa and Kimmy moved down to Miami and jacked off Madam Valerie's money, living life like celebrities. Yet, no matter how much fun Rissa was having, she could never forget the love of her young life, Bobby. His memory would haunt her forever.

THE END

CUTTHROAT DIVAS

by

Racquel Williams

CHAPTER ONE

London

"Man, it's hot as fuck out here. I'm about to go in this motherfucking house," Ajanay said.

"That's what I was thinking, but I swear I really don't want to hear this bitch mouth yapping about some bullshit that I'ont feel like hearing right now," Sheika said as she took a few more pulls of the blunt that was halfway done.

"Man, pass that shit. Let me hit it one more time before I leave," I said to Sheika.

I took a few drags and then gave the roach back to her. This was some good-ass weed that my homie gave me. I really wasn't into getting high, but lately I was stressed the fuck out. I was about to turn eighteen and, instead of things looking up for me, I felt like my life was spiraling downhill.

Before I get to talking about my fucked-up-ass life, let me introduce myself. My name is London. I feel like God did me wrong when He created me because of all the shit that I've been through in my seventeen years in this wicked world. Don't get me wrong, I had a great life growing up for the first fifteen years of my life, when my parents were still married. My daddy was a great man who provided for his family, but he was not so good to my mother. He used to beat the hell out of her, putting her into the hospital a few times. Everyone around us knew what was going on, but they didn't dare say anything or report him to the police. See, my daddy was a big-time dope boy from Whitcomb Court and everybody knew that he and his crew were nothing to be played with. So Mama endured all the pain that he instilled in her.

The older I got, the more I realized that she was weak and I wanted to be nothing like her. My home life became horrible because of all the fussing and fighting that would take place. I would just lock myself in my room and bury my head under my pillows until I thought it was safe, and that was when I didn't hear any more screams coming from my parents' bedroom.

All of this came to end one fateful day when the feds busted up in our house to arrest my father. My mother was screaming and carrying on but, truthfully, I was happy deep inside. Don't get me wrong, I love my father, but I was sick of him controlling our lives.

I watched as they removed everything from our house. We didn't have any money because my mother didn't save anything, and all the money that Daddy had was taken by the government.

We didn't have any family who was willing to take us in, so we ended up going to a shelter that catered to women and children. My life was horrible then, and I was very miserable because I wasn't used to this kind of living. It took us a few months to get a two-bedroom house in the projects, which was a block over from where we had our house. Mama's pride was hurt because she went from having everything to having nothing. She was forced to get a job so she could support me and my two little brothers. Personally, I thought she should have been happy that my dad was no longer around to whup her ass anymore.

Daddy ended up getting twenty-five years in the fed. Mama took it really hard and turned to smoking crack. It wasn't no secret because all the neighborhood dope boys would run in and out of our apartment, all times of the day. She was so strung out that days would go by and she would lie up in her room, not giving a damn. I became a surrogate mother to my two brothers, which was sad because they started running the street also.

I was determined to finish school and get my ass far away from Mama and her antics. Sometimes I do miss Daddy, and I wish he were still around because, regardless of what was going on, he still made sure we had everything, and I mean everything, that his kids needed.

"Bitch, you all zoned out and shit," Nay joked.

"Huh, what? Oh, I'm sorry. Just thinking about some shit, that's all," I said as I managed to wipe the tears out of the corner of my eye. The pain I was felt was deep, but it was the force behind me to get more out of life.

CHAPTER TWO

Ajanay

I think when God was creating people He made sure I got an extra dosage of looks. 'Cause, baby, when I tell you I am a pretty bitch, yes, I am. My dad was Jamaican and my mom was from Trinidad, so I have that exotic look; and I was also blessed with a banging-ass body to match. The bitches I know are often intimidated by me, especially when I come around their niggas. Fact is, I don't want their niggas. It's their niggas who steadily pursue me. In my mind, starting with Daddy, niggas are not worth a damn thing. They're good for a nut and a few dollars. All the other shit is definitely in the way.

I grew up in a volatile environment to say the least. My daddy was a womanizer who was fucking every- and anything around. I was young at the time, but I wasn't no fool. There were times when I would see him around the neighborhood with different bitches, and these bitches had the nerve to come up to me, trying to be all nice and shit. I used to look them bitches dead in the eyes and tell them not to touch me. I was dead-ass serious, too. My mother was my world and I'd be damned if I was going to let any one of these hoes step in and try to replace my mother.

One day after school, I was walking from the store and I saw my daddy's car parked on the side of an abandoned building. I knew it was his car, because I recited his license plate so much so I could know it was him when-ever I saw his car.

I sneaked on the side, trying to surprise him, but when I lifted my head up I got the shocker of my life. My daddy was buck-ass-naked, buried deep inside of a red bone bitch. I couldn't really see who it was. All I knew in my young mind was that I needed to grab my mama.

I threw my book bag on my back and started running to the house. My heart was beating fast as I sprinted to get to the house.

"Mama, Mama," I yelled as I pushed the front door and ran inside.

"Child, quit all that yelling up in here."

"Mama, I need you to come with me. I just saw Daddy with a woman and they were naked," I managed to say in between sobs.

"Little girl, what are you talking about? Your daddy is at work."

"Mama, no, I'm telling you. I just seen Daddy. Come with me so I can show you."

"Hold on a second." She disappeared into her room. A few minutes later, she returned fully dressed.

I ran out the door, with her following closely behind. *Please, God, let them be there,* I prayed, because if they were not there the ass whupping that was coming to me would be deadly. One thing Mama hated was when I lied, and there was no way I could prove this if they were gone.

"Look, there is his car," I yelled in excitement.

Mama placed her hand over my mouth. "Shhhh. Stay right here," she said as she ducked down and crept toward the car.

I didn't listen to her, though; I crept right behind her. I watched as she peeped into the car.

She then opened the unlocked door. "What the fuck are you doing, Trell?" she yelled.

I couldn't hear what my daddy was saying, but I imagined he was shocked that he had been caught red-handed. I saw the woman sit up, and she tried to put her shirt on. In seconds, then, all I saw was my mother raising her arm with what appeared to be a gun.

Pop! Pop! Pop!

I covered my ears and started screaming louder and louder. After about two minutes, the gunshot ceased. I was too scared to move, so I kept my head down and my eyes shut tight. Then I heard one more single gunshot. I flinched, but still kept my eyes covered.

I was frozen and my body was numb. I knew whatever had happened, it wasn't good. My fears were confirmed when I heard police sirens coming toward where the incident happened.

"We have a child right here," I heard a person say.

I mustered up enough courage to open my eyes. I looked around. I was looking for my mother.

"Come with me," a police woman said to me as she led me away from the scene.

"We got bodies over here. One male and two females," a male officer hollered into his radio.

Wait! What? Two women? What the hell do they mean? "Where is my mother? I need my mother," I yelled. I turned around and ran back toward where Daddy's car was at.

"Stop! Don't go back there." The strong officer grabbed me up. I started crying real hard because I wasn't no fool. I knew my mama was gone.

Later that night, my grandma told me and my little brother that Mama and Daddy were dead. I felt a sharp pain hit me. Guilt rushed over me because I knew Mama was dead because of what I did. If I hadn't run in the house and told her what I saw, she would've never brought the gun that she used to kill Daddy, his whore, and then herself.

"Noooooooooooooo!" I screamed out as reality hit me that my queen was gone.

My life after that was changed for the worse. The pain of losing my best friend is still unbearable at times, to the point where I want to kill myself. Sometimes I get angry at Mama because how could she leave us like that? I only wanted her to see what he was doing to her.

My grandma tries her best to show us love, but there is no love like my mama's love. I started to rebel and act out because I was mad at the fucking world! I feel like no one understands my pain, and there is no one to replace my mama's love.

CHAPTER THREE

Sheika

When bitches talk about shit that they've been through, I just sit back and laugh, 'cause until they experience the shit I've been through, they ain't been through shit in my eyes. See, when I was the young age of nine years old, my mama's boyfriend started raping me. I was happy to have dude around at first, because I never knew my biological father; so when my mother moved him in with us, I was happy to have a father figure.

The relationship between us was lovely. We spent a lot of time together playing games on my Xbox, or we would hang out at the park after school. My mother was also happy that she finally had a good man around. He worked, paid the bills, and paid attention to her child. What else could she ask for?

Two years later, while I was asleep, I felt someone touch me. I thought I was dreaming, but I quickly realized I wasn't. I opened my eyes and saw my mother's boyfriend on top of me.

"What are you doing? Aubrey, get off me," I yelled and tried to push him off, but my strength was nothing compared to his big, masculine build.

"Relax! I know you want me. I see how you look at me," his dirty ass said while he tried to kiss me.

"No, please, don't do this," I screamed out. I wondered why my mother was not coming to my rescue; then I remembered that she was working the night shift.

I continued crying. "Aargh," he grunted as he busted inside of me.

He finally got up, and looked at me. I turned my head so I couldn't look this monster in his eyes. He left the room and I thought about getting up and running out, but I was in extreme pain. I heard my room door pushed open again, and it was him coming in. *God, please don't. I can't bear any more of this,* I thought as I tried to mentally prepare myself for what was about to take place again.

"Listen, little bitch! You better not say a word to your mother or anyone else. You see this?" He pulled my face toward him. I felt something cold and hard press against my cheek. "I will kill yo' motherfucking mother if you tell anybody 'bout what happened."

I didn't say a word. I just kept crying.

"Did you hear me, little bitch?" he yelled and squeezed my face.

"Yes, I heard you," I managed to say in between cries.

"Now get yo' ass up and clean yo'self off before yo' mama come home."

I didn't move, which angered him. Slap! Slap! He slapped me twice with his open hand.

"Noooooo!" I grabbed my face and balled up my body in a fetal position. "Please, God, please take me now," I cried out.

I listened as he continued cussing under his breath until he walked out my room, slamming my door. I reached under my pillow to grab my cell phone. I was going to call my mother to let her know what kind of monster she brought in our lives. I quickly remembered the threats that he just made against my mother. I decided not to call her.

After about an hour of crying and wishing I were dead, I finally dragged myself out of the bed. I took my time to open my door, hoping he was nowhere near. I got in the shower. I was trying to wash off any and every trace of this monster.

I was alarmed when I washed between my legs. Red blood stained my white washcloth. I started crying again, because I was sore down there and the blood frightened me more. I hurried up and washed off and got out of the tub. I was hoping my feeling would wash down the drain with the soap, but it didn't.

The next couple of days were hard for me, as I had to endure the sight of this bastard. He behaved like nothing happened, and my mother was clueless. Over time I learned to block the pain out; and even though this bastard would try to talk to me I would never say a word to him. My mother asked me why I was acting so cold toward him, but as much as I wanted to tell her what happened, I just couldn't, out of fear that he might harm her.

The only thing that kept me going was the fact that I was almost out of high school and I would be moving far away.

CHAPTER FOUR

London

"Man, it's hot as fuck out here. I'm about to go in this motherfucking house," Ajanay said.

"That's what I was thinking, but I swear I really don't want to hear this bitch mouth yapping about some bullshit that I'ont feel like hearing right now," Sheika said as she took a few more pulls of the blunt that was halfway done.

"Man, pass that shit. Let me hit it one more time before I leave," I said to Sheika.

These two bitches have been my ace since the fifth grade, when we started hanging out. Ever since then we've become inseparable. Whenever you see one, you know the other two are not far behind. Blood couldn't make us any closer, if you ask me.

"Damn, bitch, you hawking the blunt," Nay blurted out.

I busted out laughing. I was so gone in my thoughts and just puffing away. "My bad, bitch. Y'all know a bitch is stressed out." I passed the blunt to Nay.

Nay is the prissy one out of the three of us. That bitch swears to God she is a glamour girl and I have to agree. But, don't get fooled, that bitch is thorough as they come. Let something pop off and she is the first one to pop off.

Sheika, on the other hand, is loud and don't give a fuck about too much. I knew Sheika was dealing with some bullshit at home, which made her angry most of the time. We asked her what was going on with her, but she never shared it. Whatever it was, I knew it wasn't good because she never wanted to be in the house. Most times she was over at either my house or Nay's house.

My phone kept ringing. I knew from the ringtone who it was blowing me up like that. "I'm about to bounce, y'all. Call me if y'all bitches need me." I gave both of them a hug.

"Damn, bitch! Who the fuck is this nigga? E'erytime he call, you got to leave?" Sheika's ass said, but not in a very friendly tone.

"Damn, why you so worried? All you need to know is it's not yo' nigga I'm fucking," I said and walked off because my phone was continuously ringing.

As soon as I bent the corner of the complex, I quickly answered the phone.

"Damn, bae, I know you see a nigga calling."

"I did, but I was with the girls and I didn't want to answer in front of them."

"You around the way?"

"Yeah. Where you at?"

"Driving down Ambrose Street right now. Trying to scoop you up real quick."

"Hmmm. I see you getting bolder and bolder. One of these days, somebody gonna catch us together."

"Man, fuck them people. You my bitch, soon you'll be my baby mama, and then everybody and their mama will know."

"I hear you. I'm walking out there now." I hung the phone up.

Keon was a big-time dope boy I was fucking. Nah, let me correct that. I started out just fucking him, but over time my feelings for him got stronger. See, my ass was not into these young-ass little boys, because all they did was fuck and tell everybody. Not my big man; he was a neighborhood boss and he be on his grown man shit. I ain't gon' lie, the first time we fucked was very painful because I was a virgin and he ripped through my pussy with force. I cried like it was the end of the world, but I quickly forgot about the pain once he dropped a grand on the hotel table before he left.

Money was definitely the motivation. He paid for me to get my cosmetology license and he started taking me on shopping sprees. I wasn't no stingy bitch so I would grab something for my bitches also. They kept asking me about where I was getting all this paper from, but I chose not to tell them. Don't get me wrong, me and my bitches were close, but I wasn't no fool. I learned from my daddy getting locked up that you can't trust nobody, not even the bitches you roll with. My daddy wouldn't be in that hell hole if it weren't for his nigga who snitched on him; and not just any nigga, but his right-hand man. So, anyways, I would have told my bitches, but Keon was grown and I was underage at the time so I couldn't risk him going to jail.

Now I was twenty-four and we were still fucking around. The only difference was I wasn't that little young, naïve girl who would fall for anything this nigga was telling me. I kind of pissed him off, because he'd been trying for the longest to have a baby with me, but I wasn't ready or . . . Nah, fuck that. I didn't want no kids. I was good by my damn self. I was taking the pill, but he didn't know that. He just thought he was busting blanks. He often suggested we go to the doctor to see what was going on. I always came up with a reason, because he didn't know, but I knew why I wasn't.

I got into his orange Charger and he pulled off. "What's up, li'l mama?"

"Ain't nothing. Got out of class and was hanging out with the girls."

"That's what's up! You tryin'a go eat and chill for a few?"

"Of course. You know my ass don't be passing up no food." I laughed.

"Yeah, I forgot, yo' greedy ass."

He pulled off and cut up Plies's music as he sped down the street. I loved being with him, even though I knew in my heart he was not being faithful. I just didn't say too much, because I knew where I was trying to go, and his money was helping me to get there. One thing I could say was he never disrespected me.

We decided to go to Croaker's Spot over on Nine Mile Road. This was our favorite place when we wanted to really pig out on some good food. After we ate, we decided to leave, and got a hotel room. I was kind of tired after I ate, but I knew I had to fuck him. This nigga was wide open over this young pussy and I wouldn't dare deny him because it kept him happy.

As soon as we got into the hotel, it was on and popping. I sat on the bed, checking my messages. I noticed a few missed calls from my mother. I wondered what the fuck she wanted. I hadn't seen her in a while. I made a mental note to stop by tomorrow and check on her.

"Nigga, stop playin'," I said, because Keon was making my panties wet by caressing my breasts.

"Who said I was playing?" he said as he massaged my breasts in a circular motion. "Shit, girl, as sexy as you are, I could eat every inch of you from head to toe." The way he was talking to me had my pussy thumping. One thing for certain, that nigga knew how to eat pussy.

"Nigga, you play too damn much." Right when I said that, his ass got up from off the bed. My heart started racing fast as hell as Keon tugged on my panties. I scooted up so he could slide down my panties. Good thing I shaved because he had a problem with hairy pussy. I parted my legs hoping he could get a great view. This nigga was crazy as hell, but I was just as crazy as him. His attention was what I throbbed for and it was a turn-on.

"Oh, my God," I sang under my breath when his lips met mine. I felt my eyes roll into the back of my head as his tongue danced inside my walls.

My adrenaline rush flowed through my body as I spread my legs wider, making sure he licked every inch of my pussy. "God," I moaned, biting my tongue. I couldn't help but to use my hand to guide his head in and out of my pussy.

I heard my cell phone ringing. I looked at the caller ID. It was Sheika calling me.

Oh, God, not right now. "If you don't take your ass on somewhere," I wanted to shout, but I struggled to get the words out because Keon was digging deep into my pussy.

My back was sliding down off the loveseat in the hotel and my hand was glued on the back of his head, working it like a yo-yo.

"God. Oh, my God," I sang out as his lips made love to my pussy. I closed my eyes as tight as possible, fighting back my groans. I wanted to scream out in ecstasy because my juices were flowing through my body, ready to explode.

"Keon," I moaned as my hips slow ground in rhythm. My pussy was soaking wet. "Damn, why are you doing this to me?" His tongue penetrated my wetness, and went back and forth over and over, driving me insane.

The way he was working his tongue was like no other. I locked my legs around his neck and squeezed as my juices flowed like a river. I was totally lost in bliss. My pussy was starving like Marvin. I was hungry for some dick. Since he was my man I wanted to return the favor.

I pulled him up toward me. I almost busted out laughing; his lips were shining like Armor All Tire Shine. Actually, it was kind of cute and a major turn-on. I got on my knees, making my way to his zipper. I slid his chocolate-delight dick through his boxers.

First, I kissed his head, before taking him whole into my mouth. I licked all over his dick like I was sucking on a lollipop. I spit on his dick, lubricating it before it slid down my throat.

When his hand grabbed the back of my head, it turned me on just that much more. My pussy was still leaking as I bobbed up and down on his dick.

"Hmmmm." I gagged, trying to swallow his dick whole. His head was so deep down my throat, tickling my tonsils. My mouth slid up and down his dick, making gooshie sounds. I inserted two of my fingers into my wet pussy, fingering myself while slurping up and down his dick. I felt his veins growing. I knew he was about to bust and my blood flowed through my body as I was about to masturbate on my fingers.

"Ahhhhhh, ahhhhhh," I screamed as I released myself at the same time, nearly choking on his thick, creamy cum. I made sure I didn't waste any seed. I licked and sucked him dry.

CHAPTER FIVE

Sheika

So we were supposed to be closer than sisters, or so I thought. But London's ass was holding out on us. Nay and I always kept it one hundred with that bitch, but she didn't do the same. See, ever since we became friends, this bitch behaved like she was the head of us. My hatred for her was getting stronger by the day, but there's no way I could tell her that. I didn't have no money, and no job. The bitch wore the latest designer clothes, which I could borrow whenever I wanted to, so I kept that bitch close so I could continue using her ass. The shit made me sick when she got to bragging about how much money dude was spending on her. She was careful not to mention his name, which kind of made me suspicious. As close as we were, I knew there was a reason why she was hiding him; and my mission was to find out why.

I knew it was her so-called secret nigga who had called her on the phone. It was a pattern: every time this nigga called, she would find a reason to leave.

"I'll be right back," I said to Nay as soon as London walked off.

"Bitch, I'm going in the house. It's too fucking hot out here. I'll catch up wit' y'all bitches later."

"A'ight, bitch. See ya." I watched as Nay walked off.

I hurriedly walked in the direction London went. I knew she didn't go home so I walked toward the front of the complex. I glimpsed her standing by the entrance, talking on her phone. I stood back so she couldn't see me, but I pushed my head a little so I could see what was going on.

After a few minutes, I saw an orange car pull up. She opened the car door and went inside. I knew that car from somewhere. I tapped my head, trying to remember. I tried breaking my neck to see who the driver was, but the windows were tinted and I couldn't see inside. I watched as they drove off. My heart raced faster as jealousy spewed through my veins.

I took one last look and walked off. Why was it that this bitch lucked out on a nigga with money? I knew for sure she was a ho and she wasn't a good bitch. Niggas kill me with that shit. They will pass up us good girls for bitches they can't even bring home to meet their mamas.

One day, I swore, I was going to get me a nigga with long pockets who was gonna move me out of these fucking projects. *Look at this shit,* I thought as I took a long look at my environment. I was so ready to go. I was tired of living with my motherfucking mama. The bitch got on my damn nerves for real, she and that nigga I despised with everything in me. Something had to give. I thought of going back to school to get a degree in nursing one day.

Something got to give, I thought as I opened the door to the house. I prepared myself mentally to make it from the front door to my room.

CHAPTER SIX

Ajanay

I was tired from smoking all that weed, and Richmond's heat index was 106 degrees today so it made me extra lazy. Man, I love warm weather, but this shit was too damn much. My complexion was getting darker with each day I spent outside.

Instead of going home, I decided to go over to Creighton Court. I really didn't mesh well with Creighton bitches, but my homegirl I went to school with lived there. I parked my car and got out. I saw a bunch of niggas standing by the corner of the first building. I wasn't in the mood to entertain these niggas today. I walked past them without even looking in their direction. I let out a long sigh after I know I was far away from them.

"Yo, shawty," I heard a male's voice holler as I walked to my friend's building. I pretended like I didn't hear, because truthfully I don't answer to "shawty" because that's not my damn name.

"Shawty! Hold up." I heard his yell getting closer to me.

I turned around to see who this stalker was. "May I help you?" I asked with my arms folded and my face balled up. I was kind of careful because these Creighton niggas were known for robbing, and it didn't matter if you were a female or not.

"Damn, shawty, drop the attitude! I've never seen you over here before. Do you live around here?"

"No, I ain't from around here; and let me find out you know everybody who lives over here."

"Well, basically, this my hood, so I try to know everybody who lives here."

I was about to respond, but I heard my friend's voice. "Nay, bitch, you had me scared. I know I saw your car pull up, but I didn't see you."

"I was coming, boo, but this dude got in my way," I said sarcastically.

"Oh, hey, Amir," Melody said.

"What up, B? This yo' peoples?"

"Yes, this my bitch Nay. We went to school together," Melody said in an upbeat mood. I was curious to know why this bitch was cheesing like she had won the lottery.

"Well, Melody, you need to hook me up, 'cause I'm feeling yo' girl." He looked at me and smiled.

"I got you, boo," she said like I wasn't standing there.

"A'ight, yo! Nice to meet you, beautiful, even though you wasn't too friendly."

I smiled but didn't say a word. I looked at Melody for an explanation. "Who the hell is that?"

"That is the one and only Amir." She started cheesing again.

"And who the fuck is he?"

"Bitch, that's the head nigga 'round here. He controls everything that goes on around here. His hands are in every- and anything. That nigga is paid, bitchhhhhhh," she emphasized.

"I don't care nothing about him being paid. A nigga need to come at me correct or don't come at all."

"Well, bitch, I say you freaking crazy 'cause that nigga is the shit; and do you know how many bitches would kill just to have him?"

"It may be so, but I'm Nay, not those other bitches. The shit that impress these hoes don't move me at all."

"I hear you, bitch. Come on, let's go in my apartment. Did you lock your car up?"

"Hell yeah, bitch. I know how they get down over here."

We continued talking as we walked to the mailbox and then to her house. That dude kind of stayed on my mind even though I behaved like I wasn't impressed. I was curious to find out more about him, but I wasn't that kind of chick who chased after dudes. I didn't plan on starting now.

My bitch cooked and we laughed and talked about all kind of bullshit. It was getting dark, so I decided to bounce. I didn't want night to catch me over in Creighton. Yes, I knew I lived in the projects too, but most of those niggas knew me. These two projects were rivals and I didn't want to get caught up in some shit that had nothing to do with me.

Melody walked me halfway and then walked back to her house. I got to my car without incident. I opened my car and was about to get in, when I heard the same voice from earlier.

"See? I was protecting your ride." He smiled.

This time, his white teeth caught my attention. This nigga was black as charcoal, but he had a smooth skin tone. He was dressed in a pair of True Religion jeans with a white wife beater. I wasn't sure what kind of sneakers he was wearing, but he was neatly groomed.

"Hmmm, what do you want?"

"Damn, I love that question. Shawty, I want you."

"First off, my name is not shawty. It's Ajanay," I said in a serious tone.

"My bad, Ajanay. I'm Amir."

I looked at him, wondering what the fuck this nigga wanted from me. "Listen, it's nice to meet you, Amir, but I need to get the fuck from around here. It's dark and I heard a lot of stories about things that take place around here after dark."

"Man, relax. You're out here with me. Trust me, baby girl, no harm can come your way. By the way, where is home?"

I thought about it long and hard before I responded. "Whitcomb Court."

"Oh, okay." He shrugged his shoulder.

"What's that for?"

"Nah, nothing. Anyway, before you go, can I get your number?"

"You shrugged 'cause I said I'm from Whitcomb. So why are still interested in my number?" I quizzed.

"Ha-ha. I see you a smart ass, too. I love that, Ajanay. But I'm pretty sure you already know we'ont fuck with them niggas over there. But I'm interested in you and I ain't worried 'bout no nigga."

"Oh, okay." I wondered if I should give this dude my number. He was cute and kind of intriguing. I blurted it out.

"Gotcha. I'm calling you now." By the time he said that, my phone was ringing.

I pressed ignore and then saved the number in front of him. Everything in me was telling me not to save that damn number, because this nigga could be trouble. But the hardheaded Ajanay was not easily intimidated; and it was kind of cute how persistent he was.

"A'ight, little mama, get at a nigga and be safe out there."

"Okay," I said. I got in my car and pulled off.

I looked in my rearview mirror and saw he was still standing there. I brought my attention back to the street and cut my music up. K. Michelle's CD was giving me life right about now. I drove down the street, singing word for word her song "Got Em Like."

I was in a great mood all of sudden and truthfully I had no idea why. I was loving it, though, and could only hope it continued like this.

My phone started ringing. I looked at the caller ID. It was Sheika. "Ay, bitch, what's up?"

"Nada. I thought you was home. Damn, where y'all bitches at?" she quizzed.

"I'm on my way from Creighton and I haven't seen London since she left earlier. Did you call her?"

"Yeah, I called her, but she ain't picking up. You know how she do whenever she's with her secret nigga. Anyway, hit me up when you get over here."

"A'ight." I hung the phone up, but I was a little bit bothered by the way Sheika had been acting toward London. Like she was salty that London had a nigga who kept her laced out. I hadn't mentioned it to London because I knew how her attitude was, and I didn't want them beefing. It was starting to seem more like jealousy on Sheika's end.

CHAPTER SEVEN

London

We chilled for a few hours, just talking about our future. I knew I loved him and wanted to be with him, but seriously I'd seen what my mother went through dating a dope boy. I wasn't ready to deal with all the drama that came with being a dope boy's wifey. He was still pressing the issue about me having his baby. I knew that I couldn't keep lying like this. I just hoped he'd drop the topic soon because I felt shitty lying to him like this.

His phone started ringing. First he ignored it, but it continued ringing. I knew it was either a bitch or a switch because of how persistent the caller was.

"Ay, yo, who dis?" he answered as I lay on his chest. I couldn't hear what the person on the other end was saying, but I heard Keon. "How much you tryin'a get? And, what, you need it now? A'ight, I'm on the way."

I knew then our chill time was over. I loved spending time with him, but I'd been with him long enough to know that whenever business calls came in, it was time to go. I had no problem with that, 'cause money over bullshit was my motto.

"A'ight, ma, we need to bounce."

"I already know," I said playfully. I got up and walked to the bathroom. I was going to take a quick shower, but Keon had other plans. He stepped into the shower and behind me. He started kissing my neck while fondling my breasts.

"Aweee," I moaned out, as he woke up my inner desires. I felt his hard dick pressing on my butt cheeks. I took my hand, parted my ass cheeks, then slid his dick into my pussy. I moaned harder as he entered my insides and got straight to handling his business.

I put my hand on the shower walls so I could balance myself. I started throwing this fat ass on him as he held me close to him while matching my rhythm.

"Baby, fuck me," I teased as he took me on an extreme sexual high.

"Shawty, I love you," he yelled out, while he dug deeper into my soul.

"I love you too. Aweeeee, oh, this is good," I screamed out as I exploded all over his dick.

"Aaarghhhhhh." He grabbed me closer and busted all up in me. My body trembled as my sweet juice mixed with his sweet juice. He hugged me for a good minute before letting me go.

After we were done, we washed each other off and got out of the shower. I swore my damn body was tired and I weak, but it was all worth it. It ain't nothing like having good sex with a nigga you're feeling. I talked all that shit, but I swore I loved this nigga.

We got dressed and were out of the hotel. "Man, you drive. A nigga is tired," he said as he threw his car keys to me. He didn't have to tell me twice 'cause I loved driving his car. I'd only gotten my license about a month ago, but the way I was whupping this Charger, you would've thought I'd been driving for years.

It was dark so I was more careful. I didn't want us to get pulled over, because his ass was always driving dirty.

"Where we going?"

"Hold up." He scrolled through his phone and then gave me the address. I realized that it was a south-side address. It kind of surprised me, because the east-end niggas didn't really do business with south-side niggas.

Oh, well. I guess he rock with some south-side niggas too.

Plies was blasting as I drove to the south. Keon was laidback in his seat and on his phone. I knew he had a Facebook page, but we weren't friends on there. I used to feel some kind of way about that, but I soon dismissed those feelings. I wasn't worried about nothing for real. I was going to keep playing my position.

I pulled on the street, and drove to the address on Warwick Road. I started having a really bad feeling because there was only one streetlight, and that was dim as fuck. "Babe, you sure this where you want to go?"

"Yeah, ma. It's cool."

I wasn't feeling this, but I took his word for it. I pulled over, but I kept the car running. He got on his phone and jumped out of the car. "Pop the trunk, babe," he yelled.

As soon as I bent down to open the trunk, I heard a commotion. Pop! Pop! Pop! Gunshots rang out in the air.

I tried to see what was going on, but I had to duck. I started praying fast. *I need to get out of here,* was my the first thought. Keon jumped in the car. "Go! Go!" he yelled.

I put my foot on the gas and pulled off as fast as I could. Someone was still firing at the car, but I used everything in me to get off that street.

"Man, I'm hit," I heard him say.

"What! Are you serious? Where at?" I couldn't take my eyes off the road because I wasn't sure that we were not followed.

"In my stomach, I think." His voice was weak.

"Hold on, I'ma get you to the hospital."

We were on the south side so I thought about going to Chippenham Hospital but, shit, MCV was the best. Especially for gunshot wounds.

"Please, God, please help him. I can't lose him, God," I screamed out. "Hold on, babe, I got you."

"Yo, pull over real quick," he said when we got to the James River.

I looked at him like he lost his mind. Nigga was dying and he was talking about pulling over. "Why? No. I'm taking you straight to the hospital."

"Man, I said pull over. You want my ass to go to jail?" he yelled.

I realized this wasn't no joking matter, so I pulled over.

"Here. Take this and throw it over there." He wiped a gun off before he tried to hand it to me.

"What the fuck? I'm not touching that shit."

"Come on, ma, I'm losing lots of blood."

I saw the desperation in his eyes. This was so not like him.

"Here, hold it in this." It was his shirt.

I grabbed the shirt, got out of the car, and walked to the side of the bridge and threw the gun into the water. I jumped back into car with my heart racing a hundred miles per hour. I swear, I'd never done no shit like this before and it kind of had me spooked.

I jumped back into the car and pulled off. I noticed he was passed out. I thought about calling the ambulance, but MCV wasn't that far away. I put my foot on the gas. I believe I was doing damn close to a hundred. I wasn't worried about getting pulled over; my only concern was getting him to the hospital.

I pulled up by the emergency entrance and got out. I ran inside and hollered, "I have someone who was shot."

"Where, ma'am?" a nurse said.

"He's over here, in the car."

I ran back outside and opened his door. Seconds later, nurses and doctors ran outside, one pushing a gurney. I watched in panic as they lifted him up, placed him on the gurney, and pulled him inside. It was then that I finally broke down crying.

"God, please, please don't let him die," I cried out.

"Ma'am, I need to speak with you. The nurse said you're the one who brought the victim in."

"Yes, I did." I continued crying.

"First, what's your name and the victim's name, and how do you know him?"

This nigga was asking a million and one questions while my nigga was fighting for his damn life. "My name is London Evans, his name is Keon, and we're friends. As far as what happened, I have no idea. He was visiting someone and I was in the car. He came in the car and said he was shot; that's all I know."

"What is Keon's last name?"

"I have no idea," I lied. I knew how much Keon hated the fucking police. So there was no way I was going to sit there giving up information on him.

"Ma'am, I hope you're not holding back any information. Your friend is in serious condition and we need your help finding this shooter."

"Officer, no disrespect, but I told you everything. Now I need to go check on my friend." I walked off on him. I know he couldn't hold me and he was pissing me off accusing me of withholding information.

"Ma'am, we're going to hold on to the car, since it's part of the evidence."

My heart sank when he said that. I knew Keon kept work in his trunk. I just hoped he gave it all to the niggas who shot him. I wished I had thought about it at first, but that was the last thing on my mind. I tried to conceal my nervousness.

"Is that all? 'Cause I need to go check on my Keon." I walked off to go ask the nurse if I could speak to a doctor or something. I felt helpless.

While I stood in line waiting my turn to speak to the nurse at the desk, I heard a phone ringing. I knew that wasn't my ringtone so I ignored it. The phone kept ringing right next to me. I turned around to see who was behind me, and that's when it dawned on me that it was Keon's phone ringing.

I stepped out of the line, and looked around to see if that officer was still lurking. I saw the bathroom sign and decided to go inside. I grabbed his phone from inside of my purse. It had four missed calls. I scrolled through to see who it was. There were no names with the numbers so, for all I knew, it could have been anyone. I was nosey as hell, and this was the closest I'd ever gotten to his phone. Before I could start snooping, the phone started ringing again.

"Hello," I answered without thinking.

"Yoooo, who dis?" a rough male voice yelled into the phone.

"This London," I nervously said.

"Where my bro at?"

That's when it hit me that he couldn't know yet what had happened. "Yo' brother got shot."

"Say what? He got what?"

"Your bother got shot and we're down here at MCV."

"Yo, I'm on my way," he said and hung up.

Even though we'd been creeping for all those years, I'd only met his brother a few times. I had not met the rest of his family. He had invited me to their cookouts, but I always found a reason not to go.

I threw the phone back into my purse and washed my face. My eyes were bloodshot and my heart was aching. I needed to know what was going on with him for real. I wiped my face and walked back out into the waiting area.

"Miss Evans?" I heard a nurse calling my name.

"Here I go." I damn well ran over to her.

"The doctor wants to talk to you."

I followed her into a room where a doctor was standing.

"Hello, I'm Dr. Joseph. I heard Keon is your friend and you're the one who brought him in."

Okay, just hurry the fuck up.

"He is in bad shape, but he's in surgery right now. Do you have his next of kin information?"

"No, but his brother is on the way up here."

"Nurse, please let me know when he gets here. Miss Evans, we will keep you updated if there are any changes."

"Thanks." I walked out of the room.

Oh, God, I didn't like what the doctor just said. I was trying to read his facial expression and I didn't feel like he was letting me know the seriousness of Keon's situation. I felt weak in my knees, and felt like I was about to collapse. I looked for the nearest seat and walked over to it. I took a seat and buried my head into my lap for a long time.

"God, please don't take him away from me. Please, God," I cried out. I heard the hospital doors open and I lifted my head. I saw a tall, light-skinned dude walk in. He resembled Keon, down to the way he dressed. I got up and walked over to him.

"Hey, Deon."

"Yo, what's this 'bout my brother? Who the fuck did this?"

"The doctor want to see you," I said.

He looked at me and walked off. A minute later, I saw a light-skinned woman running into the hospital. "Where is my baby?" she asked no one in particular.

"I'm over here, ma. She went to get a doctor for us."

She ran over to her son. I watched as they hugged and consoled each other. I watched as the doctor came out. I tried to make out what he was saying, but I was too far away.

"Noooooooooooo! Oh, my God, noooooooooo! Not my baby, nooooo!" His mother fell to her knees crying.

The doctor and his brother tried to pick her up, but she was not having it. My throat got dry and a lump formed in my stomach. I ran over to them.

"What happened? What did the doctor say?" I asked.

"My brother is gone," his brother said while fighting back tears.

"No, this ain't true. He's not gone." I started hitting on his brother.

"Who the hell is this?" his mother said between her screams.

I really didn't have time to respond. My world was in turmoil and I couldn't think. I felt everything around me spinning. I continued crying. *This can't be,* was all I kept saying to myself. My right hand, the nigga who made sure I was straight, was dead? This was not true and there was no way I was going to accept this.

"Shawty, I need to holla at you." His brother tapped me on the shoulder.

I looked up at him with tears and pleas of desperation. I didn't want to move from where I was.

"Come on, let's talk out here." He extended his arm to me.

I got to my feet and fell into his arms. This stranger held me tight and rubbed my back. I swear I needed this. I needed to know I was not alone. We walked outside of the hospital and away from the entrance. I no longer saw his mother and I wondered where she was.

We found a bench and I took a seat. "Yo, B, what happened to my brother, was you with him?"

I wiped the tears that continued to flow and I wiped my nose. "We were at the hotel together, chilling." More tears started coming down as I remembered how happy I was just hours ago. "He got a phone call from somebody. I couldn't hear what the other person was saying, but Keon told whoever it was that he was on the way." I paused. I was trying to gather my thoughts so I could tell him every bit of detail.

"He asked me to take him over to the south side, I put the address in the GPS. It was over by Warwick. But when I got on the street, I got nervous. I got this feeling." I paused as I recalled the feeling I had.

"What kind of feeling?" I could tell he was gripping on to every single word that I was saying to him.

"The lights were dim, like someone knocked out the streetlights. The address was at the end of the street. I told your brother that I didn't like it, but he said it was cool. I pulled over, and he jumped out. He asked me to pop the trunk and I did. It was dark so I couldn't see anyone. I heard a commotion. I heard your brother yelling then gunshots rang out. Your brother jumped in the car and told me to drive. I pulled off, but somebody was still firing at us."

"Did he say anything to you?"

"Nah, only to stop so he could get rid of his gun. After that he was passed out."

"Man, I put this on my motherfucking seed: I'ma kill all these pussy-ass niggas. I know they set my brother up. I told him to stop fucking wit' these lame-ass south-side niggas. Now they done took my fucking nigga." His voice trembled as he talked, but his words sent chills through my body.

"This can't be real. Oh, I got his phone. He told me not to give it to anybody. But I'm giving it to you. The call he got is in there. It was around eight p.m." I dug into my purse and took out the phone. I hesitated at first, because I felt like I was giving away the one thing that he left with me. I finally shoved it into Deon's hand.

"Good looking out. Listen, I'm 'bout to check on my moms and make some phone calls. Take my number and call me if you need anything." He stepped toward me and gave me a hug. I hugged him as the tears continued flowing.

I pulled up the Uber app on my phone and requested a ride. I didn't want to leave the hospital, but there was no need to hang around. My head was pounding and I was exhausted. This was too much for me to bear and I couldn't deal with it alone.

As soon as I got in the house, I crashed on the sofa. Being by myself was not helping. I kept seeing Keon's face in my head. His smell was fresh in the air, even though he had never been in my apartment. I felt like I was losing my sanity. This life was not fair at all.

I got up and walked into the kitchen and searched around for the bottle of Malibu Caribbean Rum that I had. I opened the bottle and took it to my head. "Nooooo! Keon, baby, how could you leave me? I love youuuuuuuuuuuuuuu," I screamed. I threw the bottle into the mirror in the living room, shattering glass everywhere. I didn't give a damn about breaking shit, because I was broken into a million pieces.

I got up and cut on my Adele CD, putting "Hello" on repeat. I lay on my back on the carpet just crying my heart out! I kept hoping this was a nightmare that I would wake up from.

CHAPTER EIGHT

Ajanay

Ol' boy was on my mind a lot, which was crazy because I wasn't into Creighton niggas. But there was something about his swagged-out attitude that kind of drew me to him. I knew it was early, but I still dialed Melody's number.

"Bitch, either you're in jail or you dying, 'cause it's only seven in the morning."

"I know, boo, but I couldn't sleep. I got a question for you, though. Is ol' boy stingy with money? And how many bitches he got?"

"Bitch, let me find out the nigga got you wide open and you ain't even get the dick." She busted out laughing.

"Bitch, you know I don't even be on niggas like that, but since ol' boy pursued me, I decided to see what's good with him."

"Well, you know he a dope boy. Matter of fact, he the head nigga in charge of most dope that is in Richmond. He got his hands in everything, legal and illegal. As far as bitches, what dope boy don't have bitches? I don't think you should worry 'bout no other hoes. Shit, you trying to fuck with him and not them hoes."

"True dat. I think I'ma holla at him today and see what he talkin' 'bout."

"Uh-huh; and, bitch, please don't forget we're friends so when this nigga start lacing you, please look out for your bitch."

"I got you, boo, you know how we roll."

"A'ight, I'ma bring my ass back to bed. These kids still over their daddy house so I got a little free time."

"A'ight, boo, talk to you later."

I hung the phone up and lay on my stomach, trying to come up with the perfect plan. I had to figure out a way to get into this nigga's pocket without falling for him. I done fucked a few dope boys before, so I was familiar with how they rolled. I also heard some gruesome shit about Amir's ass, so I knew I was in a bigger, more dangerous league. That was cool, though, because I was a dangerous bitch also, only with a smoothness.

It was kind of strange that I hadn't heard from my bitch London all night. No matter what, me and this bitch stayed on the phone all night sometimes, just gossiping about niggas or other bitches. I remembered the last time I saw her yesterday was when she got a call and left. I grabbed my phone and called her. The phone rang over ten times and I got no answer.

That bitch might still be laid up with that nigga. I knew she told me he was a dope boy, and I kind of suspected it was Keon, because I saw the way he looked at her whenever we'd be outside hanging and he would come around the way. Sheika thought it was fucked up that she was keeping her relationship a secret, but I didn't. Shit, it was her pussy and I believed she would tell us when she was ready.

I hung up and dialed her number again, but there was still no response. *Hmmm, that's strange.*

I got up, and took a quick shower. The summer weather was already hot, so I put on a little pair of booty shorts with a wife beater and flip-flops. I grabbed my phone and my purse. I got into my car and drove around the corner to her house. I rang the doorbell and waited. There was no response. I started banging on the door.

"Bitch, what the hell wrong with you?" London opened up her door and said.

I wasn't worried about what she just said. I was shocked at her appearance. My beautiful friend was looking like a ragdoll that had been to hell and back.

"What is going on, bitch? You all right?" I pushed past her and walked into her house.

She looked at me and started to cry. Hell no, something was wrong with my bitch and somebody was about to pay.

"What you crying for? What happened to you?" I stepped closer and hugged her. She collapsed in my arms, almost pulling both of us to the floor. "Man, talk to me. You making me scared," I said.

"They killed him. They killed my boo," she cried out in anguish.

"Baby, killed who? What are you talkin' about?"

"Keon. They killed him, Nay. I was there with him."

"London, talk to me. You're not making sense. What happened?"

"I took him over to the south side and the niggas robbed him and killed him."

"Oh, my God. You talking about Keon from 'round here?"

"Yes. They took my baby away from me. I just want to die, Nay," she cried.

I was feeling my friend's pain because I started crying too. I didn't know Keon that well; I just knew that he was one of Whitcomb Court's big niggas. My suspicion of her fooling around with him was confirmed, but it was too late, 'cause the nigga was gone.

"Come sit down, boo," I said as I helped her to the couch and rested her head on my chest.

"I need him, Nay. I swear, they should've killed me too."

"You better stop talking like that. I can't lose you. You my sissy, you hear me?"

She didn't respond; she just kept crying. I tried to be strong for her, but it was hard to sit back and see my bitch hurting like this.

I sat with London for a while, just consoling her and telling her it was going to be okay. I wasn't sure it was going to be, because I had no idea how strong her love for him was. Their relationship was a secret, so I only knew what she was telling me today. I had some weed, so I rolled two blunts for us. I knew she was hurting and the weed would mellow her out a little. We smoked and I sat there listening to her cry, laugh, and cry some more. Eventually, she fell out on the couch. I sat there looking at my once vibrant friend, and she was looking so frail and broken.

After I made sure she was asleep, I took my time and got up. I got a blanket and threw it on her; then I locked the door behind me. I was hurting for my bitch and I wished I could do something to help her. I felt sorry for Keon's family, also. I knew there was going to be bloodshed all over this damn city. Keon and his crew were known to be deadly. Both the police and the rival gangs knew they were not to be fucked with.

I needed something to take my mind off everything that had happened with my girl. I scrolled through my phone and dialed Amir's number. "Yoooo," he answered the phone.

"Hello." I put on my extra sexy voice.

"Hey, babe, I thought you forgot about a nigga." He chuckled.

"Nah, just been busy with school, you know?"

"Oh, you in school? I love that: a beautiful, educated woman." His smooth voice echoed in my ear.

"Why you say that like you shocked?" I asked playfully.

"Nah, it ain't that. Just most the chicks I know don't want nothing but to drink, smoke, and fuck."

"Hmm, well, you need to branch out from what you know," I said sarcastically.

"That's what I'm doing now. I'm trying to see what's up with you, queen."

"I hear you. So do you want to do lunch today?"

"Hell yeah! Lemme handle some business; then we can link up."

"All right, cool. Text me when you finish."

As soon as I walked into my house, I ran to my closet. I hadn't been on a date in a while. I was excited to be in the company of a real nigga with money. Shit, I found a brand new minidress that I bought off Angel Brinks's Web site. I decided to wear that along with my Michael Kors open-toe heels. I wanted to look nice and elegant. The plan was to blow this hood nigga's mind.

My mind was on London; I hoped she was all right. I hated that she was hurting like that. *After this date, I will swing by and check on her again.* I dialed Sheika's number.

"*Hola,* bishhh," she said playfully.

"Hey, boo, did you hear what happened?"

"What you talking 'bout?"

"They killed Keon last night."

"What you talking about? You talking 'bout Keon from Deforrest Street?"

"Yup. That's him."

"Bitch, you lying? I ain't been out all day, but I would've heard about that shit."

"I'm for real and London was with him."

"Say what? Was she hurt?"

"Nah, she's not hurt. Well, not physically. But she is fucked up over it. I just left her at the house, 'sleep. If you have time, you might want to swing over there and check on her."

"Damn, that's fucked up. What was her ass doing with him anyway? She know them niggas stay in some bullshit. That was dumb on her part for real."

I was irritated as fuck that Sheika was being so judgmental. This was our bitch we were talking about and, instead of her showing empathy, she was being a bitch for real.

"Well, Sheika, she's always been there for us whenever we go through our bullshit, so it's only fair that we do the same for her. I got to go, but I'll call you later." I hurried and got her off the phone.

One thing I didn't like was a negative-ass bitch. *Sheika better check herself before she get fucked up for real. I've been trying to ignore her little slick-ass comments against London, but if she continues I will have to let London know.*

I made sure I bathed, washed my pussy good, and douched. I didn't plan on doing anything with this nigga, but you know stiff dick has no conscience. I got dressed and put on my heels. I took one last glance in the mirror and smiled. I knew a bad bitch when I saw one, and this chick right here was a bad bitch.

We decided to meet instead of him coming around the way. Whitcomb and Creighton niggas had major beef and no outside niggas were allowed up in here. He took me to the little Jamaican spot on Broad Street. This wasn't my first time eating there and, I swear, their food was on point as always. As I sat eating, I couldn't help but admire him. He wasn't the cutest nigga I'd fooled around with, but money made him pretty as fuck. His arrogance was a little over the edge, but it wasn't nothing I couldn't deal with.

"Damn, B, you sexy as fuck," he said as he walked behind me when we left the restaurant.

"Am I?" I stopped and turned around.

"Yes, you are. Have a nigga fienin' for yo' ass."

"Uh-huh, well, if you play your cards right you might just get some of this ass." I touched his face with my hand.

"Come on, shawty, come chill wit' a nigga for a little while."

I thought about saying no, but I wasn't into playing games. I wanted to cuff this nigga, and pretending like I didn't want him wasn't going to help at all. "Okay, so which telly we going to?" I quizzed.

"Telly? Nah, fuck that. I'm taking you to the crib."

"Oh, okay. I feel kind of special right now."

"You can leave your car and get in my car. I'll bring you back later to pick it up."

"Okay, that's fine with me." I locked my car up and got into his car.

"So, Miss Ajanay, what are you studying in school?"

"Psychology."

"Nice! A woman with beauty and brains. Were you born and raised in Whitcomb?"

"Yup," I said as I scrolled down Facebook. There were a lot of RIP posts to Keon. I kind of got sad when my mind flashed back on London. I hoped my girl was all right. I planned on checking on her later.

We got to his crib over on the west end. So this nigga did his dirt in the hood and then went home to his gated community. I watched as he punched in his code then drove through the gate. This was nice for sure. Hopefully, one day I'd be able to live in something like this.

"We here, ma."

He got out and I got out of the car. I was very impressed, but I didn't show it. I remembered when my daddy was big in the game, and we had all that money. Even though we stayed in the hood we had expensive furniture and never wanted for everything. You had to say, "I was born into this life, so it's only fair that I continue living like this."

He punched in another code and we entered his condo. I stepped inside and was more wowed by the size of the inside. It was a baby mansion with nice furniture and a nice decor.

"Make yo'self comfortable. Do you drink?"

"Yeah, I drink. What you got?"

"Come see for yo'self."

I walked over to the minibar he had, and it was like a miniature liquor store. Everything that you could think of was there. *Hmmm, this is hard for me to decide.* "Let me get some that Cîroc Apple."

"Got you." He grabbed the bottle of Henny for himself.

After we got drinks, we went into his den, which had a sixty-inch TV along with a music system.

"So, do you do this often?"

"Do what?" he asked.

"Go on dates with women and bring them home?"

"Ha-ha, nah, only special women come up in here. Plus, you know, with my business I got to be careful who I bring 'round here."

"I hear you." I wasn't buying none of that shit, but that wasn't really my concern. I was only concerned about this nigga's pockets and what it was hitting for.

We started drinking and we smoked a few blunts together. The alcohol was definitely taking its toll on my mental and my physical form. My pussy started tingling and I was feeling horny. I reached over and stared rubbing on his leg. He pulled me closer to him and started massaging my shoulders. His big, masculine hand sent chills through my body. I inched closer so his hand could reach my breast.

His fragrance made me want to melt. Amir continued to massaged my breast in slow motion. "Damn, boy, you got me feeling crazy right now," I said.

"All right, keep it up and I'm going to blow your mind," he said, slapping my ass.

Damn, that shit had my hormones all over the place. I was ready to fuck the shit out of him. He had no idea he was waking up a beast in me. "Whatever."

"Whatever what?" he whispered in my ear, branding his hard dick against my ass. My body got so hot I was frozen in one spot.

"That's what I thought," he said, kissing inside my ear.

I had to take a deep breath, but my body was still stuck in a trance. Amir cupped my breast and ran his lips across my ears and on the backside of my neck. My body wanted to melt right there and then. His other hand traveled under my dress and under my panties until his fingers found my wetness. Shit, I didn't know what he was doing to me but, whatever it was, I was loving every second of it. My pussy had its own heartbeat, thumping for attention. Amir inserted two figures into my wetness while kissing on my neck. That shit nearly drove me up the wall.

"Hmmmm," I groaned. My body was on fire. I thought I was going to pass out from his gentle touch and passionate kisses. "Amir, I'm ready to feel you up inside of me." Fuck all this foreplay. I was ready for him to fill up my insides.

"Say no more." He removed his fingers from my wetness and stuck them in his mouth. "Damn, you taste so good." He licked off my juices and gently took my dress off. His stiff, hard dick was poking me in my lower back.

I stepped out of my panties and tooted my ass up on the couch. "Damn, your pussy is pretty and phat," he said as he dropped to his knees, kissing my plump pussy lips.

"Kiss me where you miss me." I spread my legs and arched my ass up higher. Amir spread my cheeks. I felt a cool breeze blowing on my pussy. "Yes, Lord." I closed my eyes, savoring the moment.

His tongue drove deep into my love box, sending chills through my body. I rocked my body back and forth as his tongue penetrated my pussy. "Amir, dammit, man," I screamed out as his tongue worked magic inside my treasure box. "Shitttt," I screamed. My knees started to buckle as my juices flowed between my legs. "Hummm." I tried to catch my breath and gather myself before Amir's dick slid into my love box from behind. I had to take a deep breath. But quickly I realized that I didn't need to. After the high I was on a few minutes ago, I noticed that I wasn't really feeling anything. I threw my ass back on his dick, but it still wasn't hitting.

"Damn, babe, I know you feel this anaconda up in there," he said between his fast breaths.

Really? Do this nigga really think that this little-ass dick is hitting something?

"Is it good, babe? This is the best you had. I know them wack-ass niggas over where you live can't put it down like this." He tried ramming me.

"Yes, baby, they sure can't," I managed to say.

This nigga was really tripping. I knew my pussy wasn't that damn big. "Aargh, this some good pussy, bitch. I fucking want this pussy," he said as he continued doing not a damn thing.

"Yes, it's yours, daddy." I rolled my eyes as I thought about my last nigga, Junie, Junie was a dog, but that nigga knew how to beat the pussy up. I started to get wet and started twerking my ass, as I pretended that it was Junie beating the pussy up.

"Aarghhhhh, I'm about to bust."

As soon as I heard that, I tried to get up from under that nigga, but that nigga pinned me under him. He remained inside and busted all up in me. "Damn, nigga, what you did that for?" I yelled.

"Damn, I'm sorry, ma, but your pussy is too good to pull out. Are you on the pill?"

"Nah, I ain't on the damn pill. Yo' ass should've just pulled out."

"Listen, ma, if you get pregnant, trust me, my seed ain't gon' want for nothing; and, shit, if you need abortion money, I got you."

"Boy, whatever. I don't even know you."

"Shiiittt, you know me enough to let me run up in you without a condom."

"Really? Well, I guess we both nasty then, 'cause you was just eating my pussy without even knowing if I washed that shit. For all you know I could be a nasty bitch," I spat back.

"Listen, ma, I didn't mean to come off like that. I hope you don't get pregnant, but if you do, just know a nigga got you."

"All right," I squeezed out. I was still kind of irritated with this little-dick nigga who felt like he could talk to me crazy. I really wanted to snap on his ass, but I humbled myself.

He walked off, then came back with a towel and wash-cloth. "Here go a towel and washcloth. Bathroom is on your left."

I took them and walked off to the bathroom. I was happy to be out of his sight for a few minutes. I shook my head in disgust. I still couldn't believe this macho-ass nigga couldn't even service my pussy right. I got into the shower and soaped my ass up, then inserted my fingers inside of my pussy. I started grinding and twerking on my fingers. There was so much built-up cum in me that, after a few minutes, I exploded all over my fingers. "Aweee," I moaned out with excitement as I licked the cum off my fingers.

This nigga couldn't fuck me the right way, so I had to fuck myself good. I chuckled as I remember what that nigga was saying to me while we fucked. I washed myself off and then got out. I walked out into the living room where he was.

"Damn, shawty, you sexy as fuck."

"Thank you." I smiled.

After chilling with me for a few more hours, I decided to bounce. The conversation with this nigga was getting wack. All he kept talking about was how much money he made, and how big he was in these streets. I was sitting there entertaining him until he started rapping about Whitcomb Court niggas. I wasn't trying to hear all that shit because these were niggas I grew up with. I kind of questioned his motives in my mind. Did he really like me, or did he know I was from over there and he was using me to give him information? There was no way for me to find out now, but I was going to holla at my girl tomorrow to see what she knew.

"Hey, I'm ready to go. Can you drop me off?"

"Damn, ma, I thought we were spending the night together."

"Sorry, boo, maybe next time. I got class early in the morning and I got to do some homework."

"Oh, okay, that's cool. Just hit me up after class and we can hang."

"Okay, gotcha."

I got dressed and we got into his car and left. He was being his usual chatty self, and I was busy browsing the Internet. Every once in a while I would smile at him, or say a few words so he could think I was listening. He dropped me off, and I got into my car and pulled off.

Whew, I was happy to be back in my car and out of this nigga's way. Damn, that was one bragging-ass nigga. It'd only been a few hours and I knew more about this nigga than a nigga I'd known for a lifetime.

I dialed London's number, but her phone kept going to voicemail. I was worried about her, but I figured maybe she wanted her space. London was the type who liked to deal with stuff her way. She'd been through so much; I just wished this wouldn't push her over the edge.

It was still early and I didn't feel like going in the house to do nothing. I dialed Sheika's number.

"Hello," she answered on the first ring.

"Where you at?"

"Sitting out here in front of my building."

"All right, I'm pulling up in a few."

I hung the phone up and turned on Sheika's street. I got out of the car and walked over to her building. I saw a bunch of Keon's niggas sitting around and talking. I know the hood was in mourning because that nigga looked out for his hood.

"What's up, bitch?"

"Nothing, just sitting out here, trying to get some damn air. My AC broke earlier and it's hot as fuck up in there."

"Damn, I can imagine. Did you go check on London?"

"Nah, 'cause I'm kind of mad because we supposed to be her bitch, and she been fucking wit' this nigga and kept it a secret all this time."

"Sheika, are you freaking serious right now? She supposed to be our motherfucking bitch and she going through a rough time and all you can think about is some bullshit? Yo, what's the real deal? Why are you so angry with London?" I decided to stop beating around the bush.

"What do you mean? Ain't no real deal and I'm not angry. I just don't think that London rock wit' us the way that we rock wit' her. I think she's selfish and only care about herself."

"Wow! This chick looks out for us all the damn time. Even when dude was lacing her with dough she was looking out for us, especially you. I can't believe that you're saying this."

"Listen, Nay, I love you to death and I fuck with London. I was just telling you how I feel."

"I just feel like we ain't got nobody but us. We've been there for one another way too long to let some bullshit come between us. That's what separate us from these other bitches is the fact that we keep it one hundred with each other, no matter what. Y'all are family to me and I would hate if we split up for real."

"Damn, bitch, who the fuck you think you is, Sojourner Truth? You just gave a whole damn speech." We both busted out laughing.

"Just call me the hood messenger. But I'm serious. We better than this."

"I hear you. Anyway, where you been? I went to the house earlier and yo' car was gone."

"Bitch, I was out getting fucked. Well, kind of fucked."

"What the hell you mean, kind of getting fucked? Either you were getting fucked or you weren't."

"The head was on point, but that dick was garbage."

"Oh, okay, one of those."

"Man, that nigga tongue was sharp as a brand new razor, but once he pushed that dick inside of me, that shit blew my damn high. I can't believe a boss nigga like that has that little-ass dick for real."

"Who the fuck is he, so I can clown his ass? That nigga know better than that to put that shit inside of you. We'ont want no little teeny-weeny-dick nigga 'round here."

"Bitch, you'ont know him."

"Oh, okay, so it was an outside nigga. That make it even worse. The niggas around here be packing that big dick."

"How the fuck you know that and you claim you like pussy and don't do niggas? Let me find out you like dick and pussy."

"Nah, bitch, I'ont do no nasty-ass dick. I'm strictly pussy. But I hear a lot of bitches talking."

"Oh, okay, 'cause I was goin' tell you that ain't no shame if you like both." I busted out laughing. I knew this ho was lying, and I knew for a fact that she got some dick before, but she was my nigga so I wouldn't pull her up on her bullshit. We continued laughing and talking, about all kinds of stupid shit.

Blap! Blap! Blap! We both dropped to the ground on our bellies.

"Oh, my God, they shooting. Get the kids," I heard this chick named Jina holler.

"Is your door open?" I hollered to Sheika.

"Yes, it is, but we can't move."

I started praying really fast. There was no way that I was just gonna lie out here and get killed. "God, please protect us," I cried out while I covered my ears, trying to block out the sounds of gunshots. It was so loud it seemed like there was a full-blown war taking place in our projects.

Suddenly the gunshots stopped and I heard police sirens everywhere. I knew whatever just happened wasn't good.

"You okay, Sheika?"

"Hell yeah, I'm good. What the fuck was that? I just hope ain't nobody hit."

"This shit got to stop for real. This can't be life for real."

The police sirens got louder and I knew then that whoever was shooting was gone. Whenever the police came through the projects, it be like a ghost town. I stood up and Sheika did too.

"Man, we need to get out of this place. Ain't nothing in these projects but death and prison. These niggas don't even give a fuck it be kids and people outside," said Sheika.

"Girl, I'm about to get out of here. I'll call you tomorrow."

"Nah, let me walk you. The police are here now, so they ain't gon' act out."

We hurriedly walked past what seemed like the entire Richmond police force.

"Bitch, first they kill Keon and now this?"

I didn't respond; instead, I ran to my car. My motherfucking baby that I saved up to buy, my used 2015 Magnum, was riddled with bullet holes. My glass was shattered. I fell to my knees and started hollering.

"What the fuck? Who did this?" Sheika said once she realized what I was looking at.

"I don't have no fucking idea, but I'm going to motherfucking find out and, when I do, one of these fuck niggas gonna pay for my shit." I was livid. I saved all my fucking money that I made when I was working at the nursing home, just so I could have a fucking car.

"I'm sorry, girl."

"Man, fuck all that. Where the fucking police at?" I looked around to see where the hell they were.

"You not serious, are you? You know they gon' be mad if you report that shit to the police."

"You think I'm worried about what these fucking niggas think? They fucked my shit up and disappeared. Who the fuck you think gonna have to pay for this shit? Me, that's who," I snapped at this bitch.

"I'm sorry, boo, I just don't want no harm to come to you."

This dumb-ass bitch was really pissing me off. "You know what? I'm about to go for real." Tears filled my eyes as I walked off. I had no idea where I was going to get the money to fix my shit. I was hating all these fuck niggas right now.

CHAPTER NINE

Sheika

Lord knows, I was tired of these bitch snapping and shit. I mean, this bitch Nay was behaving like it was me who fucked her shit up. Shit, it might have been the nigga she just finished fucking. What did she expect, though? We lived in the fucking projects and this bitch knew these niggas be shooting and shit. She knew better than to park her shit around here.

I was pissed off after she walked off. I turned around to go back to the house. I saw the police talking to a group of people. I walked slower so I could hear what they were saying. See, nobody knew it, but I would sit among different people and listen to what they were talking about; then I would tell Big Tony and his boys. Big Tony was Keon's partner and they had the projects on lock. He would hit me off with a few dollars.

I heard one of the females mention Big Tony's name and that grabbed my attention. I wanted to get closer, but that would catch the attention of the police. The bitch started talking low as I approached. I rolled my eyes and kept it moving.

I walked into my apartment and locked the door. I quickly snatched up my cell phone.

"Ay, yo, this not a good time," said Big Tony.

"Shit, I know that, but I got some info. I was just walking by and I heard the big red bitch across from me telling something to the peoples. I couldn't hear e'erything, but I heard your name mentioned. She started whispering when I got closer. And don't trust Nay ass. She talking about she gon' talk to the peoples 'cause her car is fucked up."

"You talkin' 'bout your Nay?"

"Yeah. She just got mad 'cause I checked her ass about snitching on y'all."

"A'ight, good looking out. I'll hit you tomorrow. It's hot out here."

After I hung the phone up, I walked to the window to see if they were still talking to the police. These bitches were bold. Didn't they know snitches often get stitches? And then they wonder why motherfuckers be popping up dead in a ditch.

CHAPTER TEN

London

It'd been two damn days since I lost my baby and it seemed like it just happened. Our relationship wasn't perfect. Shit, let me correct that. We didn't even have a relationship. But he was my nigga and I was his bitch, even though we were the only ones who knew this.

I hadn't eaten and, to be honest, food was the last thing on my mind. I still kept replaying the last few hours of his life. I wished I had followed my instinct. Maybe he would still be alive. Keon was hardheaded, because if he had just listened to me—

The ringing of my phone interrupted my thoughts. I didn't want to talk to anyone, but I knew my girls were worried about me. "Hello," I barely whispered into the phone.

"I'm at the front door. Open it."

I didn't want no company, but I knew Nay and I knew she wasn't going to take no for an answer. So I pulled myself off the couch and stumbled to the door. I opened the door and didn't wait; I just walked back to my couch.

"How you feeling, boo?"

"I don't know. I can't stop thinking about Keon. I want him to come back to me."

"I can't say I understand because I don't. But I know time heals all wounds."

"You know, he wasn't my man. To be honest, we were only fucking around, but I loved him and he'd tell me he loved me all the time. He made sure I was straight at all times. They took all that away from me, over what? Over jealousy? These niggas are wack as fuck. They could've just taken the drugs and not shot him." Tears started filling my eyes as I spoke. I tried my best to hide it, but I couldn't control them so I let them flow freely.

"Baby, I don't understand it either, but the police gonna catch them, or you know Keon's people gonna torture them niggas. He is gone, but you're still here and I need you to get it together. Did you eat?"

I shook my head no, because I had no appetite.

"See there you go; you know you have those bad migraines. You need to eat." She got up and walked into the kitchen.

When she came back in, she handed me a Cup Noodles soup. "I know you hurting, but you have to put something on your stomach. Here you go."

I took it from her, because I knew Nay wasn't going to take no for an answer. I didn't realize how famished I was until I started eating. I didn't bother to chew. I swallowed that Cup Noodles like I hadn't eaten in ages.

"Damn, bitch, yo' ass was starving. You can't be doing that."

"I know, right. I just don't have the energy to get up and do anything, you know?"

"I feel you, but you won't be no good to anyone if you not taking care of yourself."

I shook my head, agreeing with what she was saying. "So, you hear anything about Keon death?"

"Nah, everybody tightlipped about the shit, but you know that's how it is. I think people just waiting to see how his brother and them handle his death. I'm pissed off at them niggas anyway," she said.

"Why, what happened?"

"Man, them niggas got to shooting the other day over by Sheika building and shot up my fucking car. Man, that could've been me in the damn car."

"What? Are you fucking serious? So what the fuck they say about it?"

"I ain't seen none of them niggas since."

"That's fucked up. I wonder who they were shooting at."

"I have no fucking idea, but I know if they don't stop they all gonna be in somebody jail or dead."

"Yeah, I agree. Keon always talked about leaving these streets and starting some legit business, but he never got a chance to do it." I was tired of crying and my eyes were sore. I wished this pain would just go away.

We talked for a little while longer, then she bounced. It'd been days since I bathed and, shit, I didn't know if Nay smelled anything, but I sure could. With that said, I jumped my ass into the shower.

Tears flooded my face as memory flooded my mind. The shower was the last place that Keon and I made love. "Man. Oh, how am I gonna get through this?" I asked out loud.

Today was a new day, and I knew I couldn't stay in the bed all day, every day. I wasn't feeling too well. Earlier, I was in the bathroom dry heaving. I guessed days of me not eating was finally catching up to me. I hadn't seen my mother so I decided to go see her. I knew we were not that tight, but whenever I was hurting I could always depend on her to be there.

I was not in the mood to dress up, so I threw on a pair of leggings with a tank top and a pair of flip-flops. I called Uber to take me over to her house because I did not feel like walking in the heat through the hood, or dealing with anyone today.

I got out of the car and noticed Ma was standing in her yard. "Hey, Ma," I greeted her, and gave her a kiss.

"Hey, baby. I was wondering who the fuck this was coming up in my yard. Child, why you look like you been to hell and back?"

"I feel like it, Ma. You remember the boy I told you I was talking to?"

"Yeah, what about him?"

"Well, they killed him the other day."

"Oh, no, baby, what happened?"

"They killed him," I repeated. I didn't want to tell her that I was in the car with him because I didn't want to hear no speech.

"I'm sorry, baby." She threw the broom down and walked over to me. She hugged me tight and I welcomed our closeness. I didn't say anything. I just cried on my mama's shoulder.

"I tell you, baby, ain't nothing in these streets but graves and prison. If I knew then what I know now, I would've never dated your daddy." She finally let me go and we walked into her apartment. We sat on her couch. "You all right? You look a little pale."

"Pale? What you mean? Maybe 'cause I ain't been eating or sleeping."

"Oh, okay." She took one last look at me.

I started feeling dizzy. Maybe it was from all the heat, but I was exhausted. I stood up. I was trying to tell Mama that I was going home, when the walls around me started spinning. "Mama, I don't feel too good," I said as my legs buckled under me and I fell to the ground.

"Hold on, lemme call the ambulance."

"No, Ma, I'm good. I'm gonna call a cab and go home," I said as I tried to pick myself up off the ground.

"Let me help you. You really need to get checked out. I don't like how you look."

"Ma, I'm just tired, that's all," I tried to convince her, as well as myself. Something was terribly wrong and I had no idea what it was.

I should've gone straight home, but instead I stopped at Family Dollar. I grabbed one of those cheap pregnancy tests. There was no possible way I could be pregnant, but something in my mind keep telling me to take the test. I requested Uber again, and headed on home.

As soon as I got into the house, I rushed to the bathroom. I wanted to pee and this was the perfect opportunity. I waited a few minutes then checked the result. Shit, I was nervous, 'cause I knew my ass could not be knocked up. *Wait! What, two lines?* There was no way this was possible. I gathered my thoughts and looked again, hoping for a different result. Tears fell from my eyes when I realized the test was positive.

"Oh, my God. This test is wrong," I blurted out.

I remembered two tests came in the package, but I had to wait until I wanted to pee again. I dried my tears and tried to control my emotions. I decided to make a tuna sandwich, thinking food would make me feel better. Wrong. As soon as I smelled the tuna, it instantly upset my stomach. I started to panic. How could this be possible? I took my pills faithfully, because I knew Keon wanted a baby and I wasn't ready.

"Keon. Oh, my God," I cried out.

Man, my world was falling apart, and I wasn't sure I was ready to handle all this shit that life was throwing my way. I didn't miss a period, so how could I be pregnant? I walked into the kitchen and forced myself to drink a few glasses of water. After thirty minutes, I felt the urge to pee. I rushed to the bathroom to pee on the stick again.

I waited a few minutes, all while praying that this test would be negative. My heart sank into a hole, and my eyes popped open when I noticed it was positive again.

"Noooo! This can't be, God. Keon is gone and now I'm pregnant." *This is some bullshit,* I thought as I collapsed on my bed.

CHAPTER ELEVEN

Ajanay

Amir kept calling me. I was too pissed off about my car to entertain this nigga. That was, until it popped into my head that maybe his ass would help me get my car fixed.

"Hey, babe," I said, sounding extra sad.

"Yo, what's good, shawty? I've been trying to reach you."

"Amir, I know, but I've been going through a lot of shit right now." I busted out crying.

"Damn, shawty, what's going on witcha?"

"The other night, these niggas got to shooting and shot up my car. Now my car in the shop and I don't know how I'ma pay for it."

"Man, say what? You want me to come through?"

"No, I just need my car fixed. That's my one form of transportation." I cried harder.

"Man, cut all the crying out. I got you."

I was beaming with joy inside once I heard those words. "Nah, I'm not asking you to do that. I mean, I don't even know you and shit."

"Man, fuck all that. You my bitch and if I say I got you, then I got you."

"Okay, thank you so much. I swear I will pay you back when I get my school money."

"Man, shawty, chill out with all that. Yo, get dressed. I'm gonna scoop you up."

"All right," I happily said. I really wasn't in the mood to cater to this little-dick nigga but, then again, I needed some more of that fire head. I guessed I'd just have to fake it once again. Shit, if this nigga was going to fix my car, I could damn sure fake a couple orgasms.

I jumped up off the bed and walked into my closet. I wanted to wear something sexy and probably no panties. Tonight I planned on putting this sweet-ass pussy on this nigga. *He ain't going to have no choice but to run that motherfucking money.*

I knew it was risky bringing this nigga around the way, but I didn't give a fuck right now. I needed the money to get my car fixed and I didn't see none of these niggas stepping up to get it done.

I texted him my address and waited. He was standing outside when I walked out. His biceps and triceps stuck out underneath his wife beater. I had to get my mind right, 'cause this nigga was looking kind of good. If I didn't know better, I would have thought he had that good dick with the way he was standing like a real boss.

"Damn, shawty, you make a nigga want to eat you out right now on the top of this car," he joked.

I smiled as I got into his car and he pulled off. I saw a bunch of niggas as we drove down the street. Their asses were staring hard as hell, but his windows were tinted dark so it was impossible to see inside.

I didn't bother to ask where we were going; instead I laid my head back and just listened to Jeezy's latest CD blasting through the speakers. I noticed that he pulled up to the Lexus dealership on Midlothian Turnpike. I had no idea why we were here, and I wasn't concerned. We didn't say much as we walked into the dealership.

"Yo, pick out whatever car you want," he said.

"Huh? Are you talking to me?"

"Come on, shawty, relax. Yeah, I'm talking to you."

He didn't have to say another word! This nigga was definitely winning me over, little dick and all.

I was looking at a few 2016 Lexus on the showroom floor. My heart dropped to my stomach when I saw my dream Lexus. "This is the one." I ran my fingers across the hood to make sure I could feel the fiberglass, and to make sure I wasn't dreaming.

"You sure this the one?" Amir asked.

"Damn right I'm sure, nigga. A bitch knows what she wants," I started to say, but instead I replied, "Yes, daddy, this is the one I want," in my seductive, "go get 'im" tone.

"Okay, let's go find my homie Big Dave," Amir said as we walked to the front reception desk.

"Excuse me, miss, I'm looking for a Mr. David Lomax. He's expecting me."

The receptionist looked at her computer screen, pushing a few buttons. "Okay, you must be Mr. Amir. David left a message for you to remain in his office until he gets back," she said, pointing to an office across the hall.

"Thank you, ma'am," Amir said, guiding me by my hands to Dave's office.

I was excited as hell knowing I didn't have to spend any money. I held on to Amir's hand tight as hell. Right about now I didn't want to let his ass go.

"Shawty, you know I'm diggin' you, right?"

This was kind of hard for me to fake because I wasn't feeling the same way. I mean, he was cool and everything, but he bragged too much and that little dick problem was a big issue for me. "I'm feeling you too, bae," I replied, because it was only right. Y'all bitches don't judge me. Some of y'all will marry a motherfucker if he buys y'all some bootleg Jordans and Michael Kors purses, so don't judge me because I was about to get a brand new Lexus.

Amir got on one knee. *Oh, my God, this shit can't be happening. Damn, this nigga is about to propose to me at a fucking dealership.*

"Just relax and close your eyes, babe," he said and I did as I was told.

What the fuck? I opened my eyes when I felt Amir's hands sliding up my thighs and his hands tugging on my panties.

"Just relax, babe," he said again.

"Amir, how dare you try to fuck me in a fucking office? I thought your ass was going to propose to me," I said.

"Babe, I'm proposing to the pussy." He ripped off my panties. "Will you marry me?" he said to my pussy, digging his face between my legs.

The shit went from bitter to sweet. It really freaked me out and turned me on at the same damn time. I mushed his head away.

"What, babe, you don't want me?"

"If we're going to do it, let's do it the right way." I stood up and walked to Dave's desk. I sat on the desk and lifted my dress. "Now you may kiss the bride." I spread my legs, showing off my neatly trimmed pink pussy.

Amir tongue kissed my pussy and it sent chills through my body. "Fuckkkk," I whispered as I dug my nails into his back. He had my ass on cloud nine. I leaned my head back and my eyes rolled into the back of my head while his tongue made sweet love to my pussy.

"Hold on, babe. I'm about to take you on a flight you'll never forget," Amir said, flipping my legs over his shoulders. I felt my body levitating up in the air.

"Shit, don't drop me." I hugged his head tight, praying he didn't drop my ass. Amir tried to talk, but my pussy had his mouth muffled.

My back was against the wall. My legs were wrapped around his neck and my legs hung over his shoulders.

One of my hands was braced on top of his head and my other hand was braced on the ceiling. I had great balance while Amir had a mouthful of pussy.

"Yessss." I moved my hips to the rhythm of the music his tongue was playing. "Yessss, Amir. Oh, Lord, yes." My breathing got heavier and it was not easy trying to hold my moans. "Oh, God." I felt my body temperature rise as my blood flowed through my body. "Aweeee," I groaned.

A loud knock came from the door. "Fuck," I yelled, but Amir didn't miss a beat and neither did I. My juices flowed through my body and I exploded in his mouth and all over his face. When he came up for air, his mouth reminded me of that "Got Milk" commercial.

It took us a few minutes to get ourselves together and open the door. Dave was standing there just staring at us. We both busted out laughing, even I was feeling like a little kid who got busted for doing some sneaky shit.

"Amir, my man, good to see you." They exchanged daps and a quick hug. "Hello, miss," he turned to me and said.

I smiled at him. I was too embarrassed to really say anything.

"Okay, my man, what can I do for you today?"

Before he could answer, they both walked off in the direction of the showroom. They both came back after a few minutes. "Come on, beautiful. Mr. Amir told me you saw a car that you want."

"Yes, I did." We all walked over to the car that had grabbed my attention when we first walked in. "This the one I want." I pointed to the 2015 Lexus GS.

"The lady got good taste. All right, let me get the keys so you can test drive it, and if she likes it then it's all yours."

"Thank you. Oh, my God, thank you. How am I gonna repay you?" I hugged Amir.

"Well, no thanks needed, but if you insist, we can definitely work something out." He looked at me seductively.

"I got you, daddy." I put my charm on him.

I got the keys and jumped in my new ride. Man, this was the best feeling ever. I'd never driven a brand new car, much less a brand new Lexus. I laid my seat back, checked my mirrors, and pulled off. Damn, this was definitely what's up. I'd always considered myself a boss bitch, so this ride definitely complemented my swag.

After hitting the highway, I turned back around. The ride drove smooth as hell and I was ready to take it home with me. "I see you loving it."

"Hell yeah! Love is an understatement for real." I pulled into the car lot and we got out. Dave walked back over to us.

"So is it a go?"

"Yes, it definitely is a go," I answered.

An hour and a half later, we walked out of the dealership door and I got into my brand new car. I pulled off and Amir pulled off behind me. I knew he was paid, but I didn't know this nigga was balling like that. I know Dave was on his payroll, because this nigga didn't have no legit job but he walked up in a Lexus dealer and walked out with a brand new car. None of this was my concern; I was just happy that this nigga was pussy whupped to the point where he would buy me a car after only getting the pussy twice.

My phone started to ring. I looked at it. It was Amir. "Hey, babe,"

"Pull over at the QuikTrip."

"Okay, got you." I noticed the QuikTrip was coming up on my right, so I turned on my blinker and got into the right lane. I parked and waited for him to pull in. He got out of his car and I got out of my car.

"What's up?" I asked.

"I got some business to handle, but I'll hit you up later so we can chill."

"Okay, cool." I kissed him on his lips while he squeezed my ass.

I got back into my car and pulled off. I couldn't wait to get some music in here so I could come through the hood, blasting it.

I dialed Sheika's number to see where the fuck she was at. "Hey, boo."

"Bitch, where you at?"

"Around the way. About to walk to the store. Why, what's up?"

"Stay right there. I'll be pulling up in a few seconds." I hung up before she could say anything else. I know her overdramatic ass was going to be too excited.

I pulled up right beside her. She stared at the car like she didn't recognize the person who was driving. I honked the horn to grab her attention. "Bitch, it's me. Come on," I yelled after I let the window down.

She bent down to look in; then she busted out laughing. "Bitch, how was I supposed to know it's you? And whose shit is this?" She shot me a suspicious look.

"This my shit, boo."

"Bitch, quit playing. This must belong to the nigga you fucking."

"Girl, I just told your ass this is mine. See? Look for yourself." I handed her the paperwork with my name on it.

Her inquisitive ass carefully examined the document that I pushed into her hand. "Bitch, no way you can afford a brand new 2016 Lexus. So, spill it, you been fucking and sucking to get this?"

"I told you I was fucking with somebody. I told him what happened with my car and he took me to the dealership and bought this."

"That's fucking crazy. Why can't I find a bitch to spend money on me like this?"

"Or a nigga! Bitch, you need to quit fronting like you don't fuck with niggas. A little dick now and then ain't gon' hurt that pussy. Shit, the nigga might love it enough that he might even buy you a house."

"I ain't trippin'. My day gon' come soon."

"Anyways, I can't wait for these bitches around the way to see my new ride. They ass gonna be jealous as shit."

"You already know that. Maybe you should've gotten something a little less flashy, because you know the niggas going to wonder where you got it from."

"I told you a few days ago I'm not worried about no niggas around here. I grew up with these niggas and there are a few of them I rock with, but fuck the rest of these niggas. When it all comes down to it, they ass don't really fuck with us for real. Stop pretending like you don't know that."

She didn't respond. I had no idea why she always went hard for these niggas, and if the bitch was hungry why she couldn't call them niggas. The older we got, I started seeing another side of Sheika that I didn't fucking like. I tried to block out all negative thoughts about my bitch, because she was really pissing me off.

We drove around for a little while; then we grabbed something to eat. My phone started ringing, so I picked it up.

"Ay, babe, it's me. About to head to the crib. You coming through?"

I was about to say no, but the nigga just bought me a car, so I know it wouldn't look good if I turned him down. "Yeah. About to drop my homegirl off and grab a quick shower, and I'll be on my way."

"A'ight, cool. Hit me up when you on the way."

When we hung up, Sheika said, "Hmmm, that must be the nigga with the money."

"Yup, that's bae. I got to go put this pussy on him, show him my appreciation." I busted out laughing.

"Hmmm, just make sure you the only one he fucking. You know how these niggas are, running up in everything with a pussy or, shit, with a ass."

I ignored her comments. I stopped by her building and she got out. "All right, have fun."

I drove off without responding. I parked at my building, got out, and cut my alarm on. I was ready to move out of the projects. I didn't want what happened to my other car to happen to this one.

I took a shower and got dressed. I was on my way to my car when Big Tony stepped out of the cut. "Ay, Nay, what's good witcha?"

"Hey, Big Tony, what's going on?"

"Shit, what's going on wit' you? Lately you seem to not fuck with a nigga. We still cool, right?" he said in a not-so-friendly tone.

I looked at him, trying to analyze the situation. "Why would you say that? I've been busy with school, that's all," I lied.

"Uh-huh. What I hear about you talking to the police and shit 'bout yo' ride? Damn, shawty, you fuck with them niggas now?"

He caught me off guard with that statement. I didn't show that to him, though. "I don't know where you getting your story from, but whatever bitch carrying my name to you, she need to swallow a big dick and die. Why y'all worried about me running to the police? Y'all need to worry 'bout fixing my shit."

I didn't stand around. I walked off on his ass. I was irritated to the core that this nigga would step to me like this. *I ain't no punk bitch and this nigga know it.* Matter of fact, I had my licensed .350 in my apartment. I promise, I had no problem using it on one of these niggas.

I was sick of them and their behavior. Yes, we all grew up together and we were supposed to be cool, but this shit was getting out of hand. People were losing their lives, and these niggas didn't give a fuck for real.

I got into my car and pulled off. I watched in my rearview mirror as the niggas gathered around, probably talking shit about me; but I didn't give a damn about them or what they were saying.

I called Amir's number when I pulled up at his gate. He immediately let me in. I was still irritated, but I hid it well. I planned on having a good evening to show this nigga how grateful I really was. I walked into his house, and he was standing there in a pair of silk shorts, revealing his bare chest. His muscular, well-cut chest was screaming out to me. My pussy was definitely paying attention, but that little thought kept creeping up on me: *little dick.*

"You a'ight, shawty? You went from smiling to sad in one second."

I straightened my face and went back to smiling. "Yeah, I'm good, boo."

"Well, I figured you might be hungry, so I picked up some Red Lobster. No worries; I picked up every dish just in case there's something you don't like."

I followed him into the dining room and, I swear, this nigga was right. There was lobster, fish, hot wings, steak, and chicken on the table. I was in food heaven, like literally. I packed my plate with everything that was on that table. I sat there eating like I was starving for years. This nigga really knew how to treat a woman like a lady. I was seriously considering fucking with this nigga on a long-term basis. After all, dick wasn't everything. I would have to just make sure this nigga ate the pussy on the regular. Maybe I could buy a few toys to please myself on the regular.

After dinner, we started drinking. I wasn't no big drinker, but the Cîroc was good, especially on a full stomach. He was fucked up, 'cause he just kept drinking glass after glass.

He rubbed his hand across my breast. "So, you like yo' new car?"

"Like? Nigga, what? I love that shit. I really do appreciate you."

"A beautiful lady like you deserve a new ride. I was pissed off by what you told me them niggas did to yo' ride."

"Yeah, I'm still pissed off too." I decided to let that conversation go, because Creighton and Whitcomb niggas were rivals and I didn't want to get caught up in their beef, especially now that I was fucking this nigga.

As if this nigga wasn't full off the food we ate, he lifted me up in the air, pinning me on the wall. He dug his head deep inside of my love cave. He gripped on to my clit like a savage beast, sucking the life out of me. My body cringed as I tried to savor the moment. This nigga was a professional at eating pussy and tonight he was not holding back. My knees buckled as I tried to catch my breath. My moans continued to grow loud and intense. I held on to his head as he worked his head to the rhythm of my soaking wet pussy. I wanted the dick bad, and I mean really bad. I was at the point of no return. My veins in my head got larger as I tensed up my body. Orgasm after orgasm took control of me. I shivered inside and then my waterfall exploded. "Ohhhhh," I cried out as I gripped him for support.

He didn't move a muscle; he licked and slurped up every drop of my sweet juice. All that was good, but I wanted the dick. "Please fuck me," I pleaded as he eased me down from the wall.

"I got you, babe," he said with confidence.

The petty side of me wanted to say, "Yeah, right," but I didn't. I was fiening for some dick and his would have to do right now.

He turned me over and eased his dick inside. I placed my legs on his shoulders so he could go in as far as he could. He worked the pussy as I placed my hands on his ass and pulled him in to me. "Damn, shawty, this pussy is so fucking good."

I threw it up on him, as he plunged deeper in. "Aarghhh, I'm about to cum," he yelled as he pulled out.

He held me close, and we lay there for a good five minutes. This time was so much better than the last time.

"Ay, babe, I don't know what your intentions are wit' a nigga, but I'm trying to make you my woman, you dig?"

I remained quiet because I wasn't really looking for a full-time nigga, more like a fuck buddy with benefits. But I didn't know how to tell him at least not so fast. "Okay, I hear you. So are you saying you don't have any other bitch?"

"I'ma keep it one hunnit wit' ya. I got bitches I fuck on the regular, but none I want to be wit'. Can't trust these bitches. But I have a feeling you a thorough broad and I can trust you."

"Well, you're right, you can trust me."

"See, I know you hear shit about me. Some is true and some is made up, but I run these motherfuckin' streets and I can't have no disloyal people 'round me. You feel me?" He looked straight into my eyes.

I could tell he was very serious about what he was saying. I wasn't trying to hear none of that shit. I only cared about him eating my pussy and spending money on me.

It was getting late and I needed to get out of there. "It's late, so I'm going to go."

"Hell nah, you spending the night. I got a new T-shirt that you can put on."

I didn't fight it. I was tired too; plus, it wasn't like I had something to run home to. I took a quick wash off and put on the shirt he gave me. We smoked a few blunts, then called it a night. Shit, this was a feeling I could get used to. He held me in his arms as I laid my tired head down.

I rolled over and noticed Amir was nowhere in the bed or in the room. I grabbed my cell phone and checked the time; it was eight-fifteen. *Damn, I must've been tired as hell if I slept that long.* I wondered where Amir was. I hoped he was fixing us breakfast. That would definitely help push him into the main nigga category.

I logged on to Facebook to see what was new. Same old shit: niggas bragging about how much money they supposedly made, and bitches fronting about who they fucked with. I went over to Keon's page and people were still sharing their stories of him and them. I really felt bad for his family, and especially my girl. I couldn't help but notice that a few bitches were on there, claiming they were his wifey. Old, thirsty-ass bitches. I hurried up and logged off, 'cause this was definitely foolery.

I threw the covers off and got up off the bed. I still didn't see Amir, so I walked out of the room. I walked down the stairs. Before I got on the last couple of stairs, I heard him on the phone. The nosey part of me stopped and leaned my ear against the wall.

"Yo, bro, I'm tellin' you I got this bitch on lock. It's only a matter of time before she starts tellin' me all dem niggas' business."

Nothing couldn't have prepared me for what he said next. "Bro, I'm for real. Man, this bitch in my bed sleeping right now. You know yo' boy put that dick game down the proper way," he bragged.

I rolled my eyes! I was getting angry. So was this a fucking game? This nigga was only using me to get to

Whitcomb niggas? I was so fucking confused, I just wanted to run into the kitchen and address this nigga.

"Yo, dawg, that nigga Keon got everything that was coming to him, trust me. I ain't goin' to rest until I touch all them pussy-hole niggas," he continued to rant.

I knew I had to do something before he caught me on the stairs. I turned to go back upstairs, but not before he said, "I still don't know which bitch was in the car wit' him, but I'ma find out and, when I do, I'ma body that bitch also. Can't leave no loose ends, you feel me, dawg?"

This was too much for me to continue listening. I tiptoed back into the room. I sat on the edge of the bed, trying to digest everything that I heard. This nigga was on some bullshit, and to hear him talk about killing Keon and wanting to kill my girl hurt my heart.

"How long you been up, babe?" He walked up on me and planted a kiss on my neck. The hair on my back stood up immediately and I shivered inside as my palms got sweaty.

I swallowed hard, then responded. "Oh, hey, boo. I just got up."

"Are you okay?"

"Yeah. I have a slight headache from all that drinking last night."

"My bad. I would cook you breakfast, but a nigga can't cook." He laughed.

"That's fine. My stomach feels queasy anyways. I'll grab some hot chocolate from Dunkin' Donuts on my way home."

"Damn, babe. I got some moves to make, but you can come through tonight again."

I didn't respond, but I didn't want him to know that I overheard him on the phone. I felt flabbergasted and I needed to get out of there. I picked up my clothes and started to get dressed. He walked over to me and grabbed my ass. "You sure you good? I didn't beat that pussy up too bad, did I?"

I smiled at him. "Yeah, I'm good."

He walked away and over to a safe that was built into the wall. I turned my head and focused on putting my clothes on. He walked back over to me and handed me some money. "Here you go. Get your hair and nails done. You know a nigga need his lady to be on point."

"Nah, you did enough for me already."

"Chill out, shawty. You my woman now and you got to get used to me spoiling you." He took my hand and shoved the money in my hand.

"Thank you."

After I finished getting dressed, we hugged and he walked me to my car. I was happy to be in my car. I hurriedly locked the car. I sat for a few minutes so I could calm my nerves down a little. I finally pulled off. My thoughts were racing. I needed to let London know what I found out, but if the police were involved they would want to talk to me. Another thing that bothered me was why this nigga chose me out of all people to fuck with. What were his motives?

This nigga was a snake. I thought he was all into me, but the truth was he was trying to get close to me so I could give him inside information on what the Whitcomb niggas were doing. The crazy thing was I wasn't around Whitcomb niggas like that, and I damn sure didn't have any information about what was going on with them.

I needed someone to talk to, but who could I trust? No one for real. I would have to figure out this shit on my own. I remembered that I didn't check how much money he gave me. I grabbed the stack he handed to me. It was $3,000. My eyes lit up. This nigga was really putting on his charm. The smile left my face, though, when I remembered what he was saying to his boy earlier.

CHAPTER TWELVE

London

After a week had passed with me being totally out of touch with everything, I decided to do lunch with my girls. Ever since Keon's death, I hadn't been hanging with them like we used to. I was even more excited to see Nay's brand new Lexus that she'd been telling me about. I was happy for my girl because she deserved that and so much more.

I heard a car honking, so I peeped out the window. *Damn, that bitch was not lying,* I thought as I grabbed my purse and walked out the door.

"Hey, girl," I said as I got into the car.

"Hey, boo. I am so happy that you finally decided to get out of this house. You kind of had me worried, boo."

"Girl, I ain't goin' lie; it's been hard. You know I didn't know how much I loved him until I lost him, Nay. I swear if I could just get one more day to tell him I love him, I would. . . ." My words trailed off. No matter how much I tried to stop the tears, it's like they were right there, ready to fall out.

"Baby, trust me, Keon wasn't no fool, and I'm pretty sure he knew how much you loved him."

"Yeah. I went on his page yesterday and I saw all these bitches claiming how they were with him and all that bullshit."

"Yeah, I saw that shit too, but you know that nigga loved you. Fuck what these hoes saying now. You need to keep the good memories that y'all shared and tune out all that negative shit."

I didn't have a chance to respond because she pulled up to pick up Sheika. She walked out to the car and got into the back seat. "Hey, girl, how you feeling?"

I couldn't believe this bitch really asked me how I was feeling. We lived walking distance from each other and not one time did she stop by to see me. I swore if it weren't for Nay's ass, I would have cut off this old, ungrateful bitch a long time ago. "I'm good," I barely squeezed out.

"Okay, bitches, we haven't done this in a while so let's get some well-deserved pampering. Let's do lunch, then go get mani's and pedi's."

"Damn, I ain't got no money for all that," Sheika said.

"Bitch, you stay broke. You need to start taxing these bitches you keep fucking with," Nay said, but I swear I was thinking the same damn thing.

"Bitch, I don't be fucking with nobody for real 'cause these bitches ain't go money. I am not lucky like y'all to find me a baller."

"That's 'cause yo' ass keep yelling that you're a carpet muncher. Try taking some dick, and yo' ass will get a baller too. Just for the record, I ain't got no baller. I'm just fucking one. Anyway, bitch, I got you."

"Thanks, boo," Sheika said.

After our food came, we started eating and talking about all the gossip that had been going on lately. I ain't going to lie, it felt good to be out there again, even though every once in a while thoughts of Keon crept up on me.

"So when is Keon's funeral?" Nay asked.

"I'm not sure. Gonna call his brother this evening to find out."

"And you, missy, why didn't you tell us Keon was the dude you been messing with?" Sheika asked.

"I didn't tell y'all because, truthfully, we wanted to keep it a secret."

"Secret? I thought we shared everything. Wow! That's crazy."

"Sheika, chill out. London has a right to feel the way she feel. I'm pretty sure we all have stuff that we don't tell each other. Shit, I know I do."

"Nah, Nay, let Sheika tell how she really feel."

"I'ont feel no way. I just think it's fucked up that we supposed to be cool and you kept that a secret. But it's all good."

"But, it's my life and whoever I'm fucking is my damn business," I blurted out. I was super tight; I could feel the veins in my neck standing up. God, I didn't know if it was my hormones or this bitch was just getting on my last nerve. Whichever one it was I was seconds away from jumping my pregnant ass on this damn girl.

"All right, bitches, get out y'all feelings. Sheika, leave it alone, London is dealing with enough as it is. We are here to relax and catch up on the latest news."

I continued eating my food while trying to calm myself down. After we were finished, we paid and left to go to get our sexy on. I tried to avoid Sheika the rest of the day, even though she tried her damnedest to talk to me.

I must've fallen asleep because I felt the car stop, and I quickly opened my eyes. Sheika got out and we pulled off. I let out a long sigh, because I didn't want to be around this bitch much longer.

"Yo, what's going on with that bitch?"

"Girl, I'ont know, but lately she seems to be on some other shit. The other day, Big Tony approached me—"

Before she could finish her sentence, I cut her off. "Approached you about what?"

"Talkin' 'bout I've been acting funny. He also said he heard I was going to talk to the police about them fucking up my car."

"Okay, and is you supposed to be scared? I loved Keon to death, but he knew I couldn't stand that old, Fat Albert–looking nigga Tony."

"I wasn't tripping off that nigga. You know I got my gun. What bothers me is what he said about me going to police. See, you was going through it, so I didn't call you, but I was with Sheika when that shit popped off and she's the only one I said anything to about the police."

"You serious?" I looked at her for confirmation, while I recalled something Keon said to me a few months ago.

"Yeah, I'm serious. I know what I said and who I said it to. Ever since that, I started looking at her differently. I mean, I hate to think our bitch would tell this nigga some shit that we talked about."

"Hmmm. Keon used to tell me all the time to be careful of who I be around because he knew for a fact that one of them wasn't legit. I used to think he was just hating on us. Now that you brought this up, I'm wondering if this bitch been talking behind our backs. Keon used to say her ass wasn't gay like she claimed."

"I don't know if she gay or not, but something don't seem right for real. But until we have proof, we can't really accuse our bitch of being grimy."

"You right," I said, but I was lying. Nay could keep fucking with that bitch, but I was going to feed her ass with a long-handled spoon. "Anyways, I got something to tell you. I didn't want to tell you in front of her."

"What's up?"

"I'm pregnant," I blurted out.

Honk! Honk! Another driver blew the horn at us.

"Damn, bitch, you almost made me crash. You what?"

"You heard me. I am pregnant with Keon's baby."

"That was going to be my next question. Oh, my God, friend. Did he know before he—"

"Before he died? No, I just found out a few days ago."

"Damn, that's fucked up. They took that dude's life before he got a chance to meet his firstborn."

"Girl, I don't know what am going to do. I feel so lost right now. Keon was my source of income. How the fuck am I gonna go to school, work, and take care of a baby? Shit, I can't sell no pussy." I busted out laughing.

"You are a fool; but, on a serious note, you going to be all right. Right now, you need to get through the funeral first. Then worry about what you're going to do."

"Nay, I'm not even sure I want to go. All these bitches . . . I don't want to be part of 'team Keon bitches.' I prefer to stay home and mourn him."

"Bullshit, we're going. Yeah. I am pulling up in this Lexus and we're going to walk up in there with our heads held high."

"Bitch, stop making me laugh. So, enough of me, who is this new nigga who bought you this nice car?"

"It's a nigga I'm fucking. Trust me, he ain't even worth talking about. But you my bitch, so I'ma tell you. It's Amir from Creighton."

"What! Bitch, you lying. Not the nigga Amir?"

"Yup, that's him."

"How the fuck you pull that off? Bitch, you know it's a deadly sin to fuck a Creighton nigga. And the head nigga at that. No wonder these niggas tight with ya."

"Fuck these niggas, but that nigga hollered at me when I was visiting Melody the other day. I was shocked my damn self but, hey, I am a bad bitch, and every trap nigga want a bad bitch on his side. If you can't tell, that's why Keon cuffed your pretty ass."

"Ha-ha. Girl, whatever. But shit, this is good. Just be careful. Can't trust these niggas. I heard he is slimy and don't give a fuck about who he do dirt to."

"Yeah, trust me, I know. I don't plan to be with him for long anyways."

"Well, you know, I support whatever you do."

"Thanks, boo. But, anyways, get yo' pregnant ass out of my ride." She laughed.

"See how bitches act brand new when they get a car? Fuck you, bitch. I'm gone," I joked before I exited her car and she pulled off.

CHAPTER THIRTEEN

Sheika

I saw our friendship coming to an end really soon. These bitches always had something smart to say to me, not knowing I would fuck up not one but both of them bitches. The only thing Nay had was that gun, but she would have to get it to it first. *As for that bitch London, she'd better pipe down.* Her money tree was gone. Sooner or later, she would realize that she was just another broke bitch like the rest of us. I sure hoped that she saved some of that money that Keon was splurging on her.

After I got out of Nay's car, I called Big Tony to check if he was at his spot. He was there, so instead of going home, I decide to slide through there. I was about to turn on his street, which was adjacent to London's street. I saw Nay's car. So, these bitches dropped me off and now they were sitting out there talking. I bet you that London's old scary ass waited for me to get dropped off before she started talking shit.

I was very tempted to walk over to the car, but I dismissed that idea quickly. I was on a mission to go see my homie and kick it with him for a little. I planned to deal with them bitches at a different time.

I reached the trap where he ground at. I called his phone so he could let me in. I hated coming over here, because in the front he had his workers bagging up crack, and in the kitchen he had a few bitches whupping that powder up. He had offered me a job, numerous times, but I turned him down. I swear to God, as broke as I was, I wasn't about to deal dope. Plus, I was comfortable with the role I played in his life right now.

"Let me in," I said after he answered the phone.

He opened the door and I walked in. "Hey," I greeted him.

"Whaddup, shawty. Looking all sexy and shit." He licked his lips.

I followed him all the way into the back of the house, where he had a big room. He locked the door behind us. My eyes popped open when I saw all the money he had laid out on the table. I knew this nigga had a few dollars, but I didn't know he was balling like that.

"So what's good, shawty?"

"Nothing, just wanted to see what was up with you."

"Well, you know, a nigga just out here grinding and trying to stay out of the way. Yo, did you find out which nigga yo' homegirl fucking with?"

"No. I tried to, but she real tightlipped about the shit. She just said he wasn't from around here."

"Uh-huh. I told yo' ass that I don't trust them bitches. I don't even see why you be around them, 'cause can't you see they don't fuck wit' you like that?"

I stood there thinking about what he was saying. Truth was, I wasn't really listening to him. I was thinking about how I was going to get my hands on some of this money he was flaunting in my face.

"Hey, Tony, how about we get out of here and go to a room? I mean, you're always working and shit. Let me get a few hours with you, throw this pussy on you, daddy." By this time, I'd made my way over to him and was stroking his dick and rubbing on his chest.

"Damn, shawty, I'm grinding right now. I can't leave. Ohhhh," he said as I massaged his balls.

"Please, let's spend some time together, boo. I will make it worth it."

His dick was rock hard, and poking through his Nike sweatpants. "Damn, let me call Boa in here and we can leave."

"Okay, baby." I gave his dick another massage.

He walked out of the room, I guessed to get his boy. I took a glance at all the money. I wouldn't dare touch a dollar because I knew this nigga was deadly, and I wasn't going to lose my life over no money.

A few minutes later, he walked back into the room alongside his homeboy Boa. "You ready, babe?"

"Yeah, I am, daddy."

We walked out of the house and we got into his Hummer truck. I hoped those bitches were gone, because the last thing I needed was for one of them to see me with this nigga. I wished sometimes that I wasn't into bitches more, and that he didn't have a bitch, because I would definitely try to be his bitch so I could get some of that money he had.

"Which hotel you tryin'a go to? You know I can't risk getting seen."

"It's up to you. You the one who has to hide." I started laughing.

"A'ight. I'ma go to the one on Staple Mills Road."

I didn't respond. I didn't care where we went as long as I got to fuck him so I could get some money. He pulled up at the hotel. I waited in the car while he went and paid for the room. A few minutes later, my phone started ringing. "Hello."

"Come on, we in room 112."

"Okay."

The rooms were clean and well kept. I saw this nigga had taste. When I got to the room, he was already out of his clothes, and he only had on his boxers. He looked relaxed, just lying there on his back.

What the fuck? This man was looking scrumptious and at peace. I couldn't help but slide back the white sheets that revealed his oversized stomach. I crawled in bed on my knees, with my chin lined up with his balls.

One thing I loved about my man was that he had swag and was confident with himself. His limp dick was need of my mouth or, in this situation, my suction cup to bring it back to life. I grabbed the base of this dick and kissed the head over and over until his shit was aroused.

"That's what I'm talking about." I spoke to his dick, kissing again for responding so properly. I spat on his dick, leaving it up good so it could slide down my throat with ease. I stretched out my tongue and twirled it around his head, licking every inch of his dick. I wrapped my mouth around his head and toyed with his head with my tongue.

"Hmmmm. Shit," he moaned. His moaning had my pussy on fire. I worked my neck and mouth as if I were creating a new dance. "Ooooo, baby." His fingers wrapped around my neck, assisting the movement of my head.

I sped up my neck motion, taking him down my throat, nearly gagging trying to swallow him whole. His hips were twisting in circular motions. I was sucking his dick so hard until my jawbones started hurting, but that didn't stop me from trying to sucking his seeds out his dick.

"I'm cumming."

I tried to break my neck slaving on his dick. I knew in the morning my ass was going to a have whiplash. "Aweee, shittt."

I didn't have time to spit his shit. Cum was running out of my mouth and down the side of my face. I kissed my way up his chest until I reached his lips.

"Ewww." He moved his mouth.

"Nigga, it's your shit." I went back in for a kiss. We kissed passionately. My panties were still super soaking wet, and my pussy was starving for his dick like we were famished. We both had to have it, and I wanted it bad.

His dick was sticky but it didn't matter because my pussy was wet and my panties were sticky. My pussy was crying out for dick and, after giving him a taste of himself, my hands were back on the base of his dick. I didn't attempt to slide off my panties. I slid them over and stuck his dick on my pussy lips. "Sssss," I moaned out loud as I eased down on his dick.

I placed both hands above his shoulders and leaned over. Tony's hands ripped off my bra, revealing my chocolate milk titties. His wet tongue introduced itself to my dime-sized nipples. "Yesss." I was loving his tongue twirling around my nipples. I ground on his dick, putting my back and ass into it. "Ohhhh, baby." He matched my rhythm while sucking my titties. My hormones were fighting through my body, just like a prisoner wanting freedom.

Our pace sped up and sweat dripped down my face to my chin, and on to his bald head. "Ohhh, Tony. Yess." I popped and locked my pussy on his dick.

"Ride this dick. Dammit, man." Both his hands were squeezing my ass, tugging back and forth. "Yesss, bitch, whose dick is this?"

"Your dick, baby," he panted between moans.

"Yes, daddy, my fucking dick." I ground my hips harder and harder, feeling like I owned the world, making my own porn video. I arched my back, bracing my hands on his knees, and I let him drive me into ecstasy. My eyes rolled into the back of my head as I inhaled and exhaled, breathing easy.

This fat nigga's dick was reaching my soul and I was enjoying every minute of it. I closed my eyes and twerked this pussy on him. I might not have been his bitch, but I bet you when he went home to that bitch he would be thinking about this pussy. That thought alone motivated me to ride this nigga with everything in me. He cuffed my ass and pulled me down onto him. I lowered my head on his chest, pushed my ass up in the air, and rode that dick like my life depended on it.

"Damn, shawty, you know how to make a big nigga feel good," he said in between moans.

All along, I was thinking about how much money to ask him for. I mean, the dick was turnt up and everything, but money was my sole motivation behind this. I was tired of being broke and definitely tired of these bitches dissing me because they had a few dollars.

"Aarghhhh." He gripped me tighter and held me with force. I knew he was coming and I thought about letting him come inside of me, but he threw me off before he exploded in his hands. I saw that nigga was playing no games, and he didn't want to risk coming inside of me.

I got up and went to the bathroom. I took a quick shower so I could wash his scent off me. Not that he was stinking or anything, but ever since I was younger I hated that sex smell. I walked out of the bathroom and grabbed my clothes.

"You good, shawty?"

"Yes. I need some money from you."

"I knew it was coming." He chuckled. "How much do you need?"

"About two thousand."

"Damn, shawty! You taxing a nigga, huh?"

"Not really, but you know it's not cheap to maintain a good pussy," I teased.

"You a trip, you know that? But, shit, yo' ass performed like a beast today. Man, you had my dick thumping," he said.

He went into his pocket and pulled out a knot. My mouth watered as he peeled off some bills and handed them to me. "A'ight, shawty, we got to go."

"Thank you, and I'm ready."

We got back into his truck and he pulled off. I was only too happy to have some money. After he dropped me off, my plan was to jump on the bus and hit the mall. Yup, this pussy got me paid.

"Yo, I got to pick up some blunt at the store real quick," he said as he pulled over at the 7-Eleven. "Do you want something to drink?"

"Nah, I'm good."

He walked off into the store and I logged into my Facebook. Out of the corner of my eye, I saw a cherry red Chrysler 300 pull in and park closely to his truck. I put my head back down to finish scrolling through Facebook.

"Who the fuck are you?" A female voice startled me.

"What, bitch, who are you?"

"Bitch, this is my man's truck and what the fuck are you doing in here?"

That's when it clicked in my head that she was talking about Tony.

"Bitch, why don't you ask him who the fuck I—" Before I could finish my sentence, I felt a slap on my face and this bitch grabbed me by my ponytail, pulling me out of the truck. I tried to get my hair out of this bitch's grip so I could whup this ass real quick.

"Bitch, get the fuck off of me." I used my strength to flip her. That wasn't working, though, and this bitch was hitting me with blow after blow.

"What the hell are you doing, Lashia?" I heard Tony yell out.

"Nigga, fuck you! Who is this bitch? Is this the bitch you been fucking?"

"Nah, I told you I ain't fucking nobody. I swear, baby, I'm faithful to you," this bitch-ass nigga pleaded.

"Man, get this bitch off of me," I yelled to him.

"Bitch, shut up!" he shot back.

I saw this nigga was trying to save face and wasn't going to help me. I sank my teeth into the arm the bitch was holding me with.

"Ohhhh, bitch, I'm gonna kill you. This bitch just bit me," she yelled.

I didn't pay her any mind. Instead, I was fighting for dear life and needed this bitch to let me go.

"Man, get the fuck off her," he yelled. He then grabbed me up. "Let her go now!" he screamed while he applied pressure on me.

Although I was reluctant to do so, I still did it because he was hurting me. He then let me go, and I lunged toward this bitch.

"Yo, shawty, what you doing?"

"Nigga, let me go! You ain't said shit when that bitch was on me." I tried to get past him.

"Nah, let this little bitch go. Let her get this ass whopping like a grown woman."

"That's right, bitch, a grown woman who love fucking your man," I lashed out. At this point, I didn't give two fucks about him or his bitch's feelings.

"What? You was fucking this broken-down bitch?"

"Man, I ain't fucking her. Shawty asked me for a ride and I gave to her. Tell her I ain't fuck you, man," he turned to me and said. He stared at me with the coldest set of eyes. I knew that it would mean trouble for me if I didn't support what he was saying.

"Nah, we ain't fuck." I was pissed as fuck that I had to lie.

"Nigga, you and this bitch must think I'm a fool. I saw your ass when you pulled out of the hotel with the bitch. But it's cool, 'cause I whup that bitch ass and I better not see you with her ass again." She poked him in his face, then walked off.

"Baby, hold on." He followed her like a sick puppy.

I touched my face, which was burning. That stupid bitch scratched my damn face. I swore this bitch only had the upper hand because she grabbed my hair. I looked on the ground and noticed my ponytail sitting there. That infuriated me worse.

"Man, you need to catch a cab to the crib," he said as he hopped into his truck and took off behind the bitch's car.

I hoped that I didn't see anyone I knew, because I would have hated to see this on Facebook. I called Nay's phone.

"Yo, what's up?"

"Hey, Nay. I'm over here on Broad Street and just got in a fight. Can you pick me up?"

"Damn, bitch, I was just about to wash my car, but all right. Text me the number on Broad."

"Thank you."

I stood on the corner, waiting for her to come. I hoped this bitch would hurry the hell up. That's when I remembered my money. My dumb ass forgot that I had a purse. I quickly walked over to where the fight took place, and I spotted my purse. I snatched it up and searched for my money. Thank God, it was all there. I would've been so mad if I had just gotten into all this shit and ended up with nothing.

I heard a horn honk. I looked and realized that it was Nay. I braced myself for all the questions that this nosey bitch was going to ask. I got into the car and she pulled off.

"Yo, what the hell happened? Did you get jumped?"

"Nah, it was one bitch."

"Who the fuck is she?"

"Man, I don't know who the bitch is; and I'm good. I whupped that ass good."

"Damn, did you see your face? So, you telling me some random ho just ran up on you and scratched yo' face up like this? That bitch need to be killed."

"I said I'm good, Nay. You should see that bitch. Her ass is fucked up more than this."

"Oh, okay. 'Cause you know I will bust a bitch in the head real fast."

"I know but, trust me, your girl put a mark on that ass."

"That's what's up, bitch; but you need to put some peroxide on your scratches. That bitch did a number on your face. I swear, I would've killed that bitch if she did that to my face. You know I don't play about my face."

Nay killed me with that conceited shit. That bitch acted like she was the prettiest bitch who walked this earth. "Stop at the dollar store. Let me grab some peroxide."

After the dollar store, she dropped me off at home and I walked inside. I wasted no time. I rushed to the bathroom to look at my face in the mirror. I was shocked and angry all in one. This bitch scratched up my fucking face. That showed that the bitch couldn't fight and had to scratch. I swore I didn't care how Tony's ass felt about it; I was going to fight that bitch again. Tears welled up in my eyes with thoughts of this bitch spreading lies out in the streets that she whooped my ass.

I cleaned up my face, and even though I had plans to go shopping I canceled them. My fucking head was thumping and my body was sore. I decided to take a hot shower and call it a night. Tomorrow was another day, and I swore I was going to deal with that bitch.

CHAPTER FOURTEEN

London

Today was the day that they were laying my baby to rest. Last night, I couldn't sleep because I kept seeing his face in my head. I rubbed my stomach as I put on the black dress that I decided to wear. Oh, how I wished he were here to see his baby when it was born. This fucking life was not fair, I thought as I grabbed my Michael Kors clutch. I swore I wasn't ready, but I had to go.

I called Nay to see if she was ready. She told me she should be pulling up any minute. It was really appreciated that she decided to go along with me. I wasn't ready to face this crowd, and these bitches who were claiming they were fucking with him. Don't get me wrong, he probably was, but I knew what Keon and I shared was very special.

I heard a car horn honking, so I knew that was Nay's ass. My girl did not like waiting for anyone. I walked out and locked the door.

"Hey, boo, you ready?"

I let out a long sigh, then looked at her. "Not really, but what can I do?"

She reached over and rubbed my hand. "Baby, you are stronger than you know. You gonna get through this. We are gonna get through it together."

"Thank you, Nay. I swear, what would I do without you?"

"I don't know, maybe go crazy." She burst out laughing.

"I love you, chick, for real."

"A'ight, bitch, quit wit' all this emotional shit." That was Nay; she hated when I got mushy. In my opinion, I thought she had a soft side up underneath all that tough skin.

"You want to know some funny shit that happened the day before yesterday?"

"What's up?"

"Sheika ass called me saying she needed a ride. At first I didn't feel like picking her up, but then the bitch told me she got to fighting, and you know my nosey ass had go pick her up. Bitch, when she got into the car, her ass was fucked up and her face had scratches all over it. Whoever she got into a fight with tore that ass up."

"Are you serious? So, who did she get to fighting with?"

"Bitch, that's what's crazy. This bitch said it was a random bitch. I know she was lying."

"That shit sound fishy. Any other time she got to fighting she would call one of us. So why is this time so different? What is this bitch hiding? I told you, I don't like the way she's been moving lately."

"I tried to get the information from her, but she insists that she didn't know the bitch who attacked her."

"Hmmm, sound fishy to me. Oh, well, that's her business if she wants to keep it a secret."

I noticed that we were pulling up at Good Shepherd Baptist Church. I started to feel ill, and my stomach got queasy. I tried to coach myself, but it wasn't working. I noticed the line was long as hell. There was every kind of car out here. Mostly cars the dope boys drove. It was like a celebrity was getting buried. But I wasn't surprised at all. Keon was well known in his hood and all around Richmond. Most niggas respected him because of his thoroughness; and the few who didn't fuck with him was all because of jealousy.

"Damn, the hood came out, didn't they? This is beautiful how they showing love to one of their fallen soldiers."

"I'm scared, Nay. I don't know I am going to face him."

Before she could respond, my phone started ringing. I noticed it was Keon's brother. I quickly answered the phone, trying my best to choke back the tears. "Hello."

"Yo, are you here?"

"Yes. We are all the way back here, trying to find a parking space."

"Mama wanted me to get you so you can sit with us."

I was shocked to hear that, because the only time I saw her was at the hospital that day and we didn't even exchange a word. "Okay. I'm in a Lexus. We all the way by the Dumpsters."

"On my way to you."

I said to Nay, "That was Keon's brother. His mother wants him to get me so I can sit with them."

"Go ahead, wifey. Now you see? You were Keon's heart. Even his mama know it."

"Hey, boo, I am going to get out right here so I can go with him. Are you gonna be all right?"

"Go ahead. I'm going to wait to see if I can find a parking space. I'll be in there shortly."

I got out of the car and waved to Deon. When we met up, he grabbed me up in a tight hug. That was when the tears started rolling down my face. I knew it was messing up my makeup, but I did not give a damn.

"You ready?"

We walked past a lot of people I knew from around the way. There were also a lot of strange faces. I peeped a few bitches shooting dirty looks my way, but I didn't entertain them. Today was all about Keon and no one could take that away.

We walked into the packed church. I felt nauseous and my feet felt weak. I stood there as if I couldn't take another step. "Come on, I got you," Deon assured me.

I looked at him and noticed how much he resembled Keon. I also saw a person who was carrying the weight of his brother's death on his shoulders. We walked to the front pew, where his whole family was seated. I saw his casket and started shivering inside. His brother held my hand and led me over to see my baby.

"No, baby! No. Wake up, Keon. The joke is over, baby," I yelled as I rubbed his charcoal skin. The corpse looked nothing like my baby. His face was swollen and his complexion was dark as coal.

"Baby, it's gon' be all right." His mother wrapped her arms around me.

My heart broke all over again. "Wake up, baby, please," I pleaded.

"He is gone, baby. Our baby is gone," she bawled. We hugged and consoled each other.

"Come sit down, y'all," Deon said.

I used everything in me to get to the seat. The tears wouldn't stop. I wanted to tell him how much I loved him. I want to tell him we were finally having the baby he wanted so badly; but I couldn't share the news with my baby because he was gone.

The service started, and the pastor started to preach. I really didn't hear too much of what he was saying. Did he really know Keon? He was kind and gentle and he had a big heart.

You could hear screams and moans all over the church. I looked over at his brother and he just sat there looking spaced out. I rubbed my stomach a few times, trying to calm my nerves a little.

My phone was on vibrate and I felt it vibrating. I checked and it was a message from Nay telling me she was at the back at the church.

I texted back, Okay.

Finally, the preaching was over and it was time to go to the cemetery. One by one we walked out. I was two steps behind his mother and brother. I was looking around for Nay. I stood at the entrance trying to pick her out of the crowd. I was just about to call Nay when I felt someone tap me on the shoulder. Before I could respond, I saw three bitches standing in front of me.

"So you the bitch who's spreading lies about Keon fucking you?"

"Are you fucking serious? Bitch, you know where we are? In case your dumb ass didn't notice, we are at the church trying to bury him!"

"Bitch, I don't give a fuck. You better quit spreading them lies. I was Keon's only woman and I swear I will drag your ass through the mud if you keep on."

"Say what now? You all bitches gonna drag who?" Nay cleared her throat and said.

"Who the fuck are you? Fuck that; you can get it too, bitch," one of the bitches said as she took a step closer to Nay's face.

Man, I couldn't believe this shit was going down like that. I had too much respect for Keon and his family to bring drama to them, especially today. "Listen to me, y'all low-level bitches. This is my man and baby daddy day and I will not disrespect him, but after the funeral y'all bitches can definitely get it. Come on, Nay, these bitches ain't about nothing."

"I swear we gon' see y'all," one bitch said before she walked off with the rest of those bitches following closely behind.

"Who the fuck are these bitches? I swear, funeral or no, I would stomp a hole into these bitches' heads if they ever put a hand on you."

"Girl, fuck them. They ain't nobody. Trust me, I ain't met the bitch yet who put fear in my heart. Let's go so I can say good-bye to my baby."

We took a step off the steps, then the unthinkable happened. Pop, pop, pop, pop. I fell to the ground and pulled Nay down. Gunfire surrounded us. We both held on to each other and I silently prayed to God. It was total chaos. People were running and screaming out for help.

The gunshots were not ceasing. My heart ached for my baby. First they took his life and now they were disrespecting his burial. *When will all this madness end?* I thought as I hugged my friend, hoping we'd make it out alive.

CHAPTER FIFTEEN

Ajanay

This was ridiculous. First we got these old disrespectful bitches rolling up on my girl. I saw when they approached her and I eagerly made my way over to her. See, I didn't have no chill button and, no disrespect to Keon, but if these bitches wanted it they would get the beat down of a lifetime. London did not want that, though, and I respected that. I could tell these bitches were not no threats, but mentally I vowed if we ever bumped into each other again it wouldn't end so nicely.

I heard a pop sound, but I blew it off. That was, until the pop got louder and now it was back to back. It sounded like a war zone as bullets flew everywhere. London pulled me down to the ground with her. These niggas were dead-ass serious. I could tell this was more than gun firing. Bitches were screaming and yelling for help. I wondered where these scary-ass bitches were now. I bet you their asses weren't that damn bad anymore.

After ten minutes of what seemed like war in the Middle East instead of the east end, the gunshots ceased. I heard people start running. I grabbed London's hand and we started running in the direction of where my car was parked. I hoped nothing happened to my car this time.

As we got to the car, London got in. I was about to get in when I heard a car speeding through the parking lot.

My first instinct told me to duck into my car but, before I could, the car flew past me; but not before I got a glimpse of a face in the passenger side. It was a face I was familiar with! *Oh, my God, this nigga can't be serious,* I thought as I hurriedly got into my car.

"You okay? Did you see that car that just flew by?"

"Yeah, I saw that. I swear, this is getting out of hand. Do you know what cemetery they burying him at?"

"Yeah. Let me get the address."

I put on my seat belt and tried to pull off. I heard police sirens and ambulances close by. I knew that someone had to be hurt. There were too many gunshots, unless them niggas were busting blanks.

After twenty minutes, we were able to pull out of the parking lot. I noticed at the entrance of the parking lot, police had a few niggas hemmed up, searching them.

"Slow down; let me see who they got," London said.

I slowed down just enough for her to look. Then I pulled off. I followed the rest of the cars to the cemetery that was over on the south side. It was funny that they killed him on the south side and his final resting place was on the south side.

We got out of the car and walked up to where his grave was. I noticed London was crying again. I knew no words would help soothe her pain, so I just rubbed her back so she could know I was there with her.

As the final song was sung, London started screaming uncontrollably, but she wasn't the only one. Keon's mama and sisters were also screaming.

"No, Keon, please wake up," London screamed.

"I can't let you go. Please, baby, stay with me," his mama screamed as she hung on to the casket.

I preferred not be here right now, because it was a sad-ass scene to see. I did notice that none of Keon's brothers were present, which was kind of strange because they were all at the church earlier.

I managed to get London under control as we walked back to the car. I saw the bitches from earlier, and I thought about running up on them hoes; but, for my girl's sake, I let it ride.

I dropped London off at home and I got out of the car with her for a minute. "I love you, boo. You sure you gonna be all right?" I asked London as I hugged her.

"Love you too; and, yeah, I'm about to lie down real quick."

"Well, you know I'm a phone call away. Hit me up if you need me."

I got back into my car and pulled off. I swear, I needed a blunt. All this shit was too much for me. I stopped by the weed man, Troy, and grabbed me a twenty bag of Loud. I guessed I was going in the house early.

After I rolled the blunt, I poured a glass of wine. I needed something to help me relax. One thing kept coming back to my mind. I knew that it was Amir who I saw in the passenger side of that car. I would never forget those eyes, especially because I stared in them while I was fucking the nigga.

Everyone thought it was south-side niggas who killed Keon, but I knew better. I knew it was Amir and his boys. The thing was, how would I even tell my girl that I was fucking the nigga who killed her man? Also, I wasn't ready to be caught up in no war between the two cliques.

I took two more pulls of the weed as I pondered what I was going to do next. See, that nigga Amir didn't really fuck with me; like he said, he was only using me for information. Since we'd been fucking with each other, he hadn't really come at me with no questions, though, so I had no idea what his intentions were. I was pretty sure he saw me today, because our eyes locked for a quick second before the car he was in sped off.

***

I was at the salon getting my hair done. It was too hot to have my inches in, so I decided to cut my hair off and put a little color in it. As usual, the shop was jumping with gossip. If you wanted to know the latest hood gossip, then this was the place to be.

I overheard two around-the-way girls talking. They were talking about everybody's business, so I went back to scrolling through Facebook while sitting under the dryer.

"Girl, did you hear what happened the other day?"

"Bitch, so much shit done happened, what are you talking about?"

"I heard Tony's wife beat the brakes off that loud-mout' bitch Sheika."

"Bitch, you lying. Which Sheika? Sheika from 'round here?"

"Yes, that same bitch. You know my man be with Tony. Yes, girl, so he said Tony was creepin' wit' Sheika and the wife pull up on them. I heard that bitch didn't even see what was coming at her."

"Girl, I thought that bitch ran around here claiming she do bitches. How the hell she got caught up with a nigga?"

"Bitch, please, these bitches are trysexual," one chick said.

"And what the fuck is that?"

"Ha-ha, you don't know what a trysexual is? A bitch or nigga who try everything: man, woman, dog, horse; you name it, long as the price is right they trying it."

"Bitch, you are very special. I never thought of it like that. But back to this juicy gossip. I can't believe this bitch. How the hell you creepin' wit' somebody man and get beat up? Babyyyy, I would've whupped that ass too. I bet you her ass won't creep with nobody's man no more."

"Uh-huh, that's what I said. I can't wait to see that bitch to laugh in her face. She walks around here like she the shit, but she got dragged."

"Nay, come on," my girl Lexi hollered at me.

I got up from under the dryer and walked over to my stylist's booth. I was still shocked over that earful that I just heard. I knew it had to be true because I saw the scars, and Sheika's ass was reluctant to tell me who the fuck she got into a fight with. That bitch really was fucking with Tony. Now it all made sense. This bitch was running back and telling him our business. Oh, my God, I wanted to call London, but I waited until I left there because I didn't want these bitches up in my business.

I practically ran up out of the salon. In my car, I grabbed my phone and dialed London's number. "Hey, babe," I greeted her when she picked up the phone.

"What's up, bitch?"

"Listen, I was at the shop getting my hair done and two bitches were talking as usual, telling everybody business, and guess what the fuck I heard."

"What, heffa? You know I hate suspense."

"Sheika been fucking with Tony and his woman was the one who beat her ass."

"Bitch, you lying. Sheika fucking that fat nigga?"

"I'm dead-ass serious. Girl, I told you she didn't want to tell me what really happened. Which was suspicious because, any other time, that bitch would want us to come defend her. I can't believe this shit."

"Why can't you? I told yo' ass to quit fucking with this old grimy-ass bitch. Don't get me wrong, I used to rock with her hard, but for the last few months she's been acting really shady toward us. I don't say nothing a lot of times, because she was always your friend and I didn't want it to seem like I was hating on that bitch. But she is jealous and a jealous bitch is a dangerous bitch. Now it all make sense how that nigga knew what the fuck you said. Only God knows, what else she done told that nigga."

"I swear, I'm going to confront that bitch; and she better not pop off slick at the mouth, 'cause if she do, I'm gonna drag that ass. I don't give a fuck if we supposed to be homegirls and shit. That bitch straight violates us."

"Well, let me know when you confronting that ho so I can be there. You know I can tell when a bitch is lying."

A beep came in on the line. I looked at the phone quickly and realized it was Amir. "All right, chica, I'm on my way home. I'll hit you later." I hung up with London and clicked over to Amir. "Hello," I said in a nicer tone.

"Yo, what's good, shawty? You ain't hit a nigga up or nothing. Lemme find out you done with me already."

"Nah, I just been busy and shit, you know?"

"Yeah, I can dig that. So come holla at a nigga tonight, if you ain't too busy."

"Okay, I gotcha."

I hung the phone up and threw it on the seat. I really didn't want to be around this nigga, but I was scared that he might suspect that I was on to him. Fuck, I swore I wished I didn't hear what I heard. I wished I didn't fuck with this nigga; but, then, I wouldn't have this car and I swore I loved this fucking ride.

I busted a U-turn in the middle of the street and headed to Creighton. I needed to talk to Melody. I needed to see what the fuck she knew. I called her phone to let her know that I was pulling up. I knew this was Amir's territory. I just hoped he wasn't out and about right now because I really didn't feel like dealing with him right now.

"Hey, boo," she said as I walked into her crib.

"Hey, chick. What's going on wit' you?"

"You know, same shit. Out here trying to make it. I love the hair," she said.

"Melody, I'm going to get straight to the point. I need to ask you a question and I need you to be straight up wit' me. What did you tell Amir about me, and what did he say about me, if anything?"

She looked at me like she was surprised about what I asked her. "Nay, you know you my bitch, and we go way back. But Amir and these niggas are killers and I don't want to get wrapped up in no drama."

"Really, Melody? I am not getting you in anything. You know me better than that. I just want to know what you told him about me."

"I didn't tell him anything. He saw you a couple times when you came over here, and he asked me who you were and where you live. I told him you were my friend and that you live over Whitcomb. He didn't say anything until a few weeks ago. He hit me up and said that he would give me a few dollars if I called you over here. Nay, I swear, I was broke as hell, so I told him I'd do it. I mean, it ain't like he was going to hurt you. He was only trying to get with you, right?"

"Are you fucking serious? You took money from this nigga to get me over here? Did you ever stop and think why this nigga who can get any bitch he want was so desperate to get wit' me?"

"Not really. I mean, maybe he just want someone who didn't live around here."

"You know, you sound dumb as fuck right now. I thought we were better than this. You my nigga. I've always had yo' back and you sold me out for a few bucks."

"You can sit here and yell about 'a few bucks.' I am broke. I don't have shit. I am sorry. It ain't like it didn't work out well for you. You got a brand new car, you got money to spend. Shit, I would kill to be in your position right now. See, bitches like you are ungrateful. Y'all don't appreciate shit."

I looked at my girl and shook my head. I wouldn't ever have believed that she'd turn out to be a snake.

"Nay, I am sorry, I swear. I would never do anything to bring you harm. Amir just kept telling me how bad you are and he wanted to be with you. I only got suspicious yesterday when I overheard them talking about him fucking with you so he can get info on Whitcomb niggas. And, right after that, he showed me a cell phone pic of London and asked me her name and where she live. That was suspicious, especially since London is your girl."

"What? He had a picture of London?"

"Yes. She was walking with a dude, and she had on a black-and-white dress."

My mind went into overdrive. *A black-and-white dress; London walking with a dude. Fuck, that was yesterday when she got out of the car and walked with Keon's brother.* Oh, my God, that only confirmed my suspicion that Amir was at the funeral.

I didn't show any emotions in front of her. "What did you tell him about London?"

"Nothing."

I could tell she was lying. "Melody, what did you tell him?" I was ready to hit this bitch upside her head.

"I was scared, so I told him that's your bestie and she live over Whitcomb with you."

I was at a loss for words. I just shook my head and walked over to the door.

"I'm so, sorry, Nay, I swear."

"Bitch, save that shit. I put this on my mama: if anything happen to me or my bitch, you better pray to God I'm dead, 'cause if I'm not, I'm going to come at yo' ass. Please lose my number, bitch; and you better not say shit to him, either, about this conversation."

I didn't wait for a response from her. See, these bitches knew I used to wreak havoc in school, so I had no idea why they were playing around with me.

I got into my car and pulled off. I turned on Plies's "Kept It Too Real." This was how I was feeling. All these bitches were turning out to be snakes and shit. The only solid one was London. Speaking of London, I knew her life was in danger now that this nigga had a picture of her. I wasn't sure if he knew she was the one with Keon but, either way, I knew my girl's life was marked. I didn't know my next move, but I knew it was gonna be my best one. I loved my bitch and I wasn't going to sit back and let anyone, and I mean anyone, harm her.

CHAPTER SIXTEEN

Sheika

After being in the house for a week nursing my wounds and using cocoa butter on my scars, it was finally time to get out and do some much needed shopping. I was on my way to the bus stop when a car pulled up on me. I was scared because I didn't know who the fuck it was. "Miss Jones," a woman in the passenger seat yelled at me.

"Hello. Do I know you?" I asked suspiciously because I'd never seen this bitch before.

"No, but my name is Federal Agent Rodriguez. Get in the car."

"Lady, I don't know no federal agent and I damn sure ain't going anywhere with you right now."

"I said get in the car, or I will step out of this car and lock your ass up for money laundering and conspiracy to distribute crack cocaine."

"Say what? I ain't distribute no crack and I ain't got no damn money."

"Get in the car," she yelled.

I looked over at the driver and then back at the bitch who was yelling. I swear I had no idea what was going on and I needed to know. Shit, I ain't never been locked up and I had no intention of going to jail.

I opened the door and got into the car. I was nervous as hell and I felt like I wanted to piss on myself. I hoped this was a joke.

"Pull off," she told the driver.

"Where are we going, lady? This is kidnapping. I ain't tell you I was going nowhere with you."

"Miss, like I said before, I am a U.S. federal agent, and this is my partner, Agent Smith. We want to talk to you, so we are taking you to our office on Broad Street. Here are my credentials so you know we are not kidnappers, but federal agents."

She shoved her badge in my face. I read her name. I was sweating bullets. What could the feds want to talk to me about? I didn't break no law or anything like that. This shit sounded serious as hell. I started praying to God because I felt so alone right now.

They pulled into a garage and we walked into what seemed like an office. "Sit down," she said as she shoved a seat to me.

"Listen, lady, I don't know what you talking about. If I'm under arrest, I think I need a lawyer." I didn't know shit about the law, but I've watched enough *Law & Order* to know that I do have rights.

"No, you're not under arrest, but you can talk to us now or you can get indicted and slapped with several federal charges along with your drug-dealing boyfriend."

She threw some pictures on the table in front of me. I thought about touching them, then quickly dismissed that idea.

"Go ahead and take a look."

I looked at her, then at her partner. I then looked down at the bundle of Polaroid pictures that were in front of me. I swallowed hard and picked up the pictures. One by one, I looked through them. *What the fuck is this?*

There were several pictures with Tony coming in and out of his trap house, and pictures of him with several dudes in his clique. The last four pics, I noticed, were of me and him. *Oh, my freaking God!* What kind of stunt were they trying to pull off? I mean, just because they had a few picture of me going in this nigga's place didn't mean anything.

I shoved the pictures back to the other side of the table. "This don't prove anything other than I visited a friend a few times."

"Listen, Miss Jones. I don't think you understand what is going on here. Mr. Branch and his crew are some of the biggest dope suppliers in the Northeast. We've had them under surveillance for quite some time now. We do know that you provide him with information and you're also his ear in the streets, which make you a conspirator. With the amount of drugs and guns he's moved, you will be slapped with several charges on an indictment."

I looked at this bitch like she was crazy. Indictment? Conspirator? What was this bitch saying? I knew her ass was just bluffing. I wasn't wrapped up in any of his illegal activity. I was only fucking the nigga and I supplied his ass with a few details now and then.

"Listen, lady, no disrespect. But I know you ain't got shit on me, so you need to go holla at the nigga you really after." I got up. I was ready to go.

"Sit down! I promise you that we're going to arrest him, and you will be arrested too. This ain't no joke, so if I were you I would consider my options before you get buried for a street thug who has a woman, and who watched you get beaten down and didn't do a damn thing to help you. You need to consider fast, because I have no problem slapping you with several charges. This is the federal government, and it's as serious as it's going to get." She then moved away from my face.

"Can I go now?" I turned to her partner and asked.

"Sure, but here is our card. Please consider what she just said." He shoved a card on the table in front of me.

I took up the card without thinking and walked out. Once I was out of their office and into the corridor, I let out a long sigh. While I was there, I felt like I was going to suffocate, and that federal bitch sure didn't make it any easier. I knew she had a job to do but, damn, did she really have to be that cold? I was happy to step outside the building.

I leaned on the building for a few minutes before I walked across the street to jump on a bus. I was in no mood to go shopping after what I just went through. This was some crazy shit.

I hadn't been out of the house since the fucking feds scared the hell out of me. I would hear noises outside and I would peep through the curtains to see what was going on. I also thought about leaving, but I had nowhere to go and they were the feds. I was pretty sure that if they wanted to find little old me, they had the resources to do so.

I'd tried calling Tony since the day I got home, but instead of answering the phone he kept pressing ignore. I dialed his number again. This time I was going to leave his ass a message. I just hoped the feds didn't have his phone tapped, also.

The phone rang and rang until his voicemail picked up. "Hey, this Sheika. I need to talk to you. It's very important. I swear it really is."

I hung the phone up, and went back to browsing Facebook. My phone started ringing. I looked at the caller ID. *I guess he got my message.* "Hello, nigga. I been calling you."

"Surprise, bitch, this is Lashia, his woman. I see that ass whupping didn't do no justice 'cause here you are blowing up my man's phone."

"Listen, bitch, you ain't whup my ass. I bet you the next time I see you, it won't be like that. But like I said, if you was fucking him right, he wouldn't want to be sucking and fucking my pussy."

"You're a fucking joke." Then she yelled in the background, "Honey, come tell this little stupid-ass bitch not to call your phone no mo'."

This bitch was silly. Big Tony knew how much I'd done for him, and there was no way he was going to fuck that up over no pussy that could be easily replaced. I waited on the phone, rolling my eyes.

"Ay, yo, what's good?"

"Man, I been calling you—"

Before I could finish my sentence, he cut me off. "No disrespect, shawty, but stop calling my fucking phone. My woman ain't feeling us being friends so just lose my number."

"Wha—" Before I could get another word in, I heard a click in my ear.

I sat up on my bed, irritated as fuck. How did I just get disrespected by this nigga I was trying to help? I was furious as hell. I kept trying to call his number back to back, but I got his voicemail. Man, I was hurt as hell, but that was quickly replaced by anger.

I looked over at the card the feds gave me the other day. I swear, I was tired of people using and abusing me. *Let's see how the fuck he likes it when his ass is locked away for good.* I was done playing nice with this fuck nigga and his bitch. I grabbed the card and dialed the number.

"Miss Jones, I have been expecting your call," this arrogant-ass bitch said. I was also curious how the bitch knew it was me. I never gave her my phone number.

"Listen, lady, don't flatter yourself. I've been thinking about what you said the other day and there's no way I am going to get locked up behind Tony and his illegal activity. I don't know what you need me to do, but I'm ready."

"I'm happy you finally see things our way. I will pick you up tomorrow at ten a.m. near the store we picked you up last time."

"All right." Even though I was motivated to show Tony not to fuck with me, I was also scared for my life. I knew the feds played dirty and couldn't be trusted. I couldn't afford to let anyone find out about this because I already knew my ass was going to be killed.

CHAPTER SEVENTEEN

London

The days following Keon's funeral were extra sad for me. I went over to my mama's house for a few days just to get away and clear my mind a little bit. Mama was very understanding and didn't ask a lot of questions. I had a lot of decisions to make concerning this baby. I wanted to keep it because it was a part of Keon and me but, then again, I had no idea how I was going to take care of my child financially. I never had to work a day in my life because Keon made sure I had every- and anything that I needed. Now that he was gone, I was clueless how to survive on my own. My bills were paid up for three months, but after that I was doomed. As much as I loved Mama, going back home was not an option.

I heard my phone ringing. I grabbed it. It was Keon's brother. "Hello."

"Yo, London, just calling to check up you."

"I'm just here trying to make it one day at a time. I have something to tell you."

"What's good?"

"I'm pregnant with yo' brother's baby," I blurted out.

"Shawty, stop playing like that."

"No, I'm dead-ass serious. I found out the other day, but I wanted to wait until after the funeral to tell y'all."

"Damn, shawty, that's what's up. Maaaaaaa, we having a baby," he yelled out.

Oh, Lord, why he got to tell her? I had no idea how she was going to handle this news, especially now that her son was gone.

"Hello, baby girl? Are you sure? Oh, thank you, Jesus. Thank you, Jesus."

It warmed my heart to hear how welcoming they were. It kind of changed my mind 100 percent to have this baby. I didn't know how I was going to do it on my own, but I had to figure something out fast.

"And don't you worry about anything. We got you and the baby. As long as I'm living, my grandbaby ain't gon' want for nothing. I'ma make Deon text you my phone number, and you call me if you need anything. You hear me?"

"Yes, ma'am."

"All right, baby girl, here go Deon."

"Shawty, you ain't got shit to worry about for real. We got you, because I know my brother would've done the same thing for me."

"I so appreciate y'all for real. Do y'all know who killed him yet?"

"Nah, shawty, that's what's bothering me so much. The number that called him was from a burned phone, so that's no help. I was gon' ask you to think back on that night, see if there's anything you can remember. Shawty, I swear I'm not gon' rest until I kill all parties involved."

"Man, I've been racking my brain, especially late nights when it's quiet. All I remember was the street was too dark. I ducked once the shooting started. I wish I had done more to help him out."

"Nah, you couldn't have done anything. My brother was a real soldier and he wouldn't want you wrapped up in all this shit. But, I promise you and his seed, I'm going to get them niggas."

"Thank you, and please be safe out there."

"A'ight, shawty. I'll be in touch."

I got off the phone having mixed feelings. I was happy that they accepted me and my baby, but I was sad that I wasn't no help in identifying Keon's killer. Tears welled up in my eyes. This shit was fucking sad and I wouldn't get no closure until his killers were brought to justice or, as I would have preferred, they were gunned down in the streets the same way they gunned my baby down like he was an animal.

Them motherfuckers were even more disrespectful coming to his funeral like that. I swear, I wished I was in those streets, 'cause I would have handled these niggas my damn self.

CHAPTER EIGHTEEN

Ajanay

I swear I didn't really want to hang with this nigga. I knew for a fact that he killed Keon and I knew he had London marked. On my way to his house, all I could think of was trying to come up with a way to get this nigga back. I knew that he was deep into these streets, but I learned that nobody was untouchable. I only hoped Melody didn't let him know I was on to him.

I called his phone so he could let me in through the gate. I parked and swallowed hard. I was good at hiding my true feelings and tonight wasn't no different. I knew I had to be careful because this nigga was a killer, and if he had a hint that I was up to something, I might not make it out.

"Good evening, babe," I said as I walked in, switching my ass extra hard.

"Hey, love," he said as he locked the door behind us. We walked into the living room together and I kicked off my heels. I was trying to get as comfortable as I could so he wouldn't see a change in my behavior.

"I want to talk to you."

"Damn, sounds serious. What's good, shawty?"

"I need to know, what are you trying to do with me?" I looked at him without blinking.

"What do you mean?" He giggled.

"I mean, I fucks with you hard and you fuck with me hard. I think we should make our relationship official. Don't you think?"

"Damn, shawty, you'ont think we moving a little too fast? It ain't even been a month yet."

"Nah, I don't think we're moving too fast, especially because I'm carrying your seed," I said without putting much thought into it.

"Man, you playing. Are you fucking serious?"

"I'm a grown-ass woman and I have zero time for games. I am dead-ass serious. I took a pregnancy test at home after I missed my period and it was confirmed that I was pregnant. You the only nigga I'm fucking, so that makes you the daddy."

He sat there looking at me, while sipping on a glass of liquor. "Man, you just fucked me up wit' all that."

"I mean, if there is no future for us, I can have an abortion. It ain't like I'm trying to have your baby anyway," I said.

"Nah, nah, nah, it ain't that. I mean, I just wasn't expecting that. A nigga in these streets heavy, and having a child will only make me more vulnerable to niggas."

"Well, you're in the streets. Not me. I've always dreamed about having children of my own, so if you are ready, then I'm ready." I scooted closer to him and started rubbing his arm.

"Damn, boo. Man, I don't know what to say. You can't live in no projects with my seed. So you gon' have to move in wit' me. Damn, man." He looked he was in heavy thought.

"Well, I mean, I'm not trying to rush you into anything. I can always get a different place somewhere else."

"Nah, shawty. That's a waste of money when I got a five-bedroom here. Shawty, I need to talk to you." He grabbed my hand and looked deep into my eyes. "Listen, shawty, I don't know if you know what I do for a living.

I kill people and sell dope. With that said, I don't allow everybody 'round me, 'cause these niggas and bitches can't be trusted. I know you have friends and shit, but under no circumstances can you tell them where I stay at. Also, I'm about to give you the code to the gate. Only two people will have it, and that will be you and I, you dig?"

"Damn, nigga, you acting like you the CIA and shit. If we got to go through all this, you can keep all that shit and I will stay my happy ass over Whitcomb."

"Chill out, man. I'm just telling you, I need you to be loyal to me. Don't trust nobody but me and we be good."

"I mean, I don't know no other way but loyalty. I am falling deep for you and you gonna be my baby's father, so of course my loyalty is with you," I assured him while I rubbed his stomach.

I unzipped his pants, releasing his dick. I massaged it a few times and then licked the tip of it. "Damn, shawty, give it to a nigga," he said as he forced my head down farther.

I took his dick into my mouth and twirled my tongue around the tip. I made love to his manhood while he groaned and professed how much he wanted to be with me. I sucked it harder so I could speed up the process. Within minutes, he busted in my mouth. I wasn't tripping. I swallowed every drop of his cum.

"Yo, Nay, I want you as my main bitch, shawty," he said as he pulled me down on his dick.

"I got you, daddy." I winked at him as I straddled him and started riding his dick. Murder was on my mind, and this nigga was definitely the victim.

I was restless the entire night. His ass was knocked out after I fucked him good for about thirty minutes. I lay there, watching him as he snored. It's crazy that I came into this with clean hands but this nigga had his own motives. See, he thought because I was from Whitcomb I was a dumb bitch. I was determined to show this nigga that there was nothing dumb about us Whitcomb chicks.

"Hey, baby." He rolled over and kissed me on the cheek.

"Hey, boo." I smiled at him.

We got up. I made him a hefty breakfast of scrambled eggs, pancakes, and sausage, served alongside orange juice. "Damn, shawty, you fuck a nigga good and can cook. Shit, I got to cuff yo' ass."

I smiled at him and bit a piece of my pancake. I could see the evil in this nigga's eyes as he sat there eating. What's crazy was he really believed he had me fooled.

"Damn, you ain't gon' eat all yo' food?"

"I'm not too hungry."

"You better start eating properly and make sure you feed my baby. Damn, I love the sound of that. I hope it's a little dude so I can show him how to be a real nigga."

You mean a real killer, I thought, but kept my mouth shut.

After we finished eating, we took a shower and I got dressed.

"Here is the code to the gate, and this the code to the safe and the front door. Please guard it with yo' life, shawty. I don't mind you taking out cash when you need it, but don't bleed a nigga dry."

I looked down at the piece of paper he handed me. Something inside of me was telling me not to touch it, but being the person I was, I grabbed it out of his hand.

"You can move your things in whenever you're ready. You ain't got to bring no furniture. Just yo' clothes and shit, but we can go shopping if you don't want to bring those."

"Awee, thank you, baby. You have no idea how much I appreciate you."

I kissed him on the cheek and left. I was happy to be out from behind those gates. I looked at the piece of paper he'd handed me and then I threw it in my purse. I so wished this was real. Oh, well.

CHAPTER NINETEEN

London

I was not ready to get up out of bed, but Nay's ass had just called me to tell me she was on the way. I tried to tell her I was sleeping, until she mentioned something about bringing me my favorite breakfast. Shit, lately I'd been eating a lot. I knew it was because I was pregnant.

I jumped out of the bed and took a hot shower. I wasn't feeling my best, because this morning sickness was killing my ass. I tried to vomit a few times, but nothing came up. I got dressed in a pair of Old Navy comfy pajamas and made a cup of mint tea. This was the only thing that sort of soothed the nausea.

I got on my favorite couch and started watching *The People's Court* on television. Five minutes later, I heard the doorbell ringing. *Damn, this bitch had to come right when this court show was getting good.*

I got up and hurried to the door. I opened the door and ran back to the living room.

"Damn, bitch, what, you had to pee or something?" she said as she walked in.

"Nah, this judge show so damn good. I didn't want to miss the end."

"Oh, okay. You and these damn shows. Here go your breakfast. It might be a little cold, so you might want to warm it up."

I took the tray from her and walked into the kitchen. Something seemed off. Normally Nay would be jolly, but this morning she didn't seem too happy at all. Maybe she was just tired.

I walked back into the living room and flopped down on the couch beside her. "So, bitch, why are you up so early? Let me find out you just getting home," I said in a joking tone.

"London, I need to talk to you about something really serious."

"Damn, bitch, what, you got AIDS?"

"Nah, man, quit joking."

"Okay, Nay, what's up?" I was not feeling the mood.

"You know I been fucking with Amir for a few weeks, right?"

"Yeah, and? Did that nigga do something to hurt you?" I jumped up off the couch.

"Sit down, because you going to need to."

Like an obedient student, I flopped my ass down on the couch and listened attentively.

"I love you like a sister, London, and I swear with everything in me I would never hurt you or allow anyone else to hurt you."

"Bitch, you making me nervous. What is going on?"

"I found out that Amir didn't really like me. He knew I was from Whitcomb Court and that's why he took an interest in me."

"What that got to do with me?"

"One morning, I woke up and Amir wasn't in the room. I waited for him to come back into the room, but he didn't. I was curious where he was at, so I got up. I heard him downstairs, so I was on my way down there when I heard him on his phone. He was bragging about scooping me up and how, in due time, I was going to give him all the inside information about Whitcomb niggas. That wasn't all. I heard him talking about Keon—"

I cut her off the second that I heard Keon's name mentioned. "What the fuck he said about Keon?"

"Umm, I heard him telling some nigga on the phone that he killed Keon."

A lump formed in my throat as I gasped for air. I couldn't believe this shit that Nay was saying. I looked at my girl's face to see if this was some sort of cruel joke. But she didn't blink at all.

"Say something, Nay. Are you serious? What did he say? And how long did you know this?" I bombarded her with questions.

I had an intense tension headache. This shit just confused the hell out of me. How could Amir kill Keon? He was from Creighton. South-side niggas killed him; or did they really? Did my baby lose his life to the niggas he had beef with for years?"

"London, I only found out last week. I was trying not to believe it because you told me south-side niggas killed him, but I know what I heard and my suspicion was confirmed the day of the funeral when I saw Amir. He was in one of the cars that pulled off after the shooting."

"Oh, my God! Are you fucking serious right now! Fuck that nigga. How could he take him away from me? What did my baby ever do to deserve this? I need answers, Nay."

"London, you know one of Creighton boys was killed by Keon and them last year. I heard it's retaliation."

"Retaliation? I am carrying a child that will never know his or her daddy. All because this fuck nigga Amir wants to play God," I cried out.

I was so angry that I was visibly trembling. Nay came closer to me and put her arms around me. "Baby, calm down. Getting this angry can't be good for you or the baby."

I laid my head on her shoulder and just let the tears fall. I swear, this just broke my heart all over again that a nigga could take my baby's life and then live to brag about it. Hatred for this nigga filled my veins. "Nay, I want to kill him."

She let me go and looked me dead in the eyes. "Huh? What you just said?"

"I said I want to kill Amir. And you're going to help me."

"Bitch, do you know what you're saying?" She shook my shoulder.

"I can't live with it, knowing he took my baby's life and he's still walking around like it's business as usual. I don't know how I'm going to do it, but I'm going to kill him. I want my face to be the last face he sees before he meet his Maker."

"London, bitch, this nigga is a killer, and if we slip up we going to be two dead bitches. You do know that, right?"

"Hmm, I do know that a nigga's weakness is pussy, right?" I looked at her.

"Right," she agreed.

"This nigga love to fuck you, so you can put the pussy on this nigga and I will walk in and put a bullet in his head."

"Ha-ha. I swear you watch too many fantasy movies. It takes more than that to kill a killer like Amir."

"Yup, it does and that's why we will be planning his murder."

She looked at me, and shook her head. "Listen, London, I admit I thought about killing him too, but I'm not trying to go to prison for murder, and neither are you. I say let's rob the nigga. I have the code to his safe and his gate. We can get thousands of dollars and just get the hell out of there. That nigga ain't gon' report it because he don't fuck with the police. We can stage it like it's a robbery."

I sat there listening to her. I didn't give a fuck about this nigga or his money. I wanted his life, just like he took my baby's life. I didn't tell her, though, because I had a feeling she was more after the money.

"We need to start looking up states that we want to move to. I mean, I always wanted to go to the Big Apple, so why not go there? We can finish school and start our careers in the city that never sleeps."

"Shit, I say Atlanta. I heard a lot of good shit about Georgia."

"Hell, that's cool too. I am going to get my shit in order and so should you. And, London, please don't say anything to anyone, and I mean anyone, not even yo' mother."

"You got my word, boo."

We ended up talking and plotting for another hour before she left. I locked the door and walked to the window. I watched as she pulled off.

Bullshit. Nay really thought I wanted a dollar from that nigga. Hell nah. Money couldn't fill this void that I was feeling inside, or bring Keon back.

I dialed Deon's number. "Yo, where you at? I need to holla at you ASAP," I yelled frantically in the phone.

"You good? Do I need to handle something?"

"I just need you to come through. I'm texting you the address now."

I knew there was no way I could know this information and not share it with him. I wasn't no killer, and I knew Amir was. So, in order to touch that nigga, I needed help.

CHAPTER TWENTY

Sheika

I stepped out my door and looked around. I was nervous as hell. I hoped that I didn't bump into any of these dudes, and especially not Big Tony or any of his crew. I was tempted to turn back around and go back into the house. But I was sure the feds were not going to just disappear anytime soon.

I looked at the time. It was a few minutes before ten o'clock, so I put some pep in my step. I got to the store and looked around. I didn't see the car that they drove the other day. I was restless; this wasn't no regular meeting and I was scared someone might see me with the police.

Honk! Honk! Honk!

I looked to my left. I saw the window of a Chevy Impala roll down and I immediately recognized that bitch from hell. I took one last glance around before I walked toward the car and got inside.

"Good morning Miss Jones."

"Good morning," I barely mumbled under my breath.

They took me to the federal office and briefed me. They asked me a ton of questions, which I answered. They also showed me pictures of numerous dudes from Whitcomb and I identified them. I didn't hold back on things that I saw, including the drugs and money that I had seen. I did feel bad giving up the names of the bitches I'd seen cooking the crack. At the end of the day, I was saving my ass.

"Miss, we appreciate you for taking the time out to help us. We will not disclose your name to anyone except the grand jury."

"So, do I get to go into witness protective services? These dudes ain't playing no joke and I don't want to die."

"No one will know you talked to us. Before you know it, all of these thugs will be picked up and off the streets. They have been terrorizing this state for way too long and it is coming to an end soon."

I looked at her. I wished I could believe all that she was saying. I knew this bitch really didn't give a fuck about me. All she wanted was to lock up that nigga and his crew.

"We will drop you off back at the store. Keep your eyes and ears open and call us if you hear anything new. Do not tell anyone that you met with us. We are going to contact you next week. We need you to wear a wire the next time you visit Mr. Branch."

I looked at this bitch like she really lost her mind. Wear a fucking wire? This nigga would kill me. I instantly regretted calling this bitch because she was definitely pushing it.

"Listen, lady, you lost your damn mind. I am not wearing anything and definitely no damn wire."

"You are too far in to back out now. How would you like if I release your name and make sure he knows you gave us some inside info on him?"

"You bitch! You can't fucking do that."

"Watch your mouth; and, go ahead, try me. You are nothing but a criminal like them and I have no problem throwing your ass in federal prison for the rest of your life. Now, like I said, we will be contacting you next week. Please make yourself available."

I shot her ass a dirty look and stormed out of the office. I swear, I could have ripped this bitch's head off right now. I jumped back on a bus and headed to the mall.

After this rough day that I had, I decided to spend some of the money he gave me one day we fucked. I ain't going to front, I was going to miss all the money he used to give me. *But why should I feel bad?* This nigga carried me first over pussy.

After spending a couple hundred in the mall, I decide to leave. I bought a few outfits, and a pair of Jordan sneakers. Tomorrow I planned on getting my hair colored and cut.

It was strange that I hadn't heard from Nay or London for over a week. Let me find out them hoes were acting funny with me. *Hmmm, if that's the case, I need to find out what's going on.* I decided to stop by Nay's house since I was on the bus and it was not too far from my house.

I knew she was there because her car was parked on the side of the driveway. I rang the doorbell and waited. I heard the door unlock and then it flew wide open.

"Bitch, it's only me," I said as I stormed past her.

I stopped in my tracks when I noticed London. I swore I didn't feel like dealing with this bitch.

"Hey, London," I said.

"Hey," she barely mumbled under her breath.

"What breeze blew you over this way, Sheika? Matter of fact, I didn't know you still fuck with us," Nay said.

"Girl, what you talking about? I was on my way from the mall and I realized that I haven't seen or heard from y'all lately."

"Nay, I don't know about you, but I don't fuck with this bitch, so I'm out," London said.

"What the fuck you talking about, London?" I turned my attention toward this bitch.

"Bitch, I don't fuck with you 'cause you a jealous-ass, lying-ass bitch!" she said as she stepped toward my face.

"Jealous? Ha-ha, what you got for me to be jealous over? Bitch, everybody know you was fucking and sucking Keon dirty dick to get a few dollars. Let's see how you gon' live now, bitch."

Boom! Boom! Boom! That bitch jumped on me and started pounding me. I dropped my phone and starting matching that bitch blow for blow. I dreamed of this day numerous times and there was no way I was going to lose this fight.

"London, stop! You're pregnant. Stop!" Nay screamed.

"Nah, Nay, let me go. I am sick of this old snitch-ass bitch!" she yelled while she continued thumping on me. I tried to get the bitch's face, but I couldn't.

"Both of y'all bitches stop before y'all break my shit up in my house," Nay yelled and then I heard a gunshot. We both stopped.

I looked and saw Nay with her gun in her hand pointing up at the ceiling.

"Y'all can't be up in my shit fighting. London is right, Sheika, you a lying-ass snake bitch. You think I would not find out that you fucking Tony big ass? Well, I did, and I know yo' ass was feeding niggas everything we talked about. How could you? We've helped you in so many ways. How could you turn against us for a fuck nigga who don't give a fuck about you?"

So now both these bitches were ganging up on me. See, Nay's ass kept hiding behind that fucking gun, but without it she was a punk bitch.

"Bitch, I don't know where you getting your information from, but if you have no proof, don't come accusing me of some shit you know nothing about."

"Fuck this bitch, Nay. Better yet, give me this gun so I can show this ho something."

"You a joke, London. Fuck with me and end up like yo' dead-ass nigga."

That bitch lunged toward me, but her friend saved her. "London, I said stop! Do you want to lose your seed behind a bitch who ain't got shit to lose? Man, fuck this bitch. She already know what it is."

"Nah, Nay, fuck you and that ho."

"Listen, bitch, pick yo' shit up and get out of my shit before I blow your fucking head off. See, I ain't no killer, but don't push me."

"Fake-ass gansta," I said.

I picked my phone up and stormed out of that bitch's house. I straightened up my clothes and my hair. I was tired from the fucking fight between London and me. I swore that bitch was lucky her fucking friend broke it up. I wished I'd known she was pregnant. I would've stomped that fucking baby out of her. It was cool; I would catch her ass again.

CHAPTER TWENTY-ONE

Ajanay

The next couple of days were spent with Amir. I was partly moved in, or so he thought. We went to Kings Dominion one day, Virginia Beach the next, and shopping every day. This nigga was really splurging on me in a serious way.

We had just come to the crib. Earlier we went out to eat dinner at Applebee's. We decided to chill in the living room for a little while. I brought the big bottle of Henny in the living room. I poured us two glasses while he rolled up two fat-ass blunts. We started drinking and smoking, just chilling like we were homies instead of lovers. This was the type of relationship I yearned for but, too bad, this one wasn't the right one, I thought as I pulled on the blunt.

I picked up my phone and checked the time. It was after 11:00 p.m. "Babe, I want some dick! How about we go upstairs?"

"Hell yeah. I am ready to jump head deep into that pussy." He staggered to his feet.

I was sweaty and decided to take a quick shower. Tonight was special and I intended to make it as memorable as could be. I got out of the shower and oiled down my body with my herbal Hot Six Oil. I looked at bae, who was sprawled out across the bed, stroking his dick and smiling at me.

"You know how I gets down." There was no shame in my game. My legs were straight; I was bent over with my hands locked around my ankles. My naked, oiled body was glistening, wanting and missing Amir's full attention.

"Yes, I see," he replied. He got up, stepping behind me with his chocolate thunder in his hands, priming it up. I wanted like hell to wrap my lips around his dick but my chocolate cocoa needed dick like yesterday.

"Say no more." He stuck his dick inside my wetness.

"Slow and steady, big boy," I said between breaths, trying to stroke his ego. His arms were wrapped around my waist. My round, perfect petite ass stayed arched. "Yesss, that's it." I cooed because his dick was traveling south and north and out my pussy.

I saw his reflection in the mirror as I cocked my head sideways, mesmerized by how big my ex-nigga's dick actually was. I imagined it his dick sliding in and out of my pussy. This only turned me on more.

"Fuck this pussy." My cockiness came out. I wanted to feel all of him inside my stomach. He repositioned his hands to my lower back and continued to take long strokes inside my uterus.

"Ohhh, shit, yes." He penetrated harder into my pussy. "Fuck this pussy, Amir. Yes, bae, fuck me harder." His dick was tickling my insides. My wetness shined on his tool as it traveled into my pussy.

My ass rocked back and forth and shook like jelly as Amir made love to my pussy. "Fuck meee," I begged, feeling extra horny and super wet. His dick penetrated me and his nuts slapped my ass. I went crazy when his thumb jammed into my ass. "Ohh, shit," I screamed out, nearly losing my breath.

"You like it rough, don't cha?" He penetrated harder and harder as my screaming grew louder.

"Yesss, Amir, I love it rough," I shouted out in a feel-good pain. His thumb sent chills through my body. "Oh, Lord," I screamed louder.

"Don't call on the Lord now because I'm your savior and here to deliver you," he bragged. He was fingering and dicking me down at the same time.

"Shittt, Amir," I cried out as my body started shaking. I felt multiple orgasms coming on. I braced myself, and tightened my muscles. My juices covered his dick as if Michelangelo painted it himself.

"Shit, damn, bae." My knees became weak and my body crashed onto the floor. His heavy ass lay on top of my back. He spread my ass cheeks, and my pussy was poking out. He stuck his dick back inside my cum-leaking pussy.

He braced himself on the floor as I arched my ass up slightly to feel all his dick inside of me. "Yesss, bae." He was digging deep into my pussy fast as hell.

Our breathing became heavy. "This is my pussy." His body and my ass made a clapping sound each time he penetrated me. "My pussy, bitch," he muttered. Usually I would have raised hell, but the dick was so good I didn't care what he called me. All I knew was that he had my pussy on fire.

"Yes, I'm your bitch," I chimed because I was in total bliss and ecstasy at the same time. My pussy spat out cum all over his dick. I was breathless as he lay on top of me, gasping for air.

I was happy that this episode was over. I ain't goin' to lie; since I'd been fucking with Amir this was the best fuck that he ever gave me. I got up, grabbed my underwear, and rushed to the bathroom. As soon as I heard him get up, I turned on the water, bracing myself for what was about to come.

"Nay, man, somebody just fucking robbed me, shawty!" He busted into the bathroom, yelling.

"Boy, what you talking about? Where is yo' gun? Is they still here?" I jumped out of the shower. My body still had soap on it. I grabbed my robe, which was nearby. By this time, he was yelling on the phone. I really couldn't understand what he was saying 'cause he was talking too fast.

"I swear, dawg, I'm going to kill whoever the fuck did this shit. I swear on my dead mama, yo." His threats rang in my ears.

I hurried up and got dressed. The truth was, I wasn't sure how this was going to turn out. I wanted to call London to see if she was all right, but I couldn't do it at the moment.

He hung the phone up and turned toward me. "Yo, I'm going to ask you this one time and one time only: did you give anybody the codes that I gave you? Please, Nay, think carefully before you respond."

"Hell naw! So you think I had something to do with this? I was here with you."

He didn't say anything else to me. Instead, he picked up his 9 mm off the nightstand and walked out. I heard him go down the stairs, but I was still too shaken to move. My phone started ringing, but I pressed ignore and put it on silent. I had no idea how this was going to end. "God, please get me out of this situation," I whispered under my breath.

He was gone for a long time and I just sat on the bed, contemplating my next move. London and I supposed to be boarding an early morning flight out of Richmond. We were ATL bound. We had no idea where we were going, but we decided we would figure that out once we got there. I was really looking forward to starting over.

"Bitch! I asked you who the fuck you gave my code to and you looked in my motherfucking face and lied to me." He took several steps toward me and slapped me with the butt of his gun.

I stood up and tried to reach for my purse, but it was on the far end of the dresser. I looked down at my shirt and saw bright red blood.

"What the fuck are you talking about? I didn't give yo' shit to anyone," I said, still sticking to my story.

"Shut up, you lying-ass bitch! Before I kill you, I want you to know why I killed yo' ass," he yelled as he slapped me with an open hand.

I started crying, but I was no match for this big nigga. I could see if the nigga was fat, but he was tall and had muscles. My mouth was twisted to the side and I barely could get the words out to plead for my life. I was certain, I was going to die. In my heart, I was hoping my girl was smart enough to get away fast. He grabbed me by my weave and started dragging me while calling me all kinds of degrading words.

He dragged me down the stairs and opened a door and dragged me inside. I knew it was over for me now. I closed my eyes and start asking God for forgiveness.

"Bitch, you see this? Look, ho." He gripped my face and turned it to a screen. I almost fainted. This nigga had cameras throughout the entire house, even in the fucking shower. I swallowed, but it hurt. A lump formed in my throat. "Look, bitch! See? That's yo' motherfucking homegirl. The same little bitch who was in the car wit' that nigga Keon. So tell me, Nay, how did this bitch get into my house and into my safe? You see? That is my motherfucking money she's putting in a garbage bag." He started applying pressure to my jawbone, hurting the hell out of my face.

"Stop, you hurting me," I tried to scream out.

"Bitch, answer me. How did this bitch get into my house?"

"I don't know! I swear to you, Amir, I didn't give nobody the codes. I would never do that to you. I am having your baby." I pleaded for mercy.

"Bitch, let's go!" He dragged me back up the stairs. "Nay, I'm going to kill you, but you can stop that by calling yo' bitch and telling her you coming over so you can get your cut of the money."

This nigga was losing his mind. I knew he wanted me to set my girl up, but I would have rather died. "I'm not doing that," I said.

"Bitch, you will." He punched me in my eye, instantly closing it.

"Noooooo! Please don't do this. I swear I don't know nothing about this." My cries fell on deaf ears because this big nigga kept pounding me as if I were a nigga in the streets. I stopped pleading and just started crying silently. He finally let me go and shoved me to the ground, and pointed his gun at my face. He pressed the barrel to my forehead.

"Now, bitch, wipe those fucking tears and dial that bitch's number. You gonna act like everything is cool and let her know you coming through."

I could barely pick my head up, but I did and looked at this nigga.

"Bitch, do it," he yelled as spit flew out of his mouth and his eyes popped out wide. It was sickening to see him in such a rage. I knew his intentions for me were not good and I didn't see a way out.

"Bitch, dial the fucking number before I blow your fucking brains out now." He cocked the gun at my head with his hand on the trigger.

God, this can't end like this, I silently said to myself.

I scrambled for my phone that was in my cross-body bag. I swear I didn't want to do this, but I figured if I could make it out of here, I may have a chance to get away from him. I just hoped London was smart enough to figure out what was going on.

CHAPTER TWENTY-TWO

London

I was nervous as hell putting in the code to get into the complex. I'd never done anything like this before, but with the help of Deon, I was set to go. He wanted to come inside with me, but I begged him not to. Nay was inside and I swear I didn't want to bring any harm to my girl. I also thought long and hard about everything that I was about to do, and I felt in my heart there was no other way out.

I said a prayer to God before I got out of the dark car. I didn't want to raise suspicions, so I walked calmly to the front door. I took a long breath. My sweaty hands trembled as I turned the doorknob. My girl was on point when she told me the door was going to be left open. I really didn't know what to expect when I crept through the kitchen with the gun that Keon gave me in my hand.

Keith Sweat's song "Make It Last Forever" played from the bedroom, which made it that much easier for me to walk through the house with my gun cocked, aimed, and ready.

The bedroom door was slightly open. I hugged my body against the wall as I eased closer to the bedroom door. My heart thumped like a DJ making beats. I took a deep breath and peeped into the room. My eyes lit up like Christmas Day.

The glow from the burning candles shined light on their nude bodies. Keith Sweat's voice alone couldn't drown out the sounds of Nay's moans. Her dark chocolate, oiled body had the perfect arch in it. Her petite ass was spread wide as Amir penetrated her pussy from behind. The way Amir's dick slid in and out of her pussy made my panties wet. His hands slapped her ass constantly, making her ass jiggle; and her moans grow louder. My body heated up fast. With the way Nay moaned in pleasure I wanted to take her place. I wished that Keon was pounding me like that. Oh, I missed his touch, his smell, and his donkey dick driving me insane.

So many mixed emotions flowed through my head. I tried to aim the gun at this nigga's head, but I couldn't. His head was turned the other way as I creeped by him and over to the safe. My hands trembled as I put in the code and the safe popped open. Nay was right; this nigga was paid. I grabbed the stacks as fast as I could and stuffed them in the big garbage bag that I had. I turned around and they were still going at it. I tiptoed out, closing the door behind me. I hurried up and walked out the front door. I got in the car, throwing the money on the back seat. Deon pulled out slowly and, just like that, we were gone. This was the first time I let out a long breath.

"You good yo?" he asked.

"I don't know. I am worried about Nay. This nigga is a killer and I'm not sure what he might do to her if he finds out she has anything to do with it."

"Yo, here go a blunt. It will calm yo' nerves. I already told you, I got you."

The entire ride home was spent in silence. All kind of thoughts were running through my mind. I never imagined doing anything like this before, but this nigga deserved it and more.

Deon came inside with me. We started talking about what would happen if the shit took a turn for the worse. I knew he would take care of me, just because of his brother.

I sat there anxiously waiting to hear from Nay. I picked up my phone to call her a few times, but I threw it back down because I didn't know what was going on, if anything. We had planned for her to call me when she was out of harm's way and on her way to see me.

My phone started ringing and I grabbed it immediately. I looked at the caller ID, and realized it was Nay. I answered it immediately. "Hey, boo, I'm so glad you call. You had me nervous and shit," I yelled.

There was a pause. That kind of threw me off and let me know that something was terribly wrong.

"Nay, are you there? Are you all right?"

"London, I'm on my way to see you. This nigga just broke up with me and I need you."

I had my ear glued to the phone and I heard a whisper. I couldn't hear what was said, but I heard enough to know it was a male's voice.

"All right, boo. You know I'm here."

"I'm on the way."

The phone hung up without another word. I knew Nay long enough to know she ain't crying over no nigga leaving her. I knew that Amir was on to her and, more than likely, us.

"Deon! We got a problem," I screamed out.

"Shawty, ain't no problem. I gotcha."

CHAPTER TWENTY-THREE

Sheika

"Tony, I know you're mad at me about what happened the other day, but please just forgive me," I said as I finally got him on the phone.

"Yo, shawty, I don't want to problems between my woman and me. She already thinks I'm out slinging this dick e'erywhere."

"I ain't trying to start nothing either, but I just need to see you real quick. I promise I will make it worth your while."

"A'ight, man, but you got to make it quick."

"Okay, see you in a few."

I turned to look at the fed bitch and her partner. I saw the glow on their faces as if they'd just won the lottery.

"I really don't want to do this. This is too dangerous."

"Listen, you just need to go in there. Follow the script that we gave you and everything will work out. Remember, we won't be far and at the first sign of trouble we will be in there."

I sat there as they put the little microphone underneath my shirt. I looked to make sure it wouldn't be visible. They let me out of the car at the corner where the convenience store was. I was nervous as hell as I walked down the street. I opened the gate and walked in. I rang the doorbell and waited.

One of the runners opened the door and then walked away. I locked the door behind me and walked toward the back to his space. I knew he was watching me on the cameras that were throughout the building except in his office.

"Hey, babe," I greeted him as he sat behind the table, counting money.

"What it do? You good?"

"Well, I'm trying to maintain. You know it's hard out here for a pimp," I tried to joke.

"I hear you. So, what was the urgency?"

"I just wanted to talk to you about some business."

"Business? Shawty, what you talking about?"

"Big Tony, I'm tired of being broke and I have a cousin in Petersburg who be grinding hard out there."

"Okay, I'm listening."

"We've been talking and he told me he looking for a new connect. I told him about you, not mentioning your name. I told him I would be the middle man because I know you don't like dealing with out-of-town niggas."

"How much work we talking about?"

"Two keys," I blurted out.

By the time I finished my sentence, his phone started ringing. "Yo!"

I couldn't hear what the other person was saying, but I was watching his face. His forehead start forming wrinkles and he stood up. This wasn't a good sign, but a man like Tony got upset all the time, so I sat there waiting for him to get off the phone.

"Are you for real, dawg? A'ight, my nigga. You know what to do." He hung the phone up. He walked from around his desk. "What you say your cousin name was?"

I knew I didn't say, but I needed a name ASAP. "His name is Kemar."

He smiled at me, then took two steps toward me. I didn't see it coming, but I heard the click of the gun and I fell backward into my seat. My face was burning, as I realized then that I was dying.

Pop! Pop! Pop!

Oh, God, this can't be real!

"Now, bitch, you can finally meet your Maker."

I then heard footsteps. Several footsteps. "Get down before I shoot your ass." I recognized the federal bitch's voice yelling over the commotion.

"Fuck you, bitch!" I heard several other shots ring out. I tried moving my legs, but I couldn't move.

"Hang on, an ambulance is on its way," a police officer said to me.

She was tripping, but I knew that I wasn't going to make it. I was pleading to God in my heart to please not let me die. Everything around me started to get dark, and it was like my memory was quickly disappearing also. I no longer could hear anything, and everything around me was black.

CHAPTER TWENTY-FOUR

Ajanay

I cried the entire ride over to London's house. I was praying inside that she was smart enough to get my drift and call the police. I usually say fuck the police, but tonight we needed them. I realized that we got in over our head. Amir was on his phone with his niggas talking in code, but I was street enough to understand some of the codes that he was using. I knew for a fact that he said he was going to get his money back and then he was going to body London and me.

I said several silent prayers. I was desperate to stay alive and save my best friend's life. "Where the fuck this bitch live at?" he yelled.

"Whitcomb Court."

I swear I didn't want to give up my girl's address, but I was thinking maybe, just maybe, if I gave him his money back, he would show mercy on us, especially because he thought I was his baby mother. He pulled up at London's address and pulled in a parking space. I thought of jumping out of the car and running off. But, again, I couldn't leave my girl.

He had the gun in my back as we walked to her door. He was pretty bold coming to Whitcomb, knowing damn well he was a marked man over here. I trembled as I rang the doorbell. He stood to the side, but with the gun still pointed in my back.

London didn't answer at first, which made me nervous. I saw that he was getting angrier by the second.

The door opened and I saw my girl standing there, looking at me. "Hey, boo," I managed to squeeze out before he pushed me in and aimed the gun at both of us.

"What the fuck is this? Who is this dude, Nay?"

"Bitch, I'm the nigga whose house you broke into and stole all his money, which by the way, I'm here to collect."

"What are you talking about, dude? You got the wrong one."

"Yo, go get my motherfucking money before I blow this bitch's head off, now!" he yelled.

I knew this was it. I looked at London, trying to let her know how serious this was. Shit, I knew she saw my face and saw that this wasn't no game.

"Okay, okay, okay. It's in here, in my living room," she said.

"Come on, bitch, both of you going." He held the gun on us. London walked off to her living room. My heart was thumping. I knew then that our lives were going to be over in just a few minutes.

"Please, Amir, please let us go once you get your money," I pleaded.

"Here is your money." London grabbed the garbage bag and threw it at his feet.

I was shocked to see how calm London was behaving. This was making me scared. I guessed she had accepted the fact that we were about to meet our Maker.

"Don't move, pussy nigga!" I heard a voice say, and I heard a gun cock.

I looked over my shoulder and I saw Keon's brother standing behind Amir with a gun to his head.

"Nigga, you gon' have to kill me and, if you do, you won't live to see another motherfucking day."

"Maybe so, but you will see your Maker first."

Pow! Pow! Pow!

There were three shots to Amir's head. He fell front-ward onto the coffee table, smashing it into pieces.

"Aw, oh, my God," I screamed.

London ran over to me and held me tight. I just kept crying. This was the first time I'd witnessed somebody getting killed and it was horrible.

"Take her out of here. Matter of fact, go get a room for both of you. Don't call me. I'll call you."

"What are you going to do? I can't leave you," London said to him.

"I said go! Trust me, I don't need you here to witness this shit."

He pulled out a chainsaw and walked toward Amir's bloody body.

"Come on, we need to go." She grabbed my arm and pulled me. "Listen, dry them damn tears. We need to get out of here. We've committed one crime today and we are accessories to another one. We need to get it together because orange don't look good on either of us," she scolded.

I was trembling inside, but I know she was right. I quickly wiped my tears and wiped the snot out of my nose. My face hurt like hell, but that would have to wait until later.

London got in Deon's car and we pulled off. It was then that I realized I had left my car over by Amir's house. "Can you take me over Amir's to get my car?" I asked.

"Damn, let's go."

When we got there, I quickly jumped out of the car and into mine. She pulled off and I follow suit. I started crying as I drove. I swore this was too much for me to handle. *How did I get myself caught up into this, all because of greed?*

We got a room at the Days Inn. We waited patiently to hear from Deon. We didn't talk too much because we were both going through our own shit.

The TV was playing and a reporter came on and started talking about a botched federal sting in Whitcomb. That caught my attention immediately. I looked up at the television and saw a picture of Sheika.

"Yes, that's right," the reporter was saying. "Sheika Jones, a twenty-eight-year-old woman . . ."

"London, look at this," I yelled as if she weren't close by.

She looked at the TV and realized what I was showing her. "What the fuck happened? Turn it up."

"Yes, Jenise, Miss Jones was a confidential informant for the feds, and sources close to the case told us she was working when she was gunned down by a known drug dealer."

We both looked at each other and just hugged and cried. Even though we were mad at the bitch, we sure didn't wish death on her. I cried harder because of how close we came to losing our lives.

EPILOGUE

London

"Are you ready, bitch?"

I took one last glance at Whitcomb Court and then replied, "Yes, let's go, boo." Nay and I walked to her car.

Richmond, Virginia, would always be home, but I didn't want to stay here, especially after I lost Keon. I was four months pregnant and I didn't want to raise my son in this kind of environment. I knew I was just as guilty as Keon because I kept spending his dope money, and if I could go back and turn back the clock of time, I would beg him to leave the streets alone.

All that was too late, though, and all I had of him were his memories and his son.

"Bitch, soon as we get to Atlanta, we're going shopping," Nay interrupted my thoughts.

"Me too, nigga. My fat ass need a whole new wardrobe. I heard Atlanta had some fine-ass stores in their Buckhead area. I can't wait to drop this load so I can squeeze my ass in the latest designer clothes."

"Uh-huh. Look at you all turned up." Nay busted out laughing. Then she got serious. "London, can I ask you a question?"

"Sure, what's up?"

"I know Sheika did us wrong, but do you miss her sometimes?"

I didn't respond right away. Matter of fact, I had to think long and hard on that one. "Nay, I do from time to time. But I have to remind myself that she was a jealous snake. She acted like she was for us but, in reality, she was against us. I think it's horrible how she died, but she knew what she was getting herself into by turning into a rat. I just hope her mother finds some peace."

There was a moment of silence as we got on the highway. The morning breeze hit my face as I thought about what my future might hold. I looked across at my girl, and I wondered what I would do without her.

THE END